FIC000000 FICTION / General

FIC062000 FICTION / Noir

FIC008000 FICTION / Sagas

Author website: edieayala.com

Book and cover design: berthaclark.com

⊙ STORIES WITH CHARACTER.COM

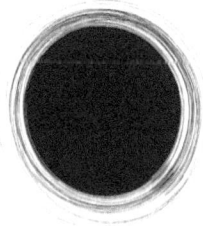

THE EYE OF THE SEA

by Edie Ayala

for Mom

PROLOGUE | THE SURRENDER

March 19 or March 20, 2020

On her last day—it was either Thursday or Friday (no one knows for sure)—Elena fell and hit her head on the wooden floor of her bedroom and she broke her nose. She lay unconscious for a long time before her soul finally made its getaway, her heart kept pumping and the blood kept flowing unobstructed, slowly spreading across the oak to form a dark, sticky pool. Perhaps (we can only imagine) she opened her eyes for a last brief look around before releasing her final breath. A sigh of relief. Escape from the violent street protests that screamed up and down the country, and the long-desired release from the torment of her confused memories.

She gracefully submitted to the calm when she stumbled, giving way, allowing the secret of her demise to be snagged like a little note wrapped in the uncertain fingers of the wind, that it might be carried off to soar like a condor and later to be set free, fluttering down into a deep crevice of the Chilean Andes.

That day—either Thursday or Friday, no one knows for sure—the universe did what it does best. It began to accommodate the shift in energy caused by the absence of her breath. Atoms realigned, rippling out in waves from the axis that was her body, millions of them nudging one another and shifting to create new molecular formations. Bacteria came alive and multiplied, the air in the room filled with an unpleasant, putrid odor. Beyond that, a few long wispy fingers of low-lying clouds eventually reached down through the window to touch her hair, limp and sticky, and they retreated carrying a rich decomposition that the atmosphere would repurpose, already rubbing its hands with glee at so much potential. The sun took refuge behind the mountains and the days grew shorter by seconds in the global south. Energy flashed up to wherever energy goes after one dies and joined in the oneness of the universe. Anyone paying attention would have known she had passed into the beyond.

On the day of her final surrender there was another person who stood so close to her that she felt his breath on her neck. It happened at Canal San Carlos. She had stopped on the wooden footbridge to gaze down, seemingly mindlessly. But it wasn't mindless at all. She was contemplating the possibilities of dying there. If she threw herself over the wooden railing, would she land in the shallows and smash her head on a rock? Or would she fall into one of the deep hollows that had been eroded by the current, and would the brown water swirl around her, gather her into its foamy embrace and whisk her out to sea? She imagined both scenarios and couldn't decide. So she stayed there, leaning over, and her small handbag, which contained only an empty wallet, dangled from her wrist. All so precarious. She became aware that the tranquilizer was wearing off because she felt panic clawing its way up her throat. She should really go home. She needed to take another pill. Almost certainly, she would return another day to accept the destiny offered by the canal.

She felt a presence and when she turned, she was looking into the dark eyes of the man who was standing so close that she could have kissed him without much effort. But that's not what happened. He ran off and just after that, the old man from the cafe appeared and the past and present collided in timeless chaos. When she finally navigated her way back to the sanctuary of her apartment, she felt another familiar presence.

1 | THE SWINGS

December 22, 2019

The dark eyes. Elena had encountered them before that day at the canal. The first time was one warm day before Christmas, and the impact was one of stinging ecstasy. You could say there was a mini mental orgasm, a pulse through the air, an electric shot through the heart. Some people might call it chemistry. Stuff of souls. Connection from a past life if you want to believe that. Whatever it was, the encounter would lead to an interlude that would in some ways satisfy her relentless yearning and in others ways, deepen it. What it meant for the man with the mesmerizing eyes remained to be seen.

They met (we cannot say that they ever truly knew one another) on a children's playground, halfway along Elena's walking route between her apartment and the canal. It was just past noon, the streets were quiet, the park was empty because the nanas had carted their little brats back home for lunch and workers had already taken their seats at local restaurants and filled the air with the sounds of their guffaws and staccato conversation, while others had disappeared to the edges of the canal and stretched out for a siesta like dogs in the sun.

Elena didn't usually venture out at midday, not because it was her usual time to eat (she didn't eat much at any time) but rather because she didn't venture out much at all. She preferred the security of her apartment. You could say that she had become a hermit of sorts, thinking and re-thinking, often writing, always analyzing. She habitually scribbled pages of notes on loose sheets that she tossed to the floor and then forgot. They ended up strewn at the foot of her night table, and from there, they were kicked or blown around before finally bowing down beside the baseboards where they were covered with dust, pencil shavings and crumbs. Rows of books lined the wall above the radiator, spines out—contemporary novels by Hernán Rivera Letelier, Gabriel García Marquéz, books by Latin American philosopher José Pablo Feinmann, a biography of Rosita Serrano, the sad story of the forgotten Chilean who sang for the Nazis, and titles by Chilean author Eugenia Prado Bassi, among others. Books had landed face-down on the floor and others had fallen open, face-up, their grey pages staring up at the ceiling in eternal insomnia. Books in limbo, abandoned but never discarded. She stepped around them.

Today she was feeling light, almost carefree. Maybe it was down to the new medication. Maybe she was a little high. Maybe it was that one extra pill. She decided to let her feet take her where they may. Inhaling deeply, she tried to absorb the scent from the roses that bloomed just inside the iron grill fence around her building. The fence was meant to keep people out. But it kept people in. Another thing to add to her growing list of good intentions gone wrong.

Elena let the iron portal slam behind her and she turned right onto the sidewalk. Head lowered, she watched as her old adidas planted one in front of the other. Heel, toe, heel, toe. She easily found her rhythm and, as was her habit, began counting the steps. She was at step number 1072 when, from the corner of her eye she was distracted by a long, sweeping motion. She paused and looked over to see a man on a swing at the far corner of the playground. His lithe adult body settled upon the wooden seat, as though it had been made just for him. He leaned back, punching the toes of his boots into the sky. He was wearing blue jeans and a black tank top with a silly yellow happy face screened on its front. Leaning back—legs up, arms up, hinging at his hips, his body formed a 'V'. He was a grown man on a childish pendulum that squeaked. The pendulum gained momentum, the man surrendered his face to the sun, his eyes closed. She thought she could hear him humming.

To describe Elena as shy would be incorrect. She was quiet, she was withdrawn but she was never shy. She approached, pushing the soft interior of her right elbow into the hollow metal upright of the swing set. She leaned in and absently observed as a few green paint chips loosened and fluttered crazily to the ground. The bar vibrated with the man's movement. She was amused by the unusual choice of activity for a mature adult male. He was what? Maybe 50 years old. No, he must be younger. Then again, maybe not.

She observed him for several seconds (maybe a whole minute), unnoticed from this close vantage point. When he sensed her presence, he dropped his feet, scarring the sand with two shallow trenches. The pendulum stopped squeaking and went still. When he turned to her, she started and caught her breath. She was captured by his eyes. They were sharp and the dark centers sunk deep into somewhere. His soul, she thought.

"What's your name?" It was unusual for her to initiate a conversation and she was surprised when the question left her lips. But she wasn't sorry.

"You can call me BJ," he volunteered without hesitation. He had a slight smile.

"BJ, as in Bee Jay?"

"Yeah."

"Why Bee Jay and not *Bay Hota*?" (the Spanish pronunciation of the letters)

"I prefer it," was his explanation.

He didn't ask her name as she expected. It would have been the polite thing to do. Instead, he pointed with his chin towards the empty swing at his side. "You should try it."

She obliged, and slid onto the seat. She waited, looking down at her lap. She hadn't done this since she was a girl. Sometimes her father used to push her. "Take it easy. Go gently," he'd say.

"I bet I can fly higher than you." It was a challenge. His dark eyes glinted with something. She wanted to keep looking into them. But he looked down at his boots then, ready to push off, to take up his own game.

"I bet you can't." She pushed off too, pumping her legs with a vigor that she must have stolen because surely such energy did not belong to her. She glanced over at him, exhilarated, a tight circle of joy ringing her chest. Then she leaned her head back, felt herself mingling with the blue, higher and higher, losing herself in the motion and the infinite sky. She couldn't stop. She thought she heard his voice, "Take it easy." But she ignored it. Who was he anyway?

She landed flat on her back, winded and panicked, swimming in the blue. She moaned and felt she was twisting from side to side but then realized she wasn't moving at all. Her shoulders had surely been wrenched from their sockets, her spine cried out in pain. But worse, she couldn't breathe. She was going to die. This isn't the way she had planned it. Helpless, she looked up and saw his black eyes floating just above her face. There was fire in there. They were the eyes of a wolf, a predator. Divine or sinister? She couldn't decide. Maybe it was both. She saw only the eyes. No mouth, no nose, no cheeks, just fiery, black eyes that mesmerized. It lasted only a few seconds but she felt like she had travelled somewhere and back with him. Trapped in their depths, his eyes penetrated her, and she burned with their energy. Suddenly, the blue of the sky was vacuumed into his darkness. She didn't feel him give her his breath.

She didn't know how long she laid there but at some point she became conscious of someone's hand on her shoulder, large, its touch light and warm. The hand stayed there, patting her gently and then suddenly she knew she was alone. She was breathing and was able to move her shoulders again, and with some difficulty, she raised herself to her knees. The pain subsided. Flashback to another man's hand patting her shoulder, memories of warmth and understanding. There was that—the sense of another man, an intangible, familiar vibe.

But it was gone now. Elena got to her feet and hobbled away without looking back and she counted her steps all the way home.

2 | YOUTHFUL AMBITIONS

December 22, 2019

There was a young-ish, or at least, a not-too-old man. It was difficult to pinpoint his age because the tell-tale traces of his unsettled past were ambiguous. Even for himself, there was a question about the validity of his birth record. His cheeks were covered in short black stubble, lightly peppered with grey, he had a wide nose and a square chin, and lips that rarely parted in a smile. His eyes were dark and they had a tendency to bore into you; it was like someone was shining a flashlight in your face and you couldn't see who was holding it. His eyes trapped you. You could see yourself reflected so sharply in their perfect roundness that it hurt. You knew he was in there somewhere, observing. He could see you but you couldn't see him.

People raised a hand and called for his attention. "Bladimir, bring me this. Bladimir, take this over there." Outwardly, he was a waiter-gopher in El Terminal, an unremarkable restaurant in Recoleta, which was owned by a man called Giorgio. He was Bladimir's long-time boss. The restaurant, aptly named for its location just around the corner from the General Cemetery of Santiago, was one of the sector's more popular Commie hangouts. The restaurant's claim to fame was that it was once frequented by famous artists and politicians—most of them now long dead and buried just around the corner. Their faded photos clung to the walls, a montage of music warriors and political idols from the Cold War era. So the restaurant had that and its more than 50 years of history. People felt comfortable with long-term, established anything. El Terminal's muggy atmosphere was complete with mangled and outdated lists of lunch specials attached with pieces of grey duct tape to grimy windows. Cockroach-infested corners were a trivial concern behind its persistent menu of traditional beef and corn soup, greasy fried fish sandwiches, cheap wine and instant Nescafe. The regulars always went home satisfied, and they pressed coins (if they had extra) into Bladimir's palm.

The boss had learned that he could rely on Bladimir, and Bladimir was content with the façade of steady, legitimate work. Some years ago, he had tired of too many brushes with the law, of *los pacos*, time and again, dragging him into holding cells and then into court. He was a minor criminal with a long record. But they noted that basically he was *un buen tipo* and not deserving of jail time.

Once upon a time, believe it or not, Bladimir had political aspirations, the origins of which were rooted in his problematic childhood. He had inherited these aspirations from his mother. Before she disappeared from amidst the hippies and their fold-up mattresses, she baptized her son 'Bladimir.' It was not a religious ceremony. Rather it was her verbal pronouncement, toasting her infant mentee with a raised, heavily-frothed mug of beer, "I present to you my son, Bladimir. He will grow strong and will one day champion the cause of el pueblo. *Salud! A mi hijo.*" Once upon a time, she had had political aspirations of her own but those floated away with too much alcohol and too many drugs. Don't blame her. She also had her demons.

In the early days, she passed on her dreams, which in years previous had become so tattered that she almost couldn't recognize them, to her son. As they stood on the sidewalk, in front of the butcher at Cal y Canto, she would mutter half-finished thoughts about inequality that drifted off to meld into the diesel behind the buses. Little Bladimir used to reach up in search for her hand. Perhaps he could calm her. Perhaps she could comfort him. But her hands were needed for other things. She used one hand to push the toddler in front of her and brace his chin so that his grubby, forlorn little face was lifted towards passersby, affording them a look into the depths of poverty. Her other hand, she kept outstretched to accept sympathy donations. When she was too wasted to do the begging herself, she rented him out for 10,000 pesos a day to an acquaintance who could use a waif to help increase her earnings.

His mother had intended to call him Vladimir, in honor of Vladimir Lenin, hero of the poor and working class. But in Spanish, 'tall b' sounds the same as 'short v' and when the time came, it was the 'tall b' that came to mind for his mother and she named him Bladimir. She didn't know who his father was. Therefore, his paternal surname became the same as his maternal one. He was called Bladimir Jaime Morales-Morales. She was sure that this name would help forge a meaningful and important path for the boy. God knows, she had strayed too far from it herself. So Bladimir, with a B, made his start as a spelling error and really, what were the chances?

Several years into his young life, social services received a call about a young boy sleeping rough in the abandoned ruins of a workers' hut between the half-constructed hospital and a highway at the south end of Santiago. Other than "Bladimir Jaime," the boy didn't give up much. The social workers found in the public records, the name of a young boy of Bladimir's approximate age, and this was enough to make him official. In order to clear the file off the desk at the Civil Registry (it had already collected dust for several months), the most convenient was to decide that he was indeed the one and the only, and they gave him a card with an ID number that corresponded to that name. If this boy was not that Bladimir Jamie Morales-Morales, then good luck to the real Bladimir, who would be forced into a lifelong battle with the State for his identity—one that he'd never win.

The authorities placed our Bladimir in a children's home, where he fell in with some young friends (you couldn't call them friends, exactly—more like small-time hoodlums, amazingly young ones, who would stab you in the back for a nice pair of Nikes or a decent knock-off of a national team shirt) who had dropped out of school to stand around in abandoned lots and exchange drugs for money. Even at nine years old, Bladimir knew better than to participate in this activity but his desire to belong drowned out the distant voice of morality that had, in all honesty, never been that loud in the first place.

Bladimir didn't do drugs himself. He had an aversion to lack of self-control (an unconscious reaction to his addict mother) and after awhile he realized he preferred the rawness of living the moment, during which, when he so chose, he could observe with a superior feeling of distance and control, the tormented souls who could not resist the surreal experiences that drugs offered.

For one brief period as a young man, he felt sure that he had stumbled into the coveted position of protégé for an up-and-coming senator of the

Republic, who had managed to gain his seat on the far left of the ruling coalition, albeit with a small percentage via the *sistema binominal*. But all of Bladimir's dreams were shattered when the senator was caught accepting illegal contributions from a Brazilian multinational and the senator disappeared into the arid folds of the northern Andes, taking Bladimir's hopes and grinding them into the coarse gravel of the Atacama Desert. Later, Bladimir would discover that the incident with this senator was the original template solution for future senators-gone-wrong.

Bladimir was a soul who was driven, without necessarily knowing towards what. Even as a youngster, although he didn't feel nervous, he could never stand still, always had to be moving somewhere, like a shark circling around an undefined goal. His theory was that if he circled often enough, maybe he'd eventually bump into it.

Bladimir was a badass. No one knew for sure why. He was just wired that way. But he was a hell of a smart badass. And he was fast. He was so fast that people hardly saw him, barely noticed as he whipped by. He was like the wind. It was this very speed that guys like the now-disgraced senator had an eye for.

Decades later, on one of his days off from El Terminal, he circled around and up to a more affluent part of town and was not far from Canal San Carlos (which defines the eastern edge of Providencia) when he passed a small children's park. The park was empty and he noticed a swing set at the far end. The park amenities were much more modern than what you could find in Recoleta, and the park itself was swept and manicured for the little minion snobs whose families lived in this neighborhood. He decided to make the most of it. So he jumped on a swing and pointed his boots up towards the sun.

3 | INSOMNIA
The Summer of '69

At times, Elena's outer self could sparkle with fun. But it had been a long time (several years, in fact) since she'd had a good laugh or enjoyed a wholesome adventure. Actually, 'wholesome' disappeared from her vocabulary when she was a pre-teen. Elena had an inner core that was solitary and intellectual, and sometimes it felt like she was on a slow motion slog through purgatory. Her darker side had installed itself when she was a young girl but it didn't take root until her early teens. And once it was firmly established, it began sucking on her, then it chewed away, and finally consumed her. The seed for this root had been sowed on a hot, sticky afternoon in 1969, during Elena's sixth summer. On that same day, the sun chose not to show himself, and he slunk behind the southern clouds, "I was not witness, my view was obstructed," he would later declare. And the moon would turn from him, unable to look such blatant cowardice in its flaming, farting face. The moon had no choice but to hang in and occupy the same sky and she would have fled the orbit in shame had she not felt such a deep responsibility towards the tides. It seems everyone has an excuse.

That day back in 1969 was the day Elena's father disappeared. He and Elena's mother had had a loud discussion up in their bedroom. Elena's stomach turned somersaults and she felt very unwell because she'd never heard her parents argue so violently. She remembered scurrying with her nanny, Rosa out the door and at some point, she ended up taking shelter in the far corner of the garage. She squatted, rubbed the palms of her hands over her ears, and she forced herself to focus on the thin rays of light that striped across the toes of her favorite black patent leather shoes. At first she didn't notice that her father had entered the garage. He fumbled furiously with the door handle of the old, black Mercedes. She looked up in time to see him heave his leather duffle bag—the soft, supple one that he sometimes let her linger over when he was about to go on a trip—onto the passenger seat, start the engine and speed off, leaving her sputtering in a trail of exhaust. Beyond this, her memory faltered. She must have run down the driveway for a distance. Mustn't she? She probably waved her arms and yelled at him to stop. Didn't she? She would have run across the gravel, little stones entering her shoes and digging into the soles of her feet. Wouldn't she? Or was it all imagined, that she just wished she had run after him? If she had, then it would mean that she had cared and had wanted to stop him, had wanted to go with him. He wouldn't have gone alone. She ran past the tool shed. And that's all she could remember.

She didn't recall the dark, stocky man lurking beside the shed, branches painting shadows over his crouched, tormented body, his ragged breath, shaky beneath the carnal moans that rose from his throat. She didn't recall Rosa running full throttle straight up to her and admonishing her as she gestured towards the shed and pointed frantically down the driveway. She didn't remember Rosa grabbing her by the elbow and dragging her around and up to the house. And she couldn't remember the something more. She always knew there was something more but she couldn't get to it.

One of the days right after that, her mother was almost hysterical. Her voice was high-pitched. "We have to bury your father tomorrow."

"No! But Mamá..."

A month after that, Elena's sleep became filled with nightmares in which she heard her father's voice. He was yelling at her to run. But when she tried to run, she found that she had no knees and she collapsed. Little stones embedded themselves in her crippled legs and she sat right down there on the gravel and, forgetting everything else, she began to pick the stones out, one by one, watching the little indents in her flesh change and redden. She looked up and there was her father's face, distorted. His pain pierced them both. And then she saw the shadow. The dream always ended that way— with her doing nothing but picking pebbles out of her shins, waiting for the cold shadow to roll across and take its confusion with it. But the shadow never left. It parked itself right there in her dream and refused to move on. It took her several years to learn how to force herself to awaken. And then she had to rub and rub at her forehead to erase the shadow that chilled across her wakefulness.

Before she learned how to awaken from the nightmare, before she could rid herself of the shadow, she stopped eating.

"But Mamá, I'm not hungry."

"Nonsense. You haven't eaten breakfast."

"But I don't want anything."

"You can't go on like this. Look at you. People will think we don't have any food to give you."

"But I'm not hungry."

"Nonsense. Okay, that's enough. I'll have to force-feed you." Mamá signaled the seriousness of her intent by picking up the ceramic spoon that she used to stir the yoghurt and she swirled it a little, teasing.

She dipped it into the sweetened yogurt and, bracing Elena's neck, she put the spoon to her lips and pushed. Eventually Elena was convinced to open her mouth. She gagged and spat it out across the table. She didn't mean to do that. She was a good girl.

She didn't mean to fight and cause trouble, and after several such episodes she learned to submit. That's also when she learned how to forget for real, to tuck away nasty thoughts and ugly memories. She was six years old. The next week they found her favorite kitten lifeless at the edge of the pond. It was too much to deal with. Elena's six-year-old brain learned how to compartmentalize.

Fast forward to the woman who was lying on the wooden floor in a pool of blood several decades later, and whose digestive tract, had it been examined by a coroner, would not contain traces of a recent meal.

4 | HOT AND BOTHERED

December 29, 2019

Sunlight streamed across the garden, casting shadows at precise angles. It drew a hard edge across the manicured lawn at the east wall. The outline of the high-rise behind was clearly defined, its shadow ending abruptly two meters further along. The undersides of leaves were golden and as they fluttered in the breeze, their natural joy at being alive quivered across the afternoon. Elena scoffed at them. She thought back to the first day of summer, December 22, 2019. Was it only a week ago?

Summer solstice—relevant to witches and warlocks, and normally reason for her to stop and take stock of the seasons—had assumed a new significance this year. Now summer solstice was also the day she met BJ. Later that day, when she had returned to her apartment, she had very slowly and very neatly penned 'met Bee Jay' (with an extra long swirl on the J) on the empty square number 22 of the photo calendar. A chewed-up yellow pencil was tied with a string to a nail on the wall beside the door, where a calendar left its mark year after year. She hung it there because sometimes she forgot what day it was, and having it by the door was reliable and convenient. She could tick off the days of the month and, in this way, pretend to command her own time. She could pause to get her bearings in order to avoid going out the door and running into a casual acquaintance who might invite her for a drink or coerce her into baby sitting or otherwise engage her in some unwelcome form of human socialization. Truth be told, she only accidentally encountered someone she recognized once or twice in any given month. It was because she was practiced at avoidance, expert in isolation. The most she offered was a nod and quick hello to the man at the local newsstand, a half-smile to the elderly cashier at the corner market, and the customary hand signal and curt order to the waiter at her local sidewalk cafe. These half-strangers at the edges of her non-existent social circle were all she permitted. Now she considered whether BJ might become an exception. Maybe. Almost certainly. Yes. Those eyes.

She knew she was being juvenile as she watched from her window for a sign. She was a mature woman, was she not? Yes, but she was smitten. Give me a sign, any sign will do. If he lived nearby, she might see him walking along her street. His name (such as it was—just initials) inserted itself into her notes on the yellow foolscap sheets that were scattered about the floor. Unable to shake the memory of last week's encounter, he had taken command of her consciousness with such ease, his brief presence now inflating an absence that kicked in a heightened anxiety. It was an uncertain mixture of anticipation and vulnerability. The memory of him moved her towards delirium, sort of like a schoolgirl still in the bliss of a first kiss, weak and pliable. She scoffed and her silly breath fogged up the window. She drew two intersecting hearts into it with her middle finger. She observed it for a few seconds, watching the edges soften and she used the heel of her hand to smudge it away, sneering at her childishness as she brandished her middle finger in front of her own nose. How old am I? I know, but life goes on, does it not? One must live a little. But she didn't really believe that. She shook her stiff middle finger in front of her nose.

She returned to the children's park twice that week, hoping to see him. But she didn't. Both times, she settled onto the seat of the swing he had used and swayed away several minutes, loose thoughts to-ing and fro-ing as she waited for him to show up, waited for the energy from the memory of his weight on this very seat to push her into the air, to lose herself again in the blue. But both times, a little girl planted herself in front of her, hands on her indignant little hips, challenging her with a spoiled scowl until Elena felt obligated to surrender the swing. And on both days, she wandered to the canal afterwards so she could lean over the footbridge and watch the water ripple a few meters beneath her feet. She got lost in the trickling and bubbling, mentally riding up along the walls and then sliding back down into the wider stream. Both times after several minutes, she had the sensation that someone was there watching her but when she turned, she found that she was alone.

Her mother used to caution her about leaning too far over the railing of the footbridge. When Elena was a young girl, and shortly after they buried her father, her mother took her for a walk around the canal and they crossed this very bridge. Back then it was all foreign territory. Her mother told her they would be moving here, that this neighborhood was to become their new *vecindario.*

"See?" Her mother tipped up the edge of her wide-brimmed toquilla straw hat and pointed her gloved finger towards the east. "See that tall brick house with the terracotta roof? That's where we're going to live. That's our new home."

"Why?" Elena had looked up at her for the answer. But her mother didn't reply. Her head blocked the sun. Instead, she took her by the hand, "Come along. My friend is waiting."

Elena was saddened by her mother's decision to move because it meant leaving the place where she had lived with her father. Would it mean that the memories of him would fade? Would her father's spirit find her in their new house, or would she have to leave a trail of clues, maybe notes, just like they left for *Viejito Pascuero* whenever they visited her aunt at Christmas?

Even now, at 56 years of age, Elena had to admit (and was regularly reminded by her mother) that she was confused. Things had become jumbled over the years by her futile efforts to pull memories from the days and weeks around father's death. She wasn't sure which memories she might have desperately shaped for her own convenience and which ones might be real. Beginning in her early years, she woke up from nightmares in which, from a hiding spot on top of a pile of oily rags, she saw someone cock a gun at the back of her father's head and fire. She could never see her father's face but she knew it was him. And she never saw the face of the man with the gun either. But sometimes in her dream, it was she who held the pistol. In that case, she was standing on something, or else her father was squatted low, because she could see the short hairs on the back of his head trembling. The trigger was always too stiff for her young fingers to activate and she woke up when someone else wrapped their hand around hers and before they could force her to squeeze to its intended end. Her bedclothes would be twisted and half on the floor as though she had struggled throughout the night. But when she looked at the clock, it was relatively early, digital numbers blinking out 10:45 pm. So she decided to trick the nightmare by going to bed later. But the cunning nightmare woke her punctually at 11:37 pm.

Her response was to stay awake yet longer but the nightmare accommodated itself and woke her at 12:20 am. And so on. Finally, she kept herself awake until dawn. But no matter when she finally fell asleep, the nightmare always found her.

This whole week, her waking mind was filled both with the nightmare (trying to avoid it) and thoughts of BJ. Where did he work? Where was his family? Who was his family? Did he also think about her? Could it have been that their meeting was some sort of providence? This afternoon, as she gazed out the window, her eyes pounced on anything that moved. Even a leaf that fell to the ground could be a sign. Perhaps it would be BJ approaching. Or the bird that dropped to the sidewalk and then looked her way. Could it be a signal? But in the end, BJ was never out there, and as the late afternoon sun beat down, she felt sleepy. She finally abandoned her post at the window and, pushing a dozen loose papers to the floor, she sank down on the sofa and closed her eyes.

At this point in Chile, there was a continuing rash of violent protests and disturbances born out of *el estallido social*—the social uprising—that began on October 19, 2019. Elena herself, had been downtown the following day and she experienced the terrifying energy and she feared the forces behind it. The protests, which were purported to have been sparked by a hike in metro fares, had origins that were much more profound and far flung. She backed away from the politics of it all. She turned inward and, as she had conditioned herself to do as a child, she made her world smaller in the hopes that it would be easier to comprehend. But it wasn't and it didn't.

There are various theories as to the origin and sustenance of Chile's October, 2019 social uprising. *Los de la primera linea* (the extreme activists on the front lines) would say it was a wave that had built up over the years until it could no longer be contained, that it reached tsunami proportions and finally rushed in to decimate the barriers of Chile's inequality. Certainly, the tens of thousands who joined the street protests in the days that followed would agree. They were comprised of the Pedros and Marias who lived every day in the inefficient bureaucracy that was built on policies designed by the powerful, for the powerful. And by 'the powerful', it was understood to mean *los grandotes*, those who had money to invest, who had a family name that could be traced back to old wealth and political influence, who were connected to foreign capitalists and as a result, who would benefit most from the status quo. Now the Pedros and Marias were out to change that. Who could disagree?

Then there were those who thought the social uprising was the result of planning from outside forces, especially other Latin American countries. The recent history behind it went something like this: a couple of years earlier, several countries from South and Central America and also Canada, formed the Lima Group, who believed that President Maduro of Venezuela had, among other things, rigged the Venezuelan judiciary in order to illegally sustain his position as President. The Lima Group wanted to replace Maduro with Juan Guaidó, the man who many believed to have been the democratically-elected and rightful president of Venezuela. Meanwhile, Maduro, along with the President of Bolivia and others, were dedicated to the Revolución Bolivariana, a movement whose goal was to see all of South America united under one socialist flag. They had steadily been setting plans in motion across the continent to ensure the 'red wave' would take wing.

Meanwhile, the situation in Venezuela was worsening by the day—inflation was running away with life savings, the military became more powerful and narcos moved in to increase Maduro's wealth and the military's power and influence. Venezuelan citizens, broken and desperate, rushed to leave in long waves of sadness that backed up border crossings in Columbia, Brazil and other South and North American countries. In February 2019, President Piñera of Chile joined in a Venezuela Aid Concert at the Colombian border along with Richard Branson and other high profile supporters in a highly public display, where he showcased Chile's support for Guaidó with a shipment of humanitarian aid. And it was a clear demonstration of his support of the popular uprising against President Maduro. It is said that, in response, President Maduro threatened to orchestrate not only Chile's downfall but that of President Piñera as well.

Elena did not subscribe to either theory because she preferred not to think about it. But had she been privy to the fact that Bladimir's boss, Giorgio, and by association, Bladimir was embroiled in the greater movement, she might have stood up and paid attention. She might have cared.

Although he was not a revolutionary, Giorgio outwardly supported the movement because it was a way to open borders and ease the work of people traffickers and flow of drugs from one country to another. Had Elena known, well, she would have stopped thinking right there, because who was she to judge the flow and the purpose of illegal drugs? Anyway, because of his selfish interests, you could say that Giorgio played a pivotal role in the cause for social justice. With contacts, especially in Venezuela and Europe, he helped with clandestine importation of people and weapons. He was a key player, albeit indirectly, in what Chile's president would later gingerly refer to as *un golpe blando*—a non-traditional government takeover. But that suggestion came well after the fact.

The current situation in Chile was extremely volatile. There were regular attacks on police stations up and down the country, with activists tossing Molotov cocktails and taking potshots at police. Although, there was nothing as terrifying as the initial days of fires and total destruction of metro stations, buses, and university and healthcare facilities, people continued to loot big and small stores, and to destroy infrastructure. In response, businesses and government authorities boarded up the center of the Capital. Small businesses folded. What remained was chaos. Civilians took it upon themselves to direct traffic because violent gangs had hauled down sophisticated traffic light systems and removed street signs and, in general, destroyed much of the transportation infrastructure.

Plaza Italia, which marks the division between west (less affluent) and east (wealthier) Santiago, and is the traditional muster point for football and political celebrations, was now a 24-hour war zone. People defaced buildings and destroyed sidewalks, lamp posts, signs, churches, and hotels. The plaza's emblematic statue of General Manuel Baquedano was covered with paint and graffiti by activists who tried in vain to pull it down entirely and then settled for climbing to its marred bronze summit to hang like gargoyles over the spoils of battle—grass and flowers trampled, garbage, bits and pieces of broken furniture, human feces and blood over gravel, under persistent clouds of tear gas. These were the victors, the guardians of violent change. They defied anyone to set foot onto their hallowed ruins. Surrounding residents vacated their apartments to seek refuge with family in relatively less agitated districts. At one point, the mayor of Providencia, who ventured onto the streets to assess the damage, was so aghast and shaken that she turned from reporters and ran for blocks, seemingly aimlessly but doubtless in an attempt to escape the insanity that had consumed the now fallen streets.

Up and down the country, los de la primera linea intimidated pedestrians and passengers alike. They blocked roads and, under threat to burn anything from small cars to transport trucks, they demanded people show their support for the cause by stepping out of their vehicles and performing a dance, during which they mocked and clapped. "*Así es. ¡Baila!*" "Come on. More enthusiasm. Swing. Move!" Holding their flaming torches high, they memorialized the humiliated dancers with videos on social media. One victim, an American resident who carried his pistol in his glove box, refused to dance and in the ensuing tumult, he shot a protestor in the leg. He was found guilty of this crime, and thrown in jail. The authorities found themselves unable to contain such events. They dared not go against current trends, so they fell in with the protesters who claimed freedom of expression and protection under human rights. The rest be damned.

As the weeks piled up and violence continued to blanket the country, working men and women began to resent the lack of public transport, the raging insecurity and the ruin of their small businesses. They appealed for protection, but the President was reluctant to call in the military for the simple reason that he didn't want people to relate it to Chile's 1973 military coup. He sought dialogue, some path to sanity amidst the mindless and stubborn animosity. Finally, he did call in troops, but he gave them limited powers. Yet the influence of social media organized by the front-liners was overwhelming and no matter how much the President succumbed to demands, he was portrayed as an assassin and torturer. The young social media experts spread the news to the rest of the world and people abroad mistakenly believed that in Santiago, you might find bodies left to rot along main streets and you might step on and squish eyeballs that had been shot out with rubber bullets. Nothing could quell the zeal. So the President tried even harder to demonstrate his desire to close the gap and to protect his own reputation. He yielded to the activists. Yet things continued to spiral out of hand. He and his authorities lost control. And that's when the politicians clambered to do the only thing that someone could think of.

In November 2019, they announced a solution that would crush the protests and satisfy every Chilean resident. Their idea was to design a process for the creation of a new constitution, to be written not by politicians but by elected Pedros and Marias. Even as it got underway, the protests would not be entirely quelled. The young voices demanding change insisted on being heard. Elena was bored with it. For her, the new constitution was an inconvenience and a path to nowhere. If the people and Chilean authorities themselves were not bound to obey current laws, what purpose would a new constitution serve? If white collar criminals embezzling millions of pesos were not held accountable, why should petty delinquents be deterred? Outwardly positive, politicians took advantage of innocent people who were overjoyed with the prospect of this brilliant, even miraculous solution. Many citizens, never truly understanding the process, placed their blind faith in the idea, and believed their lives would improve immediately. They naively assumed that once el pueblo accepted the new constitution, there would be equal access to property and opportunities and decent salaries and quality healthcare and education. They never questioned what steps had to be taken for this to happen; it was going to be a miraculous thing. If the Yes vote would win, they would wake up the next morning in an idyllic Chile. The honorable phrases in the new constitution, expressed in high legal language, would magically side-line corrupt individuals who lived on both sides of the ideological divide. How could they have known that certain of the left-wing faction (because surely it would be their proposals that would become part of the constitution) were already hard at work making lists—lists that would award politically-connected individuals with exclusive access to prime properties and high-paying jobs. How were people to know that a new constitution would not eliminate exclusive rights of politicians and their conveniently plugged-in friends? Politicians would replace the businessmen, they would become the exclusive grandotes, and they would pat themselves on the back for returning wealth to the state, the workings of which they would control and plunder.

Tonight, just as dusk fell over the city, and Elena had been passed out on her sofa for more than three hours, she was awakened by chants and shouts, "You're next. We'll get you!" How many voices she couldn't tell. But the numbers grew. The voices were rolling in waves along the street in front of her building. Both deep and shrill, it was a clamorous incursion into the softening dusk of an innocent evening. "You'll get yours!" the voices yelled. She stiffened. She stared wide-eyed at the ceiling, her ears pricked up and a chill ran over her body, the tiny hairs on the back of her neck standing on end. The chants increased in volume and intensity. Trembling, she raised herself from the sofa, and crouched at the window to peer out from under the curtain. She saw a steady stream of men and women on bicycles, peddling casually past her building. Hundreds of them. If not for the shouts and gestures, they could have been out for a leisurely spin. The bicycles all looked new, the day's last rays of light glinting off their silvery spokes. But the riders raised their hard fists with each threatening chant and they kept their eyes forward, cold, not acknowledging the people, who, one by one, were stepping onto balconies and peering from windows. Elena shivered.

A man on the third floor balcony of a building across the street rushed back inside his apartment and returned brandishing a pistol. He waved it in the air and yelled "Just try it, *hijos de puta*! We're ready for you."

It took a long time for the multitude of cyclists to pass and for their din to finally fade in the distance. Elena's heart was pounding. She watched as the neighbors, still gesturing threats to the disappearing mob and muttering to one another, finally retreated inside and pulled their blinds down. The cyclists had, at worst, succeeded in making these upper middle-class residents uncomfortable, and at best, they had sown fear. But it only set residents harder against them. How dare they roll down these streets with their righteous threats couched in violence? The episode was followed by an eerie silence, a dull, throbbing ache that overtook the street and, with an unnatural chill, spirited its way into her apartment. It was reminiscent of the minutes and hours after a 7.5 earthquake. The aftershocks repeated in her ears. "You're next, *cuicos culia'os*."

She glanced at the door and for the first time, felt vulnerable in her own home. The door was too lightweight. The lock was too flimsy. She had nothing with which to defend herself. Elena needed a reassuring voice. She picked up the intercom to talk to the doorman. But he didn't answer. He was probably out there talking to his colleague from the adjacent building. She hung up and stood guard near the door, listening. Even in the absence of the protesters, the street pulsed a foreboding. It suddenly occurred to her that she needed a weapon. What if they returned and barged in and ransacked her place? What if they beat her up? She walked into the bedroom, opened the narrow closet door, and dumped her few jackets and sweaters from their hangers. She removed the short dowel from the closet and leaned it on the wall under the calendar. Someone had once told her that you could use a rod to poke a person's eyes out. That was all she had. She would use it if it came down to it.

This incident was not the first and wouldn't be the last. It wasn't something you could easily dismiss. The estallido social had taken over the news cycles and conversations had gotten into people's heads. The ongoing street violence was feared. People argued about its relevance, they discussed its necessity. They exaggerated the police response, they cried 'torture' and 'rape' and 'murder'. They questioned the curfew and any military presence and they pointed fingers at authorities, who pointed right back. For Elena is was just another reason to stay indoors.

Given all of this, the question of whether to replace the haunting speculations about violence and threats of revolution with, you might say, small-minded and stupid musings about BJ, was a no-brainer. His face and his eyes, were right up there, triumphant over the unwanted thorns of social upheaval. The memory of this stranger's face often even clouded that of her father's.

She admitted to being infatuated again. How long since the last time? The years passed quickly but her juvenile penchant for an exciting affair had not entirely died out. Most often she was, as a matter of practice, smitten from afar and never actually made contact with the target of her obsession. Apart from relationships that ended in nothing after a few months, she hadn't experienced a whole lot of romantic love in her life. None of the relationships had been rocky. But they all lacked a certain spirit, the definition of which escaped her, but which she believed should have existed. Perhaps she sought mystery, seduction, or something else quite elusive. So in the end, rather than terminating in pain and conflict, her relationships simply lacked oxygen or fuel or both, and they flickered and died out. She often joked wryly with her mother that she should have gone into the convent because she liked to be alone, she was studious and, especially since she was approaching 60 years, she didn't fantasize about sex. The convent idea was a joke because although she had a kind heart and was generous without fault, she felt no calling to seek out and help underprivileged souls. She was too wrapped up in thoughts and analysis about her own sheltered life and besides, even if she could have joined a cloistered religious order, she had absolutely no faith.

5 | CITY OF THE DEAD

January 5, 2020

"*C*ambia... *Todo cambia...* It changes... everything changes," the sonorous voice of Mercedes Sosa was too much for the radio to constrain and too important for the tool shed to hold. The music spilled out into the air around the cemetery patio, rising up to the tips of the palms and shimmering back down through their fronds. The notes lingered, reverberating between the niche-lined walls, serenading the tired bodies that had long since been laid to rest. November 1st, the Day of the Dead, which happened to be her birthday, was also unceremoniously long gone, terminated without fanfare because of the violence of the social uprising. Huge ornate gates locked. Families' hearts broken. She had longed to spend her birthday with her father. Now it felt like years since she had visited him here. The cemetery was still under guard against violence, and it was bereft of the usual visitors who leaned in for advice and murmured as they picked dead leaves and dusted ornaments in the windows of burial niches. Santiago's city for the dead was vulnerable to delinquents. It would not be the first time anarchists had left their marks. She worried that if she didn't see her father today, it would be a long time before her next opportunity. What if the mausoleum had been disturbed? Pain shot across her chest. She had hoped the barbarity would have fizzled out by now. But she had been wrong, and, who knows, crossing town might even become more dangerous in the next months.

The tool shed that was the source of the music was a standard green metal one with a narrow door on which hung a rusty padlock. Elena could hear a woman shuffling around inside. She would be the freelance patio caretaker. She was singing along to the radio, jars clattering as she rearranged them on shelves. She tossed old rags out over her shoulder and her husky voice jumped off-key with the effort "... and that which changed yesterday will have to change again tomorrow...". One of the rags landed at Elena's feet and she kicked it aside. She was standing beside the wheelbarrow, waiting and listening. She had entered the main gates only a few minutes ago, and had been clipping along the path that would lead to her father's tomb when the music of Mercedes Sosa gave her pause. This song had been one of her father's favorites. "You'll see," he used to tell her. "You'll see how it all changes. You'll understand it when you're older." And he was right. Mercedes Sosa was right. It all changes. But love remains steady.

"Love." She said it out loud. But her voice was as weak as her sigh. It would change nothing. Lack of love, like love itself, was also a constant.

She suddenly sensed someone's presence behind her and when she turned, she knew the real reason she had come here today.

"It's you," she said, as she looked up into the dark eyes.

He smiled down at her. His eyes crinkled pleasantly at the corners. "*Hola*. We meet again."

He was holding a paper bag. He clutched it tightly to his side and then thinking better of it, he rolled down the top and made it small enough to shove into his jacket pocket. Then he pointed with his chin towards the cement bench on the other side of the path and headed towards it. Elena was a few steps behind. She sat down at the opposite end of the bench and dropped her head back to squint up past the fluorescent purple of the jacaranda blossoms and into the depths of the bright blue beyond. It was a beautiful day. Her father would wait for a few minutes longer.

She turned to the man and pretended, "BJ, right?" Of course she knew his name. It had been in her head and on her lips for nearly two weeks.

"Yup. BJ." He nodded. Just like the day in the park, he didn't ask her name and she didn't offer.

Like two old friends, they sat in a comfortable silence, she leaned back looking into the sky and he leaned forward studying his shoes. Then as if by signal, they turned to look at one another and they both smiled.

"Well," she said. "I'm going to visit my father. Do you want to come?"

"Where is he?" he asked.

"Straight down this path, to the left and into the patio with some of the more traditional but poetic—can I say poetic? ... for me they are—mausoleums. Right now, my Dad is still on his own. But there's space for all of us. Many more than all of us." She smiled again and stood up. "Come on. I'll take you." She felt satisfied, as though everything had clicked into place. Here she was, about to present the man with whom she was obsessed to the man she loved most.

Bladimir stood up, patted his left pocket where he'd shoved the paper bag. "Yeah, okay. Why not?"

Their hands almost but not quite touched as they strolled down the wide path. A stray dog walked past and sniffed Bladimir's pocket and Bladimir leaned down to pat his head and caress his ears before shooing him off. "Go on. I don't have anything for you."

"Who are you here to see?" Elena glanced up at him and then abruptly looked straight ahead because otherwise she'd be consumed by his eyes. They advanced several steps before he replied.

"You." He said.

She stopped. "What?"

He grinned and she was tripped up by the eyes. They caught her off guard. Again.

"I saw you come in the gate back there," he said and he pointed to the main entrance.

"Oh," she said. "Are you stalking me?"

"Another coincidence," he said, as though trying to put her at ease. "A lucky one," he added with a wink.

She turned away with a half smile and picked up her pace. He strode along beside her, now leaning into her, and she felt the tingle of his hand next to hers. But she didn't move away. She wasn't inclined to run from him.

She liked the strange closeness, its magnetism.

"Here," she pointed." Turn here."

They walked towards a mausoleum and he stopped several meters from the steps and looked up at the name that was carved into the pink marble above the arched doorway. Traditional serif font, all upper case. Familia Lenz-Weber. "This is your family?" Inside, on the far crypt, her father's name was carved into grey marble. "Vicente Harold Lenz-Weber, our dearly beloved father and husband. 1935-1969." Elena always thought the inscription was too cold, that her mother could have and should have managed something more, something that truly reflected their deep loss and abiding love.

Bladimir pronounced the man's full name under his breath, letting his tongue follow through, then he closed his lips with a slight pop, bringing the name to its final, foreign end.

"Do you feel like you have to apologize for that?" He was accusing her.

At first she thought he was referring the dates inscribed there, to how young her father was when he died. Did he know she felt guilty? Or did he know about her father's history, his role in Chilean politics, and was he in disagreement? "Apologize for what?"

"The name. I mean, it's German, right?"

Surely, he couldn't be serious. Was he calling her a Nazi? Incredible. Or was he connecting her to Paul Schaefer, the notorious German cult leader who was finally extradited from Argentina after he escaped Chilean justice. Either way, she bristled at his too unsubtle, malicious insinuation.

"No. I mean... no. I don't." She had already mounted the three steps to the mausoleum entrance and was standing there, her fingers gripping the wrought iron grill, looking into the golden light that penetrated the small window at the back. The mausoleum housed six crypts upstairs and eight in the subterranean level, all of which were still empty except for this one. There was room for a big family. Her mother had overshot, gone to extremes. Again. She half-turned to face BJ.

"My family name is German but we're Chilean through and through."

She forced her chin out. "I'm fourth generation, as a matter of fact."

"Yeah, but I bet you're fluent in German. Right?"

"Yes, and proud of it."

"Do you know Paul Schaefer?'

"What kind of a question is that?" He was trying to wind her up now. He was clearly an asshole with beguiling eyes. "Do you just assume that all Chileans of German descent would associate with that pedophile?"

He smirked, hands in pockets, eyes glinting and she couldn't tell if he was amused by her discomfort or if it was a smile of disdain for a family that might have been connected to Colonia Dignidad, as though they too might have routinely abused children and collaborated with Pinochet.

"My family is originally from Valdivia," was all she could summon in her defense. It was true, and Valdivia was a long way from Paul Schaefer's colony. "And my family is a very, very long way from someone like him. See the name there? See Vicente Harold Lenz-Weber? For your information, my father was a well-respected senator. If you knew your history, you'd know what he stood for. And you'd also know that he died way too early." She turned to swipe her eyes before tears became obvious. The last thing she wanted to do was let this guy see her cry. "He died in a car accident. It was tragic. And unfair. His life was cut short." By now her voice was breaking. "He was a good man. A very good man. And why am I telling you, anyway? You don't even deserve to know."

Her cheeks were hot. "It's time for you to go," she said without looking at him. "I want to visit my father in peace." She almost added, "And I don't like you." Even so, she wasn't sure that was true.

He nodded, traces of his wry smile remaining, and without another word, he turned and walked away. She watched him disappear around the corner, nonchalant, hands in pockets, and she realized that he still hadn't asked her first name. And she hadn't offered.

Elena didn't unlock the grill at the entrance of the mausoleum. Rather she just leaned her forehead into the bars, as though trying to escape this reality and gently push into that of her father. She glanced at the date and name, both carved with such precision and symmetry. She focused on her father's crypt, directly across from her, at the back, under the altar. He was at the head, as though there'd be a table around which, unless there was a miracle, she'd be the only other soul present. Her mother had designed the mausoleum, and she was in charge. Elena never asked if her mother planned to join him there because she was pretty sure the answer was No.

"Did you see that man with me, Papá?" Elena squinted into the feeble interior light and paused, hoping for the miracle of a response. There would be none coming. "Well, he's insolent. Of course he is. He's also obviously from a family of little education. But you know what, Papá? I like him. I can admit to you that I think he's beautiful. Isn't he? I don't mean just on the outside. I mean he embodies certain qualities. Excitement. Mystery. A dark enchantment. It's very seductive. To be honest, there's something of death around him. And that, well, that's where you are, isn't it?" She gazed in, pushing her cheeks into the bars, almost kissing the cool air inside. She inhaled deeply and pushed her hips forward, brushing against the large, engraved metal flower that formed part of the latch and under which hung a heavy padlock. She felt the squareness of it at her thighs and tightened her muscles so she was taut against it, imagining the bruise that would develop and show itself tomorrow. She touched her thigh there. "Proof," she thought. "Proof that I was here. Proof that I visited, that today I managed to resist the temptation to enter this quiet eternity, to fall into this peace. Proof that I will live another day. It looks like heaven will wait a little longer." She grinned to herself. "Or hell."

She leaned out, her feet planted at the base of the wrought iron and her elbows locked, hands gripping the grill, and she dropped her head to look backwards up at the sky. A green budgie flew over to perch on a bowed, long-hanging branch of an araucaria tree. The bird cocked his little head and stared at her. "We're all just waiting," he chirped. "We sing to celebrate the inevitable end."

Elena smiled at the bird and thought about going home. Home. Not her apartment and not her mother's house. But home, here, where they would all meet one day. Sweet temptation.

6 | INSIGHT

One day in 2015

Unlike Elena, who was obsessed with it, Bladimir, who'd had more brushes with it than he cared to count, didn't contemplate death. He was all about living in the moment. He had a predilection for life by the seat of his pants, and he'd learned from Giorgio, his boss, the owner of El Terminal, what fully embracing the moment meant. Giorgio had been blinded in an accident nearly 45 years ago. And when that happened, Bladimir was still only three years old, still some time before the State would assign him his official identity number.

"What do I see?" Giorgio tossed the question back to Bladimir. It was a day back in 2015, shortly after their infamous senator disappeared in disgrace, the day when he and Giorgio found themselves left in the lurch with handfuls of unfulfilled promises and half-baked plans on the shelf. They were standing, fists shoved in pockets just inside the entrance of El Terminal. Bladimir was conscious of the glow from the classic three wise monkeys statue—"See no evil, hear no evil, speak no evil." This particular version of the statue took the form of a hollow plastic lamp that was plugged in day and night. It emitted a slightly pink glow from the shelf behind the till, in such a way that the cashier appeared to have a rose-colored halo whenever he stood at that certain worn-out spot on the rug directly in front of the cash register. Bladimir thought the 'see no evil...' part was fitting for Giorgio.

"Yeah." Bladimir repeated the question. "What does a blind man see?"

As was his habit, Giorgio adjusted his cat eyes sunglasses, the ones that reflected yourself back to yourself through their black, impenetrable mirrors. The frames had diamonds in the top outside corners. Everyone assumed the gems were fantasy but no one dared ask for fear of insulting Giorgio, who sported them proudly. Had the true origin and value of the gems been known, Giorgio would have been the target of many assaults by persons who somehow just assumed they could outsmart him. The glasses were a feminine style but it was okay because Giorgio couldn't see how they looked anyway; he just loved how they felt and that's what mattered. If one's first impression of Giorgio was that he was a low-class, two-bit-player, they would be partly right. But one would always be wise not to underestimate Giorgio.

"You see, when you run your fingers around this curve here, it brings you up to these gems here." He ran his index finger along the outside and stopped at the right corner of the cat eye frame with its four inlaid stones. His finger registered each of the rounded gems. "They're pretty and they're useful. It's like, well, if I can't see something, they can. You know what I mean? They transmit. They're my eyes on a frame." The stones were set in Braille, letter G (left corner) and letter R (right corner), for Giorgio Ramirez. The glasses were the trademark of someone you should never, ever consider messing with.

Giorgio had a reputation. He was older, he was known to be wiser, and because he was blind, his other senses, and in particular, the sixth one that told him about people, was assumed to be razor sharp. Bladimir trusted him and he knew that Giorgio would guide them out of the mess that the senator had left behind. So he agreed with him about the style of the glasses. "They're beauties all right." Bladimir smiled. He wondered if Giorgio could hear a smile.

Giorgio smiled in return, the muscles of his cheeks raising the glasses a bit, and the diamonds glinted their pink glow right back to those three wise monkeys.

"So, what do you see?" Bladimir repeated the question. "I mean, in this case."

Giorgio worked around to his non-answer. "I know where you're goin' with this," Giorgio told him. "The fact is that the senator just changed. Simple as that. I had him pegged right a few years ago. He was the perfect mentor back then. I know you counted on him. But something happened and *ese hue'on* got lost along the way."

Bladimir wanted the details. He'd put his faith in this senator. This guy was supposed to be his rock, his stepping stone. He was a member of one of the new far left parties, part of the coalition that adhered to ideals of Socialism of the 21st Century and claimed to live amongst and understand the needs of working people—not like those *hue'ones* in the right-wing who were totally disconnected from reality.

Giorgio shifted from one foot to the other. "I knew he was drifting away. I could feel it. He was hedging. But I couldn't get to the bottom of it. Our senator was not greedy. No, it wasn't that. He was dedicated to the cause. I think he became desperate, though. Desperate that things weren't moving fast enough and going far enough, and in my opinion, he wanted a personal safeguard. He got careless. That's all. He trusted the wrong people and the damage was done before he could get out. I don't know… but I think the other senators in the block were screwing him around, and my theory is that they cooked it all up to trap him. You know how savage politicos are."

Bladimir stood patiently, waiting for more. Surely, there must be more, something concrete, a real, solid explanation. Giorgio's answer didn't sit right but he let it pass. After all, who was he to question Giorgio? Not only was he his boss but he was an astute political advisor, someone who had all the info, was aware of the hidden agendas, and importantly, he knew how to make the most of them.

Apparently, the vision of a blind man—specifically, that of Giorgio—was not meant to be shared with Bladimir that day. So he decided to just keep his faith.

Giorgio instructed Bladimir to meet him and a few selected others at the fringes of Party headquarters tomorrow where they'd redefine their plans in order to fill the hole the senator left. Although, as per standard Chilean planning, many steps on the way to the goal would be left to chance, the goal itself would be more or less clarified.

Members of the senate pretended to be surprised by the ousting of this senator. But really, they had all seen the writing on the wall. His immunity had to be removed by vote of the senate eventually, and in the end, there were very few people who could publicly offer him a goodwill hug or even a handshake. The vote would have to go against him if they wanted to save themselves. So it did, and they did.

The fate of the senator is, in itself, of no importance and deserves no further consideration. It's the concept of absence that is worthy of reflection and that has the most relevance. It was absence, after all, that Giorgio and Bladimir had in common. And this will be judged in future, either as very good fortune or as an extremely unlucky state of being. Upon reflection, it was absence of family that defined Bladimir as a badass survivor, singular and determined, and it was the absence of Giorgio's sight that enhanced his vision.

Perhaps this is why, four years into the future, Elena was attracted to Bladimir. Because he had an aura of absence —if such a thing is even possible. And it was the absence of her father that defined her, that pulled at her, that often dragged her first into a deep, hollow darkness and then into the brightness of fond memories. Mostly the former. Absence was a lot like death. And death was a lot like love. Like love, death's allure lay in the comfort of its all-encompassing power to relieve her of any responsibility, to envelope and take care of her. It was blind. It was seductive.

Although he continued faithfully along trodden path, Bladimir didn't feel enlightened by Giorgio's responses, and in fact, he would later remember thinking that Giorgio was hedging. As it happened, there was an elderly eavesdropper that day back in 2015 who would have agreed with Bladimir. This eavesdropper was a quiet old man who often sat alone at El Terminal for hours, just nursing a glass of water and watching. Unfortunately, the old man had lost his bearings decades ago and although he might have carried an abundance of knowledge around with him, he was incapable of calling it up. Mental decay had taken over soon after he suffered serious head trauma way back in '69 when he was only 34 years old, and afterwards, try as he may to convey the knowledge he had acquired, it was grid locked in a maze of years gone by. If he should ever succeed in stumbling through said maze to situate himself in the correct time and place, his information would be so mangled by the burned out cogs in his brain that attempts to convey it, would have been for naught. And even less likely, if a rare occasion should arise where he would be able to build a cohesive narrative, the truth would appear so ludicrous that no one would believe him. Either way, the truth would be lost.

This old man—who went by the name of Vicente—had been familiar with Giorgio for decades. Their last eye-to-eye encounter had been 45 years ago and except for the first ten of those years (while Vicente had been trying to come to terms with his new reality), he had been keeping a close eye on Giorgio.

Vicente was a pauper, a spent man, someone society considered useless and probably even a burden. He had no job, no commitments, no time pressure. He could do as he pleased. And what pleased him was watching the comings and goings of Giorgio. Although, for reasons already described, Vicente couldn't remember why Giorgio was of such consequence, he felt compelled to keep tabs on him. Giorgio was, of course, unaware of the old man's interest because he was blind and also because Vicente was cautious.

Vicente didn't question his own motives. He was content to be led around by his instincts. As such, up until the fatal bus accident, his was a day-to-day, relatively content kind of existence. Vicente had been watching one other person during the last year too. The reason for choosing the new watchee was unknown even to himself but he did not question his motive. He just watched. End of story. So, just as Giorgio was blind to Vicente's vigilance, Elena too, was unaware of his discreet but steady attention.

7 | THE GREATER GOOD

October 20, 2019

The universe had already begun to tip under the weight of the inevitable. Neither Elena nor Bladimir were aware that they had encountered one another before. But if Elena had paid attention, she would have felt Bladimir's breath on her neck the day of the bus accident, nine weeks before they would meet at the playground.

Immediately after the impact and the interminable shudder of the bus's blue metal, Bladimir shoved past the other passengers, scrambling towards the back of the old coach. He tried in vain to catch up with the young man who had the skull-print neckerchief pulled up over this nose. The boy's hood had loosened momentarily, revealing clumps of black curls and he yanked it down over his brow. His other hand was a fist, clenching the knife that he crammed deep into the right-hand pocket of his hoodie. He sprang from the back door, leaping past two young women and knocking one of them to the ground, the thick heel of his boot crushing her little finger. She yelped and collapsed onto the sidewalk in pain. Her friend snatched at the boy's jacket but he hammered at her wrist until she let go and then he escaped into the thick blue-green of the afternoon.

Bladimir followed and saw him disappear between the boards that had been hastily erected at storefronts, an urgent response for some kind—any kind—of security, at the mall entrance. The building interior was designed with an inclining ramp that spiraled up and around like a snail, little stores lining the outer curves. Bladimir followed the boy, striding past people who only glanced at him, unseeing, in their haste to lock themselves inside their shops, to yank down the blinds and make themselves unavailable to the violence that was closing in. He stopped once to lean down over the railing and survey the main floor and he saw a couple of policemen in riot gear who glanced around before heading back outside to subject themselves to the flying insults and rocks. Bladimir continued up along the ramp, more slowly now that he was out of the eye of the storm, and he found an exit to the roof. He flung open the flimsy metal door and ran to the edge. The scene below was chaotic. A dozen policemen were in a semi-circle, their shields tight to their chests, while two ambulance workers were behind them, leaning in to cover a woman's bloodied body. They hoisted her onto a stretcher, not so gently. They had thrown caution to the wind. She was dead after all.

Her fawn hat, disregarded and now without purpose, tumbled haphazardly along the curb. Maybe her soul had tugged on the hat's long blue ribbon, looking for something of this life to hang on to, something to reel her back in. But the hat had already run off. Bladimir watched as a bedraggled gentleman—whom he would have guessed was homeless except for the short white, groomed goatee—collapsed in tears at the woman's body. Bladimir counted four television crews, all elbows as they jostled to get closer, cameras pointed at the lifeless woman. No matter that her terrible state would never be fully exposed because it was too tragically graphic, too painful for the evening news transmission. The old man cried and hurled himself at the stretcher, clinging and pleading that she not leave without him. A paramedic pried his fingers loose and the old man folded and rolled into one of the pits of the sidewalk. The reporters decided against telling his broken story and instead, as if on cue, they pointed their cameras at the trembling bus driver who had fallen across the curb. Seemingly oblivious to the pain at hand, the people in the crowd were hurling rocks at the police, accusing them of murder and torture.

Bladimir released a breath of triumph, of exhilaration, of power, of change. Too bad one life had to be snuffed out. But one life often had to be sacrificed for the greater good. History would attest to it. A revolution doesn't happen without casualties. What do the Americans call it? Collateral damage. Besides, it wasn't his fault. He wasn't the one with the knife. He looked around the roof, a lofty refuge above the madness, and he saw the boy with the hoodie in the far corner. He too, was leaning down to watch. The boy soldier looked up to see him, and Bladimir gave him the thumbs-up. Then he calmly exited the roof, the building, and Santiago Centro, and he made his way home to Recoleta.

Only 40 minutes earlier Bladimir had jumped onto the blue bus to escape the riot police as they emerged without warning from a side street further east. Bladimir and his *compañeros* had already pummeled flimsy metal hoarding on store windows so they could break through into a popular eyeglass store. He grabbed as many pairs of spectacles, mirrors and small display frames as he could. But before he could drop them into his packsack, a group of protesters, fleeing the onslaughts of a water canon, charged past and he lost everything underfoot. The armored police vehicle had been attacked with a barrage of rocks, its sides and screened windows were splattered with paint and remnants of plastic bags full of shit that had burst upon impact and slithered down the sides. Yet the thing lumbered on, like a giant armadillo on its last legs. Its long metal spout pivoted and took aim, forcefully spewing its poison. This time Bladimir was in front of it, and it cut him down at the knees and sent him sprawling onto his back. He was flushed sideways in the surge, flailing and gurgling until he skidded into a wide, jagged hole in the middle of the sidewalk. Protesters had hammered out and smashed paving stones to use as artillery, leaving uneven caverns where the stones used to be. The water canon had washed him into one of those.

He was gasping and spitting, the acrid gas scorching his throat and picking at his eyes. He slipped several times before finally scrambling to his feet to seek an escape. The rioters had scattered into side streets, the armadillo performed one of its abrupt mechanical spins to follow a group of them and the police spread out in pursuit, wielding their riot sticks and rifles with rubber bullets.

Eyes burning and vision impaired, Bladimir squinted through the caustic fog that hung along the length of the street, and he recognized his youthful recruit in the hoodie, only meters away. He also spied a bus. It had just rolled up to the curb about 30 meters from the corner. The bus driver was obviously lost. Or else he was poorly informed. Was everyone not aware that the city center had been transformed into a war zone this afternoon? Who dared make these streets their destination? The old blue bus had rattled it way from the south end of town. It was pocked with rust and perforated with bullet holes. Graffiti was scrawled across its windows, dropping off where the glass was cracked or missing, and picking up again to run over the dent on the right front fender. The condition of the bus predated the riots. It was a sign of resentment and malcontent, vandalism coupled with lack of maintenance.

The bus would be Bladimir's savior.

The silly bus driver opened the doors (he would say later it was just out of habit). The passenger who had signaled for a stop, shrunk back, suddenly refusing to jump into the raging wilderness on the street. By now, though, it was too late, the bus had come to a halt, doors had opened.

Bladimir seized the opportunity. He pushed the hooded boy up the stairs in front of him and then he latched onto the front door and sprung up the first two steps just before the driver, face reddened, eyes aglow, realized his mistake and slammed the door shut, their sloppy rubber seals flapping in panic.

Bladimir assessed the frenzied young man who was one of his own warriors. He glanced back at Bladimir with a knowing nod. The driver's knuckles were white as he gripped the wheel, his shoulders drawn up so tensely that they crowded his reddened ears. But somehow the signals from his brain reached the muscles of his left thigh, and it contracted, putting pressure on the clutch. Bladimir could smell the driver's fear and it kindled a hunger that smoldered just beneath his skin, like that of the leader of a pack. Bladimir would be the courageous one who had leapt out of nowhere to lead his crew with precision and result. It would catapult him into a new realm where he'd be a force to reckon with, both among *compadres* and political infidels alike. This all occurred to him in less than a second.

As Bladimir vaulted up the last step, he signaled to the youth, who then reached into his pocket, and in one swift motion, he pushed the jack knife into the soft skin under the bus driver's ribs, stopping short of puncturing it.

"Drive, *hue'on!*"

The driver didn't need to look around. He knew. So he gripped the wheel even tighter as he shifted and tried to maintain control.

"I'll take over at the next stop." Bladimir's breath burned the driver's cheek. He saw the man begin to shake. Like a leaf. The guy wasn't going to last long. The young man with the knife had already done his part. He ran towards the back of the bus and prepared to push his way out the door.

And it was then that the brakes scraped and the bus shuddered and Bladimir heard the thud of a body colliding with the rusted-out public dinosaur just as it convulsed to a halt. He knew that in the future when the revolution was over and they were in charge, such taking of a life by an outdated hunk of rattling metal would never be necessary. So, no, this wasn't his fault. He was working towards a greater good.

Just moments earlier, Elena found herself standing in the shadows, seeking shelter at the entrance of a big eyeglass store that had been looted only minutes earlier. Now the store stood naked and in tatters, gang-raped by a dozen hooded youths who were high on their own audacity. Elena ignored the ragged state of the store because she was terrified by the storm of looters that had just erupted out of nowhere and thundered past. She saw a small woman wearing an oversized coat and a fawn felt hat with a navy blue ribbon, frantically trying to back away from the rabble on the sidewalk just beyond the bus stop. The poor woman's hat flopped forward, covering her face and obstructing her view. She stumbled off the curb and fell into the path of the big blue bus that couldn't stop fast enough. That was the moment she was sacrificed for the greater good.

Horrified, Elena struggled against the sudden current of human rabble, all straining to take a look. She raced along the sidewalk towards the back of the bus. Her goal was to reach the safety of the other side of the street. When she rounded the bus, about to leap off the curb, a tall man crashed into her from behind. They stumbled and she felt him grip her shoulders to prevent them both from falling. His breath was heavy. Annoyed, he grunted and released her without a word and ran off into the distance.

Neither Bladimir nor Elena would recall this clumsy encounter in the midst of the savage turbulence. If so, it would have been one of those rare memories, so fleeting that they would push it aside, attributing it to imagination. Had she turned around, she would have seen his eyes. Had he looked into her face, he would have seen his little fascist.

8 | BRIEF ENCOUNTER

January 15, 2020

January mornings, middle of summer, were not supposed to be cloudy. But weather systems had changed in the last few years. Elena considered that Mother Earth was well within her rights to cough and spit her discontent about the collective disregard for her wellbeing. Weather was no longer predictable; storms, either rebellious or whimsical, roared in to break historic patterns. Elena forgave Mother Earth for these tantrums even though they affected her on a personal level. Today, she couldn't rouse herself out of bed. The clouds kept her down. Usually the sun peered through the window, and with a cheeky nod of his head, he would signal for her to sit up and take notice of the day.

But this morning Mother Earth was playing havoc by beckoning the clouds in from the Pacific. And now they hung over the central valley like a dull, gloved hand, grey fingers held up in a sign that said Stop. So she did. Elena let her arms flop at her sides, shut her eyes again and began to think about that man called BJ.

She tried not to picture his stinging dark eyes. But they kept looking at her and she was compelled to look back. She tried to repress the excitement they ignited by recalling his rude comment about her family's German heritage. But that only added to his mystery, and thus to his attraction. Had destiny brought them together? That was so cliché. She clicked her tongue at the dark stain on the ceiling that looked like a face with a grin and she spit at it. "Am I really that silly?" She was juvenile for even toying with such a thought. Now that they'd met twice and he had an idea of where to find her, would he seek her out again? She sighed and rolled onto her stomach, kicking backwards at the bedspread until it flopped to the floor. "Go back to sleep. There's nothing to get up for," she told herself.

Her neck hurt. She was tense. She turned her head to the other side. That made it worse. She was irritated. She slapped the pillow and finally punched it aside, rolled onto her back and she stared out the window. The sky was so grey that she couldn't see the cordillera, and the birds were quiet. She heard construction noises, some drills and the tack-tack of electric hammers in the near distance. Who wants to build anything? What's the point? Let it all fall away. What did it matter? Then she thought about everyone out there doing something, creating something, designing, engineering, changing, building, cleaning. She thought about the joggers, and the crazies who used the exercise equipment that the municipality had installed along the boulevard. She thought about the men hanging from the top of 20-story buildings, washing windows, the crane operators, the bus drivers, the farmers, the overly cheery TV personalities, especially the silly ones who danced in front of the weather screen every morning. And what about the politicians? Most of all, what about them? What motivated them to subject themselves to the political maze and compete with other super egos? Who were all of these people? And what did they want? How did they make themselves get up every morning? What drove them to rise to the challenge and carry on?

She sat up. And just as she did, a ray of sunshine flickered through a cloud, giving her a wink and a nod. "It's as good a day as any."

"As good a day as any for what?" She said aloud. Her voice sounded stupid when it bounced back at her from her blank bedroom wall. But then she found herself on her feet and as she slowly padded her way into the bathroom, she told herself, "I'm up but it doesn't mean I'm going anywhere." It was just the call of nature and one of those routines that one assumes after living for 56 years. The days added up to an eternity. Fifty-six. Fifty sick.

She wasn't hungry but she opened the fridge to check inside. Milk. Probably outdated, so why bother to look? But she shook it anyway and could feel the clots jostle against the carton. A brick of moldy cheese that she hadn't taken a slice from yet, some limp lettuce, a soft beet. The strawberries still looked edible but she didn't feel like eating strawberries. Just a coffee then. But she had none. She really didn't want to go out. She glanced through the window and saw Doña Monica, the elderly neighbor from the first floor. Her maid was facing the old lady and slowly walking backwards. She straddled the sidewalk as she steadied Doña Monica by her elbows and encouraged her to advance one slow, halting step at a time, towards the gate. What made Doña Monica want to get up each day and go for a walk? Elena felt like shouting at the maid to move out of the way so she could push the old woman from behind. "Just go. Just move. Get it over with." It would work if Doña Monica wore roller skates. Elena imagined the old lady landing on the sidewalk, the wheels of the roller skates squeaking their last slow revolutions at the end of those spindly legs, the old lady's knees broken, her face skinned after colliding with the concrete, an unhappy, unrecognizable, mangled little mess. Poor thing.

Elena picked up a pad of yellow-lined paper and glanced at what she had scribbled. 'BJ' was scrawled here and there, sometimes in big flowing, capital letters, sometimes in tiny lower case, as though she was trying him on for size. She'd added question marks. What did BJ stand for? She tossed the pad aside. BJ, CJ, DJ, EJ... who cares?

She scoffed at her idiotic musings. A coffee would do her good. Maybe she'd take her notepad and sit at the cafe, just for a change of pace. Maybe she'd join the crowd of busy young people, or at least observe all of them doing something important.

She pulled on her old jeans and a stained cotton sweater, grabbed her wallet and a fresh yellow notepad, stepped into her boots, letting the buckles hang sloppily around her ankles, closed the door on her way out and began counting her steps.

The air was humid. Everyone seemed to be in a bad mood. By the time she arrived and sat at her usual table on the sidewalk, she was feeling even more cranky. She set the notepad facedown, took a sip of the soda water that accompanied the double espresso and she looked around. Half of the tables were occupied by individuals seriously engaged with their mobile phones. There was a couple at a table to her left who appeared to be arguing. Only one person seemed content and it was an elderly gentleman with round glasses who was leaning very far forward, his nose was almost flat against a broadsheet that he'd pressed onto the table. She thought his lips were moving as he read. She heard him chuckle to himself a few times.

She sighed and pulled a pen out of her pocket and was about to turn over her notepad when she felt someone tap her on the shoulder. She turned and looked into the smiling eyes of the man called BJ.

"*Hola*," he said, and his grin widened.

"Hi yourself," she responded, just staring up at him. Her heart skipped a beat. Then it pounded, and her bad temper magically disappeared, dark humor evaporating through shallow breaths. She smiled. She hoped the smile wasn't too broad, that it didn't give away her extreme pleasure at his most welcome and sudden presence.

"Do you come here often?" he asked.

"What's it to you?" She tried to be nonchalant. She hoped he would repent his rudeness from their encounter at the cemetery. But he didn't seem to be the repentant kind. Or else he had a short memory.

"Maybe I wanna know where to find you," he said.

"Are you stalking me?" Now she tried to sound shocked but at the very thought of it, she felt a narrow river of delight tickle around in her stomach and she knew she was batting her eyelashes. Get a grip.

"Maybe," he said.

"Well, in that case, I guess we can both relax. Will you join me?" She turned, motioning towards the empty chair.

"No." He tapped her twice lightly on the shoulder. "Thanks, though." And he was gone.

Was he teasing her? What was the point of this? Irritated, she flipped her notepad right-side-up and began scratch large letters across the sheet, 'Asshole. Loser. Charmer. Tease.' in various sizes over the entire page. She couldn't concentrate enough to make lists. Pros to counteract the cons was her usual practice. But this morning, she was too agitated.

She finished her coffee, went in to pay at the counter, frowning at the customers as she waited. The clerk was dawdling just to annoy her. By then a few more couples were seated at tables, sipping their coffee and playing with napkins, glancing up and down as they chatted. The elderly gentleman who'd had his nose in the broadsheet (and now that she saw him standing, could see that he was worse for wear) was on the sidewalk, toying with the strap of a tattered leather packsack that hung across his shoulder. Eyes downcast, he reached up to stroke his white goatee, his fingertips exposed through a pair of worn fingerless gloves. He looked oddly familiar but she didn't linger because she was looking for someone else.

She scanned the street—the drug store, and beside it, the vegetable stand and to the left of that on the corner, the bakery and then the newspaper kiosk. But wait, there he was, standing between an overgrown aloe vera plant and the flower seller on the boulevard. He hadn't even troubled himself to cross all the way to the other side of the street. He was just standing in the middle, staring back at the cafe. Was he watching her? She raised her hand to wave but he didn't wave back. She shivered and suddenly felt very, very cold.

9 | SOCIAL JUSTICE

May 2017

"You have to know how to take it on." It was Giorgio reminding Bladimir how things were to be done. It was 2017, nearly two years after their senator made his mysteriously convenient exit from the scene (and two years before Bladimir would set eyes on Elena). By now, though, Giorgio had more than filled the senator's shoes. Not in the public sense but definitely as a chef in the political kitchen sense. He was organizing groups, setting up meetings, coordinating events and in general, growing his army of budding young activists.

"I'm not just talking about the boring—but of course essential, they're all essential—tasks you perform here," he said, gently running an index finger over the gems on one corner of his glasses and then turning and blindly gesturing with a broad sweep of his arm. "Look around you, Bladimir. What do you see?"

"Your restaurant, Giorgio. And it's less than half full right now."

Giorgio heard the smile in Bladimir's voice. He responded, "Yeah, you're right. A half-full restaurant. But be patient. *Mira.* It's being populated, and very carefully, very strategically populated. This is not just your usual *hue'onaje*—human rabble." The skin around his eyes crinkled, the creases of his aged skin deepening and reaching beyond his dark glasses and into the grey stubble on his cheeks. "And with guys I picked, like with tweezers. Very carefully."

Bladimir nodded, and Giorgio sensed his agreement.

"Look at it this way, Bladimir. Serve these people and we serve ourselves. And I don't mean just with food. These guys abandoned their country to jump into the fight. We need to arm them with our stuff, with our methods. We need to teach them the ins and outs of Santiago. Well, the whole country. At the same time, we need to figure out their way of doing things. It's all coming together. Can you hear the sound of change?" He reached out and gave Bladimir a feeble slap on the back and then grinning, he nodded curtly towards the 'chi-ching' of the cash register. "And that's what it's really all about."

"That's where altruism dies," Bladimir said under his breath after Giorgio tapped his way towards the back room. "What?" Giorgio half turned. "Nothing," said Bladimir.

Bladimir rounded the counter so he could survey the crowd. These were fellow hardliners, followers of Marx, aspirers to an equitable world, one country at a time. Many of these *compradres* were teachers in their own right. Some of them were giving classes at the Instituto Nacional in downtown Santiago. They were talented, charismatic individuals who had been welcomed by Giorgio and like-minded others to promote the Marxist philosophy and push for deeper change, to help instigate the inevitable revolution that Chile deserved. This time, it would not fail. The people were clambering for it.

The full name of the Instituto Nacional was El Instituto Nacional General José Miguel Carrera. It was an emblematic school in downtown Santiago. Everyone in Chile knew about it. At that point, it was a public high school for boys between the ages of 12 and 18. It was famous partly because it was founded nearly 200 years ago. And not by the Church but rather by a nationalist General, who, for all intents and purposes, orchestrated a Coup, usurping the power of the Spanish Royalists in Congress. Among his other accomplishments, he created this independent school. The mission of the school was to educate boys who would 'direct and defend the Chilean state with honor, and make it flourish.'

From its very early days, the Instituto had been known for student takeovers in struggles for class equality and human rights. In fact, the Chilean Socialist and Communist parties were rooted in the school's original 'society for equality' movement, which began in the 1840s. And only a few years ago, the Instituto was at the forefront of the 'march of the penguins' (formidable student protests, so-called because of the resemblance of black and white school uniforms to penguins), demanding a quality national public education system. It hadn't worked. The struggle was ongoing. And although Bladimir had not been privileged enough to attend the Instituto, he felt in his bones that he belonged there because of his destiny as a big player in the class struggle. Granted, he had never enrolled but ironically, now he was in a position to influence those who did. Thanks to Giorgio's contacts, he had been invited multiple times by the school director to light up the faces of the Instituto's young soldiers with his speeches and his vision for equality and dignity. The students understood that Bladimir's humble background made him righteous and it armed him with insights that inspired them. They joined him in the courtyard after class, and then later, on the streets, their heavy boots marching behind him, pounding out the rhythm of their young, idealistic and inevitable victory. Armed with Bladimir's interpretation of practical Marxism, they felt power in each determined stomp. Bladimir had never been chosen to train in Colombia under las FARC and he sometimes resented that. But perhaps it was because his role was not with militia groups in La Araucanía because Giorgio found more use for him in the Capital.

After the disappearance of the senator two years ago, Bladimir felt himself gradually being side-lined by Giorgio, especially when it came to core planning. He sometimes wondered if Giorgio had deliberately tied him to the senator's shameful actions, if he had accused him to the politicians. Perhaps Giorgio suspected that Bladimir knew the real facts of the matter. Truth be told, although Bladimir had always felt there was something more behind the disappearance of his mentor, he never discovered what that something might be. It niggled at him but he tried to focus on matters at hand, such as his role as educator to young revolutionaries, from which he derived satisfaction.

Many of the same foreign activists who ate at Giorgio's El Terminal were also invited to the Instituto to give talks and introduce their philosophy to pliable young minds. Members of *el Movimiento de Izquierda Revolucionaría – MIR* (Revolutionary Left Movement), a political group that grew out of Chile's 60s guerrilla movement were also involved because of their life experience and the group's prestigious history. MIR originally included anarchists, socialists and libertarians but before reaching its peak during Salvador Allende's government, it had established itself as a Marxist-Leninist organization. Although essentially an ideological group, it picked up arms to fight against the Pinochet regime, and many of its members were subsequently murdered or 'disappeared.' The organization was attractive to young, idealistic students, as was *el Frente Patriotico Manuel Rodriguez – FPMR* (Manuel Rodriguez Patriotic Front) a more militant group, whose combat training in Cuba was meant to help bring down the Pinochet regime. FPMR, its 80s logo the shape of an automatic weapon, maintained its presence as protector of the native Mapuche peoples and their fight for land, as well as being advocates for the release of *compatriotas*, whom they deemed were unjustly imprisoned on political grounds.

Flash forward to the spring and summer of 2019 and you can see that they had kept themselves relevant.

Bladimir tried not to mind being side-lined by these *guerrilleros*. They were, after all, intimidating, psychological heavyweights who had already paid their dues. Soon, rather than being a leader in the classroom, Bladimir was forced to take his place behind them and was assigned to instruct small groups of students in such things as running a 'tornado'—where an unwieldy number of participants stormed an office or a bank or a store. Their goal—to loot and intimidate. The unsuspecting attendants threw up their hands at the sudden onslaught of determined destruction. Bladimir did a good job of that. He taught them how to act as one mob, outwardly chaotic and intimidating, but actually efficient and effective. He instructed them on the torching and razing of modern buildings and infrastructure. He arranged for the purchase and delivery of equipment and material to achieve such things. It was no small feat.

However, it was still easy for some to dismiss Bladimir as a man of no importance, a poorly educated, middle-aged guy who did what he was told, minded his own business and who had long since reached his low grade potential, where no more could be expected of him. But he had not lost his youthful, rebellious spark, his burning desire for equal access to the good life, and the satisfaction of meting out justice at his own hand. He was not to be underestimated. Bladimir had once had a taken his place at Giorgio's table of merry men and women (both the narco and political kind. However, truth be told, as early as 2017, fine cracks began to creep across the base of his loyalty. So far, this had not threatened to degenerate the firm foundation of his ideological perspective. He didn't seriously contemplate testing it because that would be akin to throwing himself into the middle of the ocean without a floating device. Bladimir couldn't swim.

Flash forward again to October 19, 2019, the first day of the social uprising and you could see Bladimir's hand in the actions of most of the young activists and looters on the streets of Santiago Centro. They participated in setting fire to buses and metro stations, rendering them inoperable for months. They had been there the next day, too, when the woman was run over by the blue bus, and they were there for days and weeks afterwards. They looted stores, they demolished whatever they could manage to demolish and graffitied on any available surface. "Death to the police. Death to the President." They were mighty. Defiant, they rested atop national monuments. Don't mess with the true power of the people.

Jump ahead to February, 2020. Bladimir's eyes burned with the ardor of his long-desired revolution. But a quiet little grey cloud was beginning to dim the light. Perhaps it was just a minor personal weather event that would pass. But recently there had been this little item called preoccupation with a woman. The woman was apparently the daughter of a former right-wing senator named Lenz-Weber and she was slowly becoming more than just a distraction. He head was filled with thoughts of her every day. He was in a private tug of war about this woman. He'd never been around someone like her, a barrio alto kind. So he was curious. But it was more than curiosity— did she represent a challenge, perhaps a conquest simply because she was there, kind of like Mount Everest? Perhaps she was just different enough, just connected enough, just aloof enough to whet his ambition? There was no satisfactory answer. He was attracted to her, end of story. He preferred not to know her first name. Her neighborhood and the surname on the mausoleum said it all. Or course this would make her a fascist. So he simply referred to her as 'Fachita.'

10 | DRUGS AND FORGIVENESS

February 2020

It was largely Bladimir's aura of mystery and his rebelliousness that attracted Elena. She had smothered her own spark of rebellion after, way back in her six-year-old wisdom, it became clear that she could not deny the authority of her mother. Since then, although she was sometimes tempted, Elena did her best to resist its pull. When she was young, on each Saturday in the Church confessional, she would swaddle those sinful urges and hand them over to the priest like innocent little gifts. And in return, "Your penance, my child, is three Hail Marys and one Our Father." With that, he would take hold of her sins and they would disappear like magic. And she would promise not to be tempted again. Try as she might though, the wicked and rebellious thoughts surfaced regularly, and each week at the close of her confession, the priest would sigh and she would watch through the coarse mesh window of the confessional as he drew a cross through the air with his mystical, magical right hand. "Go in peace, my child." She would bow her head gratefully, and getting ahead of the game, she would mouth the first of the three Hail Marys on her way out of the confessional, and she would already feel partially cleansed.

By the time she was in university, Elena fit the mold of an obedient, well-brought-up girl from an affluent family. But by then, she had stopped going to confession. This cessation should have been a rebellious act in itself but thankfully, her mother began drifting away from the Catholic Church after she moved in with Don Marco, a prominent medical examiner with political connections. By the time Elena would have sought her mother's permission to avoid confession, her own mother had already fallen away from most of the Church traditions, because she was now living in sin with Don Marco.

So Elena's abstention was not seen as a rebellion. As of then, before any of her infrequent appearances at mass, she was given a green light to bypass the confessional guilt-free. Oh, the freedom. Although Elena didn't think to be grateful to Don Marco, she could have thanked him for this small mercy because it was mostly Don Marco who shunned the Catholic Church. But only in private.

In her late teens she discovered another door to freedom, the one that drugs opened for her.

It was an easy transition from the prescription drugs that she began taking when she was about twelve years old. Those ones were the medical solution to her persistent youthful insomnia—an aberrance, her mother said. "How is that a young child cannot sleep?" Although she must have slept well during her first years of life, Elena couldn't remember a time before her recurring nightmares. Whenever she awoke from one of them, she feared that if she closed her eyes again, she'd fall back in with the same dreadful demons. She discovered that if she crept out of bed and paced up and down the hallway, counting her steps, it prevented the nightmare from reintruding. When she reached 5,000 steps, she was pretty certain that the dream would become bored and turn its back on her, permitting her to walk away from it and safely fall back into a quiet sleep.

Her mother awoke several times during the week because of the squeaking floorboards in the hallway and Elena's breathy whispers.

"Elena," she would say softly so as not to disturb Don Marco. He didn't like to have his sleep disturbed. "Elena, my little heart, you can't be awake all night. It's not healthy."

Elena's response was to keep walking and counting under her breath.

"Come, I'll prepare some warm milk." Her mother would put her arm around her and pull her close. She was always more maternal in the middle of the night. Elena would snuggle into her shoulder and sniff her familiar rose-scented night cream. They'd walk side-by-side down the stairs and into the kitchen. But Elena never missed a beat. She paced and counted until her mother placed the mug on the table and wrapped Elena's fingers around it with her own.

"Thank you," Elena would whisper, raising her index finger to pronounce the number of steps to that point, "Four thousand, four hundred and twenty-two." And she'd stop counting earlier than usual.

The nightmares continued and it didn't seem like there would be an end to the pacing and counting. Finally one morning, Elena's mother told her that they needed help and that's when they went to the doctor and that's when he recommended cough syrup and that's when drugs began to play a role in her life. More than the controlled substance itself, it was its promise as a convenient, even magical solution that would become a problem,

When she was in her last year of high school, she confessed to Miguel, her first serious boyfriend, that she had nightmares. She thought it best to prepare him because she was hoping to arrange for him to stay the night with her sometime soon.

And that night came to pass the first time she invited him for dinner with her mother and Don Marco.

"You've teased me long enough," Miguel told her when they'd gone out to the garden on the pretense of plucking a few grapes from the trellis. He grabbed her and pulled her so tight that she gasped for breath. He said, "I think you need to get me into your room tonight. I can't wait any longer."

Truth be told, Elena had been on fire for Miguel all day and even a brush of his hand against hers sent hot electric surges to places she knew Don Marco and her mother would not approve of. "Mamá, we're just going to the garden for some fresh air."

"Okay, but stay where I can see you. And bring in some grapes, will you?"

"They don't trust you," Elena said,

"They can probably smell something burning," Miguel winked.

They saw Don Marco's silhouette glide past the window and they moved apart, and then got serious.

"Okay, so this is the plan," Miguel said. "That's your room up there, right?" He pointed at the second story window. "You go upstairs and open the window. I'll say goodnight to your parents and then I'll come back and climb up this thing and I'll be in your bed before you can close the window again."

She flushed and nodded. She gave his hand a quick squeeze and he held onto hers and moved it towards his crotch. She flushed and started with a laugh. "No! Wait."

The plan worked. Obviously this was not the first trellis that Miguel had climbed. When all was said and done and Miguel sat cross legged, blowing smoke out the window, and Elena was lounging across the bed, she blurted it out. "I don't sleep well."

"What do you mean, you don't sleep well?" His head rotated, owl-like, to look at her.

"Well, I tend to have nightmares. Stupid things, really. But I can't go back to sleep afterwards."

"I'm not sure what you are expecting," he said. "But when I'm done here, you won't be able to keep your eyes open and you'll sleep for days." He grinned.

She grinned back.

"I'm not staying for the sleeping part anyway, Elena. It's not my style. Besides, this is your parents house. You know..."

"Oh." She was relatively new to all this.

"But listen," he was serious now. "I have a friend who can give you a few pills to help you sleep."

"Really?"

"Yeah, it'll cost you, though. But..." he waved his hand to indicate their surroundings. "You can afford it. I'll put you in touch."

And that's how Elena discovered the downers. Miguel introduced her to a guy called Flaco who sold all manner of pills. They met Flaco outside of a pizza joint in Bella Vista. "For you," he said. "For you, *mi gringita*, I'll sell you my special yellows at a discount. I promise you'll sleep like a baby. And when you need more—or something else—you know where to find me."

The yellows worked like a charm. She was a bit groggy for the first several mornings and she complained about it to Miguel. "I love that I can sleep. I mean, I can't remember having a single dream. But I'm kind of in a fog for most of the morning. I don't like that part."

"Flaco can sell you something to help with that too. He's not just the slinger of sleep, he's the wonder of wake. Go talk to him. You know where to find him."

After that, Miguel kind of drifted away towards new trellises and Elena didn't see much of him. But she would always be grateful for the education he gave her. As it turned out, she didn't miss him anyway. Flaco introduced her to some new friends over in Bella Vista. They were the kind of friends that her mother and Don Marco would definitely not approve of. They were the rebels, the front liners, the brazen loud-mouths. She smiled and admired them from the edge of their circle but she never ventured in to play wholeheartedly. Hers was, after all, another kind of world.

11 | BROKEN MEMORIES AND FALSE HOPES

February 2020

Elena watched as, one by one, the yellow papers fluttered lazily to the floor, and she was reminded of Rosa. Perhaps the memory was triggered by the lined yellow sheets or perhaps by the persistent melancholy, which tended to pull her back to the days when her father was alive. Rosa, the family maid and her nanny, left the family service a couple of weeks after her father's funeral and Elena never heard from her again. This was strange because Rosa had been in their employ since before Elena was born.

She was, for all intents and purposes, a member of their family. As a nanny she was tender and loving and a fierce protector. As a housekeeper, she was ever present and hard-working. She didn't let anything slip past her or go unanswered. This is mostly why her uncharacteristic and decision to abandon the family was extremely confusing, and her silence afterwards was painful.

After she left, Elena wrote letters to Rosa on the same sort of lined yellow pages that she used today. Her father used to keep stacks of the yellow pads in the deep bottom drawer of his desk. After he died, Elena gathered the pads and carried them up to her bedroom, where she socked them away under her bed. For years, and up until this day, she bought shrink-wrapped packages of the same. She was unable to bypass Libreria Nacional without popping in, and she never left the store without at least one or two fresh pads in hand. As far as the paper was concerned, she could probably qualify as a low-level hoarder. It was only after she entered university that she earnestly put any of it to use. Anyway, the point is that the letters she wrote to

Rosa went unanswered. After long delays, they were returned, address unknown. Her mother was no help. Eventually, Elena's curiosity and pain were replaced with bitterness, and she stopped writing and hoping.

Today, Elena decided that she would stay inside. She had no need and no desire to wander out into the heat. By mid-morning, the sun was already blinding and hot. When the afternoon rolled around, she opened the windows on the west side of her apartment to let in a light breeze and she stood in its relative coolness. At this hour, the city was more quiet than usual and she wondered if it was the calm before a storm. Since October, street protests and violence at various points up and down the country still sparked and smoldered and never entirely died away. Police were on alert as their stations were attacked with Molotov cocktails and sometimes live ammunition. Activists continued their reign over Plaza Italia and its southeast entrance to the metro, barring anyone who looked or acted too suspiciously like a *cuico*—an east-side snob. The emblematic plaza remained conquered territory in the middle of *Gran Santiago*. The victors renamed it Plaza de Dignidad. The naming of the plaza became a badge of your political colors. If you called it Plaza Italia, you were a right-wing cuico, labelled *Pinochetista* or *fascista* and you were spit at and hounded and prohibited from entering. If you called it Plaza de Dignidad, you were correct in your progressiveness, and were welcome. There was nothing in between.

The adjoining subway station was a camp for activists, who, having set it alight at the beginning of the uprising, now decorated its charred walls with graffiti, dozens of ripped and wild little flags, stained rags of some significance and large, sagging banners. They insisted this space was an historical reminder of state brutality at the hands of the national police. They set up makeshift tents and called it home, and the entry from here to the metro station was now permanently closed. Friday nights at the plaza were habitual scenes of raucous struggles between protestors and riot police. Local businesses who hadn't already moved, were forced to close, never to re-open, and local residents who had nowhere else to go complained about the insecurity and noise. But to no avail. Squatters moved into the abandoned spaces and looters wrenched away anything that wasn't nailed down. In other words, this place became no-man's land. The activists pronounced that this violence in the face of state repression must continue until they prevailed.

Eventually, the head of Chile's biggest independent human rights organizations threw a damper on all of this when he informed the public that his investigations, honest and thorough, could find no evidence to back the claims of torture and death at the hands of police in that metro station. The Communist Party was enraged at his findings and demanded he turn over his documents. He refused, and they forced his resignation. Importantly, subsequent evidence indicated that the violence of those initial days was actually finely tuned and timed and much too sophisticated to have been orchestrated by a group of young students from the Instituto Nacional who were suddenly so enraged by a five cent rise in metro fares that they spontaneously set out to destroy the country.

Giorgio said, "It doesn't matter what the fascists claim. They can't drown out the voice of the people. Not this time. Change is on its way. Freedom and open borders. That's what we stand for." Giorgio raised his fist in a feeble salute to the Communist cause. Bladimir couldn't disguise his skepticism but that didn't matter. Not with Giorgio.

This had all become too heavy for Elena, who had long ago dropped any interest in politics. Her father had died, and she had not inherited his political aspirations. More than that, as she saw it, politics had caused his death. Although she did not dip her toes into political currents, and had no first-hand information, she felt that her father had been swept away and drowned amidst their murky waters.

Elena bent down to retrieve one of the yellow sheets that had fallen on top of others on the dusty hardwood floor. She had scribbled, "People disappear and reappear." What had she been thinking? Had she written that this morning? She couldn't remember. Who was she talking about? Perhaps she had been thinking of Rosa or maybe she had BJ in mind. She tossed the sheet aside and watched it flutter to the floor, kicking the air above it and grunting in frustration. What was wrong with her? Why were her thoughts so random and shattered? Written in large letters on another sheet were the words, "Red Riding Hood and the Big Bad Wolf". She remembered writing that phrase. She had been thinking of BJ. Did his eyes really resemble the hungry ones of the big bad wolf? Could it also be that somewhere in another place he was disguised as a docile grandmother, ready to consume her? She shuddered and crouched down to shuffle more of the loose sheets.

She really should clean up soon but right now, she didn't care enough. She didn't care about much at all, save BJ's dark eyes. They were the only things that were able to pierce her apathy.

Elena didn't need much. Apart from some uppers and downers. If she wasn't satisfied with prescription drugs, then she knew where to go for the supplements. The monthly allowance that she received thanks to her father's will, was enough to pay for the basics. Anything extra went towards her yellows or pinks or whatever Flaco had on hand that she fancied. Perhaps the drugs were the reason she preferred a reclusive lifestyle. She had blown off all of her friends years ago, telling herself they were boring and self-involved. Now the bi-monthly visits from her mother and very infrequent coffees with Don Marco were the only occasions for conversation. That is, until BJ. He aroused in her an urge to talk. She found that she had to deliberately hold her tongue around him because if not, she'd spill her guts and who knew what rancid tidbits might be regurgitated? Perhaps this was his attraction. He encouraged her rebellious self. She wondered if she should have regretted inviting him to stand at her father's tomb? Had she opened a crack, allowed him to enter somewhere he didn't belong, offered him something that was none of his business? Yes, she was guilty. She promised herself she'd be more discreet.

Elena knew she was obsessed. Not only with BJ. She was obsessed with analyzing the obsession. She had lost all perspective. Perhaps she was obsessed because she was dying to tell him things—things that perhaps she didn't even know herself. Things that would surprise her only after they were said.

Elena was an incessant analyzer. Of everything. It's part of the reason she was driving herself insane. Her circle of thoughts expanded and contracted in useless spirals, threatening to choke her when they tightened around a subject. But she couldn't let go. She ran the ideas round and round, diving in to explore, resurfacing for air and finally, her thoughts would evaporate and form clouds that would rain down in confusion. Then she would paddle around in the puddles.

Recently, BJ was her obsession but in the weeks before she met him, she had begun to obsess around memories of Rosa. These ones had been dredged up in a dream. In the dream, Rosa was walking towards her. One end of a very long blue ribbon was wound through her fingers. Rosa was smiling as she approached Elena but suddenly the smile disappeared and she stopped and turned, snatching and pulling at the ribbon because it had gotten snagged on the thorns of a tall rose bush in the corner of a barren patio. Elena watched as Rosa marched impatiently, reeling herself in at the end of the ribbon like a fish on a line. Finally, Rosa reached the bush, bent down and extracted a fawn felt hat with a ragged blue bow. She smacked at the dust on it, clucking. She placing it sideways on her head. The hat produced a deep shadow across her face so that her expression was a mystery. But Elena could just see the corners of her mouth turn up in a slight smile. And, in a controlled, silky voice, Rosa said, "I have always watched out for you, Elena. Take heart. Don't give up."

"But I wrote to you, Rosa. I wrote to you. Where have you been?"

"I'm sorry."

"People do what they have to do." Elena replied. But she felt deflated.

Rosa raised her hand in a weak farewell. She turned, hat in hand. Now the ribbon was so long that there was no end in sight and it trailed behind her. As she rounded a corner, the ribbon followed and followed, and kept following.

Elena woke from the dream and her eyes were burning.

12 | THE WOMAN IN FRONT OF THE BUS

October 20, 2019

Rosa was dead. The last two things she remembered were: one, a collision—she caught a glimpse just before she felt the shuddering force of hot, heavy metal slamming into her body; and two, the tears that ran down Vicente's cheeks. The latter was perhaps a figment of her imagination because she could have already been dead. It had all happened so fast.

"Out 'a the way, stupid bitch!" Rosa was jostled about and pummeled by cruel shoulders and spiky elbows as a stampede of protestors barged past her near the bus stop. She had already been in and out of the gallery of shops and she now regretted having gone downtown at all. Crazy to expect that the madness she saw on the news yesterday would be over, or that she would escape it somehow. But she was so driven by her excitement of a gift for Vicente that she'd made a terrible decision.

As she pulled back to escape the fury of the human stampede, she stumbled at the edge of the curb, her hat slid down over her eyes, she lost her balance and tottered for a few seconds on the edge. She was suddenly aware of it, the big blue something coming at her. But the thing approached at a crazy, breakneck speed and it was on her.

That morning she had announced that she was going to a shop in Providencia to buy a little something. "Never mind," she said. "It's your birthday and I set aside a few pesos to celebrate. I've had my eye on something for months now and today's the day I'm going to get it. I mean, it might have been sold already. Last week it was still there but you never know. I can't take any chances." She bustled away without so much as a peck on the cheek. She was high on her plan.

When she arrived at the gallery of shops, the air was electric. People were agitated. "Is it a full moon tonight?" She mumbled to a passerby. But he paid her no mind. She noticed that the crowds inside the mall were much smaller than usual and it was easy to make her way up the slow, spiraling ramp. She stopped in front of the shop window to gaze once more upon the gift she had planned for Vicente's birthday. It was a fine chess set with beautifully carved light and dark marble pieces. She had already handled them several times and she knew their weight. Nose almost touching the glass, she smiled and watched as small patches of fog formed and then evaporated. She hummed as she looked down onto the board. Vicente used to play chess. He used to be very good at it. He'd love this. He could teach her. She'd catch on. She straightened and reached for the door handle, expecting it to click open and trigger the friendly little bell. But the door was locked. She tried again. Nothing. So she moved back to the window and cupped her eyes to peer beyond the window display—knickknacks of all shapes and colors lined the rows of open shelves. She saw the owner moving behind the counter, his back to her. She rapped, timidly at first, and then a little harder. Finally he turned, frowning. He wagged his index finger and mouthed, "We're closed." He waved her off and disappeared before she could knock again, which she did. She waited. No, he wasn't going to change his mind.

Disappointed, she sighed, gazed for another minute at the chess game on display and began a slow descent around the curving ramp. Well, at least the set was still here. She would come back tomorrow.

"Go home, Señora," a shop owner advised her as he turned to lock himself inside. It was when she was nearly midway down the ramp, that she noticed there were no shoppers in the gallery. Stores were either already closed or owners were locking up. Plastic signs turned to slap the glass doors with their *cerrado* faces. She was the only person wandering around. The air held an eerie discordance. Best to heed the man's advice and go home. She tugged nervously at the blue ribbon on her hat, loosening the knot under her chin so she felt less like she was choking. And she trod carefully down the ramp until she reached the gallery entrance.

She took one step onto the street and panicked. People were yelling and she saw several women pushing and clinging to each other as they snaked through the chaos to reach the other side of the road. She should have followed right away but she was petrified by the oppressive rumble and terrifying energy. People—so many of them—were raging. They were like animals, shrill and guttural, barging at each other and at her. Cries of *Vieja culia'a! Haceté un lado, puta culia'a!* She was grabbed and bashed and spun around on the spot. She thought she saw his face, but it disappeared in the fury of the mob. Where was he? She needed to go home. The bus stop was right there. If only she could step up and be in the quiet world of a safe bus. It would take her back to him and everything would be okay.

As it was, Vicente was standing several blocks east on a relatively quiet side road. He was window-shopping (or perhaps he was just gazing at nothing in particular) and he get caught up by the long row of flashy televisions. Such gigantic screens, all wearing stickers that said 'Smart', all of them flashing the same news. He blinked and couldn't look away. Paper bands of red and black and yellow, pasted at the same angle across the top right corners of the screens, from behind which a reporter called out, multiple images of himself seemingly incredulous, his mouth moving vigorously. Vicente was mesmerized for several minutes. Then he realized he was watching live protests on Avenida Providencia. He knew the street. He stood, shoulders tense, craning his neck, trying to comprehend the barbarity that was multiplied before his eyes. It was the garish television sale, the come and get yours, it's a steal, you'll never beat it, but rather it was what each of them was transmitting.

Suddenly, he recognized the exterior of the gallery of shops where he knew Rosa would be. She loved that gallery and had dragged him there more times than he could remember (of course). The old building stood stoically in the background, its silent cement walls forced to endure the ravages of red paint and ugly, frenzied graffiti. He thought he saw Rosa at the exit. He bent sideways, as though by doing so, he could change the angle of the camera and get a better look. Was it her? He saw the long blue ribbon around the fawn hat. It floated for a several moments across 20 wide screens. Then he heard the low whirring of the metal roller blind being lowered in front of the store window. The televisions were disappearing, being erased from view, top-down. He couldn't see Rosa any more. That's when he ran.

One arm escaping the ill-fitting overcoat that flapped behind him, he stumbled over his own shoes, fell as he rounded the corner, picked himself up and raced several blocks, the distance to the gallery. The streets were mayhem. Further down, he saw an old articulating bus, passengers had leapt off and scattered like cockroaches. He ran in a fury. Half a block before the gallery, he was pushed to the ground by people hell-bent on destruction. And he couldn't get back up to his feet. His knees were stiff. He crawled towards a wall, sharp stones cutting through his trousers, the palms of his hands burning, several people kicking him in the shoulders. There was yelling. Lots of yelling. Finally he reached the safety of the wall and sat, doubled over, his chin almost touching his knees, covering his head with his arms. But he mustn't stay. Rosa was here somewhere.

By the time he arrived at the scene, two paramedics were raising Rosa's limp body onto a stretcher. He managed to reach them just before they carted her off.

He leaned in, his nose almost touching hers. But hers was all bloody, and the skin on her cheeks was raw. "Rosa. What've they done? What've they done?" He sobbed and clung to her until one of the paramedics pried him off. Pressing his shoulder and guiding him aside, he said, "Señor, do you know her? We're taking her to Posta Central. I'm sorry, we have to get out of here. She'll be in the morgue."

Vicente collapsed into the cool of the wall. His torment and pain were suddenly overrun by terror. He stared, incredulous at the constant blur of exaggerated gestures, the roaring, deep and guttural, as people—almost not recognizable as humans—more like malicious beasts—battled their way past. He saw their deranged, violent expressions, their wrath forcing itself through a dense mesh of hatred and resentment. Vicente froze as, finally, the brutish noises were sucked into a thick grey murmur, and the world appeared in slow motion. He felt drunk and turned to see a man's face emerge from the eerie haze. It seemed disconnected from his body, suspended there while the rest of him was enveloped by smoke. Vicente was mesmerized by the man's piercing, dark eyes, and how, as he surveyed the riot, smug countenance spread over his face in an uneven victory. For a second, the man's eyes stopped at Vicente and Vicente saw reflected in them the yellow and red flames that licked out of the smashed windows of the lower floor. This man had the eyes of a wolf. Yes, he was a wolf. Vicente shivered. Suddenly the wolf man turned away and was swallowed into the swells of blue-green smoke. Vicente stared after him. He'd seen those eyes before.

Elena was outside the shopping gallery. While Vicente was still leaning into his slow-motion world, she had just made a successful escape to the other side of the street. She had no desire to join the curious onlookers. They were all gawking at the poor woman who had been sent flying by a bus. The woman was now dead and on a stretcher. Nothing more to see, so the hungry group of reporters turned their attention to the harried bus driver who was sprawled across the curb, trembling, tears streaming down his cheeks. A live one.

Lost in his pain and the surreal state of affairs, Vicente never did make it to Posta Central. He couldn't remember where it was, he didn't know who to ask, and even if he did, he couldn't find the words at that time. Where would Rosa go? Who would see to her? Vicente knew he was incapable of arranging things. Rosa had told him so, in the kindest of ways, a million times. He could not allow himself to imagine, and so he turned and ran until he reached a park by the canal that separates Providencia from Las Condes and he passed out from exhaustion.

All Vicente knew was that Rosa was gone. Her absence was more than he could handle. It was her brother Ricardo who took charge of the final arrangements, the same Ricardo who, decades earlier, had vowed to care for Vicente. The next day, Ricardo found Vicente sitting on a sandy slope of the park, gently rocking side to side, as he watched the water flow through the narrow channel. Ricardo attempted to explain, but Vicente grabbed his head and refused to listen. So Vicente was not present at Rosa's burial. He did not have the emotional capacity even to contemplate such a thing.

From that day forward, things went downhill for Vicente. He hung on by a thread. Well, three threads. In his tormented brain, all that he was able to remember was that he had something to do, something that he had wound himself up in and must pursue. He didn't remember why. He hung onto his old compulsion to watch a man called Giorgio (thread number one) and a woman named Elena (thread number two). Unclear though it was, there was something important about both of them and it was his watching that would shake him awake each morning, motivate him to splash water on his face, put something in his mouth, and in general, just carry on. And now, he would watch the other man he had seen on the street that day and at El Terminal, the man with the wolf eyes (thread number three).

Vicente's was a sad story. The forbidden love that he had shared with Rosa was only part of it. It was the most enduring part. But on that fateful day at the corner of Providencia with Lyon, it was finally beaten. Unaware of the significance of the event, distinct witnesses retreated with their divergent silent testimonies.

13 | WEAKNESS AND WANT

January 30, 2020

Elena had a gut feeling that if she went, she'd spy Bladimir at the green-grocer. She would casually wave at him, fall in beside him and find a reason to walk in the same direction. Perhaps they would have lunch together or something. She hadn't eaten properly for a few days. She had been to her doctor the week before.

"Doctor, I still can't sleep. The Ambien doesn't help. Look at me, Doctor, I'm a wreck." She pulled a long face and gazed at him, pouting.

The doctor was rushed. He couldn't seem to find a satisfactory solution for this woman. "Have you been eating?"

"Yes," she lied.

"I don't think you've been taking care of yourself."

"Well, I'm doing my best, Doctor." She moaned, "When you're tired all the time because you can't sleep, it's hard to find the energy to exercise and eat properly."

He nodded. He understood. He had a reception area full of patients and a dinner date that wouldn't wait. "Try these." He scribbled a prescription for Restoril. "Read the label. These will last you a week. Come and see me after that."

The pills only lasted four days, so Elena had to go and see Flaco for a top-up. He told her that what he sold her was Restoril by a different name. "Same stuff, different brand, different color. You'll like them. They're better than what the doc ordered." He winked. She didn't really care what brand he sold and she ended up sleeping past her scheduled next appointment with the doctor. No matter.

Her apartment smelled like rotten bananas, and flies had begun to circle the kitchen. She didn't see the cockroaches because she was sleeping all night and much of the day. But there were signs. Eventually Flaco's supply ran out, and she woke up. She trudged to the bathroom. On the way, she turned on the TV. She listened to the stupid laughter over the senseless jokes of afternoon talk show hosts and she groaned. The other channel was reporting on street violence up north. What day of the week was it? It didn't matter. She plugged in her laptop, which had powered down days ago and as she was waiting for it to start up, she gazed out the window and saw Doña Monica's maid supporting Doña Monica by the elbow as she labored along the sidewalk. "Why are you struggling?" She thought, "Why not just lie down and die? What motivates you people?" Always the same questions. Life was a bore.

Email alerts sounded from her laptop. They would all be junk. She trashed the messages without reviewing them and closed the lid. The yellow foolscap sheets with her hundreds of scribbles and half-analyses were scattered underfoot. She picked one up and tried to focus on it but she was still feeling groggy so she gathered several pages in her fist and stumbled back to bed. Another hour or two, that's probably all she needed. These days of absolute, blissful sleep (no matter if it was manufactured by Flaco) had done her good. Her brain was pretty mushy, and nothing would bother her.

When she woke up again, it was late afternoon. Everything was awash with golden light, as though a colorist had had her way, tinting the world through a film of her choosing. The ambient color was oddly inspiring, enough to pull her out of bed. Her head was clear now. She felt almost fresh. The foolscap sheets made crinkling noises under her palms and she leaned over to read what she, in her earlier wisdom, had put to paper.

"Oh, yeah. BJ." Flipping the pages over, she rose with the crumpled sheets in her fist, and she wandered to the window. The street was quiet. No sign of BJ or anyone else. But for an instant, she felt an urge to go outside and look for him. She sighed and carelessly swiped a few books from the chair and sat down. Without intending to, she scanned the room.

What would a stranger see, taking it all in for the first time? Whoever lived here must be disgusting. The place stunk. It was a pigpen. Flies had discovered some mushy old apples and they swarmed in and out of a bowl of something with green fuzz on it and buzzed around dirty dishes and pots that were piled in the sink and scattered across the counter. The air in the apartment was suffocating and rank, mold was growing out of a bag of garbage at the door. There was a trail of dark dots, like coffee grounds from there to the baseboard, droppings left by cockroaches who seemed to feel no pressure to scurry away.

Elena was no stranger to this scene because in spite of promising to do better, it would repeat itself about least twice a year. Recognizing it, she'd realize she'd have two choices. Either take cover under a grey cloak of depression or pull up her socks and do something. Often she slunk back into her funk until her mother came to her rescue. Elena could sense her mother's preoccupation now. She checked her mobile phone and saw several text messages from her that she hadn't answered. She quickly keyed in a short message. "Sorry for the quiet. All good here. I'll be in touch soon." That would keep her at bay.

First order of business, open the windows. The breeze had been laying in wait outside and as soon as she released the latch and pushed the window out, it rushed in with its promise of regeneration and hope. Elena sighed and leaned on her elbows to look past the window frame. The golden horizon declared, "Here I am... the rest of the world. I've been here all along."

She craned her neck to look left and right down the road. BJ was still top of mind. She really should do something about this apartment but suddenly the urge to join the rest of the world, and in particular, to encounter BJ, was much stronger.

After a quick shower and change, she was outside, locking the mess and the stench with the flies and cockroaches inside her door. She'd take care of it later.

She'd last seen him at the cafe across from the greengrocer, which was perfect because coffee was what she needed now. She counted her way down the street and before reaching the corner, she checked her phone, flipping the camera to inspect her face. Yes, she looked fresh, she felt like sleeping beauty, already awake but still available to receive her first kiss from the prince. What a stupid idea. She hated fairy tales but she grinned into her own image anyway. She was actually jovial by the time she reached the cafe.

"I'll have a double espresso. And that chocolate muffin, too, please." She knew she was grinning like a clown.

The cafe attendant smiled back, "As you wish, Señora. Have a seat. I'll bring it out to you."

Elena chose her usual table and chair because BJ would look for her there. She tried to appear serious but she knew she still looked like a doped-up kid at a circus. This was ridiculous. Down the road a tall man approached in long gliding steps. It wasn't BJ. Her grin slacked off a bit. The server delivered the coffee and muffin, "Enjoy, Señora. Let me know if you need anything else. I'll just be there." He pointed towards the coffee bar. He was in her way. She didn't thank him. She leaned to peer past him at the tall man who, by now, was only several meters away, and was looking with purpose at the table beside her. She turned her back. She wasn't interested in anyone else in the world except BJ and she wasn't in a mood for polite small talk with a strange man.

She sipped her coffee and nibbled on the muffin without enjoying either of them, and she felt her stupid grin finally disappear, no effort on her part. But she looked around, still a little hopeful. Why hadn't she ever asked BJ where he worked? Why had she not asked him if he wanted to meet again sometime, like a date or something? She could have invited him. She wasn't shy. What had stopped her? Come to think of it, BJ had still never asked her name or anything else about her. Either he didn't care or perhaps he already knew. Perhaps he knew about her father. Her father's story was old news that people didn't talk about any more but it was still out there. She doubted if the topic came up at all, even in political circles, where plenty of the old guard still lurked. But she wondered. Did he know anything about her life? Did he understand the burden she carried? "Yeah," she said under her breath, "I carry a burden. I need to analyze that." Her expertise—self-analysis. That's about all she did when she wasn't sleeping. But to truly analyze, to go deep, get to the nitty-gritty? No, she couldn't let herself get that close. And perhaps that's why it was a never-ending task.

She noticed a small-ish old man with a goatee sitting at a table at the far end. A packsack was slung over one shoulder. He wore a pair of Windsor glasses that had slipped halfway down his nose, and he appeared to be reading the newspaper. Even from the distance you could tell he was jittery. She was sure she'd seen him many times before. Perhaps even on this same street, at this same cafe. He must live around here. Probably he's someone's grandfather and he lives in the back room of his son's house, taking care of the garden, feeding the dog and entertaining bratty kids against his will, all in exchange for a place to live. Or maybe his son took over his house and made him homeless. That happens. She shifted her gaze beyond him to the greengrocer and watched as a maid paid for tomatoes and swiss chard and then stashed a few avocados into her bag when the seller turned to make change.

Elena had been sitting at the cafe for an hour. Bitterly disappointed, she finally decided to go back home. Mission not accomplished.

As it turned out, today was nothing special from anyone's perspective. That is, unless you knew that January 30th was the anniversary of: Hitler being sworn in as Germany's chancellor; Franklin D. Roosevelt's date of birth; the day that Mahatma Gandhi was assassinated; the Bloody Sunday massacre; and the first airing of The Lone Ranger. If you look at the bigger picture, the puny musings and petty desires of a spoiled girl in Santiago's east end and the ambitions of a narrow-minded political activist on the other side of town, were nothing. But it was all going somewhere. And you never know—it might lead to greatness.

Speaking of greatness, Bladimir was running deliveries for Giorgio that afternoon and, although he had considered it, he had no time to venture up to Providencia. He had asked if Giorgio needed to deliver a few bags of product to one of the minor dealers near the canal in Providencia but Giorgio said, "What are you talking about? You know that doesn't come up for a couple of days." He rubbed one of his dark lenses with his index finger, leaving greasy smudges, "Unless you know something I don't?" His tone raised in question.

"No, nothing. I guess I got the days mixed up, that's all."

"Well, wait for Flaco before you go out this morning. He owes me and I told him to leave the money with you. I have other business." As an afterthought, "And he won't dare not show. He'll be here with what he owes."

Giorgio liked to leave hints, create interest, make himself important. Bladimir also understood it to mean that he better not dip his hand into the jar because Giorgio already knew exactly how much would be in Flaco's bag.

Giorgio offered, "In case you're wondering..." (Bladimir hadn't been wondering.) Giorgio smiled and scratched the stubble on his cheek. "I have business at the old Congress building. I'll probably need your help after that."

Bladimir nodded and tried not to appear interested. Not that Gorgio could see. "Sounds good." And he turned to busy himself behind the bar. The place was filling up. Giorgio was holding private meetings in the back with people whose faces had become familiar over the course of the last few months. Most of them were men in their mid-twenties and thirties. Bladimir prided himself on his accurate judge of character, so he watched and listened, paid attention to detail. Most of the guys were foreigners, almost all Venezuelan. He'd heard the stories of how President Maduro had released convicts on the condition that they'd leave the country. Bladimir also understood that many of them were on missions and under the command of Venezuelan military. The military (official or unofficial) guys were easy to pick out. They all walked with the same confidence and they took almost identical stances at the bar and at the tables – all tall, straight, stiff backs, chests out, eyes alert. It almost looked choreographed. The other guys, the ones he assumed were the ex-cons, tried to exude a similar confidence but they fell short, what with their forced bravado, exaggerated strides and sloppy demeanor. He had come to like most of them, though. He didn't know if they cared one way or another about the politics of their mission but they knew they were better off working in Chile than brawling and wasting away in the overcrowded, insect-infested jails of Venezuela.

One or two guys that Bladimir knew to be ex-cons were on par with the military commanders in terms of the power they wielded. But they had a different style again. These ones were street-smart and canny, capable of predicting next moves and outsmarting and surprising the police. Of course, Bladimir knew a few sharp Chileans like that too. Lots of them. But these foreign guys brought a new twist, had different modus operandi. The Venezuelans and Chileans observed and learned from each other.

While these guys did their jobs on the streets and front line, Giorgio made progress on the political front. But Bladimir understood that the politics was sometimes just a means to an end. He knew a few live ones in legitimate posts who helped facilitate human trafficking and conduct illegal drug deals. And if not for the money, then it was for power—plain and simple. Bladimir's youthful understanding of politics had long ago been replaced with the murky reality that surrounded him. He had a hard time attributing any Chilean politician with altruistic motives. This fact didn't sit well with him and, although he knew it suited Giorgio, he secretly wished he was wrong.

Flaco sauntered casually through the front door with his hands in his jacket pockets. His elbows clacked in and out at the sides of his bony ribs.

"Giorgio's expecting me." he sniffed the air.

"He's out, so you can leave that with me." Bladimir nodded towards Flaco's pocket, and slid his hand across the bar, palm up.

"You're movin' up in the world," Flaco winked and passed him a crumpled paper bag. "You better count it. No one wants Giorgio to come up short at the end of the day."

"He won't come up short unless you're the one who's shorting him."

"Well, for both our sakes, you better count it then."

Bladimir dragged the bag to his side and fanned out the bills in a quick count. "Okay, we're good." he said.

Flaco raised his eyebrows and grinned. He tapped the bar a couple of times with his bony middle finger, turned around and without looking back, he raised his hand in a lazy backwards wave. Bladimir watched as the sun's rays pierced through Flaco's skinny figure. His silhouette was almost see-through.

14 | ANOTHER DAY AT THE FAIR

January 31, 2020

It turned out to be a day like no other, with the thrills and disappointments of a roller coaster. Elena was up and Bladimir was down. Then Bladimir was up and Elena was down. And as usual, the possibility of a meeting was unpredictable, but like a roller coaster in disrepair, something might fail and you might get stuck just hanging there. It might be exhilarating. It might be a titillating story for the future. Or not.

After the nothing afternoon at the cafe yesterday, Elena would've fallen back into her grey funk but she ran out of sleeping pills and on top of that, when she returned home from the cafe, her mother was there.

"I got your message." Her mother was standing inside Elena's apartment door, keys still in hand. "I just got here." She sighed, lifted her arms and let them fall heavily to her sides, indicating the state of the place. Not even a peck on the cheek or maternal pat on the shoulder. "I thought you were going to stop doing this. How long has your place been in this state, Elena? You're more than 50 years old and you live like a pig. I don't understand you. Where's the maid you said you were going to hire?"

Her mother shook her head and walked straight to the sink and turned on the tap. At nearly 80 years old, she was still a powerhouse. Elena watched as she removed plates and saucers, carelessly banged pots into one another, efficiently piled up dirty cups and tossed out old napkins. She held her nose at the garbage bin and motioned for Elena to do something about that immediately. Elena obeyed, pushing it all into a big plastic bag and forcing it down the chute outside the door. Trying to ignore her mother's foul mood and preparing for the inevitable harsh judgement, she swooped down to snatch up the yellow foolscap sheets that were scattered all over the place. No need letting her Mom read what was written there because she'd only pass judgment. She stashed them into her bureau drawer underneath her underwear.

A childish shame had replaced the increasing wretchedness that she'd accrued on her way home from the cafe. And now her mother hijacked her self pity and she could no longer wallow in it. Her mother had as good as lathered it, rinsed it, and washed it down the drain without so much as a sideways glance. And any crumbs of despair that were missed, ended up being brushed into the crevices of the loose ceramic backsplash, and dropped into the mouths of cockroaches. There was no getting it back. Not today.

Two hours later, they were dabbing croissant crumbs from the corners of their mouths and sipping tea from china teacups on rose-patterned saucers that her mother had set out on the fresh linen tablecloth. as she murmured something about 'civilized human beings.'

Her mother didn't refer again to the wretched state of the apartment or ask anything else. She already knew how things had been going. It saddened her. But there was no point talking about it. Today was the day that Elena would have to pick up and move on.

"Don Marco and I are planning a short holiday up north. He has some business up there, meeting some associates from Colombia. It's been ages since we were there and it's a great excuse for a little holiday. The weather's lovely right now. Well, maybe too hot but still... they say the streets up there are quieter. God knows how long this violence can go on." She clucked. "At least in San Pedro.... We'll just go and wander around, take the usual tours. Probably out to the geysers. Maybe visit the Valley of the Moon at sunrise. And look at the stars by night. It'll be nice to get out of this zoo." Her mother wore an absent, dreamy expression. Elena tried not to imagine Don Marco looking at the same stars.

The high desert plain with its blinding sunlight and vast horizon was in stark contrast to Santiago. Elena hadn't been there for years. She remembered encountering one of the oases with its a small herd of goats, and how, before the afternoon winds blew in, the tall reeds that grew around the edges of a shrinking brook stood quiet. Such scant protection across such a vast space. She remembered thinking it was the most tranquil place on earth. San Pedro—where they'd stayed in a modest *residencial* before the days when the town would be overrun with foreign tourists—was memorable for its welcoming local owners. The shops and restaurants back then were genuine. Rustic was real, not invented by new owners from Santiago who raised prices and watered down the northern culture. Back then, there were no pretenders, no wannabes.

The town had a museum that proudly displayed ancient desert mummies, some of whom had been found hugging their knees inside huge open clay jars, some were stretched out on shelves, ragged clothes covering ragged skin and hair, teeth in open mouths, tongues relaxed, perpetually uttering their last word, exhaling their last breath. They'd been that way for hundreds of years, the usual bacteria nonexistent on this infertile plain, leaving bodies to rest, wrapped up in their own dry leather, their thoughts eternal and uninterrupted. But then someone came upon them and moved them to the museum for tourists to wonder at. Elena had only visited the museum once. That was enough for her. She was not a fan of museums or zoos, where bodies were captured and held for the entertainment of others, contemporary slaves, forced to tell stories that no one could hear.

She loved the silence of the desert nights. The stars, clear and bright, hung so low amidst the gossamer threads of the Milky Way that they brought the heavens to within reach. Miraculously, she slept undisturbed here. Nothing like the city. Here, she was part of the universe.

The most memorable—no, it would be more aptly described as haunting—of her trips to the Atacama Desert was the time she came upon a small, almost perfectly circular body of water, no bigger than a pond. It was turquoise—shocking that it should even exist in the midst of the parched landscape of the driest desert on earth—and was edged with tall grass, the blades gracefully bowing under a breeze to lick its mineral-rich water. The locals called it *El Ojo de Mar*—The Eye of the Sea. Standing near the edge, she was tempted to jump in. "No!" A stranger was suddenly standing beside her. "No, it's bottomless and it will swallow you to its depths and you'll never see light again." Elena looked at the little man who had appeared out of nowhere.

"How do you know?" She asked him.

He was an *Atacameño*, a native of the *altiplano* and, although the sun had warmed the air, he still had an old black fedora pushed down atop his traditional *chullo* (knitted Andean hat with ear flaps), and he was wearing a brown vest under a worn tweed jacket. She noticed that he wore only dusty sandals, the kind made of old tire tread, no socks. His feet were dark and swollen. "It is known," he said matter-of-factly. She thought he was going to leave it at that. But after a few seconds, he continued, "It has been known for centuries. The Incas knew. And those before the Incas knew." He opened his arms in a gesture to take in the expanse of desert that extended to the volcanic peaks in the east and seemingly forever in all other directions. "There are many myths about it. But some things are certain. The lake's depth cannot be measured and its water holds thousands of dark secrets, too dangerous to get caught up in. Some say that it goes all the way to the center of the earth, some say it tunnels out to the sea. Either way, its secrets are treacherous and they will pull you down, entangle you, sink you to eternity, and you'll never be freed from them. Think twice," he warned.

She shielded her eyes with her hands and gazed across the plain. She wanted to ask if he had ever seen with his own eyes, anyone disappear into the lake. But when she glanced back at him, he was gone. She scanned the terrain, turning a full 360 degrees but he was nowhere to be seen. Then she noticed a small ripple in the middle of the Eye of the Sea. She stepped back from the edge and stood for several minutes staring at it, bewildered. He had disappeared, along with his warning. But she saw one of his sandals teetering on the bank. Afraid to touch it, she moved away. She picked up a small stone, kissed it for luck, and tossed it into the water, aiming for the small ripple. The stone made a dimple on the surface, which grew bigger, darker and more dense. Ripples danced and sparkled around it, until finally it diminished and the water went still. She shivered and turned away. That was years ago but the memory remained as real, and caused as much dread as the day it happened. The *Atacameño* had escaped momentarily to save her but he was pulled back into his fate. There was truth to the northern myth, that stories were snared and held captive. Just as in her dreams.

She turned to her mother and lied. "Oh, yeah. It sounds nice. How long will you be gone?"

"We booked a hotel for a week but we might stay longer. It depends..." Her mother glanced at Elena questioningly. "Do you need me close by for any reason? I can always stay in Santiago, you know." Of course, that wasn't true. Not if Don Marco had his mind set.

"No, Mamá. No, go and enjoy a break." She looked towards the living room and appreciated the tidiness. Time to break down and be gracious. "I'm fine, really. I guess it was good timing that you came over today. I really let things get out of hand. It's so much nicer now. Thanks, Mamá. I think I needed this." It was true. Her mother had broken down the walls and gotten through to her again, just like she used to do when they snuggled together in the kitchen, hands wrapped around a mug of warm milk. Comfort. Caring. The days before drugs. Elena sighed.

After that, she was riding high at the top of the roller coaster again. She promised herself that the next morning, she'd go out and get something nutritious. She'd made a bigger effort all round. "And if I'm a really good girl," she knew it was naive to negotiate with the universe but she did it anyway, "Maybe BJ will come my way."

Bladimir was in no mood to negotiate with anyone. He was annoyed with himself for being distracted by thoughts of Fachita. His attempt to make a run to Providencia had been shot down by Giorgio. It was a stupid idea anyway. What did he want with a woman like Fachita? Her politics would definitely weigh heavily to the right, and that, he couldn't tolerate. She'd call him a Commie, he'd call her a fascist and they'd end up stomping off in opposite directions. Still, though… there was an attraction, and it was mutual. He looked around the bar to see if any of the women there sparked his interest. No. He saw his mother reflected in many of them and he looked down, then shook his head and turned away, the glowing wisdom from the monkeys touching him with their pink aura.

Giorgio was planning new assaults on police stations. A few months ago, Bladimir would have been cheering the idea. But now it was eating at him. He resented that he hadn't been included in the inner circle. The plans were relayed to him, like he was an outsider, like he was a minion, a lackey who stood at attention, ready to ask how high when Giorgio said jump. His enthusiasm was waning. He was still firm in his politics and in absolute agreement with the methods but the more he thought about the lack of confidence Giorgio had in him, the more it burned him. He'd been running drugs and errands for Giorgio for years. And he'd never raised doubts or asked questions about how much of the money went towards financing the cause, had he? No, he was a true soldier. Whatever was necessary to prepare for the revolution, he was all in.

Bladimir, of all people, given his unfortunate (that's being kind) childhood, could have grown more resentful with each passing year. By all accounts, by the time he was 12 years old, he could have been a serious threat to anyone who looked at him sideways. But no matter what else his mother might have done before she disappeared, she instilled in him a purpose, and that purpose pushed resentment down, kept the inclination towards violent retribution mostly at bay. Violence was employed only when necessary. All relative. And it depended on who is doing the rationalizing. But now, for the first time in his life he was not inclined to swallow the bitterness that rose in his throat. As the ugly taste of being minimized and undervalued rolled over his tongue, he sucked on it and prepared to spit it out. Giorgio was the right target for a good gob shot but now wasn't the right time.

He thought about the lack of credit paid him by anyone, especially for his important role in the uprising back in October. His time was overdue. The bus incident had been a roaring success and the front-liners were still squeezing the incident for what it was worth, blaming the ill-trained and disorganized authorities for not preventing such a tragedy. But he hadn't received so much as a pat on the back from Giorgio, himself. A few guys had grinned and given him the high-five, but no one had actually complimented him directly, and worse, there was no sign that he'd be moved up to a position where he could fully exercise his leadership skills.

Bladimir accepted that he still had to do what he was told, and he'd be agreeable. But that's where it would end. He wouldn't take initiative or make suggestions. Work to rule. That's what they called it. He'd keep a low profile and his many talents would go to waste. So be it. Maybe it was time to reassess the whole relationship with Giorgio. But a guy didn't just walk away from someone like Giorgio.

The morning started normally for both Elena and Bladimir, and you could even say that both, in their own ways, were off to a good start. But the nature of the roller coaster is such that once you're a prisoner of its curves, you are heaved up and turned around and upside down. It's turbulent.

Theirs was not meant to be a short haul domestic flight without incident.

Bladimir's mood was lifted suddenly with an unusual request from Giorgio.

"I need you to meet Flaco at the pizzeria."

Bladimir glanced at his mobile phone. It was only Friday. Plus it was early on Friday. "Is there an emergency?"

"Nothing that will get out of hand if we deal with it on time."

"You're sending me to handle it? Who do you want me to take?"

"No one. You're going on your own." Giorgio took a step closer and inclined his face towards Bladimir as though he could really see him. He said in a hoarse whisper, "I need you to watch Flaco this morning. *Algo huele mal.* I smell bad milk."

"But I counted the money he delivered yesterday and it was all there." Bladimir was starting to get worried about his own neck. Did Giorgio suspect one of them of stealing?

"Yup. Well, that's not the problem. Just watch him for me for a few hours, okay? You don't have to do anything. Just report back to me."

The experience of walking along Pio Nono before 10:00 in the morning was totally different than being there at night. At night, all the bars that hustled to attract clients, whose dancers strobed and freaked, whose urban music competed beyond neon that flashed across the sidewalks, these places that oozed with charm and laughter were, in the light of day, just dull, worn out, broken and grimy. Signs hung, boring and lifeless, hardly noticed. Marred metal roller blinds were lowered to reveal layers of graffiti and smudges of tar. Lipstick-smudged paper cups and Styrofoam food cartons, filthy napkins, and used condoms lay in exhausted piles at the curbs, decaying where they had been kicked or where the wind grew weary of them. Empty beer bottles had been tossed at walls and glass was wedged in wide gaps of broken sidewalks. Bladimir noticed a wine-stained t-shirt that said 'Welcome to my world' in big letters, snagged on a padlock at the base of a bar entrance. A Nike trainer with a gash through the heel and its sole punctured, was wasted on its side a few steps away. Just do it.

It was uncommonly early for Flaco to be at the pizzeria. Why he was there, and what Giorgio knew about it were two more reasons that Bladimir felt side-lined. What harm would it do for Giorgio to fill him in? Anyway, Bladimir saw Flaco leaning against the door frame, the top hinges of the door were loose, so it hung crooked, making it appear that Flaco could somehow hold it up with his razor thin shoulder. Bladimir retreated along the sidewalk until he could duck into a narrow passageway, near enough to observe and far enough to remain unnoticed. He hunched there and waited, hoodie pulled down, black eyes watching, his breathing irregular. Flaco wasn't someone he'd call a friend. He didn't particularly like him but in all the years they'd worked for Giorgio, Flaco had never given Bladimir any reason to be offended. He felt a little guilty for spying on him but Giorgio must know something. It pricked at Bladimir—this secrecy, how everything was a need-to-know basis and how Bladimir didn't need to know.

Flaco dropped a cigarette butt at his feet and crushed it with the dusty toe of his boot, leaned forward to squint down the street, and then he ducked back inside. The door hung open a crack. Bladimir reached over to drag an empty crate from the corner and he sat on it in silence for about an hour, occasionally checking his mobile phone but never straying from his mission. During that time, Flaco had poked his head out the door at least four times and now, at last, he was stepping outside. He closed the door, pulled down the roller blind, bent down to padlock it at the bottom, dropped the key in his pocket and headed down the street towards Bladimir.

Bladimir shrunk back further into the shadows and half turned around, head down. Flaco strutted across the street, his long legs reaching out, the rest of him sort of dangling behind. He always looked as though he was a puppet on a set of long strings, his joints cracking apart to lift his limbs. Bladimir emerged just enough to peer around the stained stone entrance of the passageway. He watched as Flaco reached the curb and then stopped, partially blocking from view the person he was meeting. Bladimir heard a woman's voice greet Flaco with a nervous giggle. Her voice was familiar, the sound of it tingled up his spine. His ears pricked up.

"Sorry, I'm a bit late."

"You are." Flaco was impatient. He spoke quickly as always, words shooting like a machine gun. "I have places to be this morning. I can't wait around all day."

"Lucky I caught you then, right?" The woman's giggle trailed off.

"The usual, *supongo*?"

"You know what? Give me a gram of the good stuff and a week's supply of yellows."

"You never cease to amaze."

There was a short silence and Bladimir knew the woman would be paying for the powder and a small bag of pills that Flaco would be pulling out of his pocket. The exchange would be done quickly. A slight of hand. Flaco the magician. Perhaps a peck on the cheek to make it look like a couple of old friends just meeting by chance. Not that anyone cared. Authorities were far too busy these days.

"Until next time."

"Yeah, but don't hold me up next time. 'Cause there's no guarantee you'll find me."

"I know. And I appreciate it. Thanks. *Chao.*"

Bladimir heard the woman's steps approach and he retreated into the shadow again, conscious of the smell of stale piss on the wall. Fachita was counting under her breath as she walked past, her black adidas hitting the sidewalk, each step a number. She was heading towards the bridge. She'd be looking for a bus because the metro station at Plaza Italia was still a mess, its lower level the newly named '*El Jardín de Resistencia*'—'Garden of Resistance' still aglow in all of its anarchist regalia. Lest we forget the social uprising and the power of the people.

Bladimir could see Flaco rattling his way down the street in the opposite direction and he was obliged to follow him but he was compelled to follow Fachita. What kind of excuse could he give Giorgio? He'd already made up his mind to follow Fachita. He didn't know if it was because he wanted to talk to her, to look into her eyes and rekindle his infatuation (was it suddenly in danger of waning?), if he was just overcome by curiosity, or if it was simply because she needed protection in this part of town. More than any of those, he asked himself why Fachita was buying drugs from Flaco? How much was she using? Was she like his mother? He was a man accustomed to disappointment. He was made of stone. He was a brother without pain. And why should Fachita not disappoint? What could possibly make her any different? Get a grip, man. Besides, he had known from the very start that Fachita was not really the sort of woman for him. Things would never work out between people like them, people from opposite ends of the social and political spectrum. He knew that. So he stopped right there. He decided to do his job and stay the course with Flaco. Anyway, he saw her hail a taxi and disappear into the traffic, so following was no longer an option.

Elena was more than content because she was lucky that Flaco hadn't gotten away. She'd been late getting there. She'd called him earlier and he had sounded annoyed. "I'm busy today and I only have a limited window. So you snooze, you lose, *Chica*."

Last night, she had promised herself that she'd resist the temptation for cocaine and the yellows this week. "One day at a time, one hour at a time," she'd recited. And she had also promised her mother that she'd make an effort to pull things together. It was only on the rare occasion that she feared her mother might actually cut off her allowance, and for a moment or two yesterday, that fear had loomed. But this morning, in the positive light of a new day, the fear melted down to nothing. She hummed to herself and gazed out the taxi window at the signs of Providencia coming awake.

Most of the store window blinds would have already been raised, rolling the graffiti up inside, but these days all the stores still had plywood hoarding over the windows, cowering behind its protection, fearful of another tantrum by discontents. Small groups of people dispersed as they jumped off buses and scattered like busy little mice into coffee shops and around corners into office buildings, where they tried to pretend it was work as usual. But everyone was still on pins and needles. Sandwich sellers organized themselves at the top of metro entrances. The protesters had helped win these informal vendors the right to be there. So they were there in greater numbers, interspersed with pickpockets and other ne're do wells. People weaved along the sidewalk, headphones blocking out the roar of buses and the sound of impatient motorists leaning on their horns. Dogs stretched awake, tails wagging as they sniffed for left-overs that had been overlooked by the night-time street sweepers. One of them ran away with a sandwich between his teeth and the seller raised a helpless fist.

Today she would go to her favorite coffee shop and keep an eye open for BJ. On a natural high, she smiled at her reflection in the taxi window. She fingered the little bags of goodies in her pocket and her smile broadened. She felt secure. Set. Refurbished. The taxi driver glanced at her through the rear view mirror and he responded with a big smile of his own. A good start to the day.

True to his word, Bladimir was on the case with Flaco, whose route took him around and down along the north side of the river, he crossed a footbridge and headed towards what was left of Tajamar Museum—a mere shadow of its former self, not having been spared the wrath and ruin of the protesters. Bladimir followed at a discreet distance. He slouched down against the trunk of a broad shade tree, pulled the hood over his eyes and pretended to sleep one off as Flaco paused at one end of a wooden bench. A middle-aged, balding man in an ill-fitting shiny black suit was already seated at the other end. He was fidgeting with his mobile phone. Flaco sat down and looked straight ahead. Flaco and the man in the suit exchanged a few words. Not exactly Spy craft 101. Then, eyes still ahead, Flaco pulled something small from his pocket and handed it to the man. It could have been a bag of drugs but the man didn't pass him any money in return. It looked more like a folded note. The man gave a slight nod and Flaco got to his feet, scowling, and walked back in the direction of the pizzeria on Pio Nono.

Bladimir chose to follow the bulky guy in the bad suit because there'd be nothing to see back at the pizzeria. Satisfied, he stretched and looked up at the sky. If there was a god, he'd just made his day. Bladimir was sure that whatever novel event had just occurred, it was exactly what Giorgio wanted him to report.

The man in the suit pulled out his mobile phone. Seemingly agitated, he punched in a number and leaned back, spoke a few words and hung up. After he shoved the phone into his pocket, he waddled up to Avenida Santa María, where he stood and watched vehicles pass by for several minutes. Suddenly he raised his arm to an approaching town car, it slowed, the door opened for him, and it sped off again. A little further down the road were the offices of the *Policia de Investigaciones* and Bladimir watched the car turn in. The gate opened to suck in the car that was transporting our man.

So that was it. Our Flaco was a snitch for the *Rati*. That was interesting. And Bladimir was the only guy in the know. Maybe. Very probably.

He'd have to decide what to do about this. Of course it's what Giorgio needed to confirm but maybe Bladimir could use Flaco for selfish purposes. Bladimir still had time to think it over and to come up with a plan. So he decided he'd circle around a certain neighborhood in Providencia and, if the time was right, he might just sit down for a coffee and have a think. Maybe he'd see Fachita, sit down right across from her and try to figure her out too.

Bladimir had not yet discovered where Fachita lived and it didn't much matter. He knew the park and the coffee shop. And he even knew where the family tomb was. He could find her if he was desperate. Given the events of the morning, he was far from desperate. His desire to see her had suddenly cooled to a few notches above curiosity. But it remained a desire, just the same. Even before he crossed the boulevard, he spotted her at the same table as the last time he'd been there. She was scribbling notes on a yellow note pad, leaning in, concentrated. He strode over and without a word, he plunked down on the chair opposite, hands still shoved in his pockets. Confident. He was in possession of all kinds of information that hadn't been there when he woke up this morning. What a day. He hunched forward and looked into Elena's eyes. Startled, she snatched the notepad from the table and turned it face-down on her lap. She fidgeted nervously with the pen. She blushed and smiled, her eyes bright with this unexpected delight. The roller coaster had just taken a turn that made her stomach rise and fall. A thrilling speed bump.

"Well, hello," she said. "Nice to see you." It was an understatement. Her heart was racing. She looked away from his eyes because they were drilling deep and she felt naked.

"Hi yourself."

"What brings you to this part of the world?"

"You." He said quite simply with a slightly crooked smile. But his eyes were serious.

She looked down at her lap and capped and uncapped the pen several times. She would like to admit that she was there in the hopes of seeing him too, but that would be giving away too much, too soon.

He continued. "I saw you this morning."

She looked up, surprised. "Oh? You did? Where?"

"With Flaco." He cocked his head a little, daring her to tell him something new. What would she possibly offer? The better part of him wanted there to be another explanation. Maybe the drugs weren't for her. Maybe she was helping a friend. But he already knew the answer, and sitting there looking at her, watching her getting ready to lie to him, he felt like he was about to plunge into a pool of cold water.

Elena felt something crack open inside her chest. Oh, so maybe he didn't want to see her, see her. Maybe he wanted to interrogate her. Her back stiffened and she tightened her jaw. She looked away, half aware that an old man three tables away was watching them. She pretended to be distracted by him, buying extra seconds to regain her composure. And anyway, she'd seen him before—his frail, homeless aspect, big round glasses and white goatee—but right now he was just a distraction because what she needed was to come up with a response for BJ.

She didn't know if she was disappointed because BJ's intentions were not what she'd hoped, or if she was angry because her dealings with Flaco were none of his business. Was he stalking her? How did he see her with him anyway? Who was he to question her relationship with Flaco or with anyone else, for that matter? Maybe she just felt guilty and was embarrassed for buying drugs on the street. All of those things, probably. She deliberately sat on her anger and put him on the defensive.

"Yeah. And?" She said as she slowly looked up, all innocence.

"I saw you talking."

She repeated the question, "Yeah... and?"

"I had some business in Bella Vista." His response was vague. Now he was the one on his back foot.

"So how do you know Flaco?" she asked.

He shrugged, all cool. "Everyone knows Flaco."

Suddenly, that made it all better. Everyone knew Flaco, and there was nothing wrong with that. So Flaco was a drug dealer. So what? Everyone knew him and dealt with him. That made it all okay. Flaco was nothing more than everyone's common connection.

Bladimir had been about to beckon the waiter but he stopped. Fachita wasn't going to tell him anything that would ease his mind. He didn't like this side of her, this side that wanted to attack him and lie to him. And besides, he'd need to think over the whole Flaco business before he reported back to Giorgio. He studied Fachita's upturned face for a few seconds. He saw a façade. His day took a nose-dive.

"Anyway…" he rapped the table with his knuckles. "I gotta go. I don't really have time for coffee." He stood up to leave.

The elderly man at the nearby table pushed up his old-fashioned glasses as he leaned in, his red-rimmed ears catching everything, and now he straightened and readied to leave too. Elena glanced over at him, and when their eyes met momentarily, her pulse pounded in her ears and the hairs on the back of her neck prickled. Disturbed by the unexpected disquiet, and in fear of her own inexplicable reaction, she turned away. The little old man turned away too and busied himself with his packsack and then got to his feet, with some difficulty. Elena blinked several times. Better to focus on BJ. She tried to rise above the panic.

She turned and said to BJ, "See you 'round." But he was already gone. And the old man had turned down the sidewalk in the same direction, losing ground behind BJ's long stride. BJ turned the corner and disappeared. By the time the old man reached the corner, he was hobbling, packsack bumping awkwardly against his ribs. A young cyclist wheeled past and crashed into the old guy and knocked him to the ground. He dropped his bike and bent down to help but the old man pushed him away, and he said in an uncharacteristically harsh tone, "Leave me. Leave me alone, you young fool. You don't know anything."

15 | ROSES AND THORNS

One day in 1968

Elena tossed a rose into the air. "Papá! Catch."

She was a scrawny five-year-old girl who couldn't contain her delight. Grinning broadly, she tossed her hair back, and brushed a few strands from her face, eyes shining. Her father was amazing. How could he blindly catch the rose by its thorny stem and not even flinch? He was seated behind his desk, head down, glasses having slipped lower on the bridge of his nose. Without even looking up, he had raised his right hand and snatched the flower in mid-flight. Just like that.

"Papá, how did you do that?"

"I have eyes on the top of my head and I'm programmed to catch roses," he said.

"Do you like it?" She was beaming. "Rosa cut some for the vase in the dining room and she said I could bring one to you."

"Thank-you, Baby." He always called her 'Baby,' like an Englishman in a movie. Her Dad was like a movie star.

"And the thorns didn't hurt you?"

"You know that I can handle thorns. What do I always tell you about them?"

"That some people are thorns in your side." She recited it in a sing-song-y tone. "Am I a thorn in your side?"

"Sometimes."

"Like when?"

"Like now. Like when I'm trying to finish a brief and you come in here, throwing roses at me."

She sidled around the desk and leaned on the arm of his chair. "But Papá, you love roses."

"*Sí*. I love roses."

She looked up. There was more love and adoration in her five-year-old eyes than he could handle. He gathered her up to his lap and wrapped her in a hug.

She drew in a deep breath, raising her round little face, and he kissed her on the nose. "But I love you more, Baby."

She stretched her arms wide. "And I love you this much." She hopped down and jumped backwards, turning in circles, arms still outstretched, fingers reaching. "Want me to put the rose in a vase?"

"No, how about we put it in the book with the others." He nodded towards the bookshelf.

"How many roses do we have now, Papá?

"Get out the book and count them."

She went to the bottom shelf that was reserved for the biggest books. She selected the big volume of historic legends. Yanking on the heavy leather binding, she managed to pull it out far enough so she could turn the pages. With great effort, she shifted it sideways and ran her fingers along the wide girth of sheets. The pages were edged with silver, of which she was in awe.

Carefully lifting the thick cover, she felt along the book and stopped at the first gap between the pages. She opened it so she could study the rose that was pressed there, preserved as it was in its gracefully faded transparent splendor. Some of the brittle edges of the leaves were broken away but even in their distress, their fine shapes drew elegant outlines. She dared to touch the fragile, flattened ghost of a flower but did not try to lift it. After marveling for a few moments, she slid her little hand underneath the next swath of pages and opened it there. She did this again and again until she was close to the end of the book. She gazed down at each thin flower that lay pressed between the pages and counted under her breath.

"We have 10 flowers now, Papá."

"And the new rose will make how many?"

"It makes 11." She smiled. It was a proud collection they shared. She placed the new rose between two of the last several pages and closed the book as gently as she could, so the flower would be pressed in place.

The happy silence was broken by her mother. "Elena, what are you doing here? You know I have to take you to the dentist. If we don't go today, you'll have no teeth when you grow up. Who's been letting you eat so much chocolate?" She stared hard at Elena's father as she approached, her high heels clapping across the hardwood floor. She grabbed Elena by the wrist.

"Ah, Mamá. But I don't want to go."

"Well, you can't always get what you want."

Elena's mother looked towards her father for some help but he kept his head down. She clicked her tongue and said under her breath, "You always spoil her. I'm the one who has to make her toe the line. That's got to change. And soon."

Rosa bustled in, and Elena escaped her mother's grip, and ran to hug her around the waist. "Don't make me go, Rosa. I'm helping Papá."

Looking up and winking at Rosa, he said. "You've helped enough for one day, Elena. Go with your mother and do what has to be done."

Her mother unwrapped Elena's arms from around Rosa, glaring at her before closing the door with a huff.

Rosa looked at Elena's Dad questioningly and he shrugged and smiled. He put his pen down and beckoned for her to approach the desk. Rosa walked around the side, and after glancing over to the door, she bent down and kissed him on the mouth. He put his arm around her waist to pull her close and kissed her again, this time with ease and familiarity.

"This isn't a good situation, Rosa. And I think she suspects something. Maybe she doesn't suspect you. But something... and someone."

"I think it's time for me to find another *patrona*," said Rosa.

"I hope it doesn't come to that. But..." he shook his head. "Rosa, this has been going on for too long. You and I both know it's not just a fling. And a man in my position can't be caught in an affair, and especially not with a nana." He cringed. "I'm sorry, Rosa. But that's what it is. I don't care that you're my wife's maid—or anyone else's maid—that's not the point. The point is that it's just not done. It looks really bad. We have to find a way out." He paused. "But I don't want to stop being with you."

"We should never have let it happen. But here we are." Rosa lifted her arms and let them drop so they hung, helpless and blameless. She stepped back and leaned against the bookshelf.

He rotated in his chair to face her. "She's dropping more hints more often. She's trying to let me know that she's on to me. All I can do is deny it. I'm sure she doesn't suspect you, though, Rosa. I mean if she did, you'd have felt it already."

This thing, this unexpected thing. Rosa had no other word for it. It had started a few months ago. Both of them had blindly waded in. She wasn't sure how. And now they were caught up in some kind of crazy current. If they weren't careful, they'd both drown. It all began the day that little Elena had trampled into the garden to cut fresh roses, hat askew, eyes wide, oversized basket swinging off her arm, dragging a set of shears that was unwieldy and dangerous. Who knows what was going through the child's brain? Her mother caught her after she had managed to cut two roses close to the stem, their decapitated heads laying at the bottom of the basket as evidence.

"But it's a surprise for Papá!" she had claimed. "He said that he would like to smell them all day. I asked him because he was smelling the roses in the vase."

But nothing was a good enough excuse. Not for something as dangerous as that. "You can't walk around with giant shears, girl! You'll kill yourself." Her mother snatched the shears from her hands and she slapped Elena across the face. "Besides, the rose garden is off-limits. You know that too. What's wrong with you? Where's Rosa?" Her mother was in a particularly foul mood. "I've got a migraine and I shouldn't even be out of bed but it's lucky for you that I came out to try a bit of fresh air." She yanked at Elena, almost pulling her arm out of the socket, and she began dragging her back into the house. "You could have fallen on these things and that would've been the end of you."

Elena's cheek was stinging but worse, she hadn't meant to do anything wrong. It was all with the best of intentions. Tears streaming down her cheeks, she felt repentant and humiliated. It occurred to her that her mother was right. By the time they saw her father walking up the path, she was sobbing uncontrollably.

He stopped and looked down at her. Her distress melted his heart and, although he normally didn't involve himself with the discipline of the girl, and without asking what provoked it, he was moved to go to her aid. "Here," he said, forcing himself between Elena and her mother, and taking her hand, "Here, let me do this." He ignored Elena's mother, who had opened her mouth and then shut it again without a word, and he bent down and gathered her up in his arms. Elena smiled through her tears.

Elena's mother stomped one foot. "I swear the two of you will be the death of me. Can't you see that I'm suffering? I shouldn't even be out of bed." She turned on her heel.

"Well, go back to bed then." Elena's Dad smiled as he said it. He had long grown tired of the migraines, just one of her many calls for attention. He was bored with his high maintenance wife. It's not what he'd signed up for. Sometimes he just got into the car and drove away. He always came back but one day, he might not.

When he walked into the foyer, Elena snuggling his neck, Rosa was standing there, wiping her hands on her apron. The afternoon light fell across the entrance in such a way that, to his eyes, Rosa looked like an angel. She was the epitome of calm, surrounded by a warm, golden aura. Elena jumped from his arms, ran to Rosa and grabbed the corner of her apron.

Rosa was an ally. Elena and her father both knew they could always count on her. But now, as he took the few steps to close the space between them, it suddenly struck him, when she glanced up with her steady smile, that she understood him, perhaps better than anyone else. He rested his hand on Elena's shoulder and then dared to softly place his other hand on

Rosa's back. As though it was the most natural thing in the world, he slowly caressed her shoulder and let his hand run down her arm and then back up. Her hair slipped through his fingers as he stroked the nape of her neck. Rosa was blushing when she looked up at him. And it was at that moment that they both knew they had started something that would be very, very difficult to end.

A senator enjoys certain protection from the law because of his esteemed position as an elected official but he cannot be protected from defamatory gossip. Gossip is wild fire. It catches on and burns through the country in no time. Even if you might prove yourself to be above customary moral standards and can demonstrate your innocence, wounds are opened and scars linger from the moment you are accused. Even the most loyal of voters cannot deny the niggling questions that lurk in the back of their minds when opponents point to your scars. Up to now, Elena's father had no public scars. But having an affair would be like picking up the knife himself.

Elena's father had been a senator for eight years and he had earned popular support because he was a young man of his word. They say that once elected, you become just like the rest of them—corrupt and callous. But he was an exception. Stranger than fiction, but true. No matter on which side of the political spectrum he would have chosen to make his home, his principles were incorruptible. He knew how easy it was for ambitious, hungry colleagues to gnaw away at you, to drag you into squabbles and back room deals. For many, their primary aim was to build their own power and wealth, and if that worked out, then it could spin off to benefit *el pueblo*. Somehow Elena's father managed to hold strong.

He was a Christian Democrat, aligned with the advances (as he saw them) and reforms of President Frei, some of which were later picked up by President Allende. Among other goals, the party advocated tighter regulations for mines and fisheries and they aspired to agrarian reforms. Elena's father added his voice to those who were pushing for social safety nets, and better education. There was pressure on the government from both the extreme left and the far right. Elena's father stuck to his belief that a healthy society was only as good as its lowest common denominator and he said the bar needed to be raised, and raised a great deal. The only way to do that, he felt, was with certain determined steps, one leading to the next. Not a revolution but an evolution. He was generally a reasonable man but he did not see eye-to-eye with the Marxists, he reasoned that long-lasting reforms could not be implemented brusquely and that you could not simply turn a society on its head for the sake of an unproven ideology. There were those who would dispute him on that. But such was democracy.

To his distraction and also, significantly, to his denigration, Elena's father became a practical champion of anti-corruption and was not willing to join the cooks in the kitchen to negotiate winners and losers in struggles that arose from selfish and immoral decisions. "Let fall who will fall," was his motto. Thus, most politicians were wary of him, especially should they catch his eye for the wrong reasons. "Surely this man can be convinced to find in favor of a good cause, even if the cause is tied up with a ribbon of personal benefits. It's the nature of our business. He needs be taught when to turn a blind eye."

Election campaign laws prohibited donations from foreign sources. Elena's father wasn't the first to get wind that a certain Senator Vargas had accepted donations from a huge Brazilian construction firm but he was the one to initiate the investigation. Elena's father knew there were more donations coming in to other senators and also being channeled into the coffers of some far left parties. But cohorts in the senate raced to cook up a solution to keep themselves out of the frying pan. The case was closed in record time and this certain Senator Vargas was sent packing.

Unrelated, but complicating things was the fact that in those years, the late 1960s, the country was infiltrated by different foreign ideological influences, overt and covert. The Cubans saw their opportunity to make a difference, as did the Russians. And the Americans, in their self-concerned watchfulness, astutely invested in political influence and broad propaganda but their attempt to invest directly into political campaigns was refused by the candidates. It was a mess that was to everyone's downfall.

Beyond the Brazilian connections, Elena's father also became aware of a new money trail from Mexico, destined for the very same Senator Vargas, and there was some evidence that significant amounts were channeled into party coffers. The drug cartel concept was a fairly new phenomenon back in the sixties. Nonetheless, it was becoming global, and owning contacts in high places was key. Enter young Giorgio, a character from northern Chile, who had rapidly learned how to pull off the necessary. It didn't take long for him to gain a reputation as the chef, the mover and shaker between underground deals and politicians on the take. Beginning back then, and for decades to come, he managed to slink into the private offices of Chilean politicians, and he astutely stashed evidence that, you never know, could come in handy for blackmail purposes. Over the years, the back room walls of El Terminal filled up with such treasures.

In the beginning, it had been necessary for Giorgio to get his hands dirty. Unlike today, where everything was realized with a snap of his fingers, back then he was still proving himself. He was still building his reputation, and his army of trustworthy foot soldiers was small.

Giorgio's playbook, although flexible and creative, was written years before Bladimir was born. The solution he found for Bladimir's mentor senator was based on the template he had designed for Senator Vargas, during Elena's father's time.

In the case of Bladimir's senator, Giorgio claimed innocence. He wrote off the whole affair as "Unfortunate. Misplaced judgement, abrupt and unexpected change in the senator's personality." But all the while, Giorgio had been the chef in that particular kitchen, cooking up and serving the same recipe that had more than satisfied a few powerful senators as well as the public all those years ago. It had been a huge accomplishment for such a young man, and today, despite his old age and blind condition, he still had that special touch.

The recipe Giorgio had concocted for Senator Vargas went something like this: No one is really good at keeping secrets in the Senate and if there are occasions where malicious gossip will help advance someone's goals at the expense of someone else's, then let it fly. In the case of Senator Vargas, the gossip might have been malicious but it was based on truth. Vargas was rotten. He was also a convenient scapegoat. It turned out that four colleagues who were also involved in the same ill-gotten money schemes, realized that it would soon be impossible to contain the leak. It had already gone too far. Before it could incriminate them as well, they made a deal with our Senator Vargas. Since he was going down anyway, if he promised to keep his mouth shut before and after he left, then he would be rewarded. The cost would be a tarnished reputation that would fade with the years. After all, voters had short memories. By the time his five years of banishment from public life would expire, he'd be as good as new. And all the wealthier for it. They'd arranged to assign him three gold mining stakes in northern Chile which, they assured him, were about to be exploited by reputable firms. He would have the opportunity to become a local hero of job creation and he'd see a healthy profit for himself. It was a no-lose situation. Decades later, this same formula worked for Bladimir's mentor, the senator who went north... again.

Back in the days of Senator Vargas, there had been an additional loose end. And that was Elena's father. They had pretty much made the problem of the Brazilian donations disappear but Elena's father had persisted in following both the Brazilian and Mexican connections and this thread would eventually challenge Giorgio himself.

So Giorgio needed to eliminate the problem, and as it happened, it was during the process of tying up this loose end, that he lost his eyesight. Giorgio concocted an official version to explain the loss of his sight, which he cleverly fed his important clients. This version said he had suffered a freak stroke that damaged his eyes, and they degenerated to the point where his doctor had to declare him legally blind at the age of 27. No one ever attempted to prove otherwise. Why should they? Only Giorgio knew the whole truth. And the person who blinded him didn't know who Giorgio was.

16 | THE WATCH LIST

February 1, 2020

The secrets in Vicente's mind teased him with their games of hide and seek. Sometimes he sensed them tiptoeing like mice out of the back room closets of his brain. Just when he was about to pounce on them and drag them into the light and demand that they explain themselves, they dodged into shadows and absconded with their stories back into the little secret cupboards and rooms of his grey matter.

Vicente stroked his goatee as he watched Elena sip coffee. His attention was drawn to her yellow note pads. They triggered an ephemeral memory. In general, he was forced to let these fleeting memories go because they were too fast for him to gather up and make sense of. He bent forward, scratched his head and reached down to pat the packsack he had placed with great care between his feet. Everything of importance was now stuffed into that packsack. Sometimes this caused anxiety. He stroked the worn canvas, his fingers seeking out the rabbit's foot that Rosa had given him. She had insisted he carry it at all times.

"You never know when you'll need good luck," she had said. She had leaned over to fasten it to the zipper on the pocket and she had patted it into place with a satisfied smile. He distinctly remembered the smile from that day. She had returned from the corner store, eyes mischievous. "Look what I bought for only 300 pesos." She held the white rabbit's foot above her head and shook it like a mistletoe. "It's a lucky charm. And they say that when you receive it as a gift, then its power increases. So, for you Vicente, your luck has just improved one hundred fold." She was in a very happy state of mind that day. He smiled now as he recalled it.

But when memories of Rosa pushed themselves up, they inevitably fell like a series of dominos to the final, terrible afternoon of her death. This was a memory that could not hide from him. He wasn't sure how many days or weeks had passed since it happened but it was recent enough that when he woke up at night, he still groped for her, and he was brutally reminded that she wasn't there. He recalled his last glimpse of her little hand, and thought of how it had once been so capable and then how it had suddenly hung limply over the side of a stretcher. Her face, eyes closed, had been turned up to the sky. But everywhere that day was full of smoke and noise and confusion. After the ambulance pulled away, he had run after it, waving his arms like the crazy man he had become. Where were they taking her? They had told him but it didn't compute. Where would she end up? He'd never see her again. Suddenly, he saw Rosa's hat roll into view and he almost tripped on its long blue ribbon. The wind got hold of the brim, the hat fluttered, and it rolled away with the carefree lilt of a child, into the insane savagery of the street. After that, her hat was lost forever too. But he would never forget it, or anything else about Rosa.

He glanced over at the subject currently under his observation and thoughts of Rosa switched off. This woman called Elena was fascinating. In her presence, he felt an electric charge, which he found irresistible. It was more than feeling excited by her presence; it was the privilege of having discovered her existence in the first place. It was a gift. Beyond that, she filled him with a sense of familiarity that was deeply satisfying. And more than satisfaction; it was joy, not so unlike how Rosa used to make him feel. Vicente, as we now know him, was not capable of analyzing, of computing, of understanding cause and effect. Perhaps in another life.

Impaired as his brain was, his instinct still served him well. He was aware of his desire to get close and allow the calm of Elena's presence to drizzle over him, like icing on a cake, sweet and satisfying—but his instinct was to hold back, to remain unnoticed so that he could continue his vigilance unchallenged and in peace. The goal of the vigilance had never been clear. It was more an act of compulsion than of purpose, and Vicente did not question it. He just grabbed the hand of instinct and let it lead him.

One day (he didn't remember how long ago, because time was confusing) Vicente saw a middle-aged woman greet Elena at the cafe (probably she was a neighbor). That's how he knew her name. Elena. The name provoked joy. He acknowledged this joy without question, and in her presence, he basked in it. He couldn't recall exactly when he had first noticed her. One day, as if by magic, she was just there, sitting at the cafe. After he became conscious of her presence, he couldn't remember her not being there. Like sunrise and sunset, her very existence was a constant, and it was magic. Probably he viewed it as natural, something of universal design. But Vicente didn't get philosophical. He just accepted what was. There is something to be said for this kind of brain damage, this inability to connect the dots in a way that would otherwise make you worry or ruminate unnecessarily.

He desired to be in her presence, and he never regretted the attention and time he spent watching her. One day, after he spied her at the cafe talking to the tall man whom Vicente had nicknamed Wolfman—the same man who had been there the day Rosa was hit by the bus—the compulsion to be near her grew stronger.

In spite of how damaged Vicente's brain was, it managed to retain certain people forever, as though they fell into a custom-made groove and they wore themselves deeper and became more comfortable in their indelible track. One of them was Wolfman. Vicente had added Wolfman to his watch list. Giorgio and Elena were the only other two people he watched. Nowadays, Vicente was, indeed, a full time watcher. He knew Wolfman was a cohort of Giorgio's. He'd seen them together at El Terminal. But he hadn't paid much attention to him until the bus accident. Subsequent memories of his presence at that painful event were often confused but it didn't mean they were lost.

Enter Elena, and they had a trio, forming a triangular type of relationship. In his mind, Vicente turned the triangle on its head, and rotated it. His were angular thoughts whose corners often softened.

This morning Vicente hunched down close to the table top—his elbows having slid across the varnished wood, lenses in their round frames magnifying his eyes, alert, watching from a low angle. He resembled a bizarre, crazed sort of gargoyle and even the waiter didn't want to approach. Thus, Vicente was allowed to sit at his table the entire morning without anyone intruding on his thoughts. Elena was already seated when he arrived at the cafe. She was concentrating on her notes and she hadn't seen him. Even if she had, she would have written off his presence as one of the cafe regulars. Nothing to see here. Just go home, Señoras and Señores. Vicente was safe in his watching.

Cocking her head to one side, Elena was drawing small, absent circles across the yellow, lined sheets. She regretted not asking BJ for his mobile number. Although she would surely miss his eyes, today she could lower her expectations and allow herself to be satisfied with his voice. Their last meeting had been strained but it had ended on an amicable note. Had it not? Neither of them needed to explain their business to the other. They were, after all, barely acquaintances.

She signaled to the waiter for another coffee and squinted into the morning sun as she looked over towards the cordillera. Today was going to be another hot one. February was always the hottest month. The sun would be relentless, beating down on the concrete of the metropolitan valley, and then bouncing off in waves. She'd probably sleep away the afternoon. A slight breeze lifted a corner of a sheet of foolscap and she patted it back into place. Suddenly she felt the eyes of the old man at the table across the way. She recognized him from before. She wondered where he lived. He didn't look like the kind of client this millennial cafe would attract. He was wearing the same old vest that he had on the other day and his hair was unkempt. Oddly enough, though, it looked like he had groomed his short white beard.

The old man caught her eye and she wanted to look away. His expression was one of calm curiosity, constant and studying. There was no sign that he felt self-conscious. He kept his gaze. Although he didn't appear to be a threat, she was uneasy under his stare. Did she detect the sign of a smile? No, surely he was not prospecting for friends. She would not smile in return. She lowered her head and shot him a quick sideways glance, moving only her eyes. He scratched his little beard in a way that was vaguely familiar, which prompted her to watch, now quite unabashedly. Again, he looked directly at her without wavering. His fingers rested on his beard but he stopped stroking it. It was like he was frozen. He didn't smile. She couldn't look away. They remained caught in each other's eyes. The papers under Elena's fingers stirred with a gust of wind and one of the pages pulled away and fluttered across the sidewalk towards the old man's table. When, still looking at her, he bent to pick it up, she broke the deadlock. She hurriedly gathered her pages and her wallet and rushed towards the waiter who was returning with the cup of espresso. She slid 3000 pesos into his hand and mouthed, "I'll be back tomorrow."

Elena's knees felt rubbery as she rounded the corner. Clutching her papers to her chest, she turned to see if the old man was following her. He wasn't. She sighed and stopped to lean against the cold stone wall of the building, her chest heaving. What was that about?

She let her head fall back, closed her eyes and took deep breaths—in for five seconds, and out for five, counting as she'd learned as a little girl. "There's nothing to worry about, there's nothing going on, I'm safe, it's all perfectly normal," she repeated in whispers. She wasn't sure how long she stayed there, breathing and counting but she told herself it was probably only a few minutes. She opened her eyes and looked up into the thick foliage of the trees along the sidewalk. The leaves were quiet, a few birds flitted among their branches. Nothing startling. She was grateful for the peace it offered.

Meanwhile, just as the old man reached for his packsack, preparing to rise and follow Elena, he saw Wolfman striding along the sidewalk. Wolfman went directly inside the cafe and spoke to the cashier. He waited, his back to the entrance, and after a few minutes, a waiter appeared with coffee in a paper cup. Wolfman walked to the curb at the side of the cafe and took a sip. Then he set the cup on a ledge at the wall, lit a cigarette and scanned the street. His eyes stopped briefly at Vicente's table but he gave no sign of recognition, and his eyes moved on. Vicente settled back into his chair and waited.

By the time Wolfman had finished his cigarette and thrown the butt to the curb, a thin figure, worse for wear—tight black jeans stained with yellow paint, old army boots and a ripped jack shirt half untucked and hanging down his thighs strings of dull, thinning hair that got tangled in a heavy silver chain at his throat—rounded the corner and he nodded at Wolfman. Wolfman nodded back and gestured to the space beside him. The newcomer strode over and took a spot at the wall, not too close, head down, but cool and composed. Vicente watched as they exchanged words in low tones. They didn't seem overly friendly and there were long lapses during which they both looked down at their boots. Then one would break the silence with a few words, a shrug or a quick glance, and the other would offer up a minimal response.

In his role as watcher, Vicente had never before been in a situation where he had had the luxury of choice; today it could be either Elena or Wolfman. This presented a dilemma because he feared that if he watched one, then he'd miss something important by not watching the other. He waffled. After about two minutes, Elena won out because it appeared that the two men were just passing time. There was still time to find Elena. Maybe she'd stopped at a park and was sitting on a bench and she would welcome him as he approached, she'd smile and pat the spot beside her, a silent invitation, and then she's ask his name. He'd probably fidget and he'd push up his glasses, trying to hide his great pleasure at being so close to her, being able to smell her hair, see the few freckles on her cheeks. Oh, the privilege and satisfaction. He would hope they could pass several hours together, just the two of them. Small talk probably, he wasn't sure.

He shrugged the packsack over one shoulder and once again, prepared to leave. This time he got to his feet and on a whim, decided to mosey casually past Wolfman and his companion. As he did so, he heard the skinny man mention Giorgio. This put him off balance, he lost his footing, tripped on an uneven paving stone and fell to one knee at Wolfman's feet. Wolfman frowned down at him but didn't offer to help. He grunted and turned back to the skinny man and said in a hoarse voice, "You know he's got eyes everywhere, Flaco. And yesterday I saw you."

Vicente stumbled away, feigning injury as he settled against the wall near the entrance of the restaurant so he could remain within earshot. Perhaps he would kill two birds with one stone. What a glorious day.

Flaco scoffed. "You've got nothin' on me. Neither of you."

"Listen Flaco, I don't know why I'm telling you about this. But if I were you, I'd take me seriously. I do have something on you."

Flaco straightened and looked around, fiddling with the chain at his throat. He waited, eyes darting side-to-side, a slight twitch jumping around his mouth. He tugged at a greasy lock of hair that was caught in the chain.

Leaning back and stretching one leg far enough to trip someone should they wander past, Bladimir took his time to study Flaco. Flaco was a pretty good liar but Bladimir was pretty good at reading liars. Bladimir was taking great risk by not reporting to Giorgio what he knew about Flaco. It wasn't because he had a soft spot for him. Not at all—the guy was harmless enough but he was a good-for-nothing low-life, and didn't deserve any favors. If he was being honest with himself (and Bladimir decided it was high time he was), he was doing this because lately Giorgio had lost his shine. No longer the shining star, always pointing north. It looked as though Giorgio had lost his way. Perhaps a sudden decline that might be normal for a man of his advanced age.

Bladimir had known for a long time that Giorgio had lied about 'his' senator but he couldn't find a good reason why. He had thought he had Giorgio's trust, he had believed he was his right-hand man. But more and more, it was obvious Giorgio chose to overlook him. Thinking back on it, Bladimir realized that he had always been side-lined, even in the old days. He was tired of it and, yeah, why not admit that he resented it? So, no, his decision to warn Flaco was not for Flaco's sake; it was to take control of something (how much and exactly what, he wasn't sure yet) and keep Giorgio out of the loop. Perhaps—dare he let the thought linger—it was to make Flaco the first of his own soldiers, to begin to build his own army, one with a true political objective. For a fleeting second, he let himself envision the sudden smile that might turn up on his mother's face. "That's my boy."

Bladimir glared at Flaco, his eyes drilling down, unwavering. Flaco wound his fingers so hard into the chain around his neck that Bladimir thought he'd choke himself. His face was flushed up to his ears and he looked away.

"How'd they get to you, Flaco?"

Flaco opened his mouth but held his silence.

"Do I have to explain what'll happen to you if I tell Giorgio what I know about the Rati?"

"No." Flaco dropped his shoulders and looked up. "No, no you don't." Then he straightened and grinned nervously. "And what'll happen to you if he knows you haven't told him what you know?"

"And who's going to tell him?" He poked his finger into Flaco's skinny breastbone. "No, Flaco, c'mon, you're not thinking straight now."

Flaco screwed up his face and blinked quickly half a dozen times. He was between a rock and a hard place. "We shouldn't be here Bladimir. I'm supposed to be at the pizzeria. I can't be away this long. People are going to ask."

"Yeah. They are."

"Why are we meeting here anyway?" Flaco looked around. "I've never been this far east. This isn't good, Blad. This isn't good."

Bladimir ignored the question. "So what do the Rati know?"

"About what?"

"You know about what, Flaco. And, and... when did you start anyway? What've they got on you?"

Flaco was determined to keep it all close to his chest. He feigned some but he had to control something of his own, didn't he? Giorgio was his boss too and Flaco had to remain open to opportunities. It wasn't how things were supposed to be done but he was careful. And as it turned out, and as hard to believe as it might sound, from the outside at least, the Policia de Investigaciones was a good opportunity.

"Okay, I can level with you," Flaco lied.

Bladimir waited for it.

"But I can't tell you now, Blad. I've gotta get back. I mean you don't want Giorgio to know about this meeting any more than I do."

Bladimir straightened and tapped Flaco's shoulder. "Next time." And he loped away like a wolf into a dark forest.

Flaco blew air out through his mouth and visibly relaxed.

Vicente decided Flaco was interesting. His head was spinning, it was late in the day, and he was running out of energy. He watched Flaco as he rushed off, skin and bones rattling across the boulevard. And he saw him hail a taxi going north. The little black and yellow vehicle steered into the traffic and Vicente was left squatting on the sidewalk, scratching his beard. He predicted that his watching schedule was soon going to become unmanageable.

Meanwhile, Elena had reached home and, leaning on the inside of her door, she sighed with relief. She tossed the note pad towards the table and missed. It fell, undone, pages helter skelter at the foot of the table and beyond the chairs. The apartment was almost in the same sorry state of ruin as the day her mother last visited. She closed her eyes and slid down to the floor. She flopped sideways and grasped for one of the old pages and shook the dust off. On it she had jotted three bulleted lists. The first list was general, the second a bit more specific and the third was a shortlist of steps she must take to improve her lifestyle. Find an interesting job in busy office, Stop buying from Flaco (prescriptions okay), Hire a maid, Get a new wardrobe. This last list was in her former neat hand, round As and Es, and long open loops in the tails of the Gs and Ys. She was impressed by her penmanship. When had she made this list? When had she last felt balanced and sane? The old man at the cafe had really freaked her out. It was all his fault that her day had turned sour.

She would soon close the chapter on everything; all the list items that needed action, all the crazies she met outside, all the hopes of seeing BJ again. She would leave all of it behind. She got up and headed straight towards her night table, opened the drawer and helped herself to a couple of yellows. She'd be out for about a day and when she woke up, that's when she'd review her lists. Not now. Not today. Not with the image of the old man and his goatee and his steady look, reminding her of something, jabbing at her.

17 | WHAT IT COMES DOWN TO

February 2, 2020

"One more thing, Flaco." Bladimir turned just before he exited the pizzeria. "Don't sell anything else to the gringa."

"First of all, you can't tell me who to sell to and second, I don't know which gringa you're talkin' about, man," he grinned. "I've got lots of gringas."

"Think back. Last week when I saw you heading off to squeal to your Rati, and before you met him, I saw you pushing pills to the gringa on the street just there."

Flaco cocked his head. "Oh, her. Yeah. Well, that's gonna be hard, isn't it? I mean, I've been supplying that *cuica* for decades. I can't just break it off like that. You know how it works."

"Yeah. But do it anyway."

"Look, man, I don't know why you care who I sell to all of a sudden. But you know my product, right? You know what I'm selling. If she has to go somewhere else, who knows what she'll get? I mean, right, man? If you care about her... or whatever, I don't know... but she can get some bad shit. And if you have some fixation with this broad, then that's your problem but it'll be worse if you can't guarantee what she's taking, right? And that'll be on you. I mean, Giorgio doesn't supply bad shit. I have a good business because I have quality product. Bottom line, man. You know the risks."

Bladimir paused. "Okay, but I wanna know what she's buying."

"Why?"

"None of your business why. I just do." Bladimir's face darkened and he closed in, digging his fingers into Flaco's bony shoulder. But his voice was soft. "Look Flaco. You know I'm gonna keep your dirty Rati business between us. Besides, some things have come up and it means I'm gonna make some changes. You're lucky the timing is right, otherwise I'd be the first to go to Giorgio and accuse you. But right now, I've got your back. You owe me, though. And you owe me big time. And I might get you to start paying soon. I've got a project..." He stopped there.

They stood silently for a few seconds, trying to read each others expressions. It wasn't exactly a picture of confidence.

Finally Flaco stepped back, nodded and waved Bladimir out the door.

Bladimir was going to head straight back to El Terminal because Giorgio was serious about wanting a full report on Flaco. Bladimir had avoided him for 2 nights but he couldn't put him off today. It was odd to play cat and mouse with the man who'd been your boss of decades but that's what it had come to. Being underestimated for so many years, and especially lately, does something to a man, and that something finally snapped. As of a few days ago, Bladimir found himself on his own path, which up to now, wound through a lot of thick underbrush and he couldn't see his way clear. So he'd have to sniff his way along.

His initial plan was simply to lie to Giorgio. He would report that Flaco's activities were nothing out of the ordinary and he'd offer to go back and watch again. "In case something ugly rears its head," he'd tell him. His real intent was to gain more influence over Flaco and feed Flaco false information that would play in his favor. He'd been thinking this as he headed down the sidewalk, and when he was less than two blocks from the pizzeria, it occurred to him that he could give Flaco something this very afternoon. It was the opportunity to throw a wrench in the work of *El Capitán*, the Venezuelan who had managed to position himself too close to Giorgio. The man had had Giorgio's ear for the past several weeks and it grated on Bladimir. He would tell Flaco that El Capitán was planning an unsanctioned attack on a police station in southwest Santiago, and he was going to do it on his own terms, no matter what Giorgio said. In fact, this wasn't far from the truth. Bladimir had overheard El Capitán tell Giorgio that he was going to be at the station next Friday after midnight. But he said it was just a reconnaissance mission, to see how many *Pacos* were on desk duty, case the place, wander in with a complaint about a burglary or something. "First I wanna know the lay of the land that's all. And then I'll go back and burn it down... along with Sergeant Martinez. I'll find him. He's the one who detained me two weeks ago, remember? It was inconvenient. Let's see how he deals with my kind of inconvenience."

"It sounds more like mischief to me," Giorgio had responded. "Maybe it'll remind 'em that they're still in our sights. But wait 'til I give the word. I have other things to consider and the timing needs to be right. So hold off."

Bladimir did an about-turn and headed back to the pizzeria. He entered through the back door in case some of Giorgio's guys might be chugging a few beers out front. When he stepped up to the kitchen door, he heard Flaco's voice. It was hoarse and urgent. So he stopped and leaned in.

"Yeah," Flaco was saying. "He was just here again. And now he's worried about what I'm sellin' to some rich-bitch gringa."

There was a pause and then he continued, "I don't know, Señor G."

Flaco always addressed Giorgio as 'Señor G.' Flaco was casting a shadow and Bladimir watched it slide over the shelves along the inside wall. Leaning his elbow on a shelf, head down, phone pressed to his ear, back to the door, Flaco kept glancing towards the restaurant in case he had to wave off interlopers. He continued, "Dunno." Another pause, "Of course he does. He pulled me aside the other day. I told you. Bladimir thinks I'm a snitch... No, of course I didn't... No... Yeah, I delivered your message to Colonel Rojas. He's on board. He said he's already got someone trustworthy over at the airport. Not to worry, all the paperwork's in order." He sighed and chortled. "Oh, and, Señor G., he didn't go into detail... in fact, he kind of just hinted around but I know Rojas is going to be bring a new recruit on board and he's going to need something extra for that. I'll let him explain. Just givin' you a heads-up."

Before Flaco hang up, he said, "Yeah. He's on his way back to you right now. Yeah. Well, you know the guy's a loser, right? I mean, he thinks he can outsmart you, Señor G..." He straightened and checked the kitchen door again. Bladimir pulled back. The last thing he heard Flaco say was, "I'm pretty sure he's got ideas of his own. I mean, who knows? Maybe he's a snitch himself.... Yup. Nope... I know where he lives. But I don't think he's goin' home. I'd say he's on his way to you with his lies. I'm surprised he's not there already. He has somethin' up his sleeve. My advice? I mean, I know you don't need it, Señor G. but don't believe anything that comes outta that *hueón's* mouth."

Bladimir turned and gingerly stepped back from the door. He rushed down the alley, stepped out of the shadows and onto the street to hail a taxi. The driver pulled out and, as taxi drivers do, glanced at Bladimir through the rear view mirror. "Where to?"

That was the question. Where to? Giorgio was waiting for him at El Terminal but Bladimir wasn't sure how Giorgio would play this one. He might string him along just to set a trap and watch him squirm and then he'd have no chance to slip away. Maybe El Capitán was responsible for the set-up, just to clear the path for himself. Maybe he'd been feeding Giorgio lies for some time now, and maybe that's why Giorgio used Flaco against him—to reel him in. Had Bladimir been that transparent? He didn't think so. Did Giorgio suspect him of stealing? Had he discovered the missing diamonds? Probably not. Hopefully not. But someone read him. Probably El Capitán. Surely not Giorgio himself. But at this point, what did it matter? The danger was in the timing, and timing was something he couldn't afford to get wrong. So he directed the taxi driver, "Drop me at Avenida Independencia with Benzanilla."

Bladimir rented a room at the back of a house just off the Avenida, which ran opposite the main entrance to the General Cemetery. Since settling in there more than twelve years ago, he'd never thought about moving. The elderly landlady had mobility issues and there were occasions when he helped her with shopping. In the last few years, and especially as a senior with limitations, she'd begun to feel less secure and she engaged him to help cash her pension cheque. "Bladimir, I can use your strong arms to see me back and forth from the bank. I don't like to ask but it's only once a month. All the 'bad milk' around here like to loiter outside of the banks on pension day. You've seen it yourself, right? But no one will bother me if you're with me. If you can, please?"

"Of course, Señora. We'll go together." He wondered how she would manage without him. But he had no choice. He was going to have to disappear. And disappear this evening. And without telling her. He felt cowardly and ashamed but telling her might put her in danger. He jumped out of the taxi and didn't presume to be safe. He stepped back into the cool shadow of a mom 'n pop shop and asked for a pack of Lucky Strikes. He turned to survey the street as he waited for the clerk to make change, and when she slapped the pack down onto the counter without looking at him, he slid it into his pocket, kept his head down and swiftly crossed the street. He skirted around a few sidewalk signs and then walked along, shoulder brushing the walls. The street changed from little shop fronts to ancient houses whose tall porch doors opened directly to the sidewalk. He was home within five minutes. He unlocked the front door and walked in. The old lady had her TV blaring. She was fixated, mouth hanging open and eyes drooping in sympathy, the background music almost drowning out the dialogue. She was engrossed in one of her night time soaps and wouldn't notice his return.

Bladimir strode down the long hallway, across the interior patio and into his private quarters that consisted of one big room with a table and two wooden chairs, a bed, minimal shelves and zero decor to speak of. In one corner was a bathroom the size of a closet, the totality of which became the shower when he turned the water on. There was no hot water because the on-demand electric water heater was broken when he moved in and, well, she could deduct a few pesos off the rent until it was fixed. It never was. His landlady had been extremely proud when she pointed out the bathroom in this annex. It's a big plus, she had bragged. "All the privacy anyone needs. You don't need to share with me." Not exactly the Ritz but Bladimir wasn't fussy and he wasn't there much anyway. He became accustomed to cold showers.

He pulled a low wooden crate from under his bed and rifled through the dusty odds and ends that he'd tossed into it either for safekeeping, or out of sentimentality or just because he didn't know what else to do with the stuff. A few hard cover novels that he'd always intended to read (but never quite got around to), an unframed photo of his Mom from when she was in her early teens and looked in good health (he put it to one side), an old letter from Civil Registry with a list of his youthful misdeeds and petty crimes (he placed it on top of the photo of his Mom), a pistol that he'd been given by an ex-cohort of Giorgio's before the guy high-tailed it up to Bolivia (he checked it, raised it, looked down the snout and then tucked in his waistband), a box of shells for the pistol—the box had been opened only once and no shells had been removed (he emptied them into his jacket pocket). He dug past the back scratcher with a long handle and short plastic fingers, old Rubik's cube, empty clay piggy bank and vest with various lapel pins on one side, until he felt the tin cash box with the broken lock. He liberated it from beneath the other junk. Box in hand, he dropped onto the bed and rested it on his lap, took a few deep breaths, looked around and opened the lid. Several wads of large-value bills had been folded and pushed into one corner. His emergency stash, enough for expenses for several months, depending on how careful he was. But the real treasure was in a cotton drawstring pouch that was half hidden under a bulky Kraft envelope. He brushed the envelope aside and lifted out the little bag. He loosened the drawstring and gently shook the contents onto the bed. Thirteen small diamonds glinted up at him. They were high quality white gems, each of them between two-and-a-half and three carats. Although he didn't have the certificates, he knew the value had only increased and a good diamond merchant would recognize it. In fact, he'd had them appraised at a private merchant in an east end neighborhood, somewhere that Giorgio would certainly not have ventured. The man, a small, frail character with a French accent offered to buy them but that wasn't Bladimir's intent. At the time, he didn't know what his intent was, other than to hang onto them. He still couldn't believe he really possessed them. They were quite a haul and he had a feeling they'd be good for a rainy day.

Bladimir smiled and lifted each one to his lips before dropping them back into the little pouch and tightening the string. He shoved it securely into his front jeans pocket. He divided the wad of bills and stuffed them into his jacket pockets.

Finally, he carried the crate to the patio, threw it into the garbage barrel and lit a match. After a dozen years, you'd think he would have had more possessions of consequence. He watched as the photo of his mother, her face distorting and curling up, disappeared into the smoke, and right after that, the official list of priors and all the remaining items that could be tied to him. He patted all of his pockets one by one and felt for the pistol. He had everything he needed.

The question now was where to go.

18 | MAN ON THE RUN

February 24, 2020

As Elena slipped under a lightweight cotton blanket and reached for her cup of tea and a cookie, Bladimir was somewhere at the fringes of southeast Providencia trying to fortify a little spot he had claimed for the night. It was quiet there and he was miles away from both El Terminal and the room he used to call home. That night, he'd seen plenty of homeless people further north along the canal, some were solitary like him but others were in small groups. He preferred the solitude. He didn't want to keep one eye open all night, or be pushed along—"What are you doing here, *hombre*? This is my spot. *Cachai*? See that kerchief on the tree right over your head? Can't you read the signs?" And he didn't feel like making small talk with strangers or accepting advice about which kitchen always had its back door half open. He would move on soon enough but even someone as street wise as Bladimir needed time to regroup after the tables had turned so abruptly. On top of that, outsmarting an established crime boss wasn't something you could do with your eyes closed. He wasn't Giorgio, after all. Not yet. So he'd have to keep his wits about him.

Maybe Giorgio had sensed it long before Bladimir himself had an inkling that he was going to jump ship. Ironically, over the previous weeks, Bladimir had judged Giorgio to have had lost his touch, that his sixth sense had been tarnished and his antennae were in need of adjustment. What an underestimation he'd made. And it was only by a stroke of luck that he wasn't, at this very moment, tied to a chair in a cold cement warehouse, trying to outsmart the Venezuelan Capitán who, if not before, then certainly by now, would have replaced him at Giorgio's side. The blind justice of god the father, would be meted out by a foreign son at his right hand.

Bladimir pressed his shoulder into the packed dirt slope and peered beyond the shadows towards the sidewalk. A young couple was meandering there, smooching noisily and murmuring pretty things to one another. "Trite," he thought. "Juvenile." But even as he passed judgment, his mind jumped briefly to Fachita. His thoughts were more disquiet than romantic. Now Flaco would never tell him what drugs she was taking. He hadn't pegged her for a user. But then, lots of people get by without being detected, at least at first. Maybe it's just as well that he hadn't run across her lately and it would be better if he avoided her from now on. Years ago, one of his girlfriends had managed to hide her drug habit and he kicked himself for not seeing it. Back then he was living in a shared apartment north of the cemetery and he realized too late that he had deliberately pushed the tell-tale signs of addiction out of his mind. It was only after his roommate's radio and turntable went missing, followed by the only real thing Bladimir valued—his set of outdated, never consulted encyclopedias (they were a gift from Giorgio in the early days and they looked impressive, all those hard covers with embossed gold lettering running up the spines)—that he was forced to pay attention. After that, he recalled earlier incidents, and he recognized the signs, the very ones he vaguely remembered pushing aside. She went through periods of obvious confusion and was fearful of sounds, sometimes reaching the point where he jokingly told her to have her head examined, or at least give it a good shake. She would look at him, empty-headed. Other days she disappeared to the bathroom to vomit her guts out. And then of course there were all the times she arrived late, pupils dilated—something he clearly should have called her on. But in those moments, he let it run its course because, well, it was no skin off his nose. And besides, he told himself, even if she only consumed occasionally (something he reluctantly considered but chose to ignore at the time), at least she wasn't using regularly.

He wasn't in love with the woman and it was neither his responsibility nor his desire to try to reform an addict. Only when it impacted him personally, did he kick her aside without a second thought. "*No, María. Esta cosa no va a ir a ninguna parte.* That's all. I don't love you, never have. And it's over. Don't come back." He didn't see any point in opening up a discussion in which she would apologize and promise to overcome what he knew she'd never overcome. She had nothing to offer and even if she did, why should he suffer her withdrawal and future battles. No, thank-you. He replaced the roommate's radio, and haggled with a street seller for a soppy plastic dog statue to fill in for the turntable. Dust collected where the encyclopedias used to be.

Bladimir had never had any long-term relationships. How old was he now? His ID card said he was born in 1972. Last November 1st, the Day of the Dead, he turned 48. He didn't know how many healthy long-term relationships a man his age should have had, but he was pretty sure that a normal guy would have had at least one, right? Flings, yeah, he'd had more flings than he could count but very few of them were memorable. He remembered the one with the addict only for that reason—because she was a user. Nothing else about it was remarkable.

After her, he was cautious and he had been confident the experience had taught him to be wary. Well, apparently not enough, because he missed the signs in Fachita. He realized that he felt cold towards her now. Even if he scraped around, he didn't feel a hint of desire. It's strange how you can get turned off a person just like that. He shrugged and held his jacket closed at the neck and huddled deeper into the bank near the canal, closed his eyes, and let himself fall asleep.

Elena's head fell back on the pillow, half a cup of tea having long since gone cold, the cookie having fallen to the floor with only one bite taken. She was dreaming of her father. He was distressed, running towards her, yelling something but the sound was sucked away, back into his mouth. His arms were flailing. Then she saw a shadow stretch across the ground in front of the open garage door and her father bolted. He rushed towards the car and jumped in, started the motor and sped off. She ran after him. She was running as fast as she could but her legs were heavy. Try as she might, muscles straining, heart pumping, she moved in slow motion. Barely advancing, her neck, arms and legs ached with the effort and she cried and fell down on the driveway in tears. Then she turned around and saw Rosa running towards her. Rosa gathered her up. Elena was too big for Rosa to carry but she gathered her to her bosom anyway, and half-carried, half-dragged her back towards the house, one of her legs dangling painfully. The shadow moved towards the garage. It was thrashing wildly in the bushes. Elena woke up, terrified. She always woke out of the nightmare at this same point, never able to push beyond this juncture. Fear held her prisoner.

She leaned over to feel for the mug of tea and she gulped some back. The yellows that she had purchased from Flaco the other day were in the night table drawer. She thought at first that she could avoid them. She'd promised her mother (and herself) that she'd beat the temptation. She swung her feet to the floor and held her head in her hands. It would never stop. The nightmare would not leave her in peace. She groaned and stood up and then began to pace and count her steps. She walked barefoot into her little kitchen, around past the living room window, into the bedroom and around again. She counted. "789, 790, 791…" But the stash in her drawer beckoned her, It would be so much easier, so much more peaceful, so much more effective and secure. She was in front of the living room window when she made her decision. She turned towards the kitchen, poured a glass of water and padded directly back to her bedroom. She pulled open the drawer and reached for two yellows, popped them in her mouth, swallowed them and flopped back onto her bed and closed her eyes, relieved. She'd sleep into tomorrow afternoon. No dreams and no memories tearing through the haze of her brain.

19 | DALLIANCES

Decades earlier

Elena's string of dalliances (as her mother referred to them) definitely could not be counted on one hand. Elena was someone who became infatuated at the drop of a hat. "I'm an easy lover," she chuckled. "I love to be in love." After her first serious relationship with Miguel—well, perhaps you can't call a teenage infatuation serious, but a 14-week duration at that age might satisfy the criteria—she easily moved on because the university campus was full of options. There were the prospects that her mother and Don Marco approved of and encouraged her to invite for dinner and then there were the fun ones, the bad ones, and the ones who didn't go to university but who hung around in Bella Vista and who knew Flaco. Those days flew by and the possibilities flew by with them. Today, Elena couldn't even remember their names. She referred to them as "the tall thin one with the earring who wore Hawaiian shirts" or "the quasi-spiritual animal who drove me crazy with his stupid, spiraling philosophies" or "the funny one who tried his hand as a stand-up comic. Remember him? He was never as funny as he thought. Now he's probably selling mutual funds."

Elena was ushered into the workforce at a supervisory level. Although it seemed impressive and should have propped up her self-esteem, the prestige of the position only helped foment her latent imposter syndrome. She had graduated in the top third of her class with a degree in marketing and administration. She was without a clear goal, let alone a desire to work in a specific industry. Don Marco had plugged her in to a friend of his who ran a private, upscale social club. "They're looking for someone to head a small team. Of course I told him you'd be perfect." He winked, "After all, we're related, right?" She did not now, and had never in the past, felt related to

Don Marco. Any leadership skills that he thought she had, certainly did not come from him. He was nothing like her father, and she never understood how her mother could have agreed to share her life with such a cold, boring, humorless dog of a man. His wink did not inspire a smile but she forced one anyway. He didn't give her a chance to say 'No' or 'Can I think about it?' It was a done deal. She was told to appear at the west gate of the club at 11 am on Monday for her interview with Don Marco's friend, Señor Dario Sepúlveda.

Through the high gates, you could see the main building at the far end of a manicured field. The clubhouse lounged in all of its colonial glory, across one end of an expansive enclosed grounds that were couched in the Andean pre-cordillera. Elena was ushered in and guided beyond the main door by a young guard smartly-dressed in grey trousers and a green blazer. "Here are Señor Sepúlveda's offices," he said with a polite nod and a wide sweep of his arm. The secretary offered her coffee and served it in a small cup with a dainty butter cookie tucked on the saucer and a miniature glass of sparkling water on the side. Elena pretended to like the espresso, into which she self-consciously stirred only one-half spoon of sugar rather than her usual three heaping ones. She sat for several minutes after she'd finished sipping it, forgetting to lower the dainty pinkie finger that she had so deliberately raised.

"Please," said the secretary, bowing slightly. "He'll see you now."

Señor Sepúlveda liked women—a lot. And especially those under 25. He hired Elena and she began to muddle her way through the club's routines under his watchful gaze. Because Elena was a research, analytical personality type as well as a perfectionist (in those days), she was slow to come to decisions. Everything needed to be in its place, all in good time, and then, only after she had analyzed and re-analyzed, second-guessing herself. The two assistants in the department grew weary of her plodding pace and after spending three months filing their nails and adding papers to the pending piles, they jumped in to make calls and arrange events without her approval and many times without her knowledge and she became superfluous without her knowledge. So she was forced to fake her way through the special gatherings after the fact. At first, Señor Sepúlveda credited Elena for the success of these events, and the assistants made her imposter syndrome come true.

Overwhelmed, Elena began to panic on her way into work in the mornings. She maintained a level of calm on the metro but by the time she transferred to a bus, she was all wound up inside and gazed out the window, trembling. When she reached the office she had to rush to the toilet and vomit before building enough courage to face the two assistants. The two assistants habitually posed with note pads at the entrance of the outer offices, and didn't try to disguise their disdain. Finally, in an attempt to not only appear in control but to actually be in control, Elena called them into her office one at a time and scolded them for working outside of the club's structure, which, she reminded them, had her at the helm of the department.

"We had to do something," the second, and most vocal assistant complained. "You sit here all day making lists and then reviewing those same lists and we have to wait, our members have to wait, our sponsors have to wait. And all because you're busy scribbling useless lists!"

Not a conflictive person by nature, Elena surprised herself when she jumped to her feet and grabbed the assistant by the shoulders, swung her around and pushed her out the door. "I am in charge here. And you just have to do as you're told. The members and the sponsors talk to me. Do you understand? To me! So I want you to do your part in the back seat over there." She pointed stiffly to the desk that was tucked away so far that it was half under the stairwell. Surprised, the young woman tottered on her high heels and ducked behind the desk, shuffled some papers and then glanced up towards Señor Sepúlveda's office. He was standing at the window watching, amused. Elena saw him wink at the assistant. Then he nodded at Elena and beckoned her to his office, where she was fired on the spot. What she had not been aware of during her seven short months in his employ was that Elena was not the only one that Señor Sepúlveda had invited to dinner.

In the beginning, when she had been the golden girl, and on occasion after she accepted his invitation to a perfectly prepared meal in the dining room and a bottle of robust Carmenere from the Colchagua Valley, Señor Sepúlveda invited her to check the supplies in the infirmary. "Come along, honey." He liked to exercise his charm in English. Guiding her by the elbow, and with a smiling whisper in her ear, "Let's take advantage of our luxury facilities." He tickled her. She titled and fussed, half skipping along the hall and around the corner.

The first time they ended up in the softly lit, empty infirmary, she was surprised and delighted. He had gone to some length to impress. There was a fresh bouquet of freesias in a crystal vase on the counter by the door, a bottle of champagne chilling on ice at the bedside table and two small chocolates placed on the cotton pillow of the neatly-made bed. "You see, I arranged a special dessert," he joked. After that, when he invited her for dessert, she buzzed inside and giggled a little with the anticipation of stepping into the infirmary and being wooed on the crisp white sheets of the narrow bed. She thought she might be falling in love with Señor Sepúlveda. But it turned out that the assistant that Elena had banished to the faraway corner of the office was very pliable and more creative in every way than Elena, and so when the day came, Elena was the one who was sent packing.

It took her a long time to find a new job, partly because Don Marco was unimpressed that the position he had arranged did not endure, and he refused to plug her in again. "I'm not putting my reputation on the line for you again, Elena. All I'm going to say is that I know they're looking for someone to fill a marketing fund raising position over at the Equality Bank. But I'm not putting a word in for you. You'll have to get there on your own." She didn't get that job or the one after that either. Or the one after that. In fact, she attended more than a dozen interviews over a 20-month period before she finally lucked out at a large bed linen distribution company. It wasn't exciting but the job lasted for thirteen lucky years. She just had to show up and, more of less, occupy a chair at a desk, not rock the boat, and push papers to the woman at the next station. The company had a Christmas party every year and celebrated national day for a week like everyone else. She was paid for fourteen vacation days every February. For three years in succession, she spent seven of those days at San Pedro with her mother and Don Marco. Finally, on the fourth year, she begged off (much to Don Marco's relief) and spent her full two weeks drinking with strangers in bars of Bella Vista and Calle Suecia and sleeping off hangovers on hot summer days at home (not able to remember quite how she arrived there), or sometimes in a stranger's bed in the loft of an ample studio apartment, or else on a pull-out sofa or even on the floor in crowded, shared accommodation, the residents of which she would never recognize later.

In those days, she enjoyed parties. Although she wasn't boisterous— she hung back sipping on her pisco sour or nodding off into a solitary, ecstatic space after she allowed a generous stranger to place a little pill on her tongue—she was always invited, perhaps just as an extra body to fill the corner of a sofa. She couldn't figure out what magic she possessed that made her sofa-worthy. She spent most of her weekends in discos and then followed people to private parties and clubs where everyone just kind of lulled around until they were reminded that it was Sunday night and they all needed to work the next day. Elena wasn't sure how long what she referred to as her party period lasted because each year kind of blurred into the next. But she did know that what brought it to an end was a certain Jorge Molina, the guy Don Marco had earmarked as a husband material. "He's the best choice for someone like you, Elena." Elena wasn't sure who Don Marco thought 'someone like her' was. "He'll provide the balance and stability that, deep down, whether you realize it or not, you've been looking for. Maybe it isn't obvious to you now but he's the one all right." Don Marco clicked his tongue to indicate that the decision was made.

During her Jorge period, Elena was in her mid-thirties and still working at the bed linen company. She really had no intention of getting seriously involved because first of all, she was well aware of her tendency towards short-lived dalliances and second of all, why would she jump at anyone that Don Marco, of all people, had chosen?

As it turned out, though, Jorge Molina was definitely a notable blip on her screen. Although she knew deep down that he was not her type, she put aside her wild weekend habits for several months as she orbited around his gravitational pull. He was a political scientist who lectured at Universidad Católica. Don Marco was especially impressed with Jorge's connections to high society and politicians (often one and the same). He often invited Jorge for dinner, after which, they meandered to the patio to smoke cigars and expound their political views. Of course, they agreed on pretty much everything. They were sorry to see Pinochet go and they had attended his funeral along with other hard line supporters, and they both lamented the fact that the Pinochet family had endured hardships when their accounts were audited, their foreign bank accounts frozen and funds later confiscated. Elena never participated in those conversations, "Oh, you know I prefer not to discuss politics. I mean, I know it's important but I like to leave it to other people. I trust you," she told them. She didn't trust them but she did leave it to them. Sometimes, but not often, she went to the trouble of researching opposing views. She made notes and lists, which were inevitably crumpled up and tossed aside. Her analyses were never-ending, no conclusions drawn, her views remained ambiguous. Don Marco accused her of not caring but the truth is that she felt overwhelmed.

Jorge didn't sweep Elena off her feet, largely because Jorge didn't have much of a broom. But surprisingly, he had a quiet romantic side and she allowed herself to wander into it, a little like a calf nuzzling its head into the loop of a lasso. Assuming that she was the only one who knew about this side of him, she felt special, unique and trusted. So perhaps the attraction was more this portal into secret knowledge than to anything romantic. What she deemed romantic would not necessarily be interpreted as such by others. She simply longed for it to be so. She drew the romanticism from his proclaimed love of literature and poetry.

The icing on the cake was when he said that he went beyond the classics, "These short novels by Hernan Rivera Letelier will, themselves, be classics one day. You just wait." That was quite an unexpected compliment for a snob like Jorge. Elena had long been a fan of Rivera Letelier and it set her off, "My favorite is '*Mi Nombre es Malarosa*.' I mean, the final twists and turns. And the details. Of course, the humor and northern idiosyncrasies tickle right into your bones." Looking at him sideways for a few seconds and, paying special attention to the brightness in his eyes, she thought he winked at her. A luxurious shiver ran down her spine. There really was another side to Jorge, a flirtatious side.

In fact, there was nothing flirtatious about him. The wink had been in her imagination. Later, she admitted it. "He's as dry as an old shoe at the bottom of a desert mine shaft," she agreed with herself as she pulled a face at her reflection in the mirror. It had been her delight over their shared enthusiasm for an author... really! "He's the polar opposite of fun," she pouted and then laughed aloud into the mirror.

Initially, having hooked herself on her own fantasy of him as a closet artist-intellectual, she was also sort of infatuated by his pipe-smoking and the confidence with which he won over her household with issuances and pronouncements that, as it turned out, mostly came from other people's research and publications. He could spew a good stream of trendy lines of thought, and he was a master at connecting the dots. But after about six months of blind adoration, she noticed leaks in his arguments that cracked his impeccable façade, and it made him a not-so-together kind of guy. Once she saw it, she couldn't unsee it.

Meanwhile, though, Jorge waved her in and out of academic gatherings, placing his arm firmly around her waist, and carelessly releasing her to rush away when someone of status entered the room. "Go and help yourself to a drink, *mi niña*. I'll be right back." And he'd disappear into the cloud of droning intellect while she'd get buzzed on vodka martinis. In the end, she discovered that she enjoyed the martinis more than she enjoyed being drawn in and tossed aside at Jorge's whim. "I don't need to be with Jorge to enjoy a good martini," she said matter-of-factly when her mother asked.

The relationship came to an end without a word or need for explanation. It was as simple as declining the invitations from her mother or Don Marco when she knew Jorge would be there and apart from that, it was easy enough to avoid him. He faded, without legacy, into the increasing blur of her uneven history.

After that, Elena took a spin on the fast lane with her acquaintances from the Bohemian side of town. From that time until a few years ago, Elena bounced between long periods of self-isolation and short but intense periods of partying. In spite of her self-analysis, she was unable or unwilling to draw a conclusion as to why she had become a total recluse in the last five years, only venturing out to meet her mother. Visits to her doctor dropped off because they were beginning to remind her of those old days of church confessions. Plus, the doctor insisted on recommending a psychologist. "Your insomnia is probably rooted in something deeper, something from your childhood. How many years have I known you, Elena? You have to trust me." She declined his offer with a slight twist of her lips and she hardened her expression.

"My guess is that you experienced trauma and, like it or not, you still suffer from PTSD. You've never dealt with it. If you don't, Elena, you're going to die in misery." He always ended his lecture with, "See this psychologist—and she isn't just any psychologist, she's a valued colleague, someone I know very well. It'll be the best thing you'll ever do for yourself."

"No," she always told him. "I have myself to talk to. And if I ever feel the need for advice, I'll see a psychic." In truth, arranged by her mother, and without the knowledge of Don Marco, she had twice seen a psychic. It was probably the only secret that she and her mother shared. The psychic gave her very little food for thought and she was disappointed. But just the same, Elena chewed on it, trying to extract flavor from the tidbits, such as they were. The psychic had told Elena that she was being watched over. Elena knew the watcher was her dearly-departed father. She certainly didn't need a psychic to tell her that. So that was the end of the psychic too.

The job at the bed linen company would be the last one of Elena's life. She probably could have continued there for years, no matter her mental state (such were the light duties and low demands) but the company folded (no pun intended), probably for the very reasons that had allowed her to keep working there—no one really cared. Her last day on the job wasn't a particularly sad one because she didn't treasure the work nor did she feel connected to her colleagues. As it was, by then, she was numbed by her chemical addiction and the years piled up in a haze that got hazier. How did it get so out of hand? How did one thing lead to another? It's not that her life was precarious, or that something important hung in the balance. No, it was quite the opposite. Nothing hung in the balance, nothing was important.

Up to that day, Elena's mother hadn't mentioned the trust fund. Probably she couldn't be bothered. But then it became obvious that Elena was going to require support because her lifestyle was her lifestyle and there was no changing it. Elena had deliberately wiped from the slate the two occasions that her mother had arranged (through Don Marco's medical connections) for Elena to enter drug rehab. There's no need to expand on that bit of history. It was locked away in her vault. As far as Elena was concerned, the memories in that vault were extraordinarily vulnerable and volatile and they were best secured somewhere dark, somewhere unremarkable and therefore not easily brought forward in her mind. Not long into the drug rehab period, she learned to feign acquiescence in order to manage the people who tried to manage her and her drugs. It worked, but it was extremely exhausting. It was more effort than quitting the drugs themselves. And she never wanted to think about it again. Ever.

Elena's father had set up the trust fund when she was born, the seed money had come from his own father's modest wealth, the source of which was the sale of a medium-sized mining consortium in the central valley.

Therefore, luckily for Elena, money was never going to be a problem and she sailed along in her world of egocentric, half-hearted and misguided analyses, and sleeping pills. Every once in awhile, she would shake herself awake, only to berate herself for her half-lived, circular existence. When she did that, she became aware of the monotonous path that was wearing itself down into a trench, and each time she looked up, the walls seemed taller and more formidable, less light entered and she knew she would never find the means to climb out.

Dreams and memories of her father floated constantly. They hung heavy. Depression deepened its hold on her. The recurring nightmares did not subside, and their loose ends, like a cat 'o nine tails, whipped up fragments of unfinished memories that cut in and stung across her brain. Her only refuge were the yellows from Flaco or the packaged free trials—always new miracle drugs promising to calm tormented minds—that she managed to obtain from a new doctor who was enthusiastic about his singular ability to cure her ills.

20 | WATCHEE BECOMES WATCHER

February 25, 2020

Considering that he was huddled into a shallow groove on the west edge of the canal, Bladimir slept surprisingly well. Perhaps it was the fresh air, the smell of damp soil, dew on new grass, the lightly packed dirt under his back—in general, an unaccustomed direct contact with nature. He scoffed at these thoughts and he rolled over, projected a spit ball into the weeds and watched a lizard scurry away.

It was still early, the sun's fingers just raising the light blue curtain to the east to illuminate the jagged Andean summits. A car occasionally rolled by but no footsteps had yet pounded across the boards of the nearby pedestrian bridge. The tale of the three trolls came to mind and he tried but failed to remember the whole story. He leaned his head back onto the slope and sighed. He supposed he could be a troll and threaten people who attempted to cross, he could charge them a fee for the privilege. Nothing but musings. He had more urgent things to think about. He felt around for the small bag he'd shoved into his front pocket last night. He didn't want to sell the diamonds. He had simply wanted to possess them. Was it just greed? Did he lust after them? No. They were revenge gems. Perhaps they were to be his retirement fund. But if the day came (and he would strive to make sure that day didn't arrive too soon—or better yet, not at all), he'd go to *Tía Rica*, the government-sponsored pawn service. Would they be suspicious? Would they report him to the police? Did Giorgio have people planted inside Tía Rica? Only god and the devil knew. It was possible that Bladimir—and maybe even the gods, themselves—had underestimated Giorgio one too many times. The problem was that packing around such valuables was risky for a homeless man—and he was one of those now. He hadn't been homeless since he was a kid. He grunted and pulled out a cigarette to help him think. He needed a plan.

He took a drag and relaxed, mindlessly watching the smoke rise up to smudge the morning air. He half considered that being homeless—at least the part about sleeping outdoors—was not necessarily an unpleasant experience. He breathed deep and looked up at the sky. Today was going to be another hot one.

His thoughts were interrupted by the sound of someone mumbling and dragging something across the ground. He stiffened, ears piqued as he rose just enough to check between the path and the street, his right hand automatically moving to feel again for the gems in his pocket and touch the pistol. After a couple of minutes, the sounds, intermittent and hard to pinpoint, stopped. He sunk back down, relieved but still alert.

As he was drawing on the last of his cigarette, he heard the noise again. He cupped his ears. It was accompanied by the voice of an older man but he couldn't hear what he was saying. And he couldn't make out a second voice. He crawled along the slope and then straightened, trying to appear in control, trying to appear threatening even, ready for anything. He was travelling light. His cash, his mobile phone, the pouch with diamonds, the pistol, all on his person. He didn't carry a bag that someone could snatch and run with. But still, when his life wasn't secure, what did that say about his things? He could think of several skilled pickpockets, and worse yet, people who would kill for a nice pair of Nikes.

A rat startled him when it scurried up the bank to an upturned crate about two meters away. He cringed. He'd had his fill of rats as a kid. They didn't scare him but he didn't like what they were capable of. He quietly stepped backwards and waited. The sound again. And the voice. It was coming from the other side of the canal. Giving the rat wide berth, he ventured further from the base of the foot bridge and before he climbed up the bank, he glanced around to see if he was alone. On the bridge now, he paused a couple of times to lean over the railing in case someone was watching him from below. When he reached the other side, he saw what he had been unable to see from his earlier vantage point. Heavy camouflage fabric hung from the other end of the bridge and was anchored at intervals with boulders. It was a tidy little shelter that looked established. There was a fire pit on one side. It was too early for tea but a tarnished kettle straddled short bars that were balanced over a small circle of rocks.

Bladimir trod lightly past the shelter and prepared to venture down onto that side of the bank. The voice had come from down there. Whoever it was, was behind a row of low bushes. Bladimir crouched to peer through the leaves.

An elderly man was resting on his haunches at the edge of the canal and he was splashing water on his face and swiping it across his hair. He sputtered as he shook his head, like a dog drying off after a bath. He paused, chuckled and murmured something before repeating the process again and then a third time. The old man stood up with some difficulty and pulled off his sweater and shook it out over the water like he was shaking a rug. He appeared to be counting. After he put the sweater back on, he extended his arms and looked up into the sky and mumbled something. Was he praying? He reached into his pocket and put on a pair of glasses.

Curious, Bladimir leaned over too far and he slipped, loosening some pebbles that bounced down the bank.

Startled by the sound up on the slope, the old man stepped back into the wall of the canal and went silent. His breath was shaky. He flattened himself against the stone wall, and covered his face with both hands. Someone was watching him. He could feel it and he could hear it. He was supposed to be alone, especially at this early hour. His hot breath fogged up his glasses.

Bladimir carefully inched back up the bank, scrambled to his feet and ran on tiptoe back across the footbridge and away from the canal. Once out on the sidewalk, he would be just another anonymous person, on an early morning walk or on his way to work. Head lowered, hood drawn down, one hand in his pocket protecting the little bag of diamonds, he just kept walking. His plan was to head south, creating more distance between himself and Giorgio and El Terminal. The back of his neck was needled with fear, each prick a reminder that Giorgio had men on the streets up and down the city, all with an eye out for him.

He was less than a block south of the footbridge when the morning silence was broken by the ragged breaths and intermittent groans of a man, who because of his unusually short legs, resembled a gnome. He was laboring towards Bladimir from the other side of the street. He was dressed in a black jean jacket and old black jogging pants. He moved with an awkward, uneven gait, like the left side of himself was trying to catch up with the right. A tin pot with a thin metal handle swayed from the crook of his elbow and banged against one thigh. Just as they passed one another, the man cursed the pot and he hopped onto the sidewalk, muttering. "Vicente..." The next words arrived in hoarse whispers to Bladimir's ears. "Vicente Harold Lenz-Weber, you stubborn son of a bitch. I told you, didn't I?" By then, he was several steps away and his next words lost their shape behind the roar of the buses.

Vicente Harold Lenz-Weber. Bladimir knew that name. He had run into it not so long ago. When, exactly? And where? He did an about-face to follow the little man in black. Perhaps the name was of no consequence but he was compelled to find out. In spite of the man's short legs, he was surprisingly fast. He had already disappeared beyond the bushes and was making his way across the footbridge. For the second time that morning, Bladimir found himself sneaking along the narrow wooden crossing. When he reached the midway point, he waited and watched as two men greeted each other with a hug and settled onto wooden crates that had been dragged to the edges of the same fire pit he'd seen earlier. Still there was no fire.

"Good morning, Vicente. I brought this for you."

"Thank-you for the bread. And for the soup, too, Ricardo." The old man's voice sounded overly appreciative. "You don't have to do this."

The crooked little man named Ricardo said, "But you know I do have to do it, Vicente. How else will you survive? I don't understand why you can't stay with us. We both know that's what Rosa would want. You didn't have to move out."

"But she's gone," Vicente's voice was broken and whiny. He drawled, "She's gone. I can't be there without her." It was the old man that Bladimir had just seen at the edge of the canal. With his back to him, he hadn't seen the old guy's face. But now he could, and the face was familiar. He stood quietly, trying to capture the conversation between the two men. And he racked his brain to recall both the name and the face.

Ricardo was saying, "See reason, Vicente! Come on. You know you can't live like this forever. We're worried about you. Carolina is worried about you." The man was becoming more and more agitated, fidgety, rolling his eyes. It was obvious they'd had this conversation before.

Then Ricardo's voice softened. "Well, at least this place is better than sleeping under benches like you were doing before."

"I want to stay here, Ricardo. Don't make me go back there. Please. I can't face it without Rosa."

"You're a stubborn old man. What happened to you, Vicente?"

"I lost Rosa."

"No, I mean... Vicente, we know you. This is not your destiny. Your life was not meant to be like this."

"No." The old man pulled nervously at the sleeves of his sweater until his hands disappeared up inside. He looked up in Bladimir's direction and Bladimir could see his eyes behind a pair of round glasses. That was then Bladimir recognized him.

He was the same old man who was a regular at El Terminal. He always sat alone in a back corner, not talking to anyone but not causing trouble either. He would have been invisible but because he never ordered anything, he made an impression. He just sat there, looking around, seemingly lost in his thoughts. More than once Bladimir had half-decided to go and turn him out. But he had changed his mind because the old guy was harmless. He had offered him water more than once. Maybe he was just in need of a little peace and shelter, and who was Bladimir to deny that? He might be a badass but he wasn't such a badass that he didn't have a heart.

Then he remembered also having seen the old guy at the sidewalk cafe that Fachita frequented in Providencia. Was it a coincidence that he'd seen him there too? Had the old man been there each time that Bladimir had been there? He couldn't recall. But there was something else. It was the name the other man mentioned. He knew the name, and had come across it not so long ago. But from where? Finally, he remembered that he hadn't heard it but that he'd seen it engraved on a crypt in the mausoleum at the cemetery when Elena had invited him to join her at her father's tomb. Vicente Harold Lenz-Weber was Elena's father's name.

But her father was dead. So who was this *viejo* then? Or maybe it was another old guy with the same name. That was possible, wasn't it? Sure, but how likely? Maybe this old guy was an imposter, maybe the man called Ricardo had been taken in by him. Maybe he'd given him a name, maybe he was playing with the old guy. Or maybe *el viejo* was a con artist. Maybe he was playing Ricardo. Bladimir smiled to himself. The sly old bastard.

Now Vicente and Ricardo were busying themselves, trying to light a fire. Ricardo was saying "I brought some tea bags, Vicente. Let's have a cup of tea before I go."

Bladimir stood watching the two of them for a long time. When a young man brushed by him on the footbridge, he realized that the city was awake, more people had set out for work, traffic on the main drag had picked up. He'd better move on too. He turned and resumed his journey south along the canal, unsure of where it would take him. Questions about the old man had briefly overshadowed the more important things at hand.

Suddenly, it occurred to him that if Ricardo had offered a room to Vicente, and Vicente had refused it, then the man called Ricardo must have a vacant room. They were far enough from Recoleta, and it would be a safe place to hide. If Bladimir played his cards right, he might satisfy his curiosity about old Vicente too. The stars were aligning.

The watchee would become the watcher.

21 | HOME

February 25, 2020

While Elena stumbled through the next week, making lists and tossing them aside, her days a jumble of meaningless hours that blurred, one into the next, Bladimir kept his wits about him. He had passed by the cafe, which he now referred to as Fachita's Café, but it was without the former tingling anticipation of seeing her. Although now, he was relieved that she hadn't been there, he was still curious about what she might be doing. It occurred to him that the old man (whatever his real connection to the former Vicente Harold Lenz-Webber) might not be watching him but that he might be watching Fachita. The best way to find out would be to follow the old man but first he needed to resolve his living situation. And he had a plan that would kill two birds with one stone.

That morning, after Bladimir saw Ricardo having tea with Vicente, he followed Ricardo to a modest house that was only four blocks from the footbridge. It was worse for wear—its small, rough patch of grass in the front cried for water, vines wound up an old tree and travelled along a wrought iron fence until they jumped to the front wall and sprawled up and along, partially blocking the top of the windows. An old carport was overgrown with weeds and wild daisies, and a rubber tree had spread its branches up and across the beams. No vehicle in sight. A huge, neglected aloe vera plant grew beyond reasonable bounds at the fence and a tall cactus stood just inside the front gate. The buzzer on the gate was hanging by one of three wires, and beside it was tacked a small handwritten note declaring the buzzer out of order. Bladimir leaned in and called, "*Álo, álo.*" At first there was no response but after his third call, the man he recognized as Ricardo opened the door and began his uneven approach, slightly dragging one foot along the broken sidewalk towards the gate. "Can I help you?"

Bladimir played it bold from the outset. Best not to lie so much that you contradict yourself later. Besides, there was no reason to hide from this apparently harmless man. "Hello. My name is BJ. I'm an old friend of Vicente Lenz-Weber. It's been a while..." He hesitated and looked around, pretending to be lost. "He told me that he lived around here and I thought, well, I thought that since I just happened to be so close, it would be a shame not to stop in and say hello."

Ricardo looked him up and down. There was a long pause. Bladimir waited, trying to keep a steady gaze and an expression of eager amicability.

"A friend of Vicente's, you say? From where?"

"Oh, well, I met him a few years back, at a restaurant in Recoleta. You probably know the one. El Terminal?"

"Well, I don't know it personally but Vicente has mentioned it." His shoulders dropped and the muscles around his mouth relaxed.

"Oh, so then this is the right house? Vicente is here?" He feigned what would be a reasonable assumption.

"Well, this is the right house but he doesn't live here anymore."

"Oh, well, I'm sorry to hear that. It would be good to see him. But maybe I can catch him at El Terminal if he still goes there."

"Sorry. Can't help you with that one. But I see him from time to time, and I could pass on your greeting. What did you say your name is?"

"I'm BJ. BJ Morales." Bladimir extended his hand through the gate. "Thank you for your kindness."

"You're welcome," said Ricardo, briefly accepting Bladimir's hand before turning away.

"Oh, and, just on the off-chance..."

Ricardo paused and twisted around to face Bladimir again.

Bladimir said, "Um, I'm just wondering, this is a nice quiet street and I'm looking for room and board for a short stay. I have business near here but I don't have locomotion and it occurred to me that it would be convenient to rent a room within walking distance. A room would suit me better than a hotel, if you know what I mean."

Ricardo scratched his head.

Bladimir pushed forward with his plan, "I mean, I suppose Vicente's old room is spoken for by now. And that would be a shame because this location is perfect. But, well, I would understand." He repeated, "The idea just occurred to me... on the off-chance..."

Ricardo raised his hand, index finger pointing up. "Just a minute," he said. He limped back up the sidewalk and disappeared inside. He was gone for several minutes and returned with a woman who was a bit taller than he was but much more slight. She was wiping her hands on a flowered apron and she eyed Bladimir as she approached. Ricardo was right behind. She stopped and without smiling, she took her time to study Bladimir, top to bottom and up again.

Ricardo piped up from behind her, "May I present my wife, Carolina."

The woman ignored that. "You have business in around here?" Her voice was more powerful than he would have given her credit for.

"Yes," Bladimir said. "My uncle is the owner of a house a few blocks that way," he pointed south. But the people who live there haven't paid rent for more than a year and we can't get access to the property either. Well, you know how it is, right? It's hard to be on the right side of the law when you're the landlord. My uncle is too old to deal with it and asked me to see what I can do. He wants to sell the house but, well, you know, we need to deal with the squatters and probably lots of repairs before anything else."

"Ricardo..." she gestured towards the man, "He says you're a friend of Vicente. And you want short term room and board."

"Yes, that's exactly right. When I heard that Vicente lived around here, I thought it would be good to see him and I was also hoping he could recommend *una residencial*."

She responded with a smile that came and went quickly. "We're not exactly *una residencial* but Vicente's old room is still vacant and if it's just temporary, we can offer it for a decent price. And since you're a friend, well…. Main meals are extra, of course but they're home-cooked and they're good."

Ricardo was standing behind her, nodding his head non-stop.

Bladimir smiled. "That would be perfect. And yes, of course, I understand main meals are extra. No problem."

"We'd need you to pay a week up front." She said and she turned for a sign of Ricardo's agreement.

"Of course." Bladimir extended his hand through the grill and she wiped hers on her apron before accepting and quickly releasing, as though human contact would bring a curse or something.

"And if you plan to stay more than a week, then we'll need the next week up front too," she said. "And so on."

Ricardo brushed by Carolina to unlock the gate and usher Bladimir in with a self-conscious, half-apologetic sweep of his hand. Carolina turned and walked in before them. Once inside the house, Ricardo's mood was noticeably lighter. Perhaps it was because Carolina had also accepted this stranger into their house without too many questions, like seconding a motion and voting in favor without even raising a hand. It gave the decision unanimous validity. Or perhaps they couldn't afford to think twice. But Bladimir doubted that. Not in this part of town. In any case, Ricardo suddenly treated Bladimir like an old friend, patting him on the back. "Come on in and see where you'll be laying your head. It's the only extra room we have in the house."

He showed him to a bedroom at the back. It was spacious and light. There was a double bed and a wall lined with a bookshelf. There was a desk and chair and a large, overstuffed armchair covered with a crocheted throw beside a shuttered window. The walls were decorated with framed posters from museums and municipalities. The room was warm—mostly earth-tones and oranges with sunflowers, it felt like something from the 1970s, a bedroom he could have only dreamed of.

Carolina suddenly appeared. "The only thing we ask is that you don't take anything that doesn't belong to you." Ricardo looked at him half apologetically. "It has to be said," Carolina added. "You know how people can be."

Bladimir nodded. "Of course. You can count on me."

"And please," Ricardo said, "The books belong.... I mean... belonged ...to my sister, Rosa." Pain cut thin red lines across his forehead. "She loved them. I don't think she'd mind if you browsed them. But we try to keep everything just like she had it. If that's okay. You know what I mean."

"Yes. Yes, of course." Bladimir was tempted but overcame his inclination to ask more. "I'll take care of these things as if they were my own mother's. Don't worry about that." The house was unfamiliar, but he felt like he fit in. He felt welcomed, even warmed by it. Perhaps it was because his plan had gone off more easily than he had anticipated. Perhaps it was because he needed a home. Perhaps it was because he was lonely. Perhaps it was something deeper. But no one really wants to go deeper.

The couple left him at the doorway with an invitation for a cup of tea when he was ready to join them and settle the first week's payment. He sat gingerly on the edge of the bed, his thighs taut, as though he might have to spring up and escape at a moment's notice. As he tried to accept that he'd lucked out on this place, he caressed the chenille cover with both hands, his fingers teasing the soft fabric into slim rows, conscious of the pleasure the texture gave him. So this was Vicente's room. Who was he anyway? And these were Vicente's things mixed in with those of someone called Rosa. The sister. Why would Vicente prefer a bed under the bridge?

Bladimir sighed and squinted across at the bookshelf, which was filled with books of all sizes. Gaps on the shelves were filled with sea shells and felt figures of rabbits and dogs, a miniature metal sculpture of Don Quixote, three large red clay piggy banks, several porcelain birds of all colors and shapes, a forlorn-looking stuffed cat and other artisan knickknacks. A rustic wind chime made from various lengths of bamboo swung gently just outside the window. Bladimir stepped over to open it and he tapped the bamboo, causing it to release its soft, flat tones. He stood back and smiled. And again, please. He tapped it and it swung gently around under the conduction of the wind, the hollow notes vibrated up and out. Yes, Bladimir liked Vicente's room. He would stay. Not that the choices were many.

He pondered how close this house must be to wherever Fachita lived. She had come to matter less to him recently but just the same, he was aware of her nearness. In an indirect way, if not for her, he would not be standing here playing with this wind chime, looking out into the garden from this window, and about to go and have tea with this couple and very soon, bit by bit, arrange to stay long-term in this house.

Finally, he turned away and breathing slowly, reluctant to remove himself from the pleasant surroundings, he closed the window, and prepared to join Ricardo and Carolina. Later, even if it took time, he would get to the bottom of the homeless man called Vicente and the reason why he and the old man had so many people and places in common.

22 | OLD BLUE EYES

February 26, 2020

It was late February and the previous weeks had disappeared through some of the less consequential tunnels of Elena's mind. Now, as she stood in line to buy a pack of vanilla-filled chocolate cookies at the corner store, she looked around and was almost blinded by brilliant rays glinting off a metal sign at a new pharmacy across the street. "Another option," she thought immediately, and smiled. Barely open and eager for sales, they likely wouldn't insist on a medical prescription.

"A package of Fracs, please. The dark chocolate and vanilla ones," she said as she stepped to the front of the line. She dug into her jeans pockets to pull out the coins she had counted that morning and she was gripped by sudden, hot panic. Why had she felt the need to count out and bring the exact change? What if the price had increased this week? What if she was left standing like a fool and would end up walking away empty-handed and red-faced? "How much?" she asked and then didn't listen. Wrapping her fingers around the cylindrical package, she slid it off the counter and plunked down the coins. Then she turned abruptly and left as the clerk was still catching and counting coins that rolled along the counter.

She had planned to stop at the cafe but realized that she had only brought enough money for the cookies. Where was her head this morning? She hadn't ventured out of her apartment for days. Exactly how many, she wasn't quite sure. It was too much effort to try to gather time into some kind of orderly sequence and count it off. And besides what did it matter? She had no responsibilities, no commitments. Her mother was still in the northern desert, doting over Don Marco, which meant that Elena didn't have to worry about surprise visits. She was aware that she was sneering.

Who was she kidding? Being useless was not the same as being omnipotent. She pursed her lips in self-rebuke and did a sharp detour to take her past the children's play park where she had first seen BJ.

"It's not as though I really believe he'll be here but... well, on the off-chance..." she was talking aloud. An elderly lady looked at her twice and bristled past, her oversized broach bouncing double-time on her soft bosomed shelf. Elena stopped at the edge of the park and as she eyed the empty swing set, she recalled how BJ had been soaring there, like a man-eagle tied to a set of chains. A man-child in motion, reaching up and out but unable to take off. Still, he tried. Maybe it was the story of his life, a story she might never know. Seemed like ages ago but then, who was counting? Who could keep track even if they tried? But she tried. She had scribbled dates and created time lines on her yellow foolscap. Even though she could not summon it at this moment, the answer was lying in yellow pieces on her floor.

She was tempted to walk over and jump onto a swing. The freedom that swings offer—as close to flying as she could imagine—made her tingle with the childish delight she had shared with BJ that day. She took a couple of steps towards it but stopped when a little boy careened past, yelling at the top of his lungs, his father close behind. Elena stood and watched as the pair of them took to the sky on the set of wooden wings. Another opportunity lost, she shrugged and headed around the corner, counting the steps as she let her feet carry her home. Seven hundred and sixty-seven...

About 30 seconds later, Bladimir appeared on the very spot she had just abandoned. If someone wanted to measure the temperature of that spot, they would say that she had warmed it for him and that it still hadn't cooled off. Standing at the same angle as Elena had done, he watched the father-and-son pendulums, the boy shouting and laughing and the father answering with the measured responses of a responsible adult. Unlike Elena, Bladimir wasn't tempted to approach the swing set. Not just because it was occupied but because the memory no longer excited him. Now Fachita was just a possible connection to *el viejo* who called himself Vicente. Maybe that's why he had wandered over here this afternoon. He hadn't thought about how he might react if they should run into each other but he probably would have invited her for coffee just to sniff around about the old man who had hijacked her father's name. He glanced over his shoulder. He'd better keep moving. This was a safe neighborhood. For now. He pushed thoughts of Fachita aside.

Ricardo and Carolina were closed-mouthed about Vicente. Bladimir didn't want to appear overly interested so he didn't insist. But he thought that of the two, if anyone would tell him anything, it would be Ricardo. He was more relaxed. Ricardo had confided that they used to be able to count on Rosa's contributions but now they survived on his meagre pension and that the room and board that Bladimir paid was a windfall.

Ricardo turned to the subject of Vicente without any nudging from Bladimir. "Vicente hasn't been gone for very long," Ricardo started to explain. "We still think he's better off with us, here where we can keep an eye on him. For his health, you know. But he's stubborn. He just refuses to come back, at least not yet." It seemed that Ricardo needed to justify (probably more to himself than to Bladimir) why they would allow a stranger to occupy Vicente's room. "This rental arrangement is just temporary. I mean, you know... in case he changes his mind."

"He's in poor health?" Bladimir asked casually.

"Well, physically, he's good. For a man his age..."

"Oh. Well, that's a relief." What kind of health issues did Vicente have? He waited for Ricardo to elaborate but it ended there.

Bladimir was still the shark who needed to circulate but now that he had to watch his back, he tightened the circumference. Fachita's cafe was within what he had decided was a relatively safe zone so he headed in that direction, glancing behind every so often to see if he was being tailed. Even though he'd chosen a neighborhood that was, for him, uncharacteristic (mostly because the politics here wouldn't coincide with his views), Bladimir knew that Giorgio would be relentless and that he wouldn't be safe unless he could make a miracle happen. With some luck he would do just that. Having found a temporary home with this family, he allowed himself some optimism. What does a man live off, if not hope?

As he rounded the corner at the cafe he saw Vicente lean down to gather his packsack and sling it over his shoulder. The lines in the old man's face looked deeper today and the bag seemed almost too much to manage. Bladimir approached him directly to offer help.

"Señor, how do you do?" Bladimir was careful not to loom too close. The man was bent slightly forward under the weight of his pack. Vicente peered up at him, his eyes a clear blue behind the round lenses and, seeing him close-up for the first time, Bladimir was surprised at how lucid the old man appeared to be. Why had he expected something different? Vicente stood absolutely still, his jaw set, as he fixed his gaze on Bladimir. He didn't say a word, and unlike anyone else who had just been surprised by a stranger, he didn't even open his mouth. He just studied Bladimir in silence, taking his time, like a baby brazenly staring out at the world from over his mother's arms. Bladimir stepped back. The old man remained silent.

"Señor, I think I know you from somewhere." It was not a very original opening line.

"Do you think you are clever?" The old man's voice was steady. "I've seen you here before. And I've seen you in other places too." The old man twisted slightly to spit. It landed close to Bladimir's left boot. Bladimir stepped back again.

"Is that so?" Bladimir challenged him. "Where might you have seen me before?"

"Here," said Vicente. "And..." he gestured with his chin, "... and there."

Bladimir decided it was best not to play games with the old guy because it was obvious that he was more astute than he'd given him credit for. If he played it straight, maybe they could be useful to each other. So he dared, "By 'there', you mean El Terminal. Yes, I've seen you there too."

The old man was still bent forward, his packsack only half settled on his right shoulder. He managed a wry smile and shifted the packsack so he could stand straight. Even at that, he was still more than a head shorter than Bladimir. In spite of his stature, he had a remarkable presence.

Bladimir had no way of knowing that today was one of Vicente's very rare good days, and catching Vicente on one of these days, could be formidable. It was in this state that he cast the shadow of an old statesman, which loomed long on the sidewalk and cooled the area around Bladimir's feet. Bladimir shivered involuntarily.

"Well, it seems we're not exactly strangers, then."

"It seems we are not," agreed Vicente.

"I wonder if you'd like to..." Bladimir's question was cut short because, shifting his packsack with an exaggerated roll of his shoulders, Vicente suddenly turned away without a word. With his back to Bladimir, he raised his right hand in the air and waved his fingers in a nonchalant goodbye. Like an Englishman's "Ta Ra." Bladimir could only watch him go. But when the time came, he would know where to find him. And he'd be prepared for the cagey old man.

23 | MISSTEPS

February 27, 2020

Giorgio wasn't getting any joy from Flaco. He shouldn't have caved into his whining and cajoling about moving up in the organization. That he had succeeded in exposing Bladimir's misstep was only because Giorgio had given him detailed instructions. Beyond that, Flaco was most useful in the pizza joint and for feeding verbatim instructions to the Rati.

After five days of zero progress from Flaco, Giorgio sicced El Capitán on Bladimir. They were now well into their search and Bladimir was still playing hard to get. El Capitán had gone a little rough on the old lady at Bladimir's last known residence and even so, when all was said and done, she stood by her claim to know nothing. "I didn't even know he left," she pleaded, eyes round, tears spilled into the deep wrinkles of her cheeks and channeled down to her lips. She sputtered, "He's a good man. He took care of me. Something happened to him. Otherwise he would've told me he was going."

Giorgio was certain that Bladimir hadn't left the city—he was not that adventuresome—and Giorgio was getting impatient to track him down. The son of a bitch *conchetumadre* was up to something. They had unfinished business on several levels: one, most recently, Bladimir had tried to use Flaco for his own personal program. Giorgio might be blind but he could still see what was going on; two, Bladimir was jealous of El Capitán, and amidst other pettiness, he was looking for leverage, trying to slither his way up the ladder; three, Bladimir was still questioning Giorgio's judgment regarding the senator who was supposed to have been his mentor; and most importantly; four, Bladimir was walking around with diamonds that should still be in the bellies of the three wise monkeys. Did he think Giorgio wouldn't put two and two together?

Giorgio was not a man who liked to second-guess himself. He was convinced that El Capitán had been in Santiago long enough to know his way around the neighborhoods. The fact is, though, that he didn't grow up here and he didn't know the ins and outs, didn't know the narrow passageways of the populated *cités* where people had their own reasons for, and methods of keeping things secret. Still, Giorgio was hoping that a fresh perspective with creative, foreign ideas might be the solution to finding that son of a bitch traitor. He'd give El Capitán a couple more days.

As Giorgio got caught up in a few pensive moments—reaching up to read the gems at the corner of his glasses, his lips curled up slightly, Vicente watched him from his favorite table at the back. His eyes followed Giorgio as he instructed the cashier. "This is your station for the next two hours. Don't even think about moving from this spot. And keep your fingers away from where they don't belong. I know how much *plata* is in there and how much will be there when your two hours are up." Giorgio rapped the counter twice with his middle knuckle and, dragging his hand along the top, he walked steadily towards the back room, as surely as if he had two seeing eyes.

Vicente was conscious of every detail and he felt emboldened. Hadn't he just walked away from Wolfman? And wasn't he still feeling particularly sharp and somewhat exhilarated by all the watching? He sat back and let his arms dangle, his fingers ticking back and forth along the side of the chair. He thought about Wolfman. Too bad he wasn't here to give him a glass of water. He always let him have water. But no matter. Vicente would soon return to his hovel, where, among other things, Ricardo had stashed a few bottles of water.

He thought about how he had had to negotiate for his new spot under the bridge. He had come upon it when he was still sleeping under benches, weeks after he left his room at Ricardo's. Back then the place was occupied by a man who went by the name of Manguera. Manguera was very tall but he was also so skinny he could have wrapped his belt around his waist twice. Maybe Manguera was scary in the morning but by the time Vicente arrived one late afternoon, he was in a jolly mood, a real pushover. He was wobbly from having consumed half a bottle of pisco. He told Vicente that it was his lucky day because he was planning to abandon his hovel. Vicente could have it but he'd have to pay the man in charge, who would show up like clockwork in a week's time. "You have to deal with him," Manguera said. "Tonight I'm going to sleep in a shelter at the church close to Plaza Italia because I wanna dry out. Again." He gurgled and coughed. "In more ways than one. And the people there always help with that."

Informal shelters, especially sought-after ones like those under a footbridge, were valuable. Even indigents had their own mafia. And the mafia was in control of the best sheltering places, meaning that even if there wasn't an address for the place, whoever chose to lay their head there was forced to pay what could probably be called a condo fee. Vicente prepared to meet the man in charge.

Vicente had entered the refuge with two thin blankets, a mug, a kettle, a sweater slung over his packsack, a box of matches, a candle, a roll of twine, two rolls of toilet paper, some tea bags, and a photo of Rosa. Manguera had left a couple of old newspapers, two empty tin cans and—what luck!— three stubby candles. Manguera had also waved off the hanging camouflage blanket attached to the bridge, "That was here when I got here and I don't need it where I'm going. Use it." As soon as Manguera turned his back, Vicente ducked under and settled inside.

Although, there were some things that he remembered exactly and vividly, Vicente was mostly unable to keep track of time, but exactly one week later just as the shadows finished sweeping the light off the slopes of the cordillera, and just as Manguera had predicted, Vicente heard footsteps approach and then stop abruptly outside his shelter. "Manguera!" Vincent watched as a worn leather boot kicked at the dirt where the camouflage met the ground. Dust wafted in. The boot kicked again.

"Stop. I'm coming." Vicente crawled out and got to his feet. The man didn't look particularly daunting but when he spoke, he raised his voice with authority and Vicente snapped to attention. The man's breath smelled of stale wine, his complexion was colorless and he was missing a few front teeth. He stood now with both hands in his pockets but Vicente could see that they were shaking.

"You're not Manguera," he boomed. "Where's Manguera?"

"He left. He said he was going to dry out somewhere."

"I've heard that before."

"I don't know.... I'm new, aren't I. He said I could stay here." Vicente indicated the camouflage blanket." And he even left me a few other things.... for which I am grateful." Vicente smiled, trying to appear amenable. But it had no effect on the man, who eyed him.

"I don't really care who sleeps here. The space doesn't come free."

"How's that?" Vicente wanted the man's explanation.

"I keep a eye on things in this part of town and I expect to be paid for it."

"What happens if you're not?"

The man raised an eyebrow and scowled. "Wanna find out?"

"Well, no. I just wonder what I'm paying for."

"You're payin' for me not to mess you up here and now, and throw you and your garbage into the canal."

"What will you accept as payment?"

The man licked his lips. "I'll accept what Manguera used to pay me." He worked up a spit ball and sent it sailing towards a lizard at the edge of the path.

"I don't have cash. But I can get wine. I mean, I have a stash but it's not here. You understand that I can't keep anything like that unguarded."

The man blinked and waited, meaning that Vicente was going to have to come up with something solid.

"If you come back next week, then I promise I'll have it for you."

"I'm lettin' you off with a warning 'cause you're new. But I'll only give you this one chance. If you blow it, you'll have to pay for it and you really don't want that." He wagged his grubby finger in front of Vicente's nose and turned to leave. "I'll be back next week at the same time. And you're gonna owe me for two weeks. No excuses." He spit again, this time into the fire pit.

This was going to be a big problem because without Rosa, Vicente was penniless. And Ricardo would never agree to make regular payments to the homeless mafia. If he suspected such a thing, he'd be adamant about Vicente returning home. But as it happened, the winds blew in his favor and would deliver him a solution.

The solution arrived at the cafe the next morning. Elena was in a state of disarray when she first got there. Before she took her first sip of coffee, and when she swatted at a fly, she sent the coffee cup and all crashing to the ground. The waiter was on the spot immediately. He frowned as he informed her that she'd be charged for the cup as well as the coffee. "And Señora, if you want to order another, I'm afraid I have to add it to the bill. Otherwise it will be deducted from my wages. You understand."

She nodded, too embarrassed to argue. Money wasn't the problem. The problem was that she had been clumsy—again. Lately, she'd been bumping into furniture, tripping over her own feet, and letting things slip through her fingers. She dropped her favorite pen several times yesterday and the last time, she trod on it and broke it. She chalked up the clumsiness to changes in medication. And just now, she noted, even more annoyed, she'd hadn't even hit the stupid fly. The same one returned to land on the sugar pot, smugly rubbing its little knees together, taunting her.

As she watched the fly, she saw, out of the corner of her, the small man with spectacles and the goatee. He was in his usual spot, a few tables away, his eyes trained on her from behind those big round lenses. Besides her, he was the only other person at the cafe this morning. "Oh, you again," she grumbled under her breath. She raised her head to look the little man squarely in the eyes. She was in no mood to be polite or to pretend that he didn't annoy her. How often had she seen him sitting there, staring in her direction, mostly without even trying to disguise his watchfulness? Well, this morning, he'd get it back. She scowled at him and waved him off, which he chose to interpret as an invitation. He pushed back his chair, reached down to heave his packsack across one shoulder and he headed straight towards her.

Up to now, Vicente and especially Elena had mostly tried to conceal their interest in each other. She groaned but didn't look away. He arrived at her table in a few steps, and without so much as a polite nod or a how-do-you-do, he removed his packsack and sat down, careful to sandwich the pack tightly between his knees. Only then did he look at her directly again. But he didn't speak. At first he didn't even smile. But then a childish sort of grin slowly passed across his face and his eyes crinkled up in sincere agreement with his lips. She couldn't help it, she smiled back. They sat there smiling at each other without a word until the waiter returned with a broom and dustpan. "I'll bring your coffee in a minute," he said. He glanced over at Vicente. "Can I get you anything, Señor?" Elena lifted her eyebrows and asked him, "What would you like?" She extended her hands, palms open, to signal an offering. "My invitation."

Vicente nodded at her and looked up at the waiter. "I'll have a glass of water, please."

"That's all?" Elena asked. "No coffee? Perhaps some juice?"

"Well, okay, yes, I'll accept some orange juice. Thank-you." He glanced at Elena and then at the waiter, who nodded.

They both turned to watch him bustle away, swinging the dustpan with the broken coffee cup, and dragging the broom behind in an odd choreography. Suddenly, the silence seemed cracked and awkward and they both tried to mend it by speaking at once, neither of them listening to the other as their few, senseless words fell flatly into the space between them.

Elena looked around and then turned back to Vicente. She chuckled, and finally said something that made sense. "Look, Señor, I know you've been watching me. I don't know why and I don't even know for sure how long this has been going on. But you know it's not natural. Right?" She held up her hands in a gesture of good-natured helplessness.

She watched as he made a tremendous effort, digging deep for the correct response. She could see the cogs turning in his old brain. Now that she wasn't turning her back on him, trying to avoid him—now that she was observing him up close—she could see that he probably used to be a gentleman. He had an educated air about him, a finesse, even worldliness. He was all too familiar in an unfamiliar way. And, somehow, he was all wrong. His wrongness was painful. She flinched inwardly. She could liken him to a fine crystal vase that had been broken and pieced back together by someone totally unqualified. Now the prime material was tarnished and could not catch the light. It was patched and could not reflect color. But she thought that if someone who knew how to mend such things, could adjust the pieces so that the lines flowed correctly again, then the man sitting before her would be formidable. Quite unexpectedly, she felt a great empathy for him. And then something else happened, something that startled her to the bone. She recognized something about him, something that tied him to her in a way that didn't make sense. He was repeatedly rubbing the fingers of his left hand with those of his right. The motion was something like drawing off and replacing a loose ring from each of his fingers, even though he wore no rings. It was a calming, repetitive motion. Where had she seen that before?

Besides being an enigma—a challenge in an odd sort of way—the old man was also very magnetic. Up close like this, he exuded a gentle charm, and she was attracted to it—or to him. She wasn't sure to what she could attribute the attraction.

"My name is Vicente," he said. And in the very next breath, "I lost my wife recently."

"I'm very sorry for your loss," said Elena. Perhaps what she felt was just sympathy attraction. Maybe she could sense his sadness and loneliness and this is why she felt close to him. There was a sameness between them. Was it desolation?

She, too, blurted out without thinking. "My father died. It was many years ago, though. I was just a girl. His name was Vicente too." When she looked at him, she got lost in his clear blue eyes.

"Hmmm."

"Where do you come from?" She asked him.

"Over there." He pointed towards the canal.

"Do you live with family?"

"No, not anymore. My wife died, I just told you." He fidgeted in the chair and for a moment, she thought he was going to abort their conversation and abandon her, then and there. But he didn't. "I used to live with her family but it's not the same without her. I can't bear to be in the room where we used to live. So I left."

"Oh." She raised her eyebrows and waited for him to offer more.

He didn't hesitate. "I live rough now, and I just found a place under the footbridge. Someone moved out of it and he told me it was mine if I wanted it."

"Are you homeless now? I mean... so now you live under a bridge?" She was taken aback, the tone of her voice rising as she repeated, in other words, what he'd just told her. She'd never been acquainted directly with a homeless person before. Sure, she'd dropped coins into needy hands but she'd never taken the time to actually talk, to ask questions, to learn something about who the hands belonged to.

"Yes." He was matter of fact.

"But how do you eat? I mean, do you have to beg for money or food?"

"No, not that. I don't beg. My brother-in-law brings me food. I don't ask for it. He just brings it. No, I have food. But I discovered that, even if you are homeless, you have to pay for your shelter."

"What do you mean?"

He frowned. "I don't really understand it. So, now I might have to leave the spot that I just I found. I'm not sure yet."

"What, though? What? I don't know what you're saying."

"Well, it seems there is a kind of hobo mafia."

Now Elena laughed. "What?"

"There's a kind of big guy who came by my place under the bridge yesterday and he told me that he is charging me to stay there, just like he charged the last guy."

"But... What?" She laughed again. "Wow. People always find a way to get by, don't they?"

Vicente nodded repeatedly. "I know. I was surprised too. But if I don't pay, then he will probably trash everything, kick me out, and let someone else have the place. It's a good thing I keep all my valuables with me at all times." He tapped his packsack. "But I made a deal with him. I promised to give him some wine instead of money."

"Well, is your brother-in-law going to give you the wine then?"

"No, this is my problem. Not his. He wants me to move back to his house. But I just can't. I can't." He was shaking his head. "And if he finds out about this, he'll make me. I don't now how, but he will."

"It looks like you have a big problem then," she said.

"I do." Again, the same matter of factness.

A minute passed in silence as they both looked down at his hands. He was doing the ring thing again and she was distracted by it. She looked at his face but he was concentrating on rubbing his fingers and it was like he was gone somewhere else. The waiter came over and he stood for a few seconds, trapped in their awkward lull and then he removed her empty coffee cup and left the half-full glass of juice. Vicente didn't seem to notice but Elena glanced up and nodded appreciatively.

"I can help." Elena volunteered without knowing why she was willing to assume this old man's problem.

He stopped fidgeting and looked up from under a furrowed brow. His glasses had slipped down the bridge of his nose and Elena saw into his blue eyes. He seemed so innocent and helpless. Yet there was a strength behind them. A flicker of confidence.

"I have money. I can buy your wine. When do you need it? What kind did you promise?"

"No, you don't understand," Vicente was distressed. "I have to give him wine every week. It's not a one-shot deal. It's like weekly rent."

"Yeah, I get that."

They searched each other's eyes. This would mean commitment. Two noncommittal strangers suddenly committed to each other. How odd. How clumsy.

24 | LEAP YEAR

February 29, 2020

If 2020 wasn't a leap year, this day would not have happened. Or perhaps it would have taken place on March 1, or maybe back on February 28th. But would the day have unfolded in the very same way? Maybe it never would have happened at all. When he was young, Vicente had been fascinated by leap year. Of course his teachers had explained why there was one whole extra day every four years and he understood the concept. But it didn't stop him from pitying February 29th kids. They had to fake their birthday three out of every four years. Surely that does something to one's self-esteem, having to pretend that faking your birthday doesn't bother you. How could leap year babies trust that they were truly even alive? And how were you supposed to trust events that fell on this oddball day—you were a calendar afterthought. Was this the best that the brains behind the world's calendar could do? Every four years, you tuck in a whole day at the end of the shortest calendar month? Not very creative. Way too flimsy. Still, at the age of 85, Vicente didn't like leap year. And this morning, he overheard a gardener tell his colleague that today was that extra day of the year. So he had to be on guard, ready for anything, maybe things would disappear into the crack of the year, maybe that's what happened to his memory. Vanished into a non-day. It was a possibility. He just didn't trust this day. He didn't trust anything.

Questions about trust caused Vicente a lot of anxiety. Rosa had told him that his brain wasn't functioning 100 percent. She said that he shouldn't trust himself to make decisions, especially if he was tired. He used to be able to rely on Rosa for help but now he was on his own. Rosa had often told him, in the kindest of ways, that he was impetuous, and undisciplined, and that basically, he was a confused man. Sometimes he couldn't discern what was real and what was imagined. Sometimes his brain was overwhelmed with noise. And sometimes memories of places and faces of people he should have known but couldn't identify, rolled past repeatedly; they prickled him and he became itchy and he tried to rub them away, wearing down the skin at the back of his neck and behind his ears and above his eyebrows.

The long and short of it was that Vicente didn't know whether or not to trust Elena because he couldn't trust himself. His brain-gut told him that she was trustworthy, and she might even be special. If not, why had he been watching her all this time? He didn't know. How much time had it been? He couldn't remember. But surely it hadn't been for nothing. Could he trust himself to know that deep down, he might be right about the subjects he felt responsible to watch?

And as for Elena, why should she trust this old man? Whose to say he wasn't just out for free wine? The question arose but she pushed it down into a bog of unsettled emotion—emotion that didn't cause distress but rather, kind of soothed her soul. The bottom line was that, for an unknown and deeply compelling reason, after seeing him up close as she had, she felt an affection for him. She agreed to meet him for coffee the next day, at which time she promised she'd bring a couple of bottles of Gato Negro, Carmenere.

Vicente's condo fee predicament was put to rest without help from Ricardo, which made Vicente very content and Elena very alive with curiosity. They would continue to meet at the cafe for some weeks, during which time, pleasantries would be exchanged. Neither of them would have much to offer beyond small talk. Vicente, with his broken brain and Elena with her drug-soaked one, would while away their weeks in distinct daily hazes that were often confused with reality and were, therefore, difficult to recount. Thus, they would be satisfied with encounters at the cafe, during which they would experience an important exchange of positive energy that served to recharge them over the coming days.

Enter Bladimir, who met them coincidentally at the cafe on one such morning.

When he made his appearance, all three people came together like the corners of a triangle that tottered on one of its points. It was a precarious balance. Vicente, for one, was accustomed to such things.

Elena had arrived at about 11 am to find Vicente already blending into the background at his usual table. She nodded as she approached him. "I'm going to use the washroom," she said. "I'll be right back." She handed him a paper bag with a bottle of Gato Negro. He accepted it with a smile, and bent down to stuff it into the biggest pocket of his packsack. Just as he finished patting it into place, a shadow stretched out on the sidewalk, crawled up his legs, spread itself over his back and swiped across the top of his head.

"Good morning, *Maestro*," Bladimir addressed Vicente with the respect that someone of his age deserved. This did not go unnoticed by Vicente, who, in spite of himself, felt warmed by it.

"Good morning, Señor," he sat back and shaded his eyes with one hand to look up into Wolfman's face.

"May I?" asked Bladimir as he indicated an empty chair and then sat down without waiting for a response.

"Well, I don't know…" Vicente was going to say that this was maybe not the best time. But before he could finish the sentence, he saw Elena striding towards the table, wearing a wide smile, but her eyebrows were raised in question.

She said, "I ordered you a…" She stopped when she recognized Bladimir.

"BJ?" she walked around his chair so she could turn and face his consistently-absent self.

"Hola, Fachita." he said casually, as though he was expecting her.

She noticed his lack of spark. "Fachita?" she was annoyed by the name but chose to not to ask. "How are you?"

"I'm well," he said.

She helped herself to a chair and pointing at each of them in turn, she asked, "Do you two know each other?"

"We were acquainted the other day," Bladimir said. He looked at Vicente. "But it feels more like we're old friends."

"Really?" Elena said. She noticed that Vicente looked pleased, perhaps even a bit smug.

"Yes," Vicente smiled at Bladimir. He offered, "And Elena and I have just become friends too. But it feels like we've known each other for a long time."

"Elena?" Bladimir repeated under his breath. "Elena."

She looked at him and waited but he didn't say any more.

Vicente turned silent as his two 'watchees' exchanged pleasantries. What luck that he could watch both at once, at the same table. Surely their exchange would present new information. Vicente knew he was gathering it to satisfy important, deep-rooted questions. If only he could remember what they were. He knew Bladimir as Wolfman, the name he had given him. Why, he couldn't exactly recall. He'd seen him somewhere else too, somewhere that caused anxiety when he tried to remember, such that it made his heart race, and once, to the point where he was choked with pain and fear, regret, guilt—all those bad things. So he retreated from the memory and let it descend back into the mire of his brain, where it became mostly inaccessible. This morning, life spread in front of him in a positive light. He listened, letting a few phrases sink in. He noticed that Wolfman called Elena 'Fachita.' Was she a fascist? He wondered. But it didn't matter. She called him BJ. No matter. Vicente would continue to call her Elena and him, Wolfman. Best to stick with what he knew.

Elena was animated, her face flushed and she repeatedly ran her fingers through her hair. Bladimir casually flung one arm over the back of his chair, tolerating her nonsense. Because Elena had already delivered the wine, Vicente's business with her was done. But he was in no rush and he sipped slowly on the orange juice the waiter had set before him and he watched, almost hypnotized as Elena stirred sugar into her coffee, the little spoon clinking non-stop against the edges of the cup. Finally, she set it down very deliberately, just so, on the saucer and folded her hands on her lap.

The phrases that Vicente recorded for later included, "How is Flaco?" "I don't want to talk about Flaco." "Have you seen him lately?" "That's none of your business." And then, "Have you been to visit your father?" "My father?" "I thought you went to the cemetery on a regular basis." "What about you? Do you go there regularly?" "No, I don't have a reason to go there anymore."

Bladimir hadn't ordered anything but several minutes passed before he finally stood up to take his leave. Clasping his hands in front, he stretched his arms out and above his head with a yawn, his shirt coming untucked. He couldn't have been more disinterested. He said, "Well. Time to go. It was nice to see you." He nodded at Elena. He turned to Vicente and rested a big hand on his shoulder. "I'll see you around." It sounded like a promise and Vicente wasn't sure that he wanted to look forward to it. He answered, "Have a nice day." That seemed noncommittal. In fact, what he wanted to say was, "No, I'm not sure if I want to see you around." But it didn't seem appropriate.

Vicente turned to Elena and waited for her to say something. But she just sighed heavily, drank the last of her coffee and stood up to leave too. "I'll be on my way, Vicente. Stay safe." She walked away just like that and disappeared around the corner. Vicente had been basking in the concept of new friendships, and he didn't register Elena's disappointment at Bladimir's abrupt departure.

Vicente was disappointed at her departure. He blamed Wolfman for ruining what would have otherwise been a pleasant morning. He gathered the unopened packets of sugar, fed them into the mouth of his packsack and prepared to go to El Terminal. He could watch Giorgio and perhaps he would even run into Wolfman there again. If so, he would watch him very closely indeed. Wolfman owed him some answers. For what he wasn't yet sure because he didn't know what the questions were.

Vicente arrived at El Terminal at mid-afternoon and the place was packed. He hung back near the entrance to survey the room. The atmosphere was electric. He saw Giorgio feel his way around from behind the counter near the cash register and head directly for the back room—just like a man with two perfectly functioning eyes. Vicente briefly wondered what he looked like without his glasses. One day, perhaps he would trip and lose them on the floor and his eyes would be exposed for all to see. Vicente's musings were distracted by a sudden commotion from the back room. There was yelling and something crashed against a wall. The door was thrust open by a tall man who was extremely angry. Vicente had seen him many times before, usually following Giorgio like an overgrown hound. This time Giorgio was on the man's heels, waving his arms and yelling.

"This is bullshit. Capitán. This is your last chance." Giorgio's was blustering. "I want to find that *hue'on* and confirm what he knows. He can't be dickin' around this city with *my* information, and *my* property. We need someone who knows the city like the back of his hand. And that someone turns out not to be you. So if it's not you, and you wanna be the one who brings him to me, then you better enlist the guy who knows more than you. Or I'll send you packing, back to where you came from. And maybe with one less limb. So don't fail me." Giorgio was huffing like an angry bull. He hobbled towards the entrance, both hands moving up to his glasses, fingers twitching over the gems in the corners, his tranquilizers. "You've got two days. And that's two more than you deserve."

El Capitán ignored the ultimatum as he turned calmly to fact Giorgio. "Who would you suggest, *Jefe*?"

"Flaco is probably the best. He's got other responsibilities. But ask him. He'll give you what he can."

Vicente's mouth was dry. He could have used some water, so he waited for Wolfman to come in from where ever he liked to hang out. But he didn't appear. Vicente nearly opted to let Giorgio escape, without even trying to tail him because he wanted to see Wolfman and ask him for some water and ask him about Elena. But it was obvious now that Wolfman wasn't going to show. So Vicente slid the chair back and rushed to the front door just as it closed behind the blind man. He watched as Giorgio hailed a taxi. Trying to prevent another dead end, and without knowing where his courage came from, Vicente rapped on the window of the taxi after it pulled up to the curb and just as Giorgio felt his way into the back seat.

Addressing both Giorgio and the driver, Vicente asked, breathlessly if he could share the taxi because he was in an extreme rush. He lied. "*Es urgente! A question of life and death.*"

The driver glanced up at the rear view mirror and Giorgio nodded and tilted his face towards the roof as Vicente ran around to get in the other side, and he heard Giorgio instruct the driver to take him to the Old Congress Building.

"*Gracias, Caballero,*" Vicente bowed slightly, a polite gesture that was, of course, lost on Giorgio, who didn't acknowledge him.

The driver raised his eyebrows as he looked questioningly at Vicente through the rear view mirror. "*A dónde va, Señor?*"

Vicente was observing Giorgio close up and he didn't hear the question. It was the first time he'd been this close to him. Giorgio was a man of about his same age, a heavy breather, and fidgety. He kept playing with his glasses, which led Vicente to lean towards him to peer more closely at the gems. He wondered why a man would choose to wear such heavy, impractical glasses that were obviously designed for a woman. The lenses were black and reflective, their only purpose was to keep everyone from seeing what was behind. And they succeeded. Vicente was still studying the glasses when the driver interrupted him again.

"Where to?" he repeated.

"The Old Congress Building," said Vicente.

"That's a coincidence." The taxi driver grinned into the mirror at Giorgio, who frowned. "I can count on one hand the number of times this has happened to me in all my 25 years of driving." The driver was ready to chat but he picked up on Giorgio's dark mood and bit his lips. They rode to Santiago Centro in silence. As soon as the taxi pulled up outside the old Congress building, Vicente slid out the door and slammed it before the driver could ask if they were going to share the fare. Giorgio couldn't be bothered to quibble. He remarked, "He's in a rush." And then, "We're at the east door, are we not?"

"Sí, Señor."

"Wait here. I'll be back."

Vicente eyed passersby suspiciously and waited a short distance from the taxi, his back to the wall. A stout business-type with a moustache like a broom and a major comb-over approached Giorgio and shook his hand. They were both in a solemn mood. Giorgio seemed upset. His voice was low but he gestured angrily, arms flailing. The man didn't interrupt. He nodded and patted the top of his head several times, probably a habit to ensure the comb-over behaved itself. Giorgio dropped his arms to his sides and relaxed his shoulders. Finally Comb-over touched Giorgio's elbow to guide him west along the sidewalk. Vicente noticed that two other men dressed in black suits were following several steps behind. He bustled past the two men, faking a limp and then he paused to rub his knee, just in front of Giorgio and his colleague.

"They're funding more riots for Concepción," the man told Giorgio. "Between our own front-liners and the foreigners, there's no shortage of takers. They're there for the money, not the cause. More reason that we have to keep it flowing. Plenty of money, plenty of bodies. We also organized something involving a train in the north. The plan is to set it on fire and let it rip down the line, unmanned, of course. We'll keep things hot, don't worry." Comb-over laughed at his own joke. Giorgio didn't join in.

"What about the Biobio Region?" Giorgio asked.

"On top of the usual fires, we've got some armed guys set up outside of three police stations. We have fire power and are adding Molotov cocktails... to make it look more home-grown."

"How does this all line up with the European shipments?"

"That's the thing. We have tentative dates and times. Everyone knows that they have to be ready with the distractions."

"I've had confirmation about the arms coming in from across the cordillera. Right now, they're in Bariloche, just waiting for word."

"Yeah, that's all in hand. They're coming over the pass and will be at Customs when the right *Tira* is on shift. You don't have to worry about that. Your Rati arranged with his guy at Policia Internacional."

Giorgio said, "I have men ready to receive at this end. but I want to be informed about the status. If anything goes wrong, we need to be prepared. This shipment is too valuable. If we have to do a little dance at the last minute, we do it."

"Okay. Another thing. You know the new Tira needs his cut. We vetted him, and vetted him good. But *la plata* comes out of your pocket."

"Yeah." said Giorgio. "*No problema.*"

It felt like the conversation was coming to a close. Vicente rubbed his knee one last time and prepared to move on. He kept his head down. The last thing he heard was Giorgio saying, "This'll pay off for both of us." Vicente imagined mutual pats on the shoulders and upturned lips. Probably, Comb-over even winked. Out of habit more than anything else.

Vicente pivoted to watch the two men in suits disappear around the corner. None if this was surprising to Vicente. He felt quite at home at the fringes of conversations and oddly, this sort of thing felt commonplace. Respected men in suits, men responsible for the welfare of the people, men trusted with important decisions, men who passed laws to pay themselves handsomely, men planning illicit acts that somehow did not surprise him, no matter how much he used to feel disappointed, disgusted even. When was that? What did he really know about all of this? He couldn't be sure. It was just a feeling.

Now, the question was how to get back to Providencia. In the last couple of years, evasion on public transit, mostly buses, had risen to more than 20 percent. Rosa used to click her tongue and roll her eyes at the freeloaders. A few times, Vicente had suggested that they too, could get onto a bus through the back door. Why not? Everyone (and not just students) did it. But she frowned at him. "Look," she said. "You and I are pensioners and we don't have a lot of money. But we're not thieves. How can you even think of doing that? You should be ashamed of yourself. Look at it for what it is, Vicente. You'd be stealing a ride, stealing from those who do pay."

Since the social uprising, the number of evaders on public transit had almost doubled. Some said it was greater than 40 percent now. It was common to see young people (especially) vaulting over turnstiles on buses and at the metro. They insisted that not paying for public transport was a legitimate form of protest. Since Rosa (God rest her soul) wasn't with him anymore, and he needed a ride home, Vicente (God forgive him) was going to have to make it a free one. He reached the bus stop just as one of the older articulating buses pulled up, he stepped up at the last door and nodded a quick apology to those passengers who caught his eye. Most nodded back but others stared away, looking down the long aisle, shaking their heads. He set himself down onto the only empty seat at the very back, and felt shame. Rosa would have been frowning and wagging her finger.

When the bus finally turned onto Avenida Tobalaba, he stepped off and crossed the street towards the canal. There was a slight chill, the sun was setting, smog turned the sky orange and purple, the air was thick with the smell of diesel, people brushed past him in their rush to get home and call it a day. He pictured them seated at the table with their families, all heads turned to watch early evening news, all slurping their tea and eating their sandwiches. Families all coming together. He couldn't remember being part of one before Ricardo and Carolina had agreed to take him and Rosa in. And now look what it had come to. But still, he didn't see that he had a choice.

Vicente reached his camouflaged shelter without incident. It didn't feel like home but it was okay, it was somewhere to come back to and it was solitary, and if the hobo mafia was doing its job, it was also relatively secure. It took a few seconds for his eyes to adjust to the dim interior. He was relieved to be safely under the beams of the bridge. He did not feel content or anything as pleasant as that but he was relieved to be there. He hunched down to fumble under the plastic milk crate where he kept the can of matches. He struck one several times before it flared. And then he dropped it with a gasp. Someone was sitting there in the darkest corner, legs outstretched. At first he thought it would be Manguera, coming for his bottle of wine.

But it was Wolfman, lounging, if you please, across Vicente's bed, such as it was.

"Good evening, Maestro," he said, cool as a cucumber.

"*Buenos noches*," Vicente answered, hand on his heart to control the pounding that was, for him, audible above his own voice and the rumble of rush hour traffic. He slung his packsack over his shoulder in case he should have to escape.

Wolfman said "I brought some tea and *sopaipillas* with hot sauce. Can you put on the kettle?" He reached over for a plastic bag and tossed it towards Vicente.

"Thank-you. Yes, I'll put on the kettle."

They moved outside to sit beside the fire pit. Wolfman had already prepared it, something that Vicente had been careless not to notice upon his return. Vicente stood over it for a minute, watching as two bigger pieces of kindling caught fire, briefly wondering how Wolfman knew about his shelter and how long he'd been waiting for him. Too many questions.

"I need you to do me a favor, Maestro. But I'm not asking you to do it for nothing." Bladimir rushed to say. "I can pay you." He looked around. "It looks like you can use a little cash. Am I right?"

"I get by," Vicente said. "I don't need charity. But anyway, I can accept payment for doing a favor." He cringed inside, and emphasized the word 'favor' because in reality, Vicente didn't consider doing something for a virtual stranger, a favor. Favors were things you did for friends. And friends didn't pay other friends for favors. And Wolfman wasn't a friend. But right now, Wolfman frightened him a bit and it was best to play along. And anyway, he could use some cash.

"I just need information. That's all. It's easy. You won't even have to go out of your way."

Vicente wrapped a cloth around the handle of the kettle, which shook as he dribbled boiling water into the mugs, spilling half of it. It sizzled on the rocks. He handed a mug to Wolfman, who nodded his thanks, and smiled at him, his eyes reflecting the fire. Suddenly, the day of Rosa's accident flashed across his mind's eye. He shivered and stumbled backwards. The memory was playing hide and seek. He would not play this game. Not right now. Not in present company.

Wolfman's eyes caught him off balance. Was it their color, or the expression around them? or the fire they reflected? No matter. Vicente slowly sat back down, and lowered his gaze, concentrating on several tea leaves that had escaped the bag and were floating around on top. He broke off small chunks of the sopaipilla and nibbled, hoping to appear thoughtful as he concentrated on information-gathering, his expertise. While he tried to maintain a façade of perhaps-not-interested, ask-me-another-day, he remained all ears.

"I've seen you at El Terminal often enough to call you a regular. A regular who just sips water, who doesn't go there for the food and definitely not to drink with friends."

Vicente focused more intently into the tea and he locked onto one particular tea leaf, letting it calm his nerves as it floated around, bumping into the sides and finally floating and stopping near the handle. If he knew how to read tea leaves, perhaps they would tell him about Wolfman.

"Without going into details, let's just say that I won't be returning to El Terminal myself. But I still have an interest in knowing what goes on there." Bladimir cocked his head and looked steadily at Vicente. "Are you listening?"

Vicente nodded.

"So, I need you to keep going there, like you always do. I'm not asking you to change anything. Just tell me what you notice, what you hear when you're there."

Without meeting Bladimir's eyes, Vicente looked up. He pretended to be distracted by a mouse that had just scurried under a bush, and he pursed his lips and nodded again.

"Are you getting this?"

"Hmm. Yes," said Vicente. "Yeah."

"I need you to tell me what you hear. I mean, more than the normal stuff.... I'm already familiar with the routines. You know what I mean?"

Now Vicente looked up. "What I hear from whom? There are always quite a few people there, lots of regulars."

"Mostly, I'm interested in what Giorgio, the blind guy tells anyone, especially a big, tall Venezuelan guy. And another guy called Flaco will probably show up now and then too. You can't mistake him because he looks like a skeleton. I'm interested in him too. But, well, anything you hear them telling anyone. Because you never know who's important. Or what's important. You know what I mean?"

Vicente nodded again. He was familiar with this type of work.

So Bladimir (aka Wolfman, the watchee) became a watcher via proxy. That this should have unfolded on that one extra day every four years, was not the least bit insignificant. But what if this day had failed to exist? What if time had leapt beyond it and was just playing tricks? Oh, silly, silly time, that nebulous thing that we all use to organize ourselves. Vicente smiled in his sleep and reached for Rosa's hand and he was sure she squeezed his fingers.

25 | ROSA'S ARRANGEMENT
March 1, 2020

Vicente settled at his usual table at the back of El Terminal just as people were slurping their last drops of instant Nescafe and dusting bread crumbs off their laps. He fingered the loose change in his pocket and recalled how last night Wolfman had counted out a few bills, dumped all the coins from a small pouch, and pushed it towards Vicente. "Here," he had said. "This is so you can start tomorrow. Go to El Terminal well before noon, okay? I need to know who's there. It's important. There's enough here for bus fare and a half decent breakfast. If you come back with anything interesting (and even if you don't) I'll have more for you. I'll see you here tomorrow night."

Vicente ordered tea and mashed avocado with added salt and fresh lemon on a fresh-baked bun, and he sat there, packsack pinned tightly between his knees, as he looked around. Giorgio hadn't seemed to have arrived yet. And he didn't see the tall Venezuelan guy either. He relaxed and let his mind wander. He hadn't said anything to Wolfman about having followed Giorgio to the old Congress building yesterday. Maybe he should share that. After last night's conversation, and Wolfman's respectful reference to him as Maestro, he felt a bit of warmth towards him. Maybe he wasn't the monster he made him out to be. He would have to think about that some more before really trusting him, though.

Maybe Giorgio's meeting yesterday with Comb-over was the kind of thing that would interest Wolfman. Vicente had to admit that he had never had plans for, nor had he ever put to use any of the information he gained from watching people all these years. He knew full well that it would fall into the dark recesses of his brain and be lost. But now his watchfulness was of value to someone besides himself. He made a mental note to report the Comb-over encounter to Wolfman tonight. Even in doing so, he knew that the mental note might slip away, blow off, disintegrate, poof, just be gone and that Wolfman might never know what Giorgio planned with Comb-over. But maybe it didn't matter if he remembered or forgot. It wasn't for him to decide.

The door of the main entrance opened with a flourish and Giorgio barged in to take charge of the place. He was just a huge scowl wearing sunglasses. He was barking orders to no one in particular. Then Vicente saw the tall Venezuelan stride in behind, having apparently been waylaid by a phone call. He hung up, and tucked the mobile phone into his chest pocket, his eyes darting around the room. Without greeting any of the staff, Giorgio and El Capitán disappeared into the back room.

As he licked the last of the avocado from the crispy exterior of the bun, Vicente kept his eyes on the back room door. No one had come or gone since the two bad actors had arrived. He wasn't sure how much longer he should hang around. It wasn't as though he could overhear anything from his table. Perhaps he would try from the washroom because it was closer to the back office. Head lowered, he fidgeted with his glasses and he tried to look inconspicuous, like a man casually heeding nature's call. He was just about to shoulder open the door when he saw the skinny guy who would definitely be the one Wolfman mentioned because he really did look like a skeleton. Flaco greeted a waiter who was tripping over himself at his unexpected entrance, as though Flaco was a rockstar.

Vicente ducked into the washroom and, standing in front of the chipped, stained urinal, he prepared to make his presence there legitimate. The walls were thin. He heard Giorgio say to Flaco. "Where've you been? What took you so long?" And then, "No, never mind. I don't wanna hear your excuses." The walls were thin but not thin enough to hear the conversation once they got serious. Their voices devolved into a series of monotones. With that, Vicente considered his work there done. He walked out of the washroom, paid his bill and left.

If a bus came by soon, he'd be able to jump off a block from Elena's cafe. Life, for him, was beginning to fill with purpose, and his day-to-day watching was slowly squeezing out the horror of that last image of Rosa—her lifeless arms dangling on either side of the stretcher. He climbed onto the bus and waited for his senior's pass card to trigger the green light and release the turnstile. He had charged the card with some of what Wolfman had paid him last night. Rosa would have been proud of him. He looked out the dusty window up at the sky and smiled. He realized that today was the first time he had been able to smile, rather than want to cry, when he thought of her.

Rosa. If she was still here, what would she be doing right now? Vicente peered over the shoulder of the passenger in front to see the time illuminated on his mobile. It was half past noon. If Rosa was here, she'd be at Ricardo's place, helping Carolina make lunch. The two of them would be chatting and laughing. The radio would be blaring tropical music, and in between songs, listeners would phone in to recount stories of how heartbreak had eventually been replaced by true love. The radio announcer would congratulate them with over-the-top sappiness and introduce the next song, guaranteed to have all the listeners dancing in their kitchens.

Vicente had never seen Rosa dance. Maybe it was because they never went anywhere to dance, they had always kept to themselves, their relationship was private, especially at first. Vicente couldn't remember very much about their early years together. Rosa told him that he must have had a serious hit on the head or maybe he just blocked everything out because of trauma. She'd heard of that before. She was pretty certain, she said, that it was the former. He admitted that he didn't want to remember his life before they met anyway, and she assured him that it was good thing. Remembering would only cause heartache. "And anyway," she said, "All the professionals say that living in the moment is the secret to a happy life. You're one of the lucky ones, Vicente." She leaned over and kissed him on the lips.

So one of the first memories that Vicente had of their life together was of them sitting on the sofa in the very house that Ricardo and Carolina lived in now. Ricardo and Carolina were sitting across from them, their faces drawn. There was such an uncomfortable silence that, even though they were virtual strangers, Vicente was moved to ask them, "Are you okay? Is there something I can do for you?" Strange that he could remember asking them that. That particular memory was as clear as day. He recalled that he felt firmly in charge but that he felt as though he had overlooked something important, had failed in some way, maybe he had been late, or maybe he forgot their names or failed to deliver something they had been waiting for. The feeling of awkwardness was more vivid than the visual memory. It's odd how almost everything sifted through the sieve of his brain but how certain other chunks of memories were too big to fall through, and they got caught in the upper recesses where he could pick them up and turn them over. Sometimes the memories shifted and his brain reconstructed them with other loose recollections. But he wasn't aware of that, and so the truth of what had gone on in his life was sometimes rebuilt into a different truth, which he either accepted without question or allowed to get washed into other memories.

On the night of the recollection in question, both Ricardo and Carolina had responded by glancing back and forth between Vicente and Rosa, and then Carolina said, "No, thank-you. We're fine. Just hadn't expected to see you here today." She blinked hard several times and Ricardo cleared his throat. "More tea?" he offered.

"Thank-you." Vicente said. Ricardo, he thought as he smiled over at him, was kind.

Rosa said, "I'll boil more the water." And to Vicente, "You just stay here and relax." Then she turned to her brother. "Ricardo, can you help me in the kitchen, please?"

Vicente's memories of that night in Ricardo's and Carolina's living room didn't extend much beyond those few minutes. He didn't remember what came next, what they said, how they so generously made room for him and Rosa to settle in.

Rosa hadn't seen Ricardo for the better part of a month. Their usual bi-weekly visits had fallen off her calendar, the days had gotten extremely muddled. She had had so many things to sort out for Vicente.

Once they were alone in the kitchen, Ricardo said to her, "I recognize our senator. It's not like he's exactly incognito, you know, Rosa. I mean, yeah, he's changed, looks worse for wear. But anyone with questions and anyone who looks close enough... well, what's the plan? Our neighbors— and not just them, I mean, but anyone—especially if they're a reporter—will recognize this Señor. What reason are we supposed to give for him being here?"

Rosa's hands shook as she lit the match and twisted the knob of the gas burner. She leaned into the cupboard and looked up at Ricardo. "I've had this going round and round in my head for days, Ricardo. I can't sleep. I can only think of one way out."

"And?"

"He has to hide here. You have to let him hide here. Plus, he can grow a beard or something. We'll think of something. We have to."

"But something's off with him, Rosa. Anyone can see that. He needs medical attention."

She looked at him sharply. "Well, he can't get it, can he? He just can't. He's meant to have died. Right?" Then her tone softened. "I'll take care of him, Ricardo. I was thinking that he and I could move into the storeroom in the patio. We can make it comfortable. I have a bit of money. I mean, I managed to save some and the Señora, well, she was sorry to see me leave, she said. And she deposited something in my bank account. For all the years of service, she told me. But there's more. I just can't get into it all right now." Rosa's cheeks were flushed, she rubbed her head with both hands. "You won't have to support us financially. I'm not asking for that. I can contribute. We just need a safe place to hide."

When they returned to the living room, Vicente was staring out the window and Carolina was making a point of sipping her tea, quiet as a mouse. She rolled her eyes in Vicente's direction. Rosa could see that he had entered one of his absent states. These vacant episodes came upon him suddenly and for no apparent reason. During those times, which could last for several minutes, he was inaccessible. Carolina must have been trying to make conversation and had obviously given up and remained there just to watch over him.

"How long has he been this way?" Rosa asked.

"He started about 30 seconds after you left the room. Just shut down." Carolina shook her head and stood up to leave.

"Wait." Ricardo gripped Carolina's elbow to keep her with them. He nodded towards Vicente.

"He's going to need our help. Rosa's too." He looked at Rosa, who was watching, eyes pleading and teary. "We need to make room for them, Carolina. We can clean out the storage room. It's time we did that anyway, right? And Rosa has some money and she said she can fix things up, make them comfortable."

"You and Rosa decided all of this on your own? Just now?" She looked back and forth at the two of them. "That's not fair, Ricardo. That's not fair."

"But you'll understand after I explain things better. Not yet." He rolled his eyes towards Rosa. "For now, let's set up something temporary, make some space. And you'll see, it'll all fall into place."

Now it was Bladimir who occupied that space. The more nights he spent there, the more he felt that this was where he was meant to be. It was a metamorphosis of sorts. The boy without a stable family found stability in the objects that occupied the room. The man, now pretty much past his prime, carefree and rootless who had always shunned material possessions and who aimed not for the spiritual but for what he considered the higher side of humanity through politics, was transformed by the power of knickknacks. The energy from books, textured rugs and blankets, handwritten notes and smiley faces scrawled across original drawings, and aging photographs in ornate plastic and thick wooden frames drew him in and grounded him in a fat world of family.

For the first few days, although Bladimir was curious about so many of Vicente's belongings (and those of the woman called Rosa), he kept his hands off. He tried to deny their essential attraction. Then one night as he lounged on the top of the bed, careful to hang his boots over the side so as not to soil the cover (as though this had been part of his upbringing), and was looking around the room, a book with a multi-colored spine caught his attention. The book, which was relatively thin (probably less than seven millimeters), was tucked on a top shelf beside a small porcelain vase out of which bloomed several porcelain flowers. He could see a chip on one of the little flowers and he was tempted to run a finger along it, to get to know it, to trace the hairline crack that pointed directly to the colorful little book.

He heaved himself off the bed, reached for it and very carefully—so as not to disturb the porcelain flowers or knock anything else off— he slid the book out and let it rest in the palm of his left hand so he could examine it.

The cover was heavy watercolor paper that wrapped around the pages, all bound with yellow cotton. It was without a doubt, home-made, bound by hand with thread and thimble. Faded pigments had soaked into the cover stock, little rivers of color running into each other, splashing along turquoise shores at the base of cliffs that leapt up into vast desert plains and finally gave over to a range of mountains. The name ROSA was neatly printed in black ink and enclosed in a heart shape. The number 1969 was neatly printed in the bottom right corner.

Bladimir opened it, not at the first page but at an entry where the book wanted to fall open naturally, and he read an entry in Rosa's diary.

26 | ROSA'S LETTER

March 1, 2020

This diary entry, unlike the rest, didn't begin with "Dear Diary," as one might expect. Rather, Rosa began by writing a letter to a little girl.

ENTRY: MAY 10, 1969

Mi preciosa corazón,

It's been 25 days since your father left our family home. You are young and impressionable and you are your father's most treasured gift. I know the love you have for him is great and you cherish your relationship with him. I wish I could send news of his good health. But it's not possible.

Then the entry just stopped. Probably Rosa realized she would never send the letter.

Perhaps Rosa would have attempted another letter, probably a short note, a greeting with well wishes, that would itself be suffocated by words that got stuck in her throat—the things that she would never tell the girl about her father. But the girl was young and she probably would not notice the things unsaid. Nor would she recognize the lies. Rosa would only imagine the girl's deep sorrow that would last a lifetime. So, yes, Rosa would have written separate letters, which, in spite of her best intentions, would never have been posted.

All of the other entries began with the traditional, 'Dear Diary' salutation and were private, carefully penned on sheets, which had been bound after the fact. It was a story that was far beyond what a young girl could comprehend. The reality it presented was harsh, even shocking, even for Bladimir.

Captivated by what he was beginning to discover, Bladimir sat with the book resting in his hands and took his time to absorb what this woman called Rosa had written. Settled comfortably in the worn armchair by the window, he got caught up in the details that Rosa had captured and re-counted, and he read and re-read the first several pages, letting pieces of a family puzzle begin to fall into place, the subsequent pages surely providing more answers. He barely noticed the outside world, how quickly dusk had swept away the daylight and how the surrounding streets had become all but deserted, and how the neighborhood lay relaxed and naked, ready to be covered by night.

He was stunned by the tragic events that had befallen this family and was amazed that no one on the outside had ever put two-and-two together. It occurred to him briefly that what he had in his hands was a gold mine. A buried treasure that, if unearthed, would be raided by the press who would feast on it for months, possibly even years to come; documentaries would be produced, books would be written. It would be a media extravaganza to drool over. Stories would be enhanced with an abundance of newsprint photos, and embellished with pixelated collages fading in over soppy TV music. Tasty beyond imagination, it would be consumed and regurgitated out of millions of mouths. Tongues would wag, jaws would drop, heads would shake, hands would wave about. People would say, "I knew it. I knew something wasn't right. I could feel it my gut." But they didn't. They lied. They couldn't.

In truth, Bladimir knew he would never tell the story to anyone because— although he could not define the sudden affection he felt for Ricardo and Carolina, and the affinity for the old man Vicente, whom he called Maestro, and the unexpected relationship with Elena (who would always be Fachita to him)—he felt himself one of them. He, too, was a player. He, too, had secrets. He, too, was in hiding. He was part of this family. A family of liars.

So it happened that with the truth laying exposed in the palms of his hands, Bladimir felt his soul begin to re-shape. He stayed in the room for three days, even forgetting to meet Vicente, as he had agreed. He left the room only to refill his teacup and return the empty plates that Carolina would set down on the floor outside his door with a soft rap. "I'm leaving your dinner here. Eat it before it gets cold."

He finally emerged from the room on the third night with the intention of going to Vicente's shelter. He acknowledged Ricardo and Carolina with a nod and half smile as he let himself out the door. He didn't notice the earth beneath his feet, how the texture changed from a wooden sidewalk to broken concrete, asphalt, more concrete, and then finally to hard-packed earth at the edge of the canal. He was still floating in the knowledge of lives that had passed as they should not have passed, and how the rest of the world was kept in the dark. He failed to check over his shoulder and pull the hood down over his forehead and he neglected to look up and down the street before crossing to the other side. It was only when he heard a hoarse male voice against a much softer one that the spell was broken. The light from a street lamp cast itself to the ground and he dodged its feathered edges. He blinked hard several times to focus on the activity at Vicente's shelter.

The voices were not, as Bladimir had first assumed, the sound of an argument but rather a jovial exchange between two odd, old men. Bladimir kept his distance until the tall man said, "*Chao*" and waving a bottle, he trudged, apparently quite contentedly along the path towards the north. Bladimir waited until the tall man was completely out of sight before approaching Vicente.

Tonight, the eyes with which he looked at the aging little man with the white goatee were others. Rosa's diary revealed amazing new facts about Vicente's history and shed a fresh light on the man. But what he had learned about Vicente had a knock-on effect. If Bladimir were to accept what was written in the diary as true, then it followed that he would also have to question much of what he fundamentally believed. He began to realize that, on a deeper level, Rosa's diary could, if he allowed it, lift him out of his earlier paradigm. It rattled his lifelong beliefs. He was at threat of falling into an abyss, his old reality helter-skelter, on the verge of a precarious newly discovered and unbalanced truth. If he embraced this new reality; that is, if he was willing to see Vicente from a different perspective, he would be in danger of seeing other things differently too. He wasn't yet prepared for the fullness, nor the shock of it.

Even so, when he went out that evening, he noticed that the color of the sky, in its brooding lack of light, was tinged with a new value. The rugged Andean summits were outlined as if with a fine ink pen. What was left of the sun in the west was long gone but a glimmering halo stretched up from the horizon and it reminded him of the splashes on the watercolor cover of Rosa's diary. The world had been painted.

"Good evening, Maestro," Bladimir stepped out of the shadows. Knowing what he now knew of (and felt about) Vicente, 'Maestro' hardly seemed respectful enough.

"Good evening," Vicente replied. He appeared not to be surprised by Bladimir's presence. Nor was he perturbed that Bladimir hadn't been there three days earlier, as promised. "I'm a popular man tonight." He motioned towards the path along which the tall man had disappeared.

"Tea?" Vicente offered.

"No, thank-you."

"Is this a solemn visit?"

Bladimir shook his head. "No, but we have business."

"Oh, yes. Business," Vicente motioned for him to take a seat on the other crate by the fire. "Well, I might have some news and I might not. It depends on what you already know. But here's what I can tell you before it escapes me." He smiled, not apologetically but rather matter-of-factly. "I remember that I was downtown at the Old Congress Building the other day and I saw your man Giorgio talking to another man who must have been important because he had body guards."

Bladimir leaned in. "What did he look like?"

"He was a short man, fat, balding and with a big moustache."

"That describes half the men in Santiago Centro."

Vicente continued. "My memory is not as good as it used to be." This time, he blinked several times, seemingly pained. Something shuddered across his face. He looked up to his left, as though gathering information from the air, and he was hit by another bout of blinking. "They talked about police stations and Molotov cocktails." Then he sharply sucked in breath. "Oh yes, yes." He raised his index finger, pointing straight up. "They said something about transporting guns." He looked up at Bladimir, his blue eyes big, alarmed. But then he smoothed his forehead with his hand and clicked his tongue before adding, more calmly, "Maybe I got that wrong."

Bladimir sat quietly and waited, hoping the old man could retrieve more of his elusive recollections.

Vicente raised his face to the sky, squeezed his eyes closed and slowly turned his head. "They said something about a train on fire." He became agitated, blinking again and alternating between rotating his shoulders and tapping his temples with his index fingers.

Bladimir shifted closer to the old man's side and touched his shoulder. "It's okay," he said. "It's okay, Maestro."

His eyes, darting, Vicente looked at him and said, "There's something else, there's something else."

Bladimir let his hand rest on Vicente's shoulder and waited as Vicente breathed deep a few times. "I remember now. I remember." Vicente shifted, his left knee touching Bladimir's right one and he rolled his head around and up so that he was looking up into Bladimir's face, his glasses having slipped towards the tip of his nose. Bladimir had the sensation that the old man was unloading a weight, passing onto his shoulders. The old man took several more deep breaths. "There's an ugly man called Flaco."

"Yes," said Bladimir calmly, "Flaco." Bladimir felt the old man relax.

"Yes," Vicente said. "Flaco was at El Terminal."

"Oh, so you went there then?"

"Yes, I went there, as you asked me to."

"How do you know this man Flaco?"

"Because you told me about him. And anyway, I've seen him at El Terminal before. And I've seen you talk to him at other places too."

Where exactly has Vicente been? Has he been staking out more places than just El Terminal? Has the old man been keeping in eye on him too?

Bladimir tightened his grip on the old man's shoulders. "What is it that you get up to, Maestro? And who else do we have in common?"

"Well, we both watch Elena." Vicente admitted it without any sign of shame.

"Elena?"

"Yes. You know her, of course. You called her a fascist. I've seen you with her at the cafe over there." He pointed beyond the main drag. "And I saw you there with Flaco once too."

Bladimir suddenly realized that Vicente was the axis of acquaintances. He not only respected Vicente for what he had recently discovered about him, he also valued him for his usefulness and compliance, and there was no doubt that he was well-placed. It could be that this old man would help save him from Giorgio—this oddball, old man, who many years ago, had been declared dead and whose name was carved above the entrance of an elegant mausoleum in a wealthy sector of Santiago's General Cemetery.

27 | WISDOM AND LOYALTY

March 7, 2020

There was no way for Bladimir to know that both the diamonds he had stolen from Giorgio and the plush toy cat into which he had just stuffed them, were linked to Vicente. The little toy cat, dilapidated and forlorn in a corner at the bottom of Rosa's bookshelf, where it had slouched, untouched for years, was an unlikely vault for precious stones. Yet, it was perfect. It had a hidden zipper in a side seam and when Bladimir undid it and felt around, he discovered a small pouch, not unlike his own. But this one contained dried rose petals. The rose scent had been lost to time. The drawstring pouch with the stolen diamonds snuggled up perfectly beside the one with the rose petals. No one would ever be the wiser.

Bladimir was ignorant about the origins of the diamonds. As much as he might have speculated, he wouldn't have guessed that they had been in Giorgio's hands since the late 1960s. Had he known, he might have thought twice before stealing them. His own history with Giorgio was much more recent and he paid little attention to the stories of the early Belgian narcotics gangs who, decades earlier, had bought access to the Chilean cocaine trade. The diamonds were Giorgio's prize winnings, a reminder of the good old days, the days before Augusto Pinochet bombed the Presidential Palace, took control of the country, and, among others, executed all of the drug dealers he could find. At least one of them, a Chilean chemist named Mateo Morena, aka *la Cucaracha* had escaped. He made his way north to Colombia, taught Pablo Escobar everything he knew, and the rest is history.

Young Giorgio had both feet in the Chilean trade and was enamored of the diamond alternative to black market dollars. For an ambitious young man from the north, diamonds were more than a form of barter. For Giorgio, they were the stuff of dreams, they were status, proof of international success. In those days, Vicente Lenz-Weber was a senator and Giorgio was an up-and-coming fixer for certain of Vicente's senate colleagues, the ones who worked harder for themselves than for their constituents. Through senate gossip that was never meant to reach Vicente's ears, he caught wind of some of the malicious dealings with Giorgio, which included blood diamonds from northern Africa by way of the Netherlands. It was all new to him at the time and it took some digging but he had Giorgio on his watch list. He never would have imagined that the watching would have resumed decades later, not to mention the circumstances.

In the early 1960s, various and relatively small artisan cocaine producers distributed the drug in Chile and pushed it into the United States. Although he may not have been the first, Giorgio looked forward into Europe, specifically to the Netherlands and Belgium, where other greedy eyes had also turned in the direction of the illegal diamond trade.

Raised in the northern Chilean port city of Iquique, Giorgio Ramirez-Marino was born to an Italian mother and Chilean father. He once divulged this to Bladimir but beyond that, Bladimir was not privy to Giorgio's history. Naturally hermetic, a stealthy young Giorgio bobbed in and out at the fringes of illegal organizations and clever Chilean cocaine bosses, such as The Devil's Face, Pepe Wong and Chato Marí. Because Giorgio's vision was grand and ambitious, it didn't take him long to see the need for a facilitator, someone to connect characters such as these to corruptible politicians, police and port officials. So he moved south to the Capital and set himself up as a bridge. Giorgio was astute, alert and unafraid to jump on opportunities, a chameleon who easily adapted to new environments. He quickly made himself at home in Santiago, where he was welcomed into both the political and underworld cultures (often times it was one and the same). He was only 23 years old when he became known as the fixer or the chef. Although the gaps in Giorgio's life far outweighed the pieces that were known, you get a sense of his power and ambition as a 23-year-old mover. Now, you can appreciate the formidable weight that had been added to his person, each one of the subsequent 57 years building his acumen, to the point where he could run his business as if he were blind. The gravity of respect he earned equaled his notoriety, which oozed out in concentric circles. Everyone knew the fixer.

For Giorgio, the particular bag of diamonds that Bladimir now had in his possession held sentimental, as well as monetary value.

When he discovered their absence about a week before Bladimir disappeared, he was livid. While he did not attempt to hide his anger, he, Giorgio would never allow himself to be perceived as a victim and so he never told anyone that he had been robbed. It would weaken his reputation. During the weeks that followed, he vented his rage on anyone in his path, and people trod very carefully indeed.

Bladimir stole the diamonds about six weeks after the arrival of the Venezuelan Capitán, only weeks after Giorgio appeared to be enamored of one and the same. Not only had Bladimir felt sidelined, he had felt disgraced. There was no reason for Giorgio to have preferred the foreigner. Rather than including Bladimir in meetings, conferring with him like he used to over a glass of whiskey, Giorgio sent Bladimir to run trivial errands. It was El Capitán who was invited to share dinner at Giorgio's table. They sat there conversing in low tones in a corner to the left of the wise monkeys lamp, and Bladimir observed how the pink light from the monkeys reached out to shine over El Capitán's right shoulder, like he had been knighted.

One day, El Capitán arrived at the restaurant in great bluster with two of his soldiers. Their boisterous entrance interrupted a conversation between Giorgio and Bladimir. Only 20 minutes earlier, Bladimir and Giorgio were settled at his table in casual conversation, just like the old days, and Bladimir could feel his childish resentment begin to melt away. He felt redeemed, even happy. But it returned full force when Giorgio wagged his index finger in front of Bladimir's face to stop him mid-sentence, and abruptly dismiss him with a wave of his hand. His black lenses turned in the direction of El Capitán, an easy smile curled around his teeth, and with a welcoming gesture, he indicated that El Capitán should join him at his table, and should sit in the very chair that Bladimir had just been ordered to vacate.

The diamond theft occurred soon after that. It was spontaneous. Even so, you could say it was a natural progression—the culmination of built-up discontent. Over the past weeks, his resentment had been like a light breeze, steadily nudging him towards something yet to be defined. On the day of the theft, all of its acrimonious energy accumulated into a great gust that pushed him to commit the act, from which there could be no turning back. Also powering the theft was Bladimir's recent and painful admission that Giorgio lacked true ideological convictions. Although the doubt first came out of Bladimir's questions about Giorgio's solution for the ousted senator—who had, up to that point, been Bladimir's one and only stepping stone towards the realization of his personal political goals—he had managed to push it aside. Bladimir's long lost mother may have failed to instill many positive social values but she had managed to plant in him the desire for a political career, in which he would champion el pueblo. Therefore, after Giorgio replaced him with El Capitán, Bladimir rationalized that he was entitled to personal compensation, which might also purchase a high position in the Party, placing him beyond reach, and allowing him to advance his altruistic agenda. If Giorgio could thwart Bladimir's ambitions, then Bladimir would just have to manipulate circumstances to move things along their rightful path.

Bladimir knew that Giorgio kept valuables in the safe in the back room of El Terminal. But he also knew that things he coveted the most were not kept there. Giorgio kept the diamonds in the hollow of the three wise monkeys statue that lit up the shelf behind the cash register. 'Hide things in plain sight' was one of Giorgio's mottos. Bladimir had heard him use the very phrase many times.

Nearly two years earlier, Bladimir had seen Giorgio's wisdom in practice. One night, Giorgio sent the restaurant staff home early. "It's been a good day but the place is empty now and I don't think we'll do any more business. Bladimir, you have already seen to the clean-up, right?" In fact, Giorgio couldn't have cared less about cleanliness and he paid off the health inspectors left, right and center.

"Yup, we had a head start. We're good to go."

"Right. See you all tomorrow." Giorgio waved them all off with the ungrateful back of his hand.

Bladimir was almost at the street corner when he realized that he'd left his jacket hanging by the back door in the kitchen. And his house keys were in the pocket. So he returned to the restaurant, cursing under this breath. "Imbecile," he muttered. "The one night I go home early and now I'm wasting my time going back." He could still see the pink light from the three wise monkeys, which meant that probably Giorgio was emptying the till. Bladimir was surprised to find the door unlocked. Giorgio started and reached for a pistol that sat ready on the counter but he paused when he heard Bladimir.

"Sorry, *Jefe*, it's just me. I forgot my jacket. I'll just be a minute."

Giorgio huffed. The three wise monkeys were angled away from the mirror behind the shelf and Giorgio tried to cover the back of it with one hand. With the other, he pressed a small drawstring pouch into his jacket pocket and as Bladimir walked past, something on the spongy rug just in front of Giorgio's right foot caught his eye. He saw the glint of a small gem before Giorgio's toe had carelessly pushed it into the foam. Bladimir could easily have said, "Boss, you dropped something. It's just here..." and he could have bent down, picked up the diamond and placed it into Giorgio's palm. But something told him that Giorgio wouldn't appreciate Bladimir knowing about the gem. So he wisely decided to keep his mouth shut. He carried on towards the kitchen, careful not to change the rhythm of his step because Giorgio would notice something like a change in rhythm.

Bladimir laid awake most of that night, thinking about the diamond that had dropped to the floor. He also wondered why Giorgio would not have locked the front door before going about his business. An uncharacteristic oversight. Early the next morning, Bladimir joined hundreds of other sleepyheads on their trek to work. He dodged buses and the black and yellow taxis, and rushed across the street before the lights changed. Although opening the restaurant was a mundane task, and he was born for a greater purpose, back then he still believed that Giorgio had his best interests at heart.

He could have performed the opening rituals in his sleep. But this morning, he was very awake when he turned the key in the lock and headed straight over to the till. He bent down and picked at the spongy rug until the small stone that Giorgio's clumsy foot had embedded there glinted up at him. He spent several seconds gazing at it, the tiny gem lighting up the center of his palm. Such an innocent little rock, no idea what people would do to possess it. Then he smiled up at the three monkeys. He pulled the plastic lamp out from the back of the shelf just enough to see where a soft pouch had been stashed into a hollow at the back of the lamp. The cord had been cleverly wound a couple of times in front of the bag.

"See no evil, hear no evil, speak no evil"—another of Giorgio's mottos. Bladimir carefully reinserted the diamond into the little pouch and, ensuring everything was back in its rightful place, he whistled his way to the kitchen to begin the morning tasks. The single diamond he had found and replaced was like a seed—a seed that had been planted in his brain to be nurtured by every future snub and underestimation, every instance of exclusion by Giorgio. Finally it would sprout and grow and call him to the inevitable theft.

The way he saw things, an intelligent person knows when they are stepping on the toes of a long-time employee. An intelligent person knows not to tempt loyalty nor to quell ambition. An intelligent person might, from time to time, move their diamonds to higher ground. Giorgio was intelligent but he was blind. And so it was that, one night during the heat and height of the social uprising, when Giorgio had so carelessly left Bladimir in charge of closing up the restaurant while he went on a tear with El Capitán, Bladimir stealthily removed the little drawstring bag containing the diamonds while the three wise monkeys had their backs turned.

It was not premeditated theft. It was premeditated retribution. It was poetic justice.

There was no way of knowing how often Giorgio visited the hollow of the three wise monkeys. But between the night two weeks ago when Bladimir had stolen the stones and the day Giorgio ordered Bladimir to spy on Flaco, Giorgio had had plenty of time to add things up and to set a trap. Bladimir would have been his second, third, and probably even his fourth suspect. Bladimir imagined Giorgio, who would at first be incredulous, because Bladimir had been his most loyal employee for years; then he would be surprised at his own blindness; then disappointed by the ungrateful, lowlife *lanza* bastard whom he had shaped into a successful adult human being. How could someone he had trusted for so long betray him like that? The most Bladimir could hope for was that Giorgio would be repentant for underestimating him. Would he regret having overlooked him, having kept him out in the cold? Number one rule: 'Keep your friends close, blah, blah, blah.' Giorgio had slipped up. Giorgio probably would have tortured, maybe even killed, at least a couple of guys before turning his gemstone lenses in the direction of Bladimir. Bladimir would have been at the bottom of the list of those who had also had plenty of time and opportunity while standing in front of the three wise monkeys, quite often with nothing to do but nose around and let fingers wander where they should not, and stumble into drawstring bags.

28 | THE GREATER GOOD
March 10, 2020

Giorgio had a lot of balls in the air and he was, and always had been, an excellent juggler. It was true that being blind heightened his other senses and perfected his balance, and that both added to his formidable reputation. Bladimir fully appreciated and respected all of this but El Capitán, being relatively new on the block, did not. So after Giorgio issued the ultimatum to El Capitán, and when El Capitán did not satisfy the terms (those being simply that he must find Bladimir and bring him in to answer for his sins), El Capitán made the fatal error of believing he could outwit Giorgio.

In the midst of plans to transport arms across the Andes through a southern pass, while setting up firebombs at multiple police stations, run-away freight trains, and the destruction of health care centers, El Capitán took it upon himself to add yet another distraction. Unauthorized by Giorgio, he executed the looting and destruction of another North American-style supermarket in the southwest corner of the Capital. He ordered his men, armed with pistols, to storm in, sending the shoppers screaming towards the exits but not before they detoured and like a colony of ants, snatched as many expensive cuts of meat and bottles of wine as they could carry. Then, beginning at the bakery, El Capitán's men set the store on fire.

El Capitán would blame it on Bladimir. He would say that he, El Capitán had tried to thwart Bladimir's imbecilic efforts but that Bladimir was determined to earn points with Giorgio and he charged ahead, 'for the good of the cause'. And now, El Capitán was sorry to have to report that he had witnessed the clumsy oaf sheltering in the second floor staff room, just when the flames jumped out of control, and licked wildly through that part of the structure. They ended up consuming the bastard.

"You see," he explained to Giorgio, "As things turned out, this was better than capturing the lowlife and having to get rid of him after the fact. You're rid of him already. He's nothing more than charcoal now. And on top of that, I seized a lot of merchandise. We filled six one-ton trucks and they're parked at a Petrobras truck stop on Highway 5 South. I already made contacts at Persa Bio-Bio so we can unload it." El Capitán stood, his chest bulging with pride, believing this would satisfy Giorgio. The problem was that El Capitán knew nothing of the diamonds, and now, neither would Giorgio.

El Capitán waited for Giorgio to congratulate him, perhaps to toast him with a glass of whiskey. But Giorgio simply nodded and ran his fingers over the gemstones at the corners of his glasses. El Capitán stood expectantly for several minutes before Giorgio finally spoke and in an eerily soft tone, he said, "We needed Bladimir here." That was all. He was stone-faced. No congratulations. No thump on the back. Giorgio dismissed El Capitán with a wave, and turned on his heel. Within the hour he summoned Flaco, and within 24 hours, El Capitán's body had been dumped in an abandoned mine shaft 100 kilometers southeast of Santiago, never to be discovered. In less than a week, the hunt for Bladimir was on again. This time, Giorgio had breathed new life into Flaco, who would head it up.

No one believed that Bladimir had burned to a crisp at the supermarket, least of all Giorgio, who only had to call his Rati to confirm it. In fact, no bodies at all were found at that site. The building had been utterly destroyed, staff had been terrorized and merchandise had been stolen but no one had died.

Bladimir was on his own. All the more reason to remain alert. He only knew what he heard on mainstream news, which he picked up from an old radio on the shelf beside Vicente's former bed. His only direct and reliable source for information on the ground and more specifically, on Giorgio, was a brain damaged old man. And his most reliable source of information about this family was a dead woman's diary—not that family business served any direct purpose. For now, and for the near future, it would just be a passing interest, like a hobby, because Bladimir had to lay low, and even if the information inspired an idea, without trustworthy contacts and freedom of movement, he would be helpless to act.

Anyway, the plan he needed was more immediate, more related to survival, more like escaping Giorgio's web. And until that took shape, he had nothing but time on his hands. So he rested in the old armchair by the window and watched clouds cast shadows over the Andes until he felt the cool of the sunsets. Once the sun went down, he pulled the hood down over his face and loped over to the bridge, each time veering off the usual path, varying his schedule, and checking over his shoulder at the sound of footsteps or the sudden screeching of tires or shouts of passersby.

After Vicente told him about having recently seen Flaco at El Terminal, Bladimir knew Flaco's hounds had been given his scent. Flaco knew the city, he knew every part of it. He knew Bladimir. But Bladimir was correct in assuming that Flaco would not be looking for him in the east end of Providencia. At least not yet. Flaco would check the rooms for rent in Santiago Centro and Estación Central. He'd comb Barrio Yungay. He would also check the crowded cités, which, more and more, had become inhabited by foreigners, many of them undocumented, dozens of them crammed into less than adequate spaces, their makeshift wiring hanging of main power cables, sparking fires. He would have men on the streets around Cali Canto and they'd be wandering metro stations, asking guards, perhaps dropping coins into beggars' cups with promises of more if they kept their eyes open. It would be some time before they would think of looking for him amidst unassuming houses of middle- and upper-class Providencia. But that's not to say that the streets of Providencia wouldn't also have eyes. With Giorgio, you never knew. The more the man lacked, the more skillfully he managed to compensate.

As the days passed, Bladimir's ingrained resentment towards people like Ricardo and Carolina—people he had always painted with the same brush—began to diminish. At first, he didn't notice that it had begun to leak away, that his big, fat balloon of resentment was deflating, its well-defined shape quietly shrinking into something softer, more accommodating, more forgiving. One night, having been swayed by a premonition that told him things outside in the streets were 'off', he stayed in to have tea with Ricardo and Carolina. He wanted to tease information from the two of them about Vicente and about Rosa, and possibly about Elena. Who knew? But Carolina was not receptive to questions. She excused herself, saying she was tired and would go and watch TV in bed.

Ricardo made more tea for himself and Bladimir, and as they relaxed across from one another at the narrow kitchen table, Bladimir was once again conscious of the unfamiliar but admittedly pleasant sensation of belonging.

Ricardo had also warmed to Bladimir. It was an unspoken friendship between two men who felt as though they'd known each other their whole lives but who, at this point, would not dare call themselves friends. Ricardo didn't seem to notice that Bladimir never revealed much about himself. Beyond the lie about selling his uncle's house, Bladimir hadn't said much, not even where his family was from. Perhaps Ricardo was too polite to pry or perhaps it didn't matter. Perhaps it was simply enough that this man he knew as BJ was a friend of Vicente's.

"I've been retired for 18 years and I'm still not used to it. Carolina doesn't understand because her routine hasn't changed. For me, it's nice to have company in the house again. Since Rosa...." He swallowed, "Since my sister Rosa passed away... and since Vicente left, it's gotten too quiet around here. It's lucky for us that your uncle's house is so close." Ricardo looked up, surprised he had admitted that, and hoping BJ didn't read too much into it.

Bladimir took no notice. "Yeah, and speaking of that, it looks like it might take longer than I thought to get rid of the squatters. It's not so easy to intimidate them. I thought the police would be more helpful but they're not. You know how it is... the law is not on our side." Bladimir scoffed and sipped his tea.

"Well, you're welcome to stay here week by week, like we said. Carolina doesn't say much but I think she's happy to have someone in Vicente's and Rosa's room too. I mean, since we never had any kids..." Ricardo paused and looked down before he continued. "It's nice to have company here, is all I'm saying."

"Yeah. It works for me too."

Silence hung over the wood grain of the table top but neither of them desired to abandon the conversation.

"So, I don't mean to pry, and you don't have to answer me... but was Rosa ill? Or maybe she was elderly? I mean, how did she...?" Bladimir couldn't bring himself to say the word 'die'. He was afraid that Ricardo was perhaps too fragile.

Suddenly Ricardo straightened up and he said, "How about a glass of wine? We've got a bottle of Casillero del Diablo here somewhere. We've had it for ages and, well, we've just never had a reason to open it. Carolina won't mind. She won't miss it." Without waiting for a response, he got up and opened a few cupboards before finding a bottle tucked back on the top shelf. "Actually, it was a gift from Rosa."

"In that case, sure, I'll be honored to raise a glass with you."

Ricardo rinsed out two glasses and uncorked the bottle. The familiar sounds of the national news filtered out from the TV in the bedroom—serious narrative over dramatic, repetitive background music. Lately, the news was filled with replays of street violence and looting that erupted any time, day or night. Reporters interviewed people on the street as well as international human rights representatives. Striving to prove himself incapable of committing the atrocities of which he was accused (likely, in order to safeguard his personal reputation), Chile's president invited international human rights groups to observe. While he restricted the level of force that could be employed by local military and police against rioters, mom 'n pop shops cried for more protection. Bladimir's toes itched a little. He should be out on the streets right now. He should be at the head of the revolution. Instead, he was cowering in the kitchen of a middle-class house, drinking wine with someone who probably also deserved more from his country, and for whom he was beginning to feel a measure of sympathy.

Ricardo nodded his head in the direction of the bedroom and said, "She'll be sleeping by now." He sighed as he passed a glass to Bladimir.

"To Rosa."

"To Rosa." They both took a sip and Bladimir waited.

Ricardo sat down and raised the glass again, drained the contents, and reached over to refill it before he uttered a word.

"Rosa died recently. Actually she died exactly 143 days ago." He looked directly into Bladimir's eyes, almost accusing him of all the days that had passed and he nodded, "I'm keeping track. Not a day goes by…"

He paused to compose himself. "Do you remember seeing a story on the news last October, about a woman who was run over by a bus?"

Bladimir shook his head. "There were a lot of stories last October. It was a crazy time."

"Yes, but this was the second day of the *estallido social.*"

"Go on…"

"Rosa went down to Avenida Providencia to buy a gift for Vicente. I knew about it because she was really excited. She was going to get him a certain chess set. I mean, I don't know what was special about it but the two of them, well, they had some thing about these particular chess pieces. I'm not a chess man, myself, so I can't tell you… She shouldn't have gone. I tried to tell her. But I guess she wasn't really paying attention or maybe we couldn't really believe that things would've turned to shit so suddenly. Who would've thought? Right?" He looked at Bladimir, this time without trying to hide the tears that brimmed his eyes.

He tossed back his wine and poured more. Bladimir declined a top-up and sat back, holding the glass close to his chest with both hands.

Ricardo continued, "The details have never, ever been clear, BJ. All we know is that some bus driver must have been lost. This happened near Lyon with Providencia. He should have detoured that day but he didn't. He kept driving, right up to the crazies on the street."

Bladimir gripped the glass hard, holding it even tighter to his chest, willing it to expand into a dome and protect him from the words that he was sure would come next.

"The bus ran over her. I tried to figure out exactly what happened but the police weren't focused on those details because they were trying to control the mobs. It was crazy, BJ. Just crazy. All I know is that the bus ran Rosa down and she died on the spot. Afterwards, I found the paramedic, and he said she was already dead when they lifted her onto the stretcher. Someone called us from Posta Central, and Carolina and I went down right away. We didn't know then. I mean, we thought she was hurt, that's all. We didn't know she was already gone. When we got there, a guy in green scrubs met us at the front desk and he took us down to the morgue. Without a word, mind you. Just, 'Follow me, please.' It was a nightmare. A shock. I mean, when we saw that we weren't going to a ward, well, maybe we should've guessed, you know? But we didn't want to thing that. The walk from the front desk to the morgue was the longest walk of my life."

Maybe it was because of the wine or maybe it was just the emotion the memory called up—but probably it was both—Ricardo started to whimper. Then he screwed up his face and squeaked intermittently as he tried to hold back. Finally he sobbed and lowered head into his arms on the table, his shoulders shaking. He looked up through his tears, and said, "Don't tell Carolina about this, okay? I mean, nothing, not a word. Don't say anything about this conversation. We agreed never to talk about it."

Bladimir was still trying to shield himself with the wine glass. It was all he had to hold on to. Small, smudged, still half full, his knuckles white from clutching it. Eyes downcast, he didn't dare raise them to look at Ricardo. Bladimir had done nasty things—things that he always felt could be justified because he was either just trying to survive (what else can people expect of a poor, underprivileged boy who had always been overlooked and denied?) or because he was working towards the greater good. But this? No, this couldn't be explained away. It hit him where it hurt. This unexpected amity he had developed with Ricardo was spiked with agony. Agony that he felt for Ricardo. It was like a shot through his own heart. He had caused this. The man who was collapsed on the table in front of him was living a nightmare that he, Bladimir had caused. This time, he couldn't write it off as collateral damage on the road to the greater good. He couldn't say it was an accidental death. At the base of it, it was accidental. But it needn't have happened. He had wanted to make a name for himself, show off to Giorgio and the likes of El Capitán. But this is what collateral damage looked like close up. This is what he had abandoned and had refused to look back on that day as he rushed along the sidewalk towards glory.

Not another word was exchanged. For the next ten minutes, Bladimir sat frozen and dared, from time to time, to steal a glance at Ricardo, who had collapsed, face on the table, and was rocking his head back and forth between his elbows. Bladimir quietly set his glass down and stood up to make his way to his room. He paused and placed one hand on Ricardo's shoulder and lightly squeezed. He didn't know if Ricardo noticed, or if it brought him even an instant of comfort. But nothing would ever be enough. Especially coming from Bladimir. He owed Ricardo. And he owed Vicente.

On his way to Vicente and Rosa's old bedroom, he passed Carolina, fast asleep, the sound of news having been replaced with that of a late night soap opera and some light snoring. He reached the bedroom, the room of the woman he had killed. He flopped onto his back, expecting to feel a million accusing needles shooting into him from the mattress. He waited. But the room didn't condemn him. It wasn't asking him to fall to his knees and beg forgiveness. It wasn't asking for anything. Instead, the bed was reassuring. "Just lie back and sleep."

But he didn't sleep, he stared up at the ceiling and tried to ignore the questions that, one way or the other required new answers. Better answers. Answers that could redeem him.

He compared this room, in this house, in this barrio, to the barrio of his youth. The people he grew up around, cared about themselves, and they cared about others in a practical way whenever they had time or resources. Communal support was basic, sometimes just words of comfort. Not that the words were not genuine. It's just that meaningful action was often not possible. Action that could solve deeply-rooted problems required understanding, planning, time and money. And that kind of support was a luxury reserved for the wealthy. That's why the downtrodden were downtrodden; because they had no time or energy to force the change that was needed. And often they simply reached the end of this thing called hope. How often had they been shut down and turned away? The only time available was spent trying to put the food on the table. They had to depend on honest politicians to advocate for the changes they needed. And what were the chances of an honest politician? When the wealthy sectors of society (which included politicians of every stripe who earned more than ten times the minimum wage, and whose positions opened doors to more opportunities for yet more financial gain) already had the tools that the impoverished sectors didn't even have time to struggle for, and when the wealthy held the balance of power, why should they relinquish it? Why should they clamber for change? Yet, how cruel had been his revolution? How many Ricardos and Carolinas and Rosas and Vicentes had it hurt? How much would it really change the balance of power? There would always be the politically powerful, no matter their origins. He saw greed and evil in government and private corporations alike. And would that really change? He had avoided questioning the status of Chile's largely state-owned copper company. What excuse did this state corporation have for being in the red? And why was the wealth that it created not actually distributed amongst the population? It was well-known that the best jobs in state-owned companies were reserved for friends and family and the perks were reserved for top authorities, many of whom inherited their positions like monarchy. Human nature would prevail, no matter what. Bladimir had been so sure of his chosen path. But now, questions leaked out to cool the comfort and righteousness of his lifelong ideology. He had always fought hard against evil capitalism. But now, he detected a small (tiny, in fact) breach in his lifelong faith in Marxist socialism. Yes, you could call it faith. Could he ever turn from it and worship another God? Could he ever, for instance, consider capitalism as a safeguard against one single, over-riding, all-powerful state machine? If all human, material and political greed and corruption was concentrated in just one power—the State—could this not lead to a more singular, unwieldy and impenetrable power that could so easily usurp his dream of the perfect democratic socialism, and would it repress freedoms? He refuted it out of hand. But still, it niggled, was there a chance that human nature could be incorruptible?

In the few conversations he'd had with Ricardo and Carolina, Bladimir opened his eyes to their aspirations, which were not the selfish ones he had always assigned to people who lived 'over here', well east of Plaza Italia but rather the couple was genuinely sympathetic to disadvantaged people. They, too, wanted to lend a hand, to make at least one other person's life easier, even if for one day. "It sounds cliché, I know." Ricardo had told him. "But it's true." He had glanced at Carolina, as though they had had this conversation before and he was repeated something they had come to agree on. "Our society is only as good as our lowest common denominator."

And now, Bladimir found himself here, on the bed of the woman whose death he had caused, and now, having intruded into her life, having read her diary, having used her partner for personal errands, he had tricked her brother into sharing his home and hospitality. He was a hypocrite. It seemed that the road to the greater good twisted through tunnels and into very dark, cold shadows. He was beginning to lose sight of it.

29 | FRIENDS

March 13, 2020

Carolina must have had a moment or two of weakness when she admitted to Bladimir what he already knew—that Vicente had moved out only a few months ago, and recently he had made a home in a hovel under a footbridge. "I can't make myself go over there. You understand that it's hard to see someone you have come to love make self-destructive decisions. It's like... you know what it's like? I can't go to funerals, either. I simply can't. Seeing someone being slid into a cold, empty place where they don't deserve to be, and then to realize it's permanent... well, it's just too much for me. That's why I can't go and see him."

Bladimir picked up on the part about funerals. "Do you mean that Vicente's going to die? I mean, isn't there a chance he'll come back home?"

"No," she said, shaking her head. "No, God willing, he's old but he won't die soon. But he won't come back home either."

It was the first time that Carolina ever told him anything. It occurred a few days after he and Ricardo had sat up drinking wine. Bladimir hadn't slept the following nights. And he didn't want to get up, walk into the kitchen, and see the couple sitting there, exchanging worries about Vicente over their morning cup of tea. But when he finally did walk down to the kitchen, he was surprised to see Carolina there by herself, Ricardo's tea cup was already rinsed and placed beside the sink.

Bladimir motioned to the tea cup and then to Ricardo's empty chair.

"Ricardo's gone out," she said. "Just about every morning, he goes out with a thermos of tea and a sandwich for Vicente." That's when she told him the second and last thing she would confide: that up to now, this was the only way Vicente would accept support from them. After Rosa died, he couldn't be in the house without her. Simple as that. "Even so..." she said, "He knows we came to love him many years ago, in spite of the problems he brought with him." She frowned a little and opened her mouth as though she was about to say more but she stopped short.

Bladimir assumed Ricardo had told her about their conversation the other night, and she no longer had to pretend that the family situation was something else. She didn't tell him how Vicente and Rosa had come to live here in the first place, nor did she describe how the four of them had travelled such a long road towards normalcy and that she had known all along, that it would be in vain. Given Vicente and Rosa's past, how could the future promise anything resembling normal (whatever normal was meant to be, anyway)?

Bladimir felt sick to his stomach, and it wasn't from poor digestion. His nerves, the ones that he always told himself, and everyone else, were made of steel, were no more than mushy conduits for electrical impulses that he couldn't suppress. This sickness was something he hadn't experienced for decades. He tried to recall the last time he'd felt that way and it led him down a mental shaft that ended in the children's group home shortly after he had received his official ID number. His mother had disappeared. Again. The group home was going to be his permanent home, he was told. It felt strange, threatening and it smelled dank and hostile. He could detect nasty signs of rot, and as the other boys in the far corner of the room eyed him up and down, he thought they were like hawks watching their prey. For three days, he had refused to get out of bed and he refused to eat. He couldn't swallow anything they tried to ply him with. He just plucked the threads of the light blanket with his cracked and blackened fingernails and wished he could disappear underneath. On his third day, he smelled *cazuela*, which made him pay attention to his stomach. He noticed how it ached. He mustered the courage to face the rest of the guys just so he could eat. As it turned out, it could have been worse. He learned how to survive among non-friends and he learned how to hide away.

Right now, his stomach churned and he had nowhere to hide except in dead Rosa's room, under dead Rosa's blanket, across from dead Rosa's diary. She was dead because of him, and now he had to atone for it—do penance for his sin—and he didn't know where to start. Today, the house was over-come with a sad, silent scream, for his ears only, and he was helpless to shut it out. Perhaps the burden was especially heavy because it was Ricardo, weak against the pain of Rosa's death, who talked about it. But he didn't know if that was the reason. Maybe it was heavy because he'd grown a con-science. "It'll improve," he told himself. "It'll improve." Against his will, he had grown to feel rooted to this house and responsible to the people inside.

He retreated to the back bedroom and pulled Rosa's diary down from the shelf. He ran his fingers over the rough cover where the pigments had stained it long ago. Book in hand, he sank into the old armchair and gazed for a short while out the window before concentrating on the words that Rosa left behind. He had never heard her voice but he remembered (against his will), the sound of a hard metal machine against her soft, pliable body. It was the life being knocked out of her (and also Vicente). He did not hear her last breath but he imagined it now. And he remembered how the hat with a blue ribbon surrendered to the wind before it disappeared under the smoke of the afternoon of his glory. He squeezed his eyes shut in search of a haven behind the dark of his eyelids. His bones felt way too heavy, his head too. He sunk back further into the chair. He didn't have the will to even lift a finger, he was paralyzed for a time, and then finally, slowly he cracked open the cover and began to turn pages, sometimes turning back to read certain entries, again, and then again, please. He wondered if Ricardo or Carolina had even seen this little book. Probably not. Rosa's things were too sacred to disturb. So he pondered how odd it was that they allowed him into this space, with the simple promise of not disturbing anything. How odd it was that they trusted him. How odd it was that people in this sector of the city, all things being relative, had also sacrificed and struggled to survive.

Finally, dusk gathered up the last of the day's light by its tail, threw it over its shoulder and huddled down into the dishevelled garden. Golden shadows defined the bushes before finally giving way to the night. Bladimir paused, book in hand, re-reading and pondering dead Rosa's prose, sen-tence by sentence, before he finally fell asleep in the chair, with darkness for his cover.

Enchanted and once again under the spell of a reality that had run par-allel to the rest of the world, Bladimir had unwittingly saved himself that night. Or perhaps it was Rosa's hand that had arranged his salvation. The watchers that worked for Giorgio, and who were now more immediately under Flaco's direction, were cruising the main drags nearby, looking for something to report back. Flaco's instructions were, "Look down the side streets, enter them if you have to. Sometimes you just need to follow your gut. Do it. You know who we're looking for. Describe him to shop owners. If we have to scour every square inch of Gran Santiago, we'll do it. But let's start with the most likely, and fan out. We'll nail him."

Tonight, Flaco felt the power of his command and decided to embark with a few of his soldiers in a '69 metallic blue Mustang. The Mustang was a gift from Giorgio, who, except for an image in his mind's eye, couldn't see it. It had been under a tarp a few decades too many. After he assigned Flaco the job of bringing in Bladimir, Giorgio led him to a warehouse a block from El Terminal. The old building was dilapidated and appeared to be deserted. But if you looked closely, you'd notice the heavy locks, and half a dozen cameras that were mounted inside disused electrical boxes. Pigeons fluttered around and landed on top. Giorgio whistled and an armed guard leaned over and saluted him. Once they entered, they could hear the near distant hum of voices under the pounding bass of tropical music coming from somewhere in the back. The front of the building was a huge open space in which were parked four automobiles, all covered with dusty tarps. They walked past the first three and when they reached the last one, Giorgio told Flaco to unveil it.

"Disrobe it," is actually what he said. "Flaco, this baby is yours to use. And if you bring me Bladimir, it's yours to have. I've been saving it for years. As you can see, it's still in mint condition. I only drove it once before my accident." Flaco didn't bother to ask what accident; he was busy being mesmerized by the metallic blue marvel.

Flaco was now pulling away from the traffic on Avenida Tobalaba and turning onto Sánchez Fonticella, with the intention of cruising conspicuously in this formidable throwback to the '60s, to announce the arrival of him and his *cabros*. Should anyone want to know, they were looking for a tall, traitorous gorilla who had betrayed righteous front-line protestors.

Vicente had been sitting alone beside his fire pit, tea cup in hand, staring into the same kind of shadows that Bladimir saw from the back bedroom several blocks away. When he heard loud reggaeton beating out from an approaching vehicle, he stood up, his old legs stiff and muscles tense, his white head slowly rising above the sloped bank. After a few seconds, the metallic blue miracle came into view. It was just coasting along beside the canal like a royal carriage in a one-vehicle parade. Vicente squinted at the driver and three passengers who were leaning on the blue leather, arms extended across the seat backs, their heads, pumping to the music and turning in unison, as they scanned the surroundings. He recognized Flaco as the driver and immediately crouched back down and out of view.

He heard the motor rumbling as the car slowed under a street lamp. It almost stopped, and for a few seconds, he was afraid they were going to jump out and check the footbridge. But he heard Flaco say, "No, not here. He's not the kind of guy to hole up under a bridge. That much I know."

Vicente stretched up to peer over the bank again and he wiped his lenses. The Mustang faded into the distance, but the rumble of the motor filled his ears. And suddenly, he remembered something about that, and he flung himself back onto the bank, clutching his head. It was as though the Mustang had lurched up his spine, and then had suddenly braked at his neck. It idled there, rocking a little and purring like a big cat. He trembled as he struggled to escape the flashback. Clawing at the dirt with both hands, his feet scraping their way down the bank, he came to rest on the familiar stones around the fire pit. He jerked around and vomited over the charred wood.

A dread crept up to hang around his consciousness. He couldn't make sense of the memory, nor of the fear that the metal monster had just awakened. His temples throbbed and he fought between trying to piece together the flashbacks and trying to erase them entirely. Some of them stayed. His eyes ached. He squeezed them shut and rubbed his palms over his sockets as the mental movie of a blue Mustang pulling into a long driveway played, rewound and played again. He cringed at the fragments of a shouting match he was engaged in with a woman in an upstairs bedroom. Then a deep terror overtook him when he saw a man casually close the door of a new blue Mustang. The man said to a passenger, "Wait here," before sauntering from behind a garage towards a rose garden at the back door of a house.

Vicente doubled over, opened his mouth and yelled into the canal, and again he puked, this time into the bubbling current. He watched as gobs of vomit splattered over top of the silty, brown water and were rushed away in small eddies that brushed the canal's concrete walls. He exhaled and hung over the wooden railing for a long time watching fragments wash away. Nothing to report, nothing that made sense.

Bladimir was fast sleep in the armchair, the diary open at the page that described a blue Mustang racing down a gravel driveway. A man, frantic with pain, had groped for the door handle and thrown himself into the back seat. He yelled to another man on the passenger side, "Get over there and drive. Drive! Now!"

Elena was nearby. You could calculate the distance by counting the number of streets on one hand. She was doing pretty much the same as she did most nights—reclining in a drugged state. Passed out on top of her bed, she was surrounded by a dozen loose pages that were filled with lists. All apparently haphazard, not at all analytical. She had been cloistered in her room again for God knows how long. She slept fitfully because something niggled at her, something about being responsible for delivering a bottle of wine to the little man with the white goatee. She would not let him down. Although she was determined that she would rouse herself, she just wasn't sure when.

There was a shared sigh of relief when the sun came up the next morning. The day started late. Ricardo and Carolina were speaking in low voices over morning tea and sandwiches. Ricardo said he was going to resist going to the footbridge today because yesterday morning Vicente had been unusually flustered.

"I must be true to my word," Vicente had mumbled again and again. He had circled on the spot a few times before he sat down (not unlike a dog having found a place to settle). "I need to be here and there. I need to be listening. I have to report back."

"What are you going on about?"

"I made a commitment, you see. You have to honor your commitments." Vicente had tossed away the remainder of his tea, drizzling it across the dirt, some drops settling on top, unabsorbed, like little eyes looking up, trying to tell him something. "I'm in a hurry Ricardo. You understand." He looked intensely at Ricardo from over the top his round, innocent lenses. "I have to be on my way." And then he turned, slung his packsack over this shoulder, and strode quickly for a man his age, up to the bus stop, which was a good 300 meters away.

"I don't think he has money for the bus. Maybe the driver has a soft spot for him. Or maybe he just insists by sneaking on. Just another one of the evaders... I don't know."

"He's okay," Carolina told him. "He'll be okay."

Bladimir walked into the kitchen and greeted them with fake joviality. He looked worse for wear. He'd only stopped long enough for *una manito del gato*—a quick splash of water on his face and a half-hearted grooming in the manner of a cat. He tried to appear positive. He lied, "I have an idea and I just might make progress with my uncle's house today. See you later."

"Will you be back for dinner?" Carolina asked. But he was already out the door.

In contrast to his bluster with Ricardo the morning before, this morning Vicente was a coward. He was jittery as he prepared to leave. He settled his packsack across his shoulder, and removed it, settled it, removed it, couldn't get it right. He looked around, especially insecure. He did remember seeing Flaco last night but seeing Flaco was nothing new and had never before caused this much agitation. On the other hand, the blue Mustang event and the memory it aroused was something that, if he was going to survive the morning, he would have to squelch. Survival mode required only that he remember to report seeing Flaco to Wolfman and nothing more—no loud, disturbing music, no rumbling flashbacks.

He set off, following a dozen workers on their way to office jobs, all marching from the bus stop, and across Avenida Tobalaba. He was going to Elena's cafe to accept the wine she would bring, to pay the big man's fee, which, if he remembered correctly was due tonight. Maybe not tonight but soon. More than the wine, though, he sought the tranquillity that he always felt in Elena's presence.

There was only one other person at the cafe when Vicente arrived. He pulled out a chair at his usual table and was grateful that the waiter ignored him. He tried to remember why he was thinking about Flaco, and why Flaco being in the neighborhood was important. He rapped his forehead with his knuckles. He had to remember to report it to Wolfman. He rapped again for good measure.

He looked up, suddenly distracted by a dozen green budgies that chirped and fluttered among the branches, disappearing and then reappearing from within the thick foliage. Amused, he got lost in their games and didn't notice as Elena meandered along the sidewalk and approached the table. She pulled up a chair and immediately slid a bottle of wine towards Vicente.

"Here," she said. "This is for you. Well, for him. You know..."

Startled by her arrival, he jumped a little and she touched his shoulder and smiled. He relaxed. It was so pleasant to hear her voice. "Thank-you," he said. And he immediately socked the bottle away in his packsack. Smiling to himself, he took his time adjusting the zippers and patting it into place before looking up at Elena, the crinkles around his eyes reaching out to her. He suddenly felt that his cheeks were flushed and he was embarrassed that he should be embarrassed. He raised his hands to his face and covered his glasses. He looked at her through his fingers. She was wearing a short-sleeved pink shirt that buttoned down the front. He thought she looked like a young girl but he didn't say so.

"Here," she said. "I brought this for you too. I don't know why, but I saw it along the way and I wrenched and twisted it until it finally broke off. It wasn't exactly stealing," she said. "It was hanging over on this side of the fence." She placed a deep pink rose, only partially opened, in the middle of the table. "Put it in water and it will open for you. But mind the thorns here." She pointed at the short stem. "I cut myself." She grinned and sucked on her index finger.

He reached out to accept it and tears welled in his eyes. Someone used to give him roses. Maybe it was Rosa, he wasn't sure. They were a sign of deep affection. And here was Elena, practically a stranger, presenting him with one. Love filled his chest. He felt warm all over.

"My father loved roses," she continued unselfconsciously. "I used to give them to him too. But I was really little then. I remember getting into trouble for cutting them from the bushes. They were supposed to stay in the garden for all to enjoy. But I liked to keep them for myself and so I always cut one off and took it away with me. Maybe because my father liked them too, it made me feel close. He wasn't at home all that much, you see..." And then it was her face that flushed. "Sorry, I don't know why I'm rambling on." She furrowed her brow, blinked several times and nodded towards the flower. "The rose maybe... maybe just that," she said, passing on the blame.

The arrival of the waiter saved them more discomfort. Without asking, Elena ordered orange juice for Vicente and coffee for herself.

"Thank you," Vicente managed. This morning was an 'off' morning. He was aware of his own confusion, and he wasn't prepared for small talk. Not that small talk was something he did well anyway. They both watched as the waiter busied himself with another customer. Neither of them moved to speak but neither of them wanted to leave, either. Just a couple of kindred souls who didn't need words. They both hoped the waiter would be extra slow, that he'd be the excuse for them to spend more time together.

Finally the waiter arrived with their tray and they smiled up at him and then quickly, self-consciously at each other. The waiter half bowed as he turned to walk away and when he looked up, it was straight into the dark eyes of Bladimir—aka, BJ; aka, Wolfman.

"*Lo siento, Señor.* I didn't see you there."

Bladimir side-stepped the waiter and pulled up a chair beside Vicente. He looked at him and Elena and then nodded at each of them in turn. "Well, good morning to you both."

The spell that had spun around Elena and Vicente fell away. Elena immediately became flustered in BJ's field of charm and she was positively agitated, fidgeting with her fingers. Vicente didn't notice. "Good morning," he nodded politely to Wolfman.

The waiter was attentive and returned to ask if Bladimir wanted to place an order but Bladimir brusquely waved him off. In spite of having made himself look comfortable in his chair, it was obvious that he didn't intend to stay. He looked at Vicente, eyebrows raised and although Vicente was not able to interpret the gesture, Elena caught it.

"Yeah," she nodded in Vicente's direction. "This gentleman and I have met a few times for coffee. I mean, why not? Same cafe, same mornings, different tables. No need for separate tables."

"So you two have become good friends?"

They looked at each other and then away. They didn't know. Elena shrugged. Vicente didn't catch that. He was trying to decide.

As much as Bladimir was intrigued by this relationship, which they apparently couldn't define themselves, he pushed aside the questions. The relationship was something to pursue later because right now, he needed to know what Vicente could tell him about Giorgio or Flaco or anyone associated.

"Are you sure you don't want to join us?" Elena asked.

"I can't stay," said Bladimir. He picked up the rose. "Are you bringing each other roses?" For no particular reason, he was annoyed by it. It got under his skin and turned his mood foul. "I'd like to say it was nice to see you but unfortunately, we can't say we had time to visit." He looked deliberately at Vicente but, again, this was lost on him.

Elena prickled with frustration at BJ's intrusion and his sudden bad humor. "No," she said. "Let's say we haven't seen each other. Don't let us keep you." And she flicked the back of her hand, giving him the wave-off.

"Well, it might have been nice..." he said sarcastically. He scraped his chair out from the table and saluted them both, turned, and strode away.

Elena glared at his back and then turning to Vicente, "Do you know this man well?"

"Well, no, not well. I saw him 146 days ago, and maybe also before that. And I've been watching him, just by chance, off and on, anyway."

"Why do you remember the date so precisely?" She asked.

"Because he was there when my wife died. I saw him."

"Oh, I'm very sorry, that's really tragic." She wanted to reach out and touch his hand but he stiffened and put both hands on his lap.

"And I also used to see him a lot at El Terminal."

"Which terminal?"

"You know, the restaurant." He reached up to rub his glasses with both index fingers, smudging them to such a degree that she wanted to pull them off his face and clean them herself.

"No, I don't know it."

He didn't seem to have heard her. He stood up, reached for his glass and gulped the last of the juice. "Thank you." He slung his packsack over one shoulder and left without another word.

Elena sat at the table, wondering what had just happened. Whatever it was, it was all wrong.

When Vicente reached his shelter, Wolfman was already crouched beside the entrance, chewing on a blade of grass. He spit it away when he saw Vicente and motioned for him to move over beside the fire pit. Bladimir wanted to know more about Elena but he didn't want to distract Vicente from the real business at hand.

Vicente looked up at Wolfman from under his brows. "What happened before I got there?"

"Got where? You were there before I was." Bladimir was confused.

"No, you were there. I saw you." Vicente insisted.

"Maestro, I don't know what you mean."

"The bus... I saw you behind the bus.... I saw you that day. I saw you behind the bus..." Vicente's voice cracked and disintegrated. Like glass that had shattered.

Oh, the incident. That was how Bladimir referred to it now. He buried his face in his hands. Everyone, even this old man had questions. He groaned under the weight of them, floundering amidst the guilt. Rosa's diary was incomplete, full of dead ends begging to be tied up. If Vicente's brain hadn't been so broken, he would be able to answer everything. But it was broken and how did someone penetrate a brain that had collapsed in on itself, where answers were only questions tied in knots that were buried in the obscurity of grey rubble? If only the answers were autonomous and could rise and shine like sharp rays of light, pointing like a laser to something clear and finite.

"Are you sure, Vicente? Are you sure you saw me? Was it me?" The best Bladimir could do was cast doubt. He wanted answers from Vicente but not all of them, not the ones that could incriminate him.

"Did you see her? Did you see my Rosa?" Vicente's face was scarred with confusion, dry lines on his brow and around his lips deepening. "Did you see me that day? I saw you. You were there. You passed me by. Did you see her? Did you see me?"

Bladimir shook his head slowly and reached over and touched Vicente's elbow. It was as close as he dared get. He was tempted to gather this damaged old guy in his arms. The urge was extremely out of character. Such an act would turn him into someone he did not recognize. Besides, he knew from Rosa's diary that this little old man, was—or could have been—a powerful political enemy. Now he was too broken to be anything of the kind. Bladimir pulled back. "No, Vicente, I didn't see you," and then he lied. "I didn't see her either. I'm sorry." He meant that part, "I'm very sorry."

At that moment, Vicente didn't believe him. But suddenly, his brain switched channels. He turned to Bladimir. "I saw him last night."

"Who?"

"I saw the skinny man, the ugly one, who you wanted me to watch. Flaco."

"Did you go to El Terminal last night?"

"No, he was here."

Bladimir straightened. Blood suddenly pounded in his ears. "Here, here?" He pointed to the ground. "Does he know you? Does he know this place?"

"No, but he was here." Vicente stood up and surveyed the canal. Then he frowned, ducked down low and peered over the slope, towards Avenida Tobalaba. "There," he pointed. "Somewhere there. He was with other people."

"Did he see you? Did you talk to him?" Bladimir didn't know if anyone besides himself would recognize Vicente as a regular at El Terminal. With Flaco spending most of his time around the pizzeria, he doubted if he would recognize Vicente. But what if Giorgio had replaced himself with Flaco? Probably not. Chances of that were slim. Flaco had worked the pizzeria for too long. His clients depended on him, and Giorgio depended on him to be there too. Besides, El Capitán was Giorgio's main man now.

"No, he didn't see me. And I didn't talk to him."

"Then what was he doing here? Was he on the footpath? Was he driving by? What?"

"I don't know. I don't know." Vicente became more distressed. "But he said that someone wouldn't sleep on the street." Then he grinned and shrugged. "Like me, I guess. Do you want some tea?"

Bladimir had thought he would have been relatively safe in this part of town, at least for awhile longer. But Flaco wasn't here peddling drugs. He was here hunting.

30 | THE BLUE MACHINE
March 13, 2020

There was no question but that Elena was haunted by the big bad wolf. She didn't know that Vicente had nicknamed BJ 'Wolfman,' nor was she aware that beyond that, she and Vicente had a common way of categorizing people, even perhaps of interpreting the world. And who knew... maybe there were other commonalities that neither of them were aware of but were a familial way of seeing things, a sort of logic that is passed down through the genes. She wondered if BJ had tried to seek her out, if he desired—as she did—an opportunity for the two of them to be alone, somewhere private. She glanced towards her bedroom. Certainly not here, at least not yet. She'd been loafing around in the same stained, button-down pajama shirt for days. Lately, it was only when she went to meet Vicente and to buy cigarettes and bread, that she bothered to get dressed. Even then, she just pulled her jeans and a loose sweater on top of the pajamas. She smelled her armpits. Yeah, maybe time for a bath. Did BJ and Vicente notice that she hadn't bathed for more than a week? Maybe that's why BJ had had to rush off in such a hurry. She sighed and ambled over to the cupboard. It was barren except for some canned peaches that her mother had stocked about a year ago, and a small vial of pills. Her entire kitchen was in the same shape. Devoid of nourishment. She chuckled dryly. Same as her life. She avoided the question of how a girl from such a privileged household could end up being as aimless as she was.

She reached in and shook the bottle of pills. Only a few left. Soon she'd to have to pay a visit to Flaco. The prescription from the new doctor had run out and he'd already warned her that she had to manage her dosage properly. What's more, he said he wasn't going to prescribe more pills until she went for a thorough examination, which would mean a series of probing and time-consuming tests that would come back with inconclusive results. So there would be more tests. The business of medicine. And the doctor would then start guessing and offering advice and maybe prescribing a new drug, or two, or three. She's been there, done that. No, thank-you. It was much more simple to visit Flaco. No questions, no tests, no judgment, no mess. Just some hard currency. And for Elena, that wasn't a problem.

She popped a pill, and her thoughts turned back to BJ. It was the not knowing that was killing her. Why had he shown up at the cafe and then just up and left so suddenly? He was playing games with her. And why so much interest in Vicente?

She ran her fingers through her hair a few times, pushing it out of her face, and she leaned in to huff on the window. She was looking towards the sidewalk. Perhaps if she closed her eyes and counted to ten... no, maybe to 20, then she'd open them and there he'd be, walking straight right up to the entrance, where he'd ring her buzzer. He would invite himself in and then he would never leave. She sighed. "I'm love sick," she said aloud. "And pathetic. Too old for this. But here I am." She flopped onto her unmade bed, which, she realized as her head landed on the pillow, smelled as though the bed linens hadn't been washed for weeks, and she promised herself that after a nice, long nap, she'd clean up the place.

Her nap lasted for 16 hours. When she woke up, it was early evening on March 14th. She vaguely remembered half-promising herself to clean her apartment. Well, she'd begin with a shower and get dressed. That might start the ball rolling towards greater challenges. After her shower, which she did admit made her feel more vital, she padded into the kitchen to double-check the cupboards. Yesterday was a lifetime ago and maybe she'd missed something. The number one item would be the pills. They came before food. She needed to make a trip to Bella Vista to find Flaco.

When Elena arrived on Pio Nono, and when she neared the pizzeria, she scanned the sidewalk for signs of him. The street was already in full swing—people hopping in and out of taxis, groups of students jostling and laughing their way into bars, silly couples leaning into one another, others exchanging bitter recriminations. Dogs wandered passed, sniffing for scraps. The beats of *reggaetón* blasted out from bars, noises blending and clashing along the sidewalk. Bar and restaurant hosts yelled out their specials from doorways, some grabbing pedestrians by the elbows to take them inside by force. Whatever worked. The street smelled of beer and grilled food. Neon lights flickered and silhouettes danced and jostled on the other side of tinted windows. Elena walked two blocks up and down and there was no sign of Flaco. She wanted to avoid entering the pizzeria. She just wanted to buy some pills and go, she wanted to leave this scene, which only reminded her that she had already been there, done that. Years misspent, people lost. Deep down, she knew that recent years hadn't been that much better but either way, she didn't want to be reminded of her miserable past.

She passed the pizzeria a fourth time and in desperation, she finally stepped in and asked after Flaco. The young waitress, eyes with thick black eyeliner and purple glitter from lashes to brows, a very short skirt and very tall boots shook her head. "*Negativo*. He's not here. He left about two minutes ago. But hey, if you run up to that corner..." she pointed with her index finger, nail painted with pink and yellow flowers and more purple glitter. "You might see him driving his new car. It's a convertible, mind. Blue. Lucky you, if he offers you a ride." The waitress grinned.

Elena touched the young woman's shoulder and flashed a fake smile. Worried now that she was going to miss Flaco all together, she did an about-turn and rushed towards the corner.

When she was half-way there, a black metal gate was sliding open and the nose of a blue Mustang was nudging forward. The car stopped and she could hear it idling from where she stood. The motor's deep purr sent shivers up her spine. Fine hairs on the back of her neck stood up. The car inched forward and the driver suddenly stomped on the gas, the engine roared and wheels spun, kicking up hundreds of stones and peppering the gate behind. The tires squealed as the driver turned the car towards her. She saw Flaco, one arm out the window, the other gripping the wheel. He was laughing aloud, head back, mouth open wide. He turned to say something to the passenger as the blue machine rumbled past.

Elena backed up tight to the wall, her fingers desperately searching for something to lean on. She was suddenly a little girl again. She shut her eyes tight and screamed. Her knees turned to mush and she slid down the wall. She crouched there, grabbing her head, cupping her ears, elbows coming together in front of her face. She had just seen the blue car speeding away.

It was the one that sped off down the driveway after her father disappeared from her life forever. She thought the car existed only in her nightmare from hell. It didn't make sense that it was here on Pio Nono. Clash of realities. Too much to take. She passed out in a heap on the sidewalk.

Suddenly there were eyes peering into her face, hands touching her shoulders, questions being whispered above her ears. "Are you okay?" "Should we call an ambulance?" "Are you hurt? What can I do?" Tears rolled down her cheeks. She was shaking. "Are you cold? Here, here's my sweater. I don't need it." Finally someone squatted beside her, and pulled her up to sit shoulder to shoulder. He didn't say anything, he just leaned in and gently removed her hands from her ears and took them into his own. She turned slowly to look at him, eyes wide, frightened, brimming with tears. He was a stranger with a concerned expression, the kind of stranger who understands without words, who doesn't question, who just knows. She was grateful for his touch and she stopped trembling. She nodded and whispered to him and anyone who was still standing around, "I'm okay. I had a shock. That's all. I'll be fine."

The stranger stayed there for she-didn't-know how long. Finally, she made a move to stand up and he helped her. "Thank-you." She had never felt so grateful in her life.

"Can I call you a taxi?" he asked. He was already raising his hand to stop the black and yellow cab that was slowly rolling by, fishing for customers. She climbed in and mechanically recited her address to the driver. Somehow she fumbled her way through her building entrance, upstairs to her apartment, and she walked straight to the kitchen cupboard where the few remaining pills rattled inside the vial. She was also very grateful for those. Tomorrow would be another day. Tonight she needed not to think, not to remember, and not to question. Nothing made sense and she was too exhausted to try to sort it out.

That night, the metallic blue Mustang rumbled in through the fog of her sleep. Its nose appeared, just as it had earlier that evening, nudging confidently out from the gate. This time, though, it was not from the gate on Pio Nono; this time it emerged from beside the garage at her childhood home, the garage where she was still crouching after her father scrambled into his car and spun off. She heard the engine of the blue Mustang purr as it sat idling, waiting for a command. She heard Rosa screaming and then a man's voice, suddenly gruff and then animal-like in a long drawn-out, tortured moan. The sound of feet skidding across the gravel outside, another masculine voice, urgently directing someone with expletives "*Conchetumadre. Hijo de puta, Culiao de mierda!*" that shot, between moans, from deep in his throat. The other man responded with yet more expletives. Then two car doors slammed and the engine revved, the car roared off and its rear tires spit gravel all the way into the back of the garage, small rocks landing near Elena's feet.

Unlike in her recurring nightmare, she didn't immediately run after her father. She cowered. Then she heard Rosa calling her but she was still too afraid to move. Rosa went back inside the house or maybe she hid, waiting in the bushes before returning to haul her to the back door. Suddenly little Elena was inside, cold and cramped. Her stomach churned and she leaned forward to vomit on her favorite patent leather shoes and finally tiptoed around the acrid bile.

Her dream then transported her down the driveway, her father's car was there again, as though it was at a starting gate, the engine was running and suddenly the vehicle charged forward and disappeared in the distance. She ran after it in slow motion before tripping and falling onto her hands and knees. A man suddenly appeared at her back. At first she thought her father had returned but when she twisted around, she saw a stranger glowering down at her, a creature without eyes, the sockets red-rimmed and dripping with blood. She ignored him, turned around, and she began to pick tiny pebbles out of the skin on her knees. She felt the man's breath as he leaned down and she smelled the heavy scent of too much aftershave. Suddenly she was terrified of this man. She gasped and forced herself to wake up.

Luckily, the pills pulled her sideways into a forgetful grogginess where she settled until the next day. When she awoke, she had no memory of the dream but she had a piercing headache and was in need of a new prescription.

She barged into the reception of a doctor's private office. "You have to help me," she said.

The doctor took one look at her and knew it was true. Exams would have to be run once she was more calm, under control. Besides, he had a busy schedule, what with an important luncheon and a football match later that night, it was simply best to prescribe something and get rid of her.

"Listen," he told Elena. "This is how it works. We need to trial these medications. This means that the dosage will have to be altered as days progress. We can't say they are the optimum treatment for you until we fine-tune them. Do you understand? But unless you agree to some time in hospital—and I can't even guarantee a bed these days—then you have to at least agree to run the course and allow us to test your tolerance. Just so we can get the right balance. Understand? It would be best if your husband or someone else close to you could help monitor your tolerance and reaction."

She nodded and reached across his desk to accept the prescription and to sign a document that she failed to read. None of what he said mattered. None of it even sank in. All she needed was something to help avoid those waking hours full of questions and the constant, compulsive analysis accompanied by list-making, and those sleeping hours full of nightmares.

31 | HOPES AND FEARS
March 15, 2020

Vicente was hunched over a big glass of orange juice, watching from a corner table in El Terminal. One eye always on the front door. He'd changed tables because recently one of the new waiters appeared to be watching him. Vicente didn't like to be watched when he was watching. Wolfman had been paying him regularly so Vicente didn't have to worry about not consuming, and this meant there were no more worries about being a *persona non grata* at El Terminal. He enjoyed the freedom the new status—that of a paying customer—gave him.

Now that he didn't have to watch Wolfman anymore, he was less occupied as a watcher. And he hadn't been watching Elena because she hadn't shown up at the cafe for three days. He hoped he would see her before the week was up because she would be due to give him the wine for his landlord. But that wasn't as much of a concern now that Wolfman was paying him. Vicente could afford to buy the wine himself now. So that wasn't the point. The point was that he wanted to see Elena. He missed the familiar comfort that he felt in her presence. Even if he knew where she lived, it wouldn't be appropriate to show up at her doorstep. He sometimes forgot things and more than sometimes, he confused timelines and had to refer to the Xs on the 2020 calendar that Ricardo had given him, but in spite of those shortcomings, he was hardwired with proper etiquette. He'd been sitting at the table, thinking all of these things when he saw Flaco breeze through the front door. He straightened, alert, like a hound that caught his scent. He noted how Flaco's hands dangled at the end of his bony arms, and how he was snapping his nervous fingers and smiling a silly smile at nobody in particular.

Vicente watched Flaco address the young man at the cash register, "Is he...?" The man at the cash register nodded affirmatively. He motioned with this chin towards the back room and he continued counting bills into the drawer, his head partially blocking the glow of the three monkeys who were watching from behind. More watchers. Vicente gulped down the rest of his juice, picked up his packsack and made his way to the men's room. He knew by now that if he entered the far cubicle and stood on the toilet, he could hear conversations through the vent. He recognized Flaco's voice and he could pick out Giorgio's without a problem. Some of the words were muffled. He heard Flaco laugh but he probably laughed alone to some non-sensical joke that Giorgio didn't find funny. Apparently Giorgio was not one for small talk or senseless jokes.

"Anything?" It was Giorgio's voice. Not a happy sound.

"Not yet but we're making progress." Flaco was probably lying. Vicente heard Flaco mention Providencia. "I'm trawling the likely barrios."

"Good man." Giorgio said. "And talk to our Rati. Let's give him something to do for all the money I pay him. I have an old picture of Bladimir—in case they're too lazy to look up his rap sheet. He can distribute it and tell his men to keep an eye out. No need for anything formal. We just need a location. He can arrange that much."

Vicente pictured Giorgio looking at nothing (what does a blind man see?). He was suddenly overcome by the creepy feeling that the blind man could see him crouched and listening on this side of the men's room wall. He shivered and felt himself once again being sucked into dark memory pools. They were too murky to make sense of but he knew from experience that he would sink into the fear of them. It used to be that Rosa pulled him out, she'd save him from himself. Now what would he do? He felt panic rise in his throat. But just then, he heard someone's fist thudding against the cubicle door. The whole downward spiral was interrupted by the waiter who had been watching him earlier. "Are you gonna be all day, viejo? What's wrong with you?"

Vicente didn't answer. He tried to push his way past but the waiter grabbed him by the elbow, his fingers digging in. "You owe me for the juice and sandwich. I'll follow you out. Did you think you could hide in here and then disappear without paying? Not on my watch, old man!"

He marched Vicente to the cash register. Vicente paid with a handful of coins and when the waiter put out his hand, he dropped a few into his palm.

Just as Vicente hopped off the bus on Tobalaba, he saw Ricardo coming towards him, carrying a thermos and plastic bag. "Where have you been, Vicente?"

"Nowhere."

"I thought we could have some tea."

"Okay, I'm going to my place. You can come if you want."

It didn't feel like a heartfelt invitation but Ricardo accepted it. He smiled and followed Vicente across the street and down the slope to the edge of the fire pit. Vicente lit a fire and took his time to position the kettle. The two of them adjusted their trousers, sat back and looked each other, Ricardo was trying to gauge Vicente's state of mind and Vicente was just looking, a stream of unrelated thoughts coming and going.

Ricardo dove right in. "You can always move back to our place. You know that, right?" Vicente didn't look good. He could use a shower and trim his beard, and it probably wouldn't hurt to eat a few bowls of Carolina's soup. Had he gotten thinner? He looked shriveled. In spite of it, he seemed agile, even animated. But he was holding back. He was digging in his heels, setting his jaw. He was not going to give anything up.

"You know I can't go there."

"Well, it's been five months now. Things have changed."

"Yeah, well, I can't."

Ricardo tried harder. "You don't have to move back to the house. Just come over for dinner sometime."

Vicente shook his head. He got up to pour water into the mugs. Ricardo unwrapped two cheese sandwiches and passed one to Vicente.

They sat there, chewing without speaking. Finally Ricardo tossed away the last few drops of tea. Vicente did the same, and Ricardo stood up to leave.

"It was nice to see you, Vicente."

"It was nice to see you too." But it wasn't. Vicente didn't want to see Ricardo today. He needed to sit down and think things through. He didn't understand. He couldn't organize stuff in his brain. He knocked his temples repeatedly with his knuckles and then ducked under the camouflage curtain, without noticing that one end of it was threatening to work itself free from the old nails on the underside of the bridge. He stretched out on the sleeping bag that he had opened out at a the flat spot at the foot of the slope. Damp seeped through the cardboard underneath and he made a mental note to find more tomorrow. The sun blinked through the cracks of the footbridge. He felt someone walking overhead. Precarious though it may be, this was home now. He couldn't allow himself to compare it to the comfort and security of the bedroom at Ricardo's. Its comfort far outweighed the loneliness that swamped the room in Rosa's absence. He would never be able to face that. He closed his eyes and pushed those thoughts aside by forcing himself to think instead of Elena. Thinking about her didn't hurt him, even if it did disturb him. But the disturbance wasn't something he chose to define or even to question. It was at once unsettling and attractive. It was a blend of sadness and bliss.

Vicente was somewhere in this bliss, which wove itself in and out of his groggy siesta, when he was startled awake by the presence of Wolfman. Wolfman had quietly entered and was squatted at Vicente's side, eyeing the surroundings.

"I came to pay you for your work." Without waiting for a response, Wolfman slid a few folded bills into the top pocket of Vicente's packsack, which Vicente had carelessly left out of his reach. Struggling to his knees, Vicente reached out and pulled the bag to the safety of his chest.

He fumbled for his glasses, arranged them precisely, and looked up at Bladimir. "*Gracias.*" For some time now, he was aware of the strange warmth he occasionally felt towards Wolfman. But as he looked at him, he tried to remember why, at other times, Wolfman filled him with panic. It was gone now, though. It must have been for the same reason that he had decided to watch him. But it had all slipped down the bland slopes of his memory and into the bogs of confusion, a place into which he could not wade. All that was left was the name he had given him—Wolfman. And now Wolfman and

Elena were his two reasons for getting up and carrying on. He counted his watchees on one hand. Flaco and Wolfman were his most recent subjects. Giorgio and Elena had been established for some time.

Wolfman was all business. "Did you go to El Terminal this morning?"

"Yes."

"And?"

"I heard Flaco tell Giorgio that he was looking around some more in Providencia. He said there had been a 'sighting.'"

"Here?"

"Somewhere in Providencia."

"What else?"

Vicente studied the boards on the bridge deck overhead, as he remembered something else. It took several minutes. Finally he said, "He's going to give the Rati a picture of someone called Bladimir and the Rati will help look for him."

Wolfman nodded and then abruptly changed the subject. "Vicente, are you going to keep living under this bridge?"

"Yes." It was simple. This place was a habit too. Nothing would change.

"Listen, Vicente, I've just decided that I'm gonna disappear. I don't mean forever. I just have to stay out of sight for awhile. So I won't be able to visit you very often. But keep doing whatever it is that you do. Don't stop going to El Terminal, okay? Next time I see you, I need you to tell me who goes there and what they say. Can you do that, Maestro?"

Vicente adjusted his glasses and nodded.

Wolfman repeated, hoping the repetition would make Vicente capable. "I'm gonna come and visit you and when I do, I'll need to know whatever you've seen and heard at El Terminal, okay? It's important. Will you remember the details?

Vicente nodded. But he wasn't sure.

The next day he was late arriving at El Terminal because he had waited for hours at Elena's cafe. He took his sweet time drinking a single glass of orange juice but she didn't show up. The waiter targeted him with a stare before finally walking up to Vicente's side and towered over him. "If you're not planning to consume, then you can't stay here. This isn't a park bench."

"I'm waiting for someone." Vicente defended himself weakly.

"Well, it looks like they're not going to show up. You need to move on."

Extremely uncomfortable (because Vicente would never deliberately overstay his welcome), he slung his pack over his shoulder, excused himself and, winding through the half dozen empty tables, he tried to disappear as quickly as possible.

It was mid-afternoon before his bus arrived at Rio Mapocho. Vicente had been so distracted by the outdoor market that ran along the river bank—table after table with assortments of fresh produce, and bright plastic and electronic gadgets, sellers yelling "*Casera*, stop here for fresh farm eggs, get your goat cheese here." "*Mi reina*, what can I get you? We have it all."—that he lost track of where he was, and he panicked. Believing he must have already passed his stop, he got off several blocks too soon. When he realized it, he became agitated. But then, as he crossed the bridge at Pio Nono, he caught sight of someone who looked a lot like Elena. She was wearing tight jeans and a loose brown sweater, and she clutched a small purse to her chest. He squinted, focused carefully, blinked several times, and looked away, then back again just to be sure he wasn't mistaken. Rosa used to tell him to slow down and really be sure of things before he acted. "Remember, you've made mistakes before, Vicente," she used to say. "Things are not always what they seem or what you'd like them to be."

But he was right this time. He was sure of it. He didn't question what Elena was doing there. He was just happy to see her. So he followed.

After a few blocks, Elena turned and stopped at the entrance of a pizzeria. His happiness turned to deep apprehension when Flaco stepped into view and she greeted him. Discombobulated, Vicente shrunk back and squirmed into the wall but he kept watching. Flaco said something and grinned at her but Vicente noticed that she did not smile in return. Good. She pulled some bills out of her little purse and pressed them into Flaco's hand and he passed her a tiny bag, which she immediately stuffed in her bosom. Without a word, she turned to walk out and didn't notice as Flaco raised his hand in a skinny half-wave. Although Vicente's first impulse was to approach her—to get close enough to see the small lines crinkle around her eyes when she smiled, to catch the sparkle of her blue eyes, to hear her voice, and to watch as she knitted her fingers, or as she ran them through her hair, he decided against it. Seeing her with Flaco just felt wrong. No further explanation needed. And it made him all the more curious.

Vicente ducked inside one of the dozens of small souvenir shops, and he watched through the window display of miniature lapiz lázuli penguins and small copper spoons and ashtrays as Elena passed by. He waited for a minute and, looking back apologetically at the clerk, he stepped out the door and followed her as she turned towards the river.

She crossed the bridge and headed straight down into the metro station. She walked briskly past street sellers (who looked up hopefully, trying to catch her eye) without so much as a sideways glance. Vicente followed. If he was lucky, he'd be able to trail her all the way home. His earlier disappointment at not seeing her was replaced with joy (ridiculous as that might sound). And an even better plan. Today he would find out where she lives. El Terminal would wait. He didn't worry about the consequences, and rationalized that since Flaco was not at El Terminal, probably there wouldn't be any news to pass onto Wolfman anyway.

Keeping his distance, he descended the stairs to train level and he spotted Elena at the far end of the platform, constantly shifting her weight, like she was trying to keep warm, like she was impatient. He hid himself behind a young couple who were busy murmuring sweet nothings, barely any space between their faces. The train pulled up, and when the doors closed, Vicente started walking slowly through the cars towards the front. He was pretty sure that Elena would disembark at Los Leones and he prepared to push past the crowd at the door. But when the train slowed, she was still hanging onto an overhead strap. The doors opened, then closed again and the train continued along the rails. Elena got off at the Tobalaba stop and Vicente played with the idea of walking up to her, pretending it was a pleasant coincidence. But he decided that would be intrusive, and anyway, how would he make small talk all the way to her house?

Elena walked at a steady pace all the way from the Luis Thayer Ojeda exit, eventually crossing over to El Bosque South and she continued for several blocks. Vicente stayed on the opposite side of the street and he hung back when she stopped and unlocked the gate to a red brick apartment block. She said something to the doorman, who nodded absently as he held a hose over the garden, and she entered the building. Vicente wondered, fingers crossed behind his back, if he would perhaps see her through one of the windows that faced the street. He waited.

After a couple of minutes, he saw someone moving across the window of an apartment on the third floor. His heart quickened and he felt blood rise all the way to his ears. He stood half-hidden under the shade of a soap-bark tree, and held his breath. The silhouette that passed by the window was so obscure that he couldn't be sure if it was a man or a woman. He made a deliberate decision that it was, in fact, Elena, that this was, in fact, her apartment (even if it wasn't) because this way, he could tell himself that he knew where she lived.

It's just as well that Wolfman didn't go to the footbridge that night because Vicente was in no state to accept a visitor. He was far too distracted with the good fortune of having discovered where Elena lived. He hummed around in circles as he prepared tea and unwrapped a sandwich. But the pleasure of this afternoon's coincidence was short-lived because as he sat relaxed at the edges of the canal, the mug of tea warming his hands, a deep dread suddenly rose up and trod all over his happiness. The fleeting image of Elena and Flaco from earlier that afternoon had, as memories usually did, slid down into a murky pond of confusion. But somehow the memory had bubbled its way to the surface to disrupt the calm, and create deep unease. He didn't like Flaco.

32 | NO ABSOLUTES

March 16, 2020

Bladimir had nothing to kill but time. Unless and until he came up with a plan to escape Giorgio, he was forced to stay out of sight. He lied to Carolina. "I'm making progress with the squatters but now the Housing Office said I need to submit different forms. I did that and now I have to wait for approvals before they'll move on it. You know how it goes."

She did. "Well, be prepared for a wait, then. If they don't know how to deal with the problem off-hand, they'll just bury the forms under a pile on someone's desk. That way, they hope they'll never have to deal with it. They'll come up with a new excuse every day."

"I hope that's not the case." Then he half-asked, half-stated, "I'll be hanging around the bedroom for awhile. It's hot and I haven't really got anywhere else to go for the time being."

She nodded "Yeah, that's fine. Ricardo and I like that someone else is here. I think you know that by now, BJ. With all the noise and violence on the streets, it's nice not to be alone in the house. Just in case, you know... There are so many protesters that are imposters. And they scare me." She added, "And besides, you know we're happy to have the money too."

He noticed that she didn't specify it was his company that brought them pleasure. Maybe she was content with just any old boarder who paid on time. No matter. Everyone was satisfied.

She paused before leaving the kitchen. "Speaking of the money. If you don't plan to go anywhere and you'll be eating all your meals here, then you'll need to pay up front so I can buy extra meat and rice."

"Yeah. I'll go to the bank in the next day or so. Is that okay?" His stash was his stash and he wasn't yet willing to dive into it. But the question of whether Giorgio had contacts in the Banco Estado recently crossed his mind. Surely they wouldn't be monitoring his bank transactions. Maybe best to empty the account early, though.

Carolina murmured a reply under her breath and turned back to the stove. It was hard to know where he stood with her.

Bladimir returned to the bedroom. There were still a few corners on the shelves that he hadn't snooped through yet. He glanced up at the diary. It sat where he'd found it on that first day because he was careful to always put it back exactly as it had been. He didn't want to give Carolina a reason to question him. He knew she inspected the room from time to time. No matter. He was prepared, and what was important was tucked away and she'd never think to inspect that.

He pulled the diary off the shelf and settled down in the chair beside the window. This chair had become his, the thin homemade diary had become his, the double bed, the shelves, the desk, everything, down to the peeling paint in the top corner of the wall above the door, had become his. All so familiar. All so family. He'd studied the diary until he knew exactly how many pages to flip past to arrive at the information he wanted to re-read. "Like the back of my hand," he murmured, referring to both the diary and the room.

He stretched his legs, about to rest them on the small padded footstool (worn out more from dust and moths than from someone actually resting their feet) just as he'd done a dozen times in the past and he sighed the sigh of a man in his rightful place. If he was someone who believed in miracles, he would say it was miraculous to feel as much at home as he did in Vicente's old room.

Just as he was about to lower his heels, he noticed for the first time that the footstool had two small brass hinges that were all but hidden under the seat padding. He paused, both feet in mid-air. Still eyeing the hinges, he lowered his feet and straddled the stool. He reached over to feel around the edges until he found a short blue ribbon that was folded back into itself. When he tugged on it, the top of the footstool opened to reveal a cubby hole. And inside the cubby hole was a thick book. Bound in rich brown leather, its title, 'Leyendas Historicas' was embossed in heavy serif type. The book looked ancient, the kind that someone might find in an antique book shop, or perhaps even, he imagined, the Vatican library. Its size alone was impressive, not to mention the silver ink that had been brushed across its girth so that, when the book was closed, it was edged in metallic silver. He let his hands hover above it for several seconds, afraid to touch it. Then he brushed his fingers across the cover and picked it up to feel its weight. More remarkable than the subject matter of the book—which appeared to be a series of short stories, the title pages for which were reproductions of black and white wood cuts—was the presence of 11 pressed roses, their petals now brittle and semi-transparent, like the thin, pink skin of Sleeping Beauty.

The roses had been inserted at intervals between the pages and must have been lying there, undisturbed for years, flat and frail, their glory long since crushed by the weight of the silver-edged pages. Bladimir carefully opened to the pages where each rose had been placed and studied them before closing the book and returning it to its secret hideaway. In his mind, he asked forgiveness for his intrusion. He didn't presume to be Prince Charming.

"BJ!" It was Ricardo calling from the kitchen. Bladimir was about to put the book back and drop the lid of the footstool when he noticed some manila folders that had been placed on the bottom. There were three folders, none of them very thick. His curiosity was piqued. But he would save them for another day. He softly closed the lid and patted it twice in a gesture that said, "I'll be back."

He slid the diary back in place on the shelf too. Rubbing his hands on his jeans, he took a few deep breaths, and sauntered down the hall towards Ricardo as though he'd been bored, just sitting there, just waiting to be summoned.

"What can I do for you?"

"Carolina says you'll be staying put here for awhile." He was smiling. "A glass of wine?"

Bladimir accepted with a nod and a smile, sipping only occasionally as Ricardo helped himself to a few refills. Ricardo held the bottle upside down over his own glass and said "They say there are always six drops remaining." He grinned as he shook it and waited for another drop to form and fall into his glass. "Cheers," said Ricardo to the air in front of his face. By the time he emptied two bottles, his speech was slurred, his eyelids were heavy and words fell out of his mouth before his brain registered what his mouth was saying. Among the stories that popped into his head at random, were facts that coincided with some of the details of Rosa's diary. But Bladimir knew more than Ricardo.

"Of course, we couldn't refuse Rosa," he said. "But before she showed up with Vicente, we had no idea that she'd been sleeping with him. And we had no idea the man was still alive. They said he was dead. His funeral was all over the news, for God's sake." He shook his head, and his eyes occasionally crossed in a drunken expression of bewilderment. Suddenly, in his stupor, he was struck with a question. He raised his empty glass, his tongue seeking the rim for that last drop. "So if everyone thought he was dead, how do you know him? When did you meet him?"

"I don't know if we are talking about the same Vicente," Bladimir said. "I don't know anything about a funeral. I met him at El Terminal. Tell me about this funeral."

"I don't know about the funeral. I mean not first hand. I only know what Rosa told me. I guess I can tell you that Vicente is not who he appears to be. Well, at least he changed a lot. Let's just say that he closed a chapter of his life years ago. I doubt that he even realizes it. You can see that, right? He's not 100% here." Ricardo pointed to his temple, and dropped his chin to his chest, and Bladimir thought he might be about to nod off. Instead, he straightened and became serious. "Sorry, BJ. I don't know what came over me. Too much wine. No funeral. Just the end of something and beginning of something else." He grinned sheepishly and raised his empty glass in a mock toast.

Bladimir could only assume that Ricardo and Carolina had an abundance of respect for Rosa's privacy, even after she died. The bedroom was not exactly a monument to her but they obviously guarded it—an homage perhaps. Although, truth be told, how sacred could a space be if you rented it out to a stranger? They must have needed the money more than they let on.

Ricardo was slumped over the kitchen table and Bladimir quietly got up and walked around to pat him on the shoulder, *"Buenas noches,"* he said softly. Ricardo mumbled and managed a half smile in return. Bladimir gave him an extra pat, feeling the cotton texture of Ricardo's shirt under his fingers and wondering how many years Ricardo had worn that same shirt.

In the few weeks he'd been here, Bladimir had softened. All his life, he'd harbored a deep resentment for the people who lived in this end of town. This was where wealthy people were supposed to live—rich, selfish and mostly heartless people, who cared nothing for the well-being of society itself. All of these people had it easy. These were the people Bladimir was fighting against, these were the ones who needed to walk in the shoes of the less fortunate others, who needed to learn a lesson about empathy, who needed to change the rules and who needed to understand why people like him were fighting a revolution, fighting to turn the tables. Now he wondered if a revolution would really solve the problem or if it would become the same problem on its head. He'd never become acquainted with any of these people before. And of course, he'd never sympathized with them. Why should he? They had everything. He had nothing. But lately, he saw things differently. Maybe it was all relative. But was it worth the death of someone like Rosa? He felt so heavy with guilt by the time he'd walked those twenty steps to the back bedroom, that his knees nearly gave out on him. Nothing to do with the wine. He pushed past the door and dropped down on the edge of the bed.

During these past few weeks, it was like he'd been sitting on a different hill, at a different height, with a different view. He saw turmoil and he saw hard work, he saw struggle and felt pain. This time it wasn't only for people who were born into his situation but it was for people like Ricardo and Carolina, for hard-working people whose only fault was to be born here and not there. Nothing else. Ironically, it was Bladimir, who possessed diamonds and who was privileged to make generous cash withdrawals at will. His wealth might have been ill-gotten but he justified it by saying that all the rich people at this end of town got their money through corruption, collusion and unfair advantage. They had access to places he had no access to. Maybe the access part still held true. But he realized that he couldn't paint them all with the same brush. And what about Elena? She had been born into privilege. But look at her now. He compared her to his mother, who had also disappeared into the obscure bliss of drugs.

Unable to sleep, he switched on the bedside lamp and reached for Rosa's diary. He started at the beginning.

33 | ROSA'S DIARY

March 16, 2020

ENTRY: NOVEMBER 1, 1963

Querido Diario.

It was lucky that I was here today because this morning, a little girl was born to los patrones. La Señora was not going to make it to the hospital because of the amount of construction along the road. The doctor was late coming to the house for the same reason. So I delivered the baby right here with no mishaps. Lucky I had some training in my mother's house.

Lucky too, that la Señora hired me last week to replace the no-good little thief that she had to get rid of. I will be loyal to this household. I feel in my bones that this is where I am meant to stay. And now, with the baby, I have been brought to the bosom of the family.
–END OF ENTRY–

Bladimir noted, with a sense of misplaced familiarity, that he shared the same birthday as baby Elena. Maybe his mother had registered him correctly. Maybe not. The Day of the Dead. All Saints' Day. But there it was, and—not that he had ever celebrated his birthday like most other little boys who were given birthday parties with cake and invited friends—every year Bladimir marked his day with a private celebration. Most years he just bought himself an extra dessert and savored it slowly, congratulating himself, mocking the situation, "Happy Birthday young man." That was the extent of it. Once upon a time, he thought that he (and therefore his birthday) might go down in history. A few decades ago, he realized it was not destined to be so but somewhere in his heart, he harbored a faint shadow of hope that he would be revered as a savior, just as his mother had envisioned. Even though one might be estranged from one's mother for whatever reason, it's natural that one still yearns to please her.

ENTRY: NOVEMBER 3, 1963

Querido Diario,

There has been so much to take care of, what with the new baby girl. They decided to call her Elena Eugenia. She is a scrawny thing and fidgety. She does not take easily to her mother's breast. But they will both learn. —END OF ENTRY–

ENTRY: NOVEMBER 8, 1963

Querido Diario,

It was my intention to write to you every day. But I find this impossible, what with all of the chores and extra duties because of the baby. I do love her, though. Already. Who could not love an innocent child? I am exhausted by the time my day comes to an end and I find that my energy cannot be extended enough to write to you. I can only flop into bed and wish that the nights were longer.—END OF ENTRY–

Then there were longer gaps between Rosa's entries. Most days and weeks, she did not write anything at all. In fact, in some cases, the gaps were longer than a year. She did not apologize for her lack of continuity. Perhaps she remembered the diary when she was moved by something remarkable and she desired to share it. Bladimir speculated that she was lonely. She never mentioned friends. And she didn't mention Ricardo or Carolina until several years after she had begun to write. Therefore, Bladimir concluded that Rosa was indeed a solitary soul—perhaps like himself. He developed a fondness for the younger woman who was the writer of these accounts but he reserved judgement about the older woman she must have become. As someone who tended towards the common adage, 'what goes around comes around,' Bladimir attempted to feel less guilty about his role in her death and to let her assume some of it. Some days he was more successful than others.

By now familiar with the contents of the diary, Bladimir flipped forward several pages.

ENTRY: NOVEMBER 8, 1967

Querido Diario,

Try as I might to avoid it, I must admit a certain attraction to my patrón. Señor Vicente is a kind man who unexpectedly treats even the household staff with courtesy and consideration. Today, he stopped in the rose garden where I was choosing some flowers for the vase in the foyer. He asked after my family. Of course, without giving details, I told him that my family was fine, thank you. He asked if I enjoyed being a member of his household and I told him that I did. I also mentioned that his little girl, Elena, was a darling child, worthy of much love and affection. He smiled and asked me to make a small pouch of potpourri for the little girl and put it under her pillow. I did that. I will see if she notices. —END OF ENTRY–

Other than her first entry, where she stated the name of her employers, this was Rosa's first mention of Vicente by name. She did so with fondness and he wondered if she surprised even herself with this. Bladimir too, would not have expected that Vicente Lenz-Webber, then a public figure, a well-respected senator of the Republic, would take his time to show interest in, and converse with, household staff. Household staff was, after all, the responsibility of his wife. Bladimir made note of the uncommon consideration shown by a person of stature, if not wealth. It was likely that Vicente was an exception to the rule, but what with the new realizations about Ricardo and Carolina, things were stacking up in favor of *cuicos* in this more affluent end of town, the ones who felt they were better than men like him. Bladimir had already begun to question his lifelong assumptions about anyone who lived east of Plaza Italia. The cracks that began to creep through the foundation of his resentment, unbalanced his perspective and the horizon began to tilt ever so slightly to the right.

For his part, Bladimir had only ever felt shunned, at very best, disregarded by people who were economically better off than himself, and as a child in a church group home, he was treated with very little sympathy by staff who themselves should not have (but did) consider themselves 'better than.'

By now, accustomed as he was to painting everyone with a wide brush, he reluctantly had to admit that perhaps he should use a finer one, in which case, he'd find both disdain and respect spattered all across the spectrum.

Although it was perhaps inherent, Rosa did not specifically call out the differences between her working class and the class of the household in which she lived and for whom she performed her duties.

ENTRY: JUNE 16, 1968

Querido Diario,

El Señor returned from El Congreso in the center of Santiago. He was angry and went directly to his office without a word to anyone. He slammed the door. Later I caught Elena entering his office and I followed to get her out of his way. I came upon Señor Vicente arguing with la Señora about garden sheers and some roses that Elena had in her hand. La Señora left the room angry and I stayed. Señor Vicente needs me.

Lately, I have noticed an unusual closeness between la Señora and Don Marco, Señor Vicente's doctor friend. Don Marco comes to the house during the day and lounges in the garden and drinks tea with la Señora. I have seen him reach out and hold her hand. She acts like a kitten in his presence. She almost purrs. Yes, Señor Vicente needs me. Today we both felt a connection. —END OF ENTRY–

ENTRY: DECEMBER 20, 1968

Querido Diario,

The house has been decorated for Christmas but the plan is for the family to go to their summer residence on the coast on the 25th. I will not go this year. La Señora granted permission for me to stay in their house in Santiago, where I will enjoy free time but also ensure everything here is in order for their return. I plan to visit Ricardo and Carolina. It's been a very, very long time since I've seen them. Now that they have moved from Talcahuano to Providencia, we will have more opportunities to see each other. I'm excited. —END OF ENTRY–

ENTRY: JANUARY 10, 1969

Querido Diario,

I brought in the New Year with Ricardo and Carolina. I can't believe it's already 1969. I have tried not to pay attention to it but the country is in turmoil. The politicians are like tigers at each others' throats. No one agrees, new political parties are forming, breaking away of other parties. I don't pretend to understand. Señor Vicente came home from the beach right after the New Year. Nowadays, he spends much time in his office. I hear him on the phone. Many important guests arrive and I take them to his office where they lock themselves in for ages, discussing and drinking tea or wine. I often serve them sandwiches and refreshments late at the night.

Yesterday was the first day that no one came to the house. I served Señor Vicente tea on the terrace and he invited me to sit with him. I was surprised but very happy. He told me that I am like a shelter from the storm and he looked at me with fondness. Then he touched my wrist and smiled. He has a disarming smile and I felt myself melt. I felt myself blush too, and I was ashamed. I told him, "Señor Vicente, you are doing a good job." The truth is that I have no idea what he has done but I know it must be good because he is a good person. Anyway, he smiled at me some more. "Let's not talk about my work," he told me. "Tell me about your family." I think he needed a distraction. So I told him about my brother Ricardo and his new wife Carolina. It told him my father had land outside of Talcahuano and that he died three years ago and Ricardo and I sold the land. It was enough for Ricardo and Carolina to buy a house and for me to put something in the bank. Señor Vicente said something about a land reform bill but I didn't understand if it was good for us or bad for us. Ricardo works in a warehouse and Carolina makes aprons and sells them to a store downtown. They can't have children and this has made them sad. I don't know why I told Señor Vicente so much but he seemed interested.— END OF ENTRY–

Bladimir wondered fleetingly why Ricardo and Carolina had not adopted a child. There were many children without homes in those days. Most kids were brought up in state homes run by the police but others were in group homes run by the Catholic Church. It was Bladimir's bad luck to have ended up in the latter. And here, he made sense of the ideology professed by his mother. Here, he became intolerant and rebellious. They tried to beat him down but he ran away from that place, which was supposed to be run by kind, spiritual people. It was really more about their power, money, properties and connections to even more powerful people. They took advantage of innocent children. There was no denying his experience. Therefore, there was no negating his point of view.

ENTRY: MARCH 13, 1969

Querido Diario,

Señor Vicente is in Brazil on business and Don Marco has been here several nights in a row. La Señora instructs me to retire after I serve them refreshments on the terrace. The evenings are turning cooler now and I hear the two of them coming indoors. Last night, I got up to close a window and I heard them in the master bedroom. This should not surprise me. I've seen it building up. It makes me sad for Señor Vicente. On the other hand, there seems to be no love lost between him and la Señora. And little Elena is feeling this, I know. She has been unsettled and has been misbehaving. It's worse when Señor Vicente is not at home. So I've been spending more time with her. Lately, she has even been refusing to go to school but each morning, I bribe her. I tell her I will have news of her father upon her return. Then I make things up, and it settles her. I take her out to the garden, where we cut roses and I teach her to dry the petals and make potpourri, a gift for her father when he gets back.

I have heard Señor's name mentioned on the radio lately. Many other senators are speaking out against him. I prefer not to hear this. It's upsetting and I don't understand. —END OF ENTRY–

Bladimir returned over and over to the entries that Rosa made around this period. He allowed the information to fall into place as the identities of the players she either named outright, or hinted at, finally became clear. Bladimir was only a child at that time. In those days, he was still running away from the group home. Giorgio, on the other hand, was building his reputation. And when he first took Bladimir under his wing, he used to brag about his rapid inroads and the efficient formation of his business.

According to Giorgio, early 1969 was a turning point. Bladimir had always understood this to mean that the business itself had taken wing. But probably what he was referring to was a personal turning point because this was when he lost his eyesight.

ENTRY: APRIL 30, 1969

Querido Diario,

It has taken days for my hands to stop shaking enough for me to pick up this pen and write. For Vicente's safety and well-being, what has happened must be guarded within these pages. Only six people know the truth. And one of them will very never comprehend it. At least, not if I do my job well. I will try to explain but it's so upsetting that I may have to spread this over several days.

La Señora and el Señor had a big fight. I heard them yelling but the words were muffled because I was downstairs with Elena and the two of them were behind the closed door of their bedroom on the second floor. I took little Elena out to the calm of the rose garden. The garden is between the house and the garage. As we played behind the rose bushes, a car roared up the driveway and stopped on the other side of the garage. It was a fancy blue American sports car, convertible. That's all I know. I heard two men get out of the car. Then one got back inside and the other man stood beside it and looked around. I made sure that Elena and I stayed out of sight. Luckily, she was playing with a ladybird and was concentrated and quiet. The man stood near the small door of the garage. He stayed there smoking. I dared not approach him. He was not the type of man who usually visits this house. I think he must have been a bad man. Perhaps even a criminal. Lately, with all of the reports on the radio about people who were angry with Vicente, I thought this man was here to do harm. I whispered to Elena that we should play a hiding game. She just nodded because she was engrossed with the little lady bug that was now crawling over the palm of her hand. I apologize, Querido Diario, but I have to pause. My heart is pounding with the memory of it. —END OF ENTRY–

Bladimir noted that Rosa did not call Vicente 'Señor' but rather the familiar, 'Vicente'. Something had changed in their relationship between the latest entries. Something that she didn't need to explain.

ENTRY: MAY 25, 1969

Querido Diario,

I am writing you from the safety of my new home. I could not write sooner because too much has happened. But now I can tell you every-thing. I am writing from Ricardo and Carolina's house. I moved here four weeks ago with Vicente.

Ricardo has almost finished refurbishing the back bedroom, which is ours. Ours. Vicente is my partner, Querido Diario. He trusts me fully and I am taking care of him. After what happened, he will never be the same. But for me, he is the loving man I have always known. I saved his life, Querido Diario. And in a way, he saved mine.

That day when the two men drove up in the North American car and when Elena and I were in the garden, was the day of the tragedy. The bad man was waiting by the garage, looking around and smoking like he had all the time in the world. The sun was shining, the birds were singing, the garden was buzzing with bees, and except for the two strange men, it would have been a lovely fall day. But it turned into a horror after Vicente burst out the side door beside the garden, with his leather bag in hand. He was almost at a run and he didn't see the blue car because it was on the other side of the garage and he didn't notice the man standing between the tall juniper and the garage door. The man who was waiting there, threw down his cigarette and stepped right into Vicente's path, startling him. Vicente almost lost his balance when he stepped back. And suddenly Elena was running out towards the garage. She wasn't crying or yelling. I think her intention was to go and hug Vicente.

I had to get her. The man was threatening Vicente. Elena must have sensed danger because she suddenly changed direction and she ran past the strange man and into the garage and she huddled in the corner. Lucky neither of the men paid attention to her.

I snuck towards the garage and then I remembered the tub of lye. I had secured it ages ago in a wooden box with a padlock. I thought I would throw lye in the man's face. But I couldn't open the box. I didn't have the key. That's when I saw the metal rod leaning against the box. I don't know what came over me. I grabbed it and marched up to where Vicente and the man were standing. The man was swearing at him. I just marched, mind you. As though I wasn't terrified. As though I was in control. I just came around and stepped in front of the bad man, and with two sharp jabs, I stabbed his eyes out. It all happened so fast. He howled and I whispered urgently to Vicente, "Run! Run!" So he did. He ran inside the garage. I don't know what happened there. I was worried about Elena and deathly scared of the man. He was plucking at his eye sockets. I pushed him towards the blue car and he swore and fell face-down onto the gravel. He screamed that he couldn't see, that his eyes were burning. He cursed and swore at the top of his voice. I won't repeat the words here. The other man ran around the car, lugged the injured man up and shoved him into the passenger seat. He didn't even notice me. Probably he did but he didn't have time to do anything. I was lucky. He gunned the engine and there was a rain of gravel as the car took off. Just before that, Vicente had sped off in his car.

I don't know how much time passed. But I saw Elena running down the driveway and she tripped and fell on the gravel and she was crying when I reached her. Tears had dirtied her cheeks. She was panicked. Poor little thing.

The next thing I know, the police were at the house. They said Vicente had been in an accident. And I don't know when Don Marco arrived. Maybe with the police. He said he would take care of everything because he was the medical examiner.

And that's when it got even crazier.

—END OF ENTRY–

Bladimir remembered standing in front of Vicente's mausoleum with Elena, reading the name above the entrance, and how, rather than relating it the former senator, he had chosen to poke fun at her German origins. He regretted it now. Trying to associate her family, even in jest, to Paul Schaefer was unforgivable. The leader of Colonia Dignidad, who set up his cult in the Maule region in 1961 was later convicted of, among other things, child sexual abuse. He was also rumored to have hidden some of Pinochet's victims in unmarked graves on his land. Someone once even claimed to have found on this land, the rifle that was used to assassinate J.F. Kennedy.

There was no shortage of rumors but it was bad style to have tried to make a joke of it, and Bladimir wished he had kept his mouth shut. That aside, Rosa's diary carried on to spell out how Vicente Harold Lenz-Webber, esteemed member of the Christian Democrat Party and valued senator of the Republic, came to have his name engraved on a grand family mausoleum in the General Cemetery of Santiago.

ENTRY: MAY 30, 1969

Querido Diario,

As I look at Vicente, asleep in our bed, I'm grateful for all that happened. Both good and bad. Because it delivered him into my arms, into my care. I will protect him until the day I die. He is everything to me, even if he is not the man he used to be. He is mine now.

I had to agree to lie about everything. It was the only way. So I'm not ashamed. And I'm not sorry. At first, I wasn't sure. But in the end, I had to put my trust in others who also had something to gain... or lose. Our pact will never be broken. Those who played an important role are Don Marco, la Señora and myself. Ricardo and Carolina only have one foot in the plot because the whole thing was concocted before they got involved. But they agreed and so they are guardians just the same. And Vicente.... well, he's the kingpin. But he'll never know it.

The day that the two men disappeared down the road in their blue car was tragic. Vicente had sped off and was shaken and unable to control his own car and he crashed into a tree about two kilometers from the house. That's when everything became what it was not.

Don Marco arranged to examine Vicente in his private room. I didn't know that doctors had such private rooms but Don Marco arranged one somehow. Because of his desire for la Señora de Vicente, and hers for him, Don Marco was actually going to allow Vicente to die. I'm sure of it. It would have been so convenient. But I followed them to Don Marco's office and I saw that Vicente was alive and breathing. He was trying to speak but he couldn't form words. He didn't recognize la Señora, Don Marco or myself. His soul had gotten lost in his body and he was struggling to find a way to make himself whole. And he was in pain.

At first when she saw me, la Señora was hysterical and she called me in-trusive and she called me delusional and other nasty names. And Don Marco tried to physically force me to leave. I slapped him and pushed him away and went to Vicente's side and I could feel the warmth of his hand. I felt the injuries on his neck and face and top of his head. I stood beside him and faced Don Marco and la Señora. The Señora knew that I loved him. And if it hadn't been for me, I think they would have let Vicente die... from neglect if not directly from his injuries. They were plotting to let him rot there.

And that was when the deal was made. It was either that, or kill me too. And how would they explain that? Finally, she came up with the idea. She would get what she wanted too. But it all came at a price.

We decided that Vicente would be declared dead as a result of the ac-cident. This way, he would be forever free of the threat from his enemies. Don Marco said Vicente had severe brain injuries and that he would never be whole ever again. He wasn't sure what Vicente would ever be capable of, or what he would remember. But I knew that I could help him and protect him. And I knew I had to convince Ricardo to help us.

Don Marco arranged for la Señora to identify the body of a homeless man that he had pulled out from a niche in the morgue. The man's body was meant to be dumped into a common grave the next day. Don Marco wrote a death certificate to say that Vicente had died from mul-tiple injuries as a result of the crash. Now the homeless man's body would rest in a crypt in the Lenz family mausoleum and he probably wouldn't mind that. And Vicente would come with me to Ricardo's and Carolina's house. —END OF ENTRY–

Each time Bladimir read these last two entries, he was freshly amazed at the audacity of the plan and how all the pieces had fallen into place. But more, he was amazed that after these decades Vicente's undoing was still unknown, even to himself. Bladimir began to sum all of the events and measure them against the facts of today. For reasons unknown to Vicente himself, Bladimir understood—or thought he understood— why Vicente was compelled to watch Giorgio.

Back in the 1960s, Giorgio was just beginning his career as everyone's fixer. And also back then, Vicente had already exposed one senator, which meant he was a potential threat for others. One, or several important people would have hired Giorgio to fix the problem. Perhaps they asked Giorgio to threaten Vicente and his family. Perhaps he was hired to do more. The names of the people who hired him would be among the documents that he kept stashed somewhere in the back room of El Terminal. Giorgio was untouchable from that moment on. And his business expanded with impunity in whatever direction he saw fit.

ENTRY: AUGUST 12, 1969

Querido Diario,

I am certain that Vicente will never be himself again. Outside of when Don Marco arranged to deliver a broken Vicente for an examination in his private room, Vicente has not seen a doctor. And we can't afford to expose him to one. So his condition will never be fully explained. But it doesn't matter. He—and his brain, such as it is—will be safe with me.

For the first two weeks, I had to leave him alone in the care of Carolina and Ricardo because la Señora was afraid it would look suspicious if I left her employment right away. But it was all extremely awkward. They cremated the remains of the homeless man who they had identified as Vicente. The funeral was held within two days. We performed perfectly for the press. Hundreds of people arrived to pay their respects. I felt sorry for cheating them this way but they didn't know what was behind the whole affair. People left beautiful bouquets at the cemetery and for days on end, more fresh flowers appeared at the roadside, at the spot where the accident happened.

I didn't want to leave Elena. She was so confused. I think she was traumatized long after I left the employ of her mother. I made la Señora promise never to leave the girl's side and always to share good memories of her father. I don't know if she will keep this promise. I hope so.

La Señora accused me of blackmailing her and Don Marco. At the same time, she said that no one would ever believe me if I said that they were about to let Vicente die right there in Don Marco's examination room.

Still, she could never be sure, and the fact that she and Don Marco were seen together in public almost immediately after Vicente's death would be enough to cast doubt on her side of the story. Each month, she will deposit money into my bank account. I should have insisted on more but it's enough to keep Vicente and I fed and sheltered. And anyway, I suspect it's only a small percentage of the insurance and estate that she benefited from. But I don't begrudge her that because I know that it is also for the girl. Elena was the apple of Vicente's eye and above all, he would want her to be well cared for. And now, at last, after everything, I have Vicente to myself.

I am so tired, Querido Diario. Now I will concentrate on creating a quiet, peaceful life for all of us. For Ricardo and Carolina too. I wish I could say that Elena was part of it. But she cannot be. Her mother insisted that she live the lie that we created. That, too, was part of the deal. It would be too complicated otherwise, she said. And after all, but sadly, she is right. —END OF ENTRY–

The memory of a woman on a stretcher, hat having fallen and rolled to the street, ribbon snaking lazily through the smoke and dust swirling around her, tormented Bladimir even more than the disappearance of his mother. He felt that he knew Rosa now. And sadly she was one of his sacrificial lambs in the name of the revolution. She was the only one he ever got close to, and sleeping in her bed is definitely what you'd call close. Since living in Ricardo's house, eating his food, sharing conversations and staying in this room, the concept of individual sacrifice for greater good was more and more unsavory. Only a few months ago, before he knew this family, it was the only logic that made sense. He reflected on the extreme circumstances that led him and Rosa and Vicente to this same refuge. The refuge in which they all sought protection from the same man. Giorgio.

Giorgio must be going crazy with the failure of his manhunt so far. Something would have to break soon.

34 | WHEN SHE LEFT

March 19 or 20, 2020

Elena was sick, vomiting over the side of the footbridge. It was early in the morning of March 19th or March 20th. She was angry. She'd been up half the night with unbearable stomach cramps and a pounding headache. Why had she not slipped into her usual state of blissful unconsciousness? What had Flaco sold her? It must have been that mixture of pills that he had counted out and handed over with his grubby, bony fingers. What else would make her so sick?

She needed fresh air. She needed to feel mist on her face, and a cool breeze to turn back the ugly waves of nausea. She slipped herself a nice tranquilizer well before she turned the lock on her apartment door and waited for the effect to take hold. That's when she made her way to the canal and stood leaning over the wooden railing, watching the water swirl lazily up and along the walls. She had no reason to be here, no reason to be at home either. She had no reason. Period. Perhaps she should lean forward just enough so that the authorities would declare her death an accidental spill—"Silly, really. A waste," more than one of them would remark. "The canal just claimed another life."

She unclasped her handbag and, out of habit, felt around for her mobile phone. She must have left it at home. She closed one eye and squinted down to watch the water flow by. It was hard to tell which plane she was on. She liked the idea of floating between planes and she sighed and half smiled to herself. Was death going to be this easy? Suddenly she was conscious of someone at her back. Startled, she turned and found herself looking into BJ's eyes. Oh, those eyes. She had not entirely stopped thinking about them.

They were smiling at her, maybe making fun. She would have kissed him but his eyes suddenly turned steely and she froze with fear.

The following all happened within seconds.

There was a heavy rumbling as the blue convertible slowed to a stop; Bladimir clenched his jaw and turned around without a word; the sound of two car doors opening, followed by hoarse whispers. "Here he is! *El hueón está aquí!*" More expletives and, louder now, hurried instructions; his hands at her hips, Bladimir pushed off, and bolted towards the east side of the canal. At the same time, Elena was gripped by a memory; her father running blindly into the garage; he swung open the door of his car and threw a bag inside. Then, the sound of a motor and the sight of the blue car from the corner of her eye, the past and the present colliding in a single dissonant moment. She stared as the convertible pointed its nose onto Tobalaba, its purr building to a roar as it turned sharply to disappear east, along San Gabriel.

Drawn back into the memory, her whole body shook as a familiar, dense ache surfaced, and she watched BJ disappear into a side street, just as her father had disappeared in his big old Mercedes, fading into the distance of the driveway, never to return. The past crashing its way into the present— her father panicking as he drove away and BJ loping off, zig-zagging into the distance without looking back. She slumped down on the footbridge and started to cry.

It was impossible to say if several minutes or several hours had passed before she felt footfalls approaching along the bridge. She was too exhausted and afraid to look up, afraid to hope that BJ had gone full circle and had returned to rescue her from herself, half hoping and half afraid that he would cause her to change her plans. She felt a gentle tap on her shoulder like that of a child trying to wake up his groggy mother who had swallowed too many pills, who would rather just roll over and sleep forever. She didn't move. The tap was repeated. Gently.

"You're going to drop your belongings." It was Vicente, indicating her purse, eyes wide, looking worried from the other side of his big round, smudged lenses. He shrugged his packsack higher as he shifted his weight and bent in closer. He looked like he was planning to settle down for a conversation, awkward as she imagined that might be.

"Why are you here on the bridge?" She asked. She didn't want him to see her crying.

Apparently he didn't notice. "Look," he said. He produced a small gingham drawstring bag and held it to her nose. "It's potpourri. I made it myself."

She turned slowly and, without looking into Vicente's face, she reached up to hold it. The pure scent of red roses, the kind she used to cut with the forbidden shears from the garden of the big house when she was a child. She inhaled trying to absorb it. It awakened a clear memory of her father sitting at his desk, his blue eyes smiling at her and then him bending down to pull something from the middle desk drawer, just like the man standing here now. He had bent down a little to magically produce this bag of potpourri. She gasped and dropped the little pouch.

The moment was cut short by the sound of the same blue convertible as it pulled to a halt along the service road bordering the east side of the canal. The motor rumbled. A tall man got out of the driver's side, walked around and then paused to lean in and talk to the man whose arm rested casually out the window of the passenger side. The man inside the car lifted his hand to touch gemstones on the corner his cats eye sunglasses. Elena could hear him. He said, "He's not here. He's gone. Get back in the car. He's down here somewhere. *Mierda!*"

Vicente and Elena recoiled at the sound of his voice, and glanced at each other but neither of them could offer anything to soften it, so they both looked away. Suddenly and without an obvious reason, Vicente dropped the packsack and began to run along the bridge towards the car. Elena tried to follow but the handle of her purse caught on a nail on the railing and she had to yank it several times before it ripped free. Vicente was already on the road, chasing the Mustang. Elena was far behind him, willing her legs to move faster. She felt like she was running in slow motion, straining and pushing but not advancing. Finally, she tripped over her own feet and fell. She rolled over and sat upright, tears rolling down her cheeks, trousers torn and her knees scraped and bleeding. She leaned forward and sobbed helplessly and began to pick pebbles from her skin. When she finally looked up, she saw Vicente still giving chase down a side street, the car long gone.

Her mind jumped back and forth between the image of Vicente, who was getting smaller and smaller in the distance, and her recurring dream in which her younger self sat, impotent, on a gravel driveway, knees bleeding, skin torn. She remained there for some time, doubled over on the side of the road. The streets were quiet when she finally got to her feet and returned to the footbridge. She saw Vicente's packsack sitting where he had dropped it and she decided to stay and guard it for him.

By the time he showed up, the sun was high in the sky and the city was awake. Several strangers had passed her by, some of them had greeted her, and she ignored them. When Vicente finally returned, he was like a madman. He didn't even acknowledge her.

He recognized the footbridge but he seemed unable to place himself in the moment, his thoughts were in another time, another place. He picked up the packsack and brushed by Elena with a quick glance. Then he paused, turned around and said, "I'm looking for my daughter. Have you seen my daughter?" Elena just shook her head. She was tired. Dead tired. And confused. She needed to go home.

When she unlocked the door to her apartment, she sighed with relief. The curtains were drawn and the apartment was dim. A refuge. She was about to collapse on a kitchen chair when she felt someone's presence and when she turned, she faced a man lounging back into the sofa.

"You left some notes on the floor," he said. He had a bunch of pages crumpled in his fist and he released them so they fell at his feet.

"Oh, yeah, I tend to do that." Today she didn't care.

The man was sitting in the corner opposite the window, casually taking in the condition of her apartment. Judging her. He had her mobile phone in his hand. Had she forgotten to take it this morning?

"Is this the normal state of things?" He asked.

"Yeah, pretty much."

"You live like an animal."

She allowed a silence to extend for the time it took for her to walk into her bedroom and back again without any purpose. "What are you doing here?" It didn't occur to ask how he had gotten in.

He ignored the question. "The point is that you need to stop calling attention to yourself and your problems."

"I don't know what you mean." She looked at him blankly. Already today's events had added up to something intolerable. And finding him here was over the top.

"I know where you're getting your drugs, Elena. It's bad news. It's too close to home."

She sank onto the sofa and stared at her feet. Then she began to wring her hands. What did he want?

"I've tolerated your irresponsible behavior for years but I've reached my limit now."

She looked up.

"So has your mother."

"What are you talking about, Don Marco?"

"Do you think Flaco doesn't know who you are?"

"What? Flaco? You know Flaco?"

"Everyone knows Flaco." Don Marco carefully placed her mobile phone on the corner table. "Look," he said. "I have contacts on both sides of the river and east and west of Plaza Italia. In my position, I have to know what people are up to. I have to protect my reputation, not to mention your mother's. And because of your weakness and stupidity, it's in danger of crashing down around us. People are talking to me."

"What? Who? I have no idea what you're talking about. Plus, I'm just really tired, Don Marco. You have no idea..."

"Yes, I do have an idea, Elena. I do have an idea."

"Do me a favor then and agree to talk about whatever it is you want to talk about later. Another day. Okay? I can't take any more today."

He was suddenly all smiles. "Listen. Okay, then. Let me help you out. I understand you've had a hard day. We all get those. I did you the courtesy of bringing a bottle of wine. I also have some yellows in my pocket. That's what Flaco calls them, isn't it? Yellows?"

Elena was hopeful. "Yes, yes he has yellows. But he sold me something the other day. I mean, I don't know what he sold me but it wasn't right. Yellows might help calm the waters. I'd be grateful, Don Marco."

He rose from the sofa with as much grace as the situation required and rummaged through a drawer in search of a corkscrew. Then he pulled out a vial of pills. "Let's have a drink, shall we? Let's toast to your mother. She's worried about you. She's always worried about you." He lied. "She was going to come over but she had one of her headaches and I told her I would check on you today."

Elena nodded.

Don Marco found two glasses and filled them both. "*Salud*," he said, and he raised his glass.

"*Salud*," she said and she sipped at hers.

He rattled the vial in front of her face, teasing, and he grinned. "Take three of these, Elena. If the day has been as bad as you say, then these will take the edge off."

"Three? Are you sure?"

"I'm a doctor."

"Thank you." She swallowed the pills and he nodded for her to empty her glass. He refilled it. And then again.

"And... Elena, if the day has been as bad as all that, I would recommend that you take the rest of these." He handed her the vial. She accepted it and swallowed several pills without counting, smiling demurely as he proceeded to make small talk and casually dust the cupboards and wipe off the table with his handkerchief. He picked up the mobile phone again and dropped it in his pocket. He paused for a second before sliding her wallet out of her bag and dropping it into his other pocket. He wandered into the bedroom and took a last look around before returning to the living room, pausing and looking out the window. The street was quiet. He didn't notice a small elderly man with a goatee and Windsor glasses standing in the shadows across the street. That Don Marco abruptly drew the curtains was purely coincidental.

Vicente wasn't sure if the window where the curtains had just been drawn was, in fact, Elena's apartment. He willed it to be. So yes. Yes, it was her place. His gut fluttered and cramped, and he felt a familiar sensation of dread and helplessness. After the day's upsetting events, he hadn't known where to turn. Maybe if she ventured out of her apartment, they could go to the cafe, fall into their strangely familiar, comfortable silence.

Don Marco patted Elena on the head and then he left, the latch clicking solidly into place as he locked the door with the key he'd lifted from Elena's mother's purse. He dropped it into his pocket and sighed. His shoes clapped softly on the polished terrazzo as he hummed his way downstairs and slipped out the main entrance. He had just closed the gate at the front of the building when a small man in glasses and white goatee bumped into him. He was trying to hurry past, unnoticed, just as pickpockets do. Don Marco turned with a start and instinctively grabbed both of the old man's hands and held them firmly at his side. "What are you doing?" Don Marco demanded. Vicente was about to apologize but he stood with his mouth open, no words escaping as he looked at Don Marco.

Vicente tried to rise onto his toes and peer more closely at the other man's face. "Do I know you?" he asked. He wanted to reach up and rub his lenses but the man was still holding his hand against his ribs. Vicente's sense of dread increased and he cowered. He felt sick.

"We do not know each other and I want you to step back. I'll let go of you if you promise not to lunge at me again."

His hands still restrained, Vicente coughed a few times as he looked up into the man's face and he struggled to find his voice. "I'm sorry," he said. "I didn't mean to frighten you."

"You didn't frighten me. You startled me. There's a difference." He glared into his face to make his point and then released Vicente's hands with a feeble shove, one old man to another. And he wiped his face with the palm of his hand. The insolence of this vagabond.

Vicente grimaced and apologized again under his breath as he stood back and allowed the man to pass. Don Marco walked swiftly to the end of the block, unlocked the door of an old model black Mercedes and got in. The man caused Vicente a certain kind of mental distress, something he was unable to pinpoint. Growing disquiet waved up across his chest. Incoming. Be careful. Don't drown.

Vicente watched as the man adjusted the rear view mirror, ran his fingers through his hair, rubbed his teeth with his index fingers, patted his nostrils, leaned over and fidgeted with something on the passenger seat, checked his reflection once more, readjusted the mirror, turned over the engine and without looking over his shoulder, maneuvered the big car out onto the street and it disappeared around the corner. Vicente turned his attention once again to the apartment window. It was quiet. No people moving inside, the curtains remained still. He kept watch for another hour until he decided there was nothing more to see. He was content just knowing where she was, and he assumed she would have a cup of tea, perhaps she would read, or maybe watch TV before settling down to sleep. She was safe inside. Satisfied, he shrugged his packsack so it was balanced evenly on his shoulders and he proceeded like an old soldier in the direction of the footbridge.

Elena didn't remember Don Marco leaving. But in the end, he had been unexpectedly kind and helpful. She would remember to tell her mother, perhaps give him a bit of credit, erase some of the foul things she had said about him in the past. After all, for all his criticisms, he generously left the vial that had several yellows and he advised her to finish them. So she did. He was a doctor after all. She was not responsible. She hummed a bit as she floated around in her increasingly light-headed ecstasy. She wouldn't have remembered when the bliss overtook her and when she fell. She wouldn't have felt her face hit the floor and she would have had no idea that her nose was broken and that it bled profusely. She definitely wouldn't have noticed when her heart stopped pumping and that the universe crowded in and began to do its job.

35 | THE PANDEMIC

March 20 or 21, 2020

Bladimir slithered through gaps in the fence around the same children's park where he had first met Fachita. He looked over at the swings, innocent as they were only a few weeks ago—before the tables had turned with Giorgio.

Bladimir had promised Carolina that he'd get cash for her, and he had been sure that going out in the early morning would have been safe. But he'd been wrong. And if he hadn't been tempted to stop at Vicente's hovel and if Fachita hadn't been on the footbridge, he wouldn't have lost those precious minutes and wouldn't have been in the wrong place at the wrong time. He still needed to make his way back with cash in hand, and hope Flaco and none of his cronies would see him. He had to suspect everyone.

The convenience shop at the gas station that was three blocks from the canal had a cash machine in the back corner and he made it in and out without incident. He even picked up a bottle of wine for Ricardo and two chocolate bars as a gift for Carolina. Thinking back on it, he wasn't sure what he'd been thinking. One thing in his favor was that the blue Mustang would stand out and he would hear it long before it could get close to him. It was the first time he'd seen the car and he wondered where Giorgio had come up with it. For sure, it wasn't Flaco's. But he couldn't fixate on the vehicle because probably it was just one of many, albeit the most remarkable, that would carry his hunters. No doubt they'd been promised bonuses. Giorgio was good with incentives. Anyway, it all added up to the fact that Bladimir needed to be cautious no matter what. He pulled his hood over his brow and took a roundabout route through side streets, finally crossing

Tobalaba and forcing his way through a couple of breaks in hedges before arriving back at the house. He let himself in the gate without looking back.

Ricardo and Carolina were in their bedroom, laughing at a television program. Bladimir left the chocolates and wine on the kitchen counter and rapped softly at their bedroom door.

"Hi BJ. We're watching an oldie."

"I have *plata* here for a few weeks' room and board. Should I give it to you now?" He lingered politely in the hallway.

Carolina shuffled to the bedroom door and he put the bills in her hand. She counted it. "A few weeks? Thanks. That's good."

"Good evening."

"Good evening," Ricardo chimed from the back.

Bladimir shivered. He undressed, climbed in bed and pulled the quilt over his head. He hadn't hidden under bedclothes since he was a boy. The weight and dark was smothering. In spite of it, he still felt vulnerable and exposed. He pulled the quilt tighter and gagged on the heat that rose from his belly. He stayed there, curled up, and in the fever of his fear, he was unable to sleep.

He thought more about fear. He thought more about family. He thought more about age. He thought that even Giorgio wouldn't live forever. The man was in his 80s. How was it that guys like him lived longer than kinder, more gentle souls whose presence was more appreciated? It wasn't what the world needed. But maybe the afterlife had a stronger case—guys like Giorgio weren't wanted in the afterlife either—and the afterlife won out, had longer fences, higher walls. So guys like Giorgio hung in here, trapped in their unhappy lives, their menace protracted as they continued to profit from other people's misery. But then he thought about Vicente and calculated that he had to be Giorgio's age, too and he was another old guy who refused to surrender to an afterlife, which in his case, might have welcomed him with open arms, might have unlatched its heavy gates and swung them wide, "Make way for one of the good guys." It was hard to imagine what might keep Vicente going. Perhaps life was simply a habit that he didn't know how to quit, his old cogs and hinges didn't know how to stop turning, were unable to grind around to that final curve. And what about himself? What did he have to look forward to? First and foremost, it was survival. But beyond that... what? Here he was, a 47-year-old nobody from nowhere with an official identity that he still questioned. It was likely that he would never be recognized or credited for who he really was, and lately he'd even had questions about that. No wonder no one else could see him.

Why then, did he suddenly feel like he had something to lose? And not the diamonds. And not the cash. And certainly not his reputation, at least not anymore.

For a few hours, he'd been making an effort to keep his eyes closed, hoping to be overcome by sleep, and to stop thinking. Suddenly he was hit with a realization and he gasped, he opened his eyes and blinked into the cotton fabric of the quilt. For the first time in his life, he felt like he had a home. A home with a family. He was undeserving but nevertheless, finally at his age, he had stumbled upon one. This is how it felt. This is what gripped him, scared him even, because it was so unfamiliar. This good feeling, a mixture of comfort, security and pleasure was also terrifying because now, having acknowledged it, he couldn't let it go. He needed to protect it.

He reflected on the short time he had been staying here, how he'd landed in this house and had grown roots. Without his consent. His wealth was stashed here too. He visualized the toy cat, flopped on the shelf where he left it, belly stuffed with diamonds. There was enough there to support himself and these people for years to come. He realized that he was thinking plural. Ricardo and Carolina and Vicente too, were as close to family as he'd ever had. He scoffed at how sentimental he'd become. He was supposed to be ideologically opposed to such people. Maybe that scared him. After all, his ideology was his touchstone. For as long as he could remember, it justified and qualified everything. What would he stand on if not his beliefs? The ground had shifted beneath him and now it was too late. His beliefs had been eroded, and like sand that had slid down a cliff, there was no pulling it back.

Besides all of that, suddenly Bladimir was, like it or not, a man with complicated family responsibilities. It was his fault that Ricardo and Carolina were in danger of an 80-something-year-old blind man with long sticky tentacles. Finally he closed his eyes again but he slept in fits and starts, coming out from under the quilt for air and huddling back down again in exhaustion and discomfort. At last, morning arrived and it was time to make a move. But he lingered a little longer so he could take pleasure in the soothing sound of soft voices from down the hall, so he could listen to congenial family conversation. Finally, Ricardo told Carolina that he was on his way to the canal. She did the dishes and he heard her leave too, probably to shop for today's meals. Then he ventured into the kitchen to help himself to tea and a sandwich, which he ate while listening to the radio.

The news was full of talk about the Coronavirus, a dangerous global contagion. Apparently, Chile had now joined the world in its pandemic. The first known case landed here almost three weeks ago, and it was about to spread like wildfire. With stubborn cultural norms where a kiss on the cheek was the polite, accepted form of greeting, where personal space was small, and where the predominant attitude was 'well, it won't touch me and if it does, I'll get over it', where the transient population and informal work meant the transfer of millions of people daily in crowded metros and buses, where impoverished families hung out with other impoverished families on cramped apartment stairwells because common space, crowded as it was, was less crowded than private space and where people simply refused to, or could not afford to stay home, Chile, like the rest world, was unwilling and unprepared.

The pandemic conveniently served another purpose, however. It slowed and finally brought the violent street protests to an end. If the government was reluctant to call a state of emergency, including a national curfew to prevent protestors and delinquents from destroying small businesses and burning churches and university buildings and private clinics, the coronavirus would do it for them. Troops were ordered out to protect the people from a virus. As it turned out, Covid-19 would be a political savior, the price for which, when tallied about three years later, would be the deaths of more than 60,000 *compatriotas*.

Politicians could not dare highlight the opportune arrival of this deadly virus. Instead, they would claim that the real reason for the calm on the streets was because one of their own had dreamed up a miraculous solution to the social unrest, to which the whole desperate crew clambered to sign on. Their brilliant solution was to write a new constitution. They allowed *el pueblo* to believe that it would magically and immediately provide all the answers to the country's social woes and inequities. And not only that—it would be written not by politicians but by regular people from regular neighborhoods. It would be a shining example of Chile's democracy in action. Politicians from across the entire political spectrum, in arranged photo ops, jubilantly signed their names to the plan and patted each other on the back. This constitution would give birth to a progressive new country in which everyone would share equally in the mineral, material and cultural wealth of the nation.

Bladimir was one of those who cheered on this new constitution. If written well, it would bring an end to inequality and hardship, blindness and ignorance, lack of access and discrimination. It would protect the environment and open doors for immigrants who were escaping untenable circumstances in their home countries. His hope was a sort of childish aspiration, in which the new *carta magna* would also miraculously erase corruption and greed. As if laws could reform unscrupulous individuals who threw wrenches into the works of a well-oiled society. Or perhaps even a heretofore unattainable and almost unrealistic existence in which we would all suddenly evolve into beings who could live in a beautiful, balanced anarchist state. It would be pluri-national and welcoming, it would be built around the good sense of Marxism. Chile would be the model of a just, perfectly functioning socialist nation. With that in mind, he pushed aside questions about Giorgio, and he hummed as he washed up his cup and saucer before returning to the bedroom to pick up on the business that had been interrupted the other day.

The manila folders. He lifted the lid of the footstool and removed the book of historic legends. The folders were still on their backs, vulnerable and willing, exactly where someone had placed them decades ago, just waiting to feel the soft brush of someone else's forefinger as it would carefully bend the top right corner to open and reveal their secrets. Bladimir lifted the folders from their hiding place and set them down, one beside the other at the foot of the bed. There was nothing written on the outside, no labels to warn him. He could sense the energy from each of the folders, relieved to have been discovered, eager to tell their tale. What, after all, does it all come down to, if not someone's story? "You see," they were telling him, "there is always more than meets the eye." He selected the folder in the center. He knelt down to open it up. He counted five loose pages, the top one was a completed form with a signature. The other four consisted of typewritten paragraphs. Narratives, he supposed. But he wasn't quite ready to read. He left it sitting open and shifted his attention to the folder on his left. It contained two pages, with space for signatures. He opened the third folder and saw what looked like a police report, consisting of a dozen or so pages.

With that in hand, he stepped back to sit on the chair, and he rested the folder on his lap to scan the first page. At the top was a faded photo of a young Giorgio, full name: Giorgio Ernesto Ramirez-Marino, born 1942 in Iquique, Chile. Bladimir squinted at the image in disbelief. He'd never seen Giorgio without his dark glasses. Plus, the photo pictured a much younger version of the man. But his name was there in black and white. Date of birth would make this man about the same age as the Giorgio he knew. He checked details on the form. Giorgio's residence was listed in Recoleta, on the corner where El Terminal stands. Bladimir set the paper aside and read the pages that followed. The information was basically a list of delinquent and criminal charges that had been brought against Giorgio from 1958 until early 1969. They ranged from petty theft, drug dealing, and attempted murder, to bribing government officials and illegal campaign funding schemes. The list was long. The document recorded several arrests and subsequent releases, all as a result of insufficient evidence to prove the cases. Bladimir was not surprised. Giorgio was slippery and he always had help from inside.

He closed the folder and set it aside to reach for the next one. This one contained an invoice with hours and costs listed on the letterhead of a private detective agency. The other pages were a summary of dates and events, all of which involved the surveillance of a certain Senator Vargas, two other senators from the far left-wing coalition and one from the right. The common denominator was a certain Giorgio Ramirez-M. The detective recorded meetings between Giorgio and each of the named senators in turn. But it also outlined meetings between Giorgio, a known drug lord, and a high level foreign corporate executive. Although not included in this folder, there was reference to photos of stacks of American dollar bills changing hands. The report, and the names in it, meant nothing to Bladimir because they were before his time and he didn't recall reading news articles about any of them. He supposed this was because Giorgio had been successful and there were no loose ends, nothing to report. When he flipped over the last page, he saw another single sheet of paper, this one folded in half, seemingly an after-thought. It was on the same detective agency letterhead. It said at the top, "Activities of Don Marco Rubilar-R. Medico, February 1, 1969 to March 31, 1969." Apart from a private clinic and the official location of Medical Legal Services, one address was highlighted and repeated three times. It was in a high-end residential sector of Las Condes. Another that appeared only once was the Old Congress Building in Santiago Centro and finally, on a single occasion was an address in Recoleta, and the name of a restaurant, El Terminal. The details were not attached. Bladimir slipped it back in place, wondering about the identity and role of a certain Don Marco.

Finally, Bladimir turned to the contents of the third folder. It was a five-page memo drafted by Vicente, denouncing illegal activity by certain prominent senators, effectively demanding that they be sent up before a commission in order to remove their immunity as elected members of the Senate so that they could be open to prosecution. Obviously, Vicente's intention was to obtain more signatures in order to force an investigation. He would make his case with the proof contained in the other two folders. There was little doubt it would have meant their expulsion from the Senate, followed by legal proceedings that might see them rot in prison, or at least, prevent them from holding public position for five years. It would seem that Giorgio had, after all, left at least one loose thread somewhere along the way, and Vicente had been dogged in his efforts to unravel it.

Bladimir sat back and looked out the window, not sure what he had just learned. He wasn't surprised by the corruption that Vicente had uncovered. But he was sent spinning when he related it to present circumstances and what had led to them. By the time he digested the information, the sun was high in the sky and he heard Ricardo and Carolina getting ready for lunch. He would join them, clear his head.

"Good afternoon," he greeted them, trying to appear unperturbed but he was still swimming in the information he had uncovered.

"Hi, BJ. You're just in time for tea." Carolina poured boiling water into his mug and sat down opposite. She and Ricardo were unusually light-hearted. Ricardo was wearing a permanent grin.

"Tell him, Ricardo."

"I've convinced Vicente to move out of that hole he's been sleeping in," said Ricardo.

"Oh?" Bladimir looked at them each in turn.

"I couldn't convince him to return to his room. So you don't have to worry about moving out." Ricardo looked at Carolina before continuing. "Well, you know the small shed at the far end of the patio? The one opposite your room? We can make repurpose it. I mean, anything is better than that hovel under the bridge. So we were talking about minor improvements, things that won't cost much. And eventually, we can buy a bed and wardrobe. It'll be a start. We can fill gaps in the walls and probably we'll paint it too. The floor in there is broken but maybe we can lay down some wood, make it warmer. Would be nice to lay new tiles but, well, maybe down the road."

He suddenly looked serious. "They declared a State of Emergency because of the virus. You know that, right? It's all the talk on the news. I don't know exactly what that means for homeless people but it can't be good. I told Vicente that someone might force him to move against his will, take him to some shelter somewhere. I convinced him that he would be much better off returning here, where he knows us, where he's safe, where he's taken care of."

Carolina interrupted, "He's such an old man, BJ. We don't want to find him lifeless one day..." Tears glistened. "He refuses to come back to his old room because of Rosa. I don't know why we didn't think of it before. It just occurred to us that if he has a different room, then maybe he'd agree."

"And he did." Ricardo leaned back, stretching his arms triumphantly above his head. "It took some doing but I convinced him just this morning."

"When will he be here?"

"I'm going back to get him soon. Can you come and help me? We can put our mattress in the shed. Carolina and I can sleep on the box spring until we get a new one. Bit by bit, we'll all get comfortable."

"Isn't that kind of sudden for him? I mean, a sudden change. Is he going to cope?"

"He has before."

"Yeah, I guess." Bladimir thought about Rosa's sudden death.

"The only stuff he cares about are the things that fit in his packsack. God knows what that might be." Ricardo grinned.

Less than two hours later, when Bladimir was in the bedroom, he heard Ricardo, in low tones that sounded like consolation, talking to Vicente as the two of them headed towards the shed. He envisioned Ricardo's arm around Vicente's shoulder, the two of them shuffling slowly towards the shed door. He heard Carolina come up to them. "Come and have some tea." Then she rapped on Bladimir's door, her voice bubbly, "Come and join us. Your friend is here."

When he stepped into the kitchen, Vicente was seated facing the door. He looked up at Bladimir and smiled, appearing not at all surprised to see him.

"Hi Vicente." Bladimir approached to pat him on the shoulder. "It's good to see you at last."

"There's lots of activity at El Terminal," Vicente reported as though the two of them were alone.

Bladimir sat down. "I'm sure." He glanced at Ricardo. He and Carolina were stirring their tea, both wrapped up in the pleasure of Vicente's presence.

"Oh, you've been there recently?" Carolina asked.

"I go there all the time." Vicente said as he studied a crumb that floated on top of his tea. "The other day the Policia de Investigaciones were there."

Bladimir stiffened but refrained from asking. Vicente needed to keep his mouth shut.

"Oh, that's nice," Ricardo said absentmindedly. And then, "Vicente, how does it feel to be back here having a cup of tea with us? You haven't seen Carolina for a long time."

Carolina jumped in. "It feels like home again, Vicente, with you here. Right? Doesn't it feel like home?" She was bubbling.

He smiled. "Yes. Yes, it feels almost like home. I think I need to sleep now." He got up, thanked Carolina for the tea and walked through the door towards the shed. He pointed to the door. "There, right?" Without waiting for a response.

Ricardo looked at Carolina and then started to laugh. "Same old Vicente."

"You're quiet," Carolina turned to Bladimir. "I thought you'd have stories to tell your old friend."

"More like he has stories to tell me," Bladimir said. "I think I'm going to lie down early too. Thank you for the tea." He made a move to leave. "Oh, and let me know how you need me to help Vicente settle in. You know, I found out that we're really close to finishing the paperwork for my uncle's house. He's grateful. He gave me more cash and if you want, you two can go buy a new mattress and paint, or whatever, while I get things organized here... and well, I mean, Vicente and I can catch up."

Carolina looked at Ricardo and then up at Bladimir. "BJ, you're an angel. The sooner the better. With all the talk about the pandemic... and the quarantine, well, people are saying all kinds of things. We don't know what to believe. We have to wear little masks. It's ridiculous. They're trying to scare us. And they said they'll close some stores all together. I don't believe it. Well, but what if they're right?" She turned to Ricardo again, "Ricardo, let's do what BJ says. Let's get what we need now. Maybe we should stock up on food too. Toilet paper. Maybe I'm overreacting. I don't know..."

"Yeah, you're overreacting Carolina." Ricardo said. "I doubt it'll get that bad. But yeah, let's make Vicente comfortable and we'll need to buy stuff for that. So, thanks, BJ. We'll take you up on your offer."

The next morning Bladimir pulled out several of the bills that he'd stashed in a can on the bookshelf and pressed them into Ricardo's palm. "This should cover it. I'll stay here. I'll make sure Vicente stays here too. We don't want him wandering around, getting into trouble or worse yet, catching the virus."

But Vicente had already been infected. Nobody knew, not even him. That day in Bella Vista, when he had had to slip inside the souvenir shop to avoid being seen by Elena, the virus had silently introduced itself. The germs were agile and they clung easily to the palms of his hands, from where they were transported to his face and then found their way around his nostrils and into the soft pink interior of his throat and down into the warmth of his lungs. He breathed heavily, excited because it had been so easy to follow Elena. The virus set about its work, multiplying and circulating freely through his body, not causing a fuss, not creating a scene, just calmly infecting Vicente, who didn't notice a thing.

You have to watch out for the innocent-looking ones, these false victims, the ones who must surely be the most weak and vulnerable, especially the elderly. Who would ever suspect? Vicente was one of these false victims, a cooperative body, just doing a small favor for the virus. He was an amenable, generous host, beyond suspect. Oh, no need to thank me. It's nothing, really. A co-conspirator, unwitting trafficker of disease. Isn't nature amazing?

And now, Vicente woke up in his new makeshift quarters, feeling like a million dollars. He breathed deeply, stretched his arms above his head and gave a nod to the sun that shone through the cracks on the east wall. He reached for his glasses that were folded on top of his packsack, swung his legs around like a youngster and stood up. So much space.

He deliberately did not to look across to what was once his and Rosa's bedroom. He would never look there. No, that space had been erased from his life. It no longer existed.

When he got to the kitchen, Wolfman was sitting at the table, sipping his tea. "Good morning," he said. Something was so wrong (Ricardo and Carolina were missing), yet so right with this picture (Wolfman looked like he belonged here). Vicente paused, shifting his weight, and he waited.

"Good morning, Maestro," Bladimir gestured for Vicente to pull up a chair. "I made tea, and we have buns and cheese. Can I offer you some?"

"Yes, please. And thank-you." He sat down opposite Wolfman and scratched his beard. "It's unusual to find you here."

"Yes, it is. But I told Ricardo and Carolina that we are friends. That's true, isn't it?" He didn't wait for a response. "I needed to find a new place to live and they needed someone to pay rent. So it worked out. And now you've moved back too."

"Yes." Vicente smiled.

"So are you still watching for me?"

"Of course."

"But don't say anything to Ricardo or Carolina, okay? I don't want them wondering or, well, worrying, you know? I mean about you going to El Terminal."

"They know I go to El Terminal. I've been going there for a long time. But Ricardo says that for now it's best to take a break."

"Good idea. But still, they don't need to know about my business there."

"Don't they?"

"No." Bladimir's voice was stern. "No, no, they don't. So don't talk about it in front of them, okay?"

"Okay."

"Why were La Policia de Investigaciones at El Terminal, Vicente?"

"Because they're looking for you."

"You mean Giorgio...?"

"Yes."

"Okay, thanks." Then a change of subject. "I gave some cash to Ricardo this morning but I still have some on hand. Are you good for now?"

"What do I need cash for? The radio says they're going to lock us inside one day soon. Lock us up. Like prisoners, just like prisoners." Vicente shook his head.

"You listen to the radio?"

"Yes."

"Which radio?"

"This one." Vicente reached down to his packsack, which was, as per his custom, on the floor between his knees. He pulled out a small transistor radio, the kind that runs on two double-A batteries. "I listen to music but now they talk a lot. A lot about the new virus."

"Okay. You know what? Change of plans. I don't think you should go out at all, Vicente. And you have to stay away from buses and the metro."

"Then I can't do my work."

"No one can do their work. Maybe it's time for a holiday."

36 | ON THE OTHER SIDE

March 24, 2020

Elena's body wasn't discovered until March 22nd.

It was her mother who found her lying in a pool of dried blood, nature having its way—its own gentle, meandering, unhurried, collaborative way—with her decaying flesh. It had a few days before anyone showed up to interfere. Her mother was overcome at the sight of her lifeless daughter, now a body without a soul. The corpse was bloated. But without a soul, she also seemed deflated, flattened, flesh sinking into the floor. Having accepted death's offer of mercy, she was becoming one with the wood,

Her mother screamed and ran blindly out the door. She didn't remember anything else from that day. Even if Elena had been willing to reveal her secret, her mother would not have been receptive. How could she? She would try to guess later (with her eyes squeezed shut under furrowed brow, quivering chin), she would speculate and imagine the events of her daughter's last day, even as she tried to beat down the questions as they arose. But she would never, ever, ever have guessed her beloved Marco.

From Elena's point of view, it had all turned out for the best, no longer being able to resist the temptation of the glory and the joy—yes, the joy—that death offered. Initially, though, it was just a relief. Not much more could be said. But then she looked around at the white noise of nothingness and realized that death had deceived her. She had been so certain, so absolutely prepared to smile brightly into her father's face, see his eyes glitter with amusement, laugh at their delightfully unexpected (well, almost) encounter. And with him, there would surely be that hint of rose scent mixed with something else, some aftershave or men's cologne that she had been too young to identify by name before he passed away. She would ask him now. She would laugh and tell him that of course she was familiar with it because she had been an adult for decades and the traditional scent of English Leather was well-known. Then he would toss her a small drawstring bag with the potpourri that Rosa used to make and she would hold it to her nose and sniff it in so hard that he would tell her to stop before she inhaled the bag itself. And they would laugh and laugh.

Instead, here she was, watching as someone else flipped through the pages of her life. She saw how he lifted out the roses from between thin pages. His dark eyes examined them. He had done this before. He noticed how transparent the flowers were, how fragile they had become, pressed flat like that, withered, their veins delicate, embossed in the petals, and all the more beautiful for it.

Death had put what had become of her life into someone else's hands. Someone else's fingers had dared to turn her over and look at her, one page at a time and lift out and examine the roses that had been pressed for safekeeping.

She saw handwritten pages, letters to her that were never delivered. They were tied up in a long blue ribbon that had wrenched itself free from Rosa's hat and now it dangled from a jagged, dusty branch.

She saw Rosa wave at her, smiling and pointing at someone on the other side, someone that Elena was not able to see. And then later, she supposed it would be some time later—she wasn't sure how long because death has no time—she felt a tap on her shoulder and she turned around and looked straight into the dark, glimmering eyes of the man-child who had once invited her to join him as he swung through the air, feet pushing into the sky, faces peering up into infinity. Free.

37 | PAYBACK

March 31, 2020

The day after she discovered Elena's body, her mother made arrangements to lay her to rest right next to the man whose tomb said 'Vicente Lenz-Weber' in the family mausoleum. Much like the internment of this poor man, the ceremony for Elena was a very private affair. But this time it was for very different, very confining reasons, ones that had to do with restricting the numbers of humans at a single gathering.

No one, including the Official Medical Services ascertained the exact cause of Elena's death. They simply declared cause of death: 'Unknown.' And they left it at that, partly because Don Marco had given them the nod. Although they detected unnatural chemicals in her system, they neglected to do a thorough examination, perhaps out of an abundance of caution due to the pandemic (no one needed more exposure, and besides, they were so busy) but more likely because Don Marco simply wanted the facts buried along with Elena. Either way, Elena's mother was relieved, for fear that there would be an official pronouncement of suicide because such a thing would stain the family name. Therefore, Elena's death and its mysterious circumstances went relatively unnoticed because the pandemic cast its shadowy worries across it. She was laid to rest on March 24, 2020, with only her mother and Don Marco as witnesses.

The next day, Providencia and several other municipalities across the region went into lockdown to try to curb the spread of the virus. But the action was not fast enough. Nor were the measures sufficient. The virus had already boarded its means of transport and was carefree, probably even gleeful in its flight from one cooperative host to another. It's amazing how nature sees everything as one continuous wave, where one organism cooperates with another in efforts to survive and propagate. It has been said that perhaps the real reason for human existence is merely to play host to billions of bacteria.

Less than a week later, Don Marco succumbed to its power. As an experienced medical doctor, he had taken all of the necessary precautions, and more. Yet he became extremely ill. Because of his important position, he received only the best medical care but it fell short. In his final lucid hours, he struggled to determine the lamentable point of contact with the virus. He failed, in all of his mental re-examination, to pull up the memory of the little old man with the white goatee, who had watched him exit Elena's building on the last day of her life, whose hands he had felt compelled to restrain, the man who had coughed in his face and apologized. Don Marco was buried quickly, according to the new pandemic regulations and Elena's mother who had also quite suddenly taken ill, barely had the strength to give him a proper send-off. She lived to tell about it after she won her own battle with the virus, which left her visibly weakened for the remainder of her days, which weren't more than 365.

As it happened, the day after Elena made her somewhat clumsy final exit, Giorgio made a business decision that would see him board up El Terminal and the pizzeria that Flaco managed. What was the point? Who knew how long-lasting and how deep the restrictions would be? The nightlife in Bella Vista came to a halt because of the ongoing curfew and the daytime restrictions, and profits plummeted. El Terminal, too, suffered from having to restrict the number of patrons and was not allowed to open its doors either. Even Giorgio was powerless to turn things around. Giorgio's business was hamstringed.

There was a much reduced demand for Giorgio-style political fixing because all of the politicians were preoccupied. They had swarmed to podiums to congratulate themselves on the proposed new constitution, which was going to fix everything without his help. The only thing keeping Giorgio in Santiago was his search for Bladimir and the stolen diamonds. But the State now required permits (granted online) to be out on the streets for only hours at a time and only three times a week. It seriously crippled Flaco's team's movement. And Giorgio couldn't count on police cooperation because they were too busy keeping people off the streets and it had all become very messy. So Giorgio packed everything that was worth anything into his warehouse and he ordered Flaco to manage the few loose ends, including finding Bladimir. But it turned out that Flaco saw a couple of friends die from the virus, and he became extremely paranoid. As soon as he saw Giorgio's back, his effort fizzled right to zero.

Giorgio managed to call in an important favor from his police contact, who provided safe passage up to his hometown of Iquique, for a convoy of black SUVs with tinted windows. Since the beginning of the social uprising (a lifetime ago that actually spanned only five months), Giorgio's contact with a Venezuelan drug gang known as El Tren de Aragua had grown into a fruitful association. The gang had successfully penetrated Peru, and saw their opportunity to expand into Chile after the social uprising threw the country into chaos. While Chilean press was preoccupied with human rights violations, and authorities strained to prove there were none, El Tren de Aragua found ample opportunity to import arms and merchandise, unquestioned, through Chile's long, porous borders.

Now, from his penthouse balcony on the rooftop of a luxury beach tower overlooking the Pacific, Giorgio breathed in the salt air and stood shirtless as the sea breeze gently caressed his withered old chest. He listened as tropical music filtered from a neighboring apartment in a fruitless effort to liven up the panorama of deserted beaches. Giorgio stretched out on the chaise lounge and the sunlight bounced off his greasy, sun-blocked chest as he made strategic phone calls in an effort to articulate the tentacles of his distribution network that was settling down across the north. Here he would prosper from his dealings with El Tren de Aragua.

After faking search efforts in the central sectors of Santiago, Flaco was ready to end it. The pandemic provided the perfect excuse and besides, Flaco couldn't see the point in searching for a loser, has-been wannabe activist. So he finally gathered the nerve to call Giorgio and put a final end to it.

"Bladimir is on the list of deceased," he said as matter-of-factly as he could make it sound. "My contact at the health authority confirmed it for me."

Dissatisfied, Giorgio told him to repeat it. So Flaco repeated it, word for word, matter-of-factly.

"God damn *hijo de puta, conchetumadre* weak cowardly bastard."

Flaco's face reddened and he stuttered into the phone, at the risk of giving himself away. Then he realized Giorgio was talking about Bladimir and he relaxed and went with the flow. "Yeah, I know. He got off lucky! The virus is nothing next to what he would have gotten if we'd caught him."

The diamonds were lost. "Well, where was he hiding all this time?"

Flaco had to think fast. "He must have been living under a tree or something. According to the information from my contact, Bladimir was listed as homeless."

"What?"

Flaco was impressed with his own creativity. "Yeah, I know. Homeless. We had him on the run, *Jefe*. We had him on the run. If not for this stupid virus... but whatever. The good news is that he died of the thing and now he's gone, poof, non-functional. Kaput."

Flaco's untruth was not too far from Bladimir's reality. The day after Vicente moved back into the shed in the patio, Bladimir woke up aching all over. Pain grabbed at the top of his head, peeled off his scalp centimeter by centimeter, piercing the vulnerable soft matter inside his cranium. He groaned and rolled over, curling into the fetal position, holding his head. He needed water. He needed something for the pain. After what felt like an eternity, he struggled out of bed and found some Ibuprofen in the bathroom and he returned to bed. He was freezing and he rolled himself tightly in the quilt.

Carolina was certain that BJ hadn't left the house. Why would he? By the time she realized he was still in bed, he was burning with a fever and was borderline delirious. She called Ricardo and they both appeared at the door but advanced no further.

"He caught the virus," she whispered.

Ricardo nodded but looked helpless. "Do we take him to the hospital?"

"No hospitals. Not unless he can't breathe." Carolina said. "People are lined up there for days and by the time they attend to him, how many other sick people will have passed it on to us? Let me see if I can bring his fever down." But without proper personal protection, her efforts would have to be minimal. She cautiously placed bottles of water near the bed and left him to it. She tried only enough to say that she had. And of course she prayed, and that counted for something.

Vincente was told to stay away, for his own safety. "For God's sake, Vicente, you're the one at highest risk here. We told you about the virus. You have to be careful."

Vicente felt light-headed and his stomach churned. But it wasn't from the virus. He didn't even think about that. Besides, he'd already given it away and he didn't have it anymore. He was distressed for two reasons: the first was that he was sometimes fond of Wolfman and now he was worried about him; the second was that it occurred to him that the bedroom was cursed. First Rosa and now Wolfman. He leaned against the wall of his shed, looking across at the room he had run away from and vowed never to enter again. But here it was and it was demanding his attention.

He couldn't imagine stepping into the room without Rosa being there. But now Wolfman was there. And it seemed he was just one long, continuous moan. Wolfman needed help. Sometimes he mumbled. Was he asking for him, Vicente, to come to his aid? Vicente was a good man after all, wasn't he? He could not stand just back if he could alleviate another human being's suffering. So he tiptoed across the patio and opened the bedroom door a crack. He reminded himself it was Wolfman's room now. He peered in.

Wolfman was lying on his side, two fingers protruding from beneath the quilt, clawing at it. Oh, he probably needed water. He would enter, just for a minute, just as long as it took to tiptoe in and assist Wolfman. He wouldn't look around. Vicente would manage to forget where he was, forget whose room this used to be. He would focus on the man huddled and shivering under the quilt, the man whose bloodshot eyes squinted at him, whose cracked lips appealed for help. Water? Yes, he needed water. Yes, Vicente could give him some.

He poked at Wolfman until he rolled over onto his back, chest heaving, gasping for air, mouth agape, pain flickering helter skelter across his face. But no, don't worry, that's okay, that's okay, Wolfman. Vicente would help. He lifted the huge thermos of water from the night table and touched it to Wolfman's lips. He allowed it to drip at first, and then he tilted it so that it dribbled, then more quickly. Then he poured it in. Poor man was so thirsty. He let the water flow freely. Oh, it was running fast. Too fast now. Wolfman was trying to chug it back. Vicente held the thermos firmly at Wolfman's lips. It continued to flow, and Wolfman sputtered and coughed. He pressed it harder, trying to channel all the water into Wolfman's mouth. But some entered into his nostrils too. It overflowed, forming little streams across his cheeks and chin, and it dribbled down his neck to his shoulders. Too much. Way too much. Wolfman's eyes suddenly opened wide. His eyes were not fiery now. Remember that day when they were so fiery, wild and glaring through all that smoke? There was so much of everything. Except for Rosa. There was no Rosa now, was there? And whose fault was that? Then Wolfman's eyes grew dim. There was no breath. Only water. Wolfman blinked twice before falling into a slumber, the kind that you can't come back from.

Vicente set the thermos back on the night table and stood over him for several minutes, watching. He knew that this was the last time he'd need to watch Wolfman. He tried to make sense of it all. Wolfman was there when Rosa died. What was he doing there that day, his fiery eyes darting all around? What did Wolfman do to Rosa? His suspicions had always come and gone, ebbed and flowed, just like water. Sometimes there was none and sometimes there was too much. Without Rosa, there was no one to help him put the pieces together. And then, as it happened, he'd grown rather fond of Wolfman. And now, look. Now look what happened. Now Wolfman had stopped breathing. Not exactly like Rosa of course. Rosa's death was much more tragic, much more violent, much less deserved. Yes, that was it, much less deserved. What did Wolfman do that he deserved to die?

This was all too much. Best get out of here.

As he stepped towards the door, he paused to look around. The room didn't frighten him now. It didn't blame or stab or cry out to him as he was so sure it would. It didn't shriek and threaten him with cruel words. Instead it whispered, "Everything is okay, Vicente." And, although he didn't know what for, he knew that Rosa forgave him. He looked at the shelf. Most of the books and knickknacks were Rosa's but some of his things remained there, where they'd always been. He reached down for the scruffy cat that was stuffed with that old rose potpourri. He held it to his nose and breathed in so deeply that the fake fur was drawn up into his nostrils. It tickled. He smiled to himself. Then he turned and felt around at the top of the footstool for the little satin ribbon tab. He pulled on it, opened the lid and picked up the heavy leather-bound book with the silver edged pages and he tucked it under his arm.

He stepped out of the room, quietly latched the door and made his way back to his new bedroom. He tucked the book and the old plush cat into his packsack, laid his head on the pillow and remembered something about a little girl, something about pressed roses, something about legends and secrets.

Epilogue | Status Quo

April 1, 2020: April Fools' Day, Bladimir Jaime Morales-Morales is another fatal victim of Covid-19, but his passing is not registered. Therefore, according to official registry records, Bladimir, aka BJ, aka Wolfman, is alive to this day. But no one asks.

The night of Vicente's afternoon visit, Ricardo and Carolina discovered BJ's lifeless body beneath soaking bedclothes, empty thermos at his bedside. They had no means to officially identify him because Bladimir was not carrying ID. They had no way to contact his family. Finally, assuming that authorities would be too busy burying Covid victims to do the legwork, and rationalizing that BJ would be much better off, Ricardo made the executive decision to take care of it himself. He prepared a shallow grave in the far corner of the back patio and Bladimir now rests in the only place that he ever put down roots, under an unmarked patch of dirt, not too far from a neglected rose bush. His forever home.

November 24, 2020: Vicente dies in his sleep because he is without purpose. For reasons we know, this death cannot be registered. Sadly.

In those last months without Rosa, Vicente's duty as a watcher was the only reason for him to get out of bed each morning. When the whole world became a prisoner of the virus, his reason for living disappeared along with the people he could no longer watch. Once again, Ricardo made an executive decision. Because Vicente's tomb at the cemetery was occupied by a homeless man, and because Vicente had been officially wiped from existence, and to avoid an enormous administrative nightmare, not to mention the rebirth of a scandal, but also just to keep him close, Carolina and

Ricardo buried Vicente in the back patio along with his favorite leather-bound book of legends and his old plush toy cat that was stuffed with rose potpourri and Giorgio's diamonds. They dug up the rose bush and made a grave beside BJ, his good friend. Then they replanted the bush on top of Vicente's grave, a secret marker over his final resting place. They watered it regularly and it thrived, roses blooming all year round.

October 31, 2021: Until this date, the whereabouts of Giorgio Ramirez-Marino is cause for much speculation. Some argue that old age surely must have taken him but others fear that he still manages to spread misery as far as his reach extends because death doesn't want him either.

The truth, however, is that one day after falling asleep on his northern rooftop terrace, a freak thunderstorm blew across the altiplano and reached the Pacific coast. A lightning bolt lashed out like a lizard's tongue and consumed him. It happened, of course, at the speed of light and our man Giorgio disappeared in a simultaneous combustion event to which there were no witnesses.

June 30, 2022: Flaco now runs two resto-bars, having re-opened El Terminal and the pizzeria in Bella Vista. He is said to be faring well, and although he will never reach the heights of someone like Giorgio, he thrives because he found Giorgio's stash of blackmail documents in the walls of El Terminal.

June 30, 2022: Having managed to survive the virus, Carolina and Ricardo remain in the same house in Providencia. Since Vicente's passing, they cleaned out his old room and they now have two rooms for rent. They are seeking someone who wants to put down roots.

……………………………..

INTERESTING FACTS

March 11, 2022: President Gabriel Boric is sworn in after winning Chile's November 2021 Presidential election. He is a founding member of Convergencia Social, a far left party formed in 2018, and strong proponent of the first new constitutional proposal.

September 4, 2022: The Chilean people soundly rejected (62% against, 38% in favor) the first constitutional proposal put forth by the elected, mostly left-wing makeup of the constitutional assembly.

December 17, 2023: The Chilean people clearly rejected (56% against, 44% in favor)the second constitutional proposal put forth by the elected, mostly right-wing makeup of the constitutional assembly.

The current constitution of Chile is based on the one written in 1980 during the Pinochet regime, and which was modified by President Lagos in 2005.

Residents of la Región de la Araucanía, use the term *narco-terrorismo* when referring to the insecurity and daily risks that exist in their zone. Local people are threatened by those who burn industrial machinery and homes, and they live with the almost daily hijacking of cargo and logging trucks, where drivers are threatened and sometimes murdered, where lumber is stolen and sold illegally, and where organized, armed militias take refuge in dense forests. Increasingly, since the social uprising of 2019, organized crime, narcos and human traffickers have moved more freely up and down Chile's porous borders. The murder of policemen, the 'crazy bullets' that kill innocent children, and the record number of murders on the streets of

Santiago all point towards the growing violence as organized crime groups fight for territory.

In 2023, an investigation began into several members of the ruling coalition for their roles in money that went missing between government departments and suspicious non-profit foundations that are linked to some of the ruling parties. Dozens of computers have been stolen from said government department offices, no traces to date. In 2024, officials in high places, including La Policia de Investigaciones, have been charged with corruption and with credible links to organized crime.

....

ACKNOWLEDGEMENTS

Many thanks to Lezak Shallat for her brilliant notes and insights, and to Pat St. Germain and William Barlow for their willingness to read and offer perspectives. Eternal thanks to Cathleen Schmitke and Katja Preston for their patience with many early drafts and their constant encouragement along the way. Heartfelt thanks to my husband Alex for helping me "*abrir las pepas*," and as always, for his inspiration and undying support.

....

....

REVIEW THE BOOK

Your review will be appreciated.
Please post a review at your favorite books site.

....

RECOMMEND THE BOOK

If you enjoyed the story, please recommend it to a friend.

....

OTHER BOOKS BY EDIE AYALA

HARD BED HOTEL

This humorous love story mistakes the living for the dead, and trips along to a delightfully unexpected end.

Everything goes wrong but maybe it's right, as heaven and earth settle into an unexpected juxtaposition in this twisted Latin tale that is doused with humor and magic realism.

ISBN Print 978-0-9880032-2-4
ISBN Ebook 978-0-9880032-3-1

SOUTH OF CENTRE

An intriguing saga of hidden family connections.

Dipping into some of Chile's rich history around the time of Pinochet's regime, South of Centre unfolds through multiple narratives and is peppered with magic realism. The story raises questions about social justice and other things that you can never quite get to the bottom of.

ISBN Print 978-0-9880032-4-8
ISBN Ebook 978-0-9880032-5-5

THREADS

One woman has an extraordinary gift, another woman desperately needs one and the man in the middle is indifferent.

Two women on opposite ends of the world strive to get by, and their distinct coping methods take bizarre twists. The story is about overcoming loss and our shared humanity.

ISBN Print 978-0-9880032-0-0
ISBN Ebook 978-0-9880032-1-7

All available in print or as ebooks from your favorite bookseller.

For more information and links to books and their sellers, please visit: edieayala.com

www.ingramcontent.com/pod-product-compliance
Lightning Source LLC
Chambersburg PA
CBHW022030240626
47154CB00007B/2339